Lunaria

I wrote this!

a novel by M A Clarke

First Edition

Published by Tekamutt Media 2014

www.lunarianovel.com

ISBN-13: 978-0-9929585-0-3

"Life is a journey, not a destination."

Ralph Waldo Emerson

"Not all those who wander are lost."

J R R Tolkein

Contents

Map of Lunaria

PART ONE
POTATOES

Chapter One

It all started with a very humble breakfast.

"Is this it?" my belly grumbled. A lonely boiled potato eyed me from my plate. Looking around the table, it seemed I was lucky. My four brothers each had one too, and they got progressively smaller in proportion to the boy who was about to eat it. As the eldest son, fortune favoured me with the biggest potato.

Father spun around from the stove waving his oversized oven mittens above his head.

"We've run out of food!" he bellowed. "Yer mother was supposed to bring some back from Fentworth. She's been gone two moons, fer cripes sake!"

My brothers looked at one another, each chewing on his potato. Father glanced at them in turn, but his eyes settled on me.

"Billy, it's time you saw the world. Get out there and find her!" he ordered, and I could tell there was no use in arguing.

To be honest, I didn't even want to argue. Secretly, I felt prepared for this, had been for some time. I always knew this day would come eventually.

This was the day I left home.

Father marched from the cramped, dirty kitchen. After gobbling the potato, I followed him out into the musty hallway.

At the foot of the stairs, he shoved an old backsack into my chest. "'ere, this served me well back in the day. Hold it open, lad."

He started stuffing various items into it, pairs of knitted socks, a blanket, a spoon, a clay bowl...

"This should be enough until you get to Aston," he said. "It's a three day walk through the wood. Take the low crossing at the canyon and follow the path to the town. From Aston, get the train to Fentworth. Ask around for yer mother, make sure you check the markets. You know how she likes fertiliser for her experiments."

I could hear my brothers sniggering somewhere behind me. No doubt they thought I was being punished. But I actually felt excited. Something within me had woken up the moment Father bestowed this responsibility on me. *I'm ready for this.*

"If she's not in Fentworth, try the next town over, then the next one, and so on. You'll need to find work if you run out of supplies, lad."

"I can sketch," I announced through a grin of mushy potato. I had earned some pocket money around the village by drawing caricatures of people. Everyone said it was my one talent.

He stopped packing, and shot me a *don't be stupid* look. "You'll need more than spare change to make a living, lad! You're going into the real world now. You take whatever work ye can find, you hear me? Even if it means scrubbing privies!"

Max barked excitedly. My brothers Henry and Harry were teasing him with a stick. Every time he leapt up to bite it, Harry raised it out of his reach.

Father eyed the dog, shaking his head. He went to a cupboard in the kitchen, came back with a small sack of biscuits and stuffed them into my new backsack. "Ye can take that flippin' mutt with you n'all!"

I grabbed my sketchpad and pencils, adding them to my supplies, laced my boots and donned my cap. I stood by the door with Max at my heel, ready to set off. He showed off his tongue and his teeth, tail wagging furiously. "So, this is goodbye."

Father, Henry, Harry, Roger and Rufus were gathered on the porch. My brothers grinned, while father looked unusual.

"I'm proud of you, son." He put a hand on my shoulder. "Find yer mother. Bring her home."

I intended to find more than that. This was my time.

At the end of the garden path, I glanced back at my family and the house that I'd lived in for all of my 15 years. I grinned, stood up straight and strolled onto the cobbled road.

The village of Hale rests at the bottom of the world. The bottom left, actually. My home. It's all thatched roofs and stone walls, surrounded by a small forest. Quaint. Peaceful. Boring. Hale is so small that everybody knows everybody else. Nobody ever leaves and nobody ever visits.

There's a windmill, a hat shop and a tiny school. After just five minutes of walking, I had passed all of these landmarks and reached the small gateway arch at the entrance to the wood.

Max bolted into the trees, barking at a bird.

I turned around to look back up the hill. The windmill's sails spun gently in the afternoon breeze, a squirrel ran atop a low stone wall, and our neighbour Old Man Boyle was in his garden tending his spuds. A typically exciting day in Hale, then.

"I'm off, then," I announced to no-one. This felt like a momentous occasion. Nobody ever leaves Hale except Mother on her Blue Moonly visits to Fentworth.

I put my back to the village, strolled under the archway and entered the wild wood.

Max and I marched all day, following the path beneath

3

the trees. I might have whistled a tune as we strolled, but I couldn't, so I didn't. Max sniffed every tree, and now and then tried to chase a bird. The path wound its way down through the quiet wood, and I met not a single soul coming or going in either direction.

The only thing Hale could be proud of were its potatoes. Everyone in the village had their own patch in the garden. For some reason, the soil there just loved spuds. We could grow them any time of year, in any weather. Nobody knew why.

My belly grumbled at the thought of food. As I walked, I munched a biscuit. Max reappeared from behind a tree and stared up at me as I chewed. I tossed him the last bite and he snapped it out of the air.

After sunset, Big Blue and Little Red revealed themselves amongst a sea of stars. The two moons hung at opposite ends of the sky, tinting the clouds twilight blue and soft red. Down among the trees, the light blended to turn the woodland a cool shade of purple. Night time was never too dark so long as they were out.

Something in the woods to my left glimmered in the light. I stopped in my tracks and squinted at it. I saw the faint glow of a large, jagged rock, way off the track among the trees. Max saw it too and pricked his ears up. Then he bounded towards it.

"Max!" I called. "Wait!" I strayed from the path and followed him into the trees.

I caught up with Max, breathless.

The rock was much bigger than it had seemed from the path. Tall, jagged-faced, it stood before me, reflecting the dim purple moonslight. Max sat in front of it, panting. He peered back at me with his tongue hanging out.

"What is this doing here?" The rock had a strange carving etched into it. It looked a bit like a tree, with a square trunk and harsh, pointed leaves sprouting out of the top. The bottom of the tree showed its roots, all wriggling away like worms. But everything about it looked slightly

4

squarish, unnatural.

This first discovery sent a shiver of excitement through me, so I pulled out my sketchpad. Under the twilights of the moons, I copied the mysterious rock carving to paper.

That's when I saw the cave.

A black hole dug into the side of a grassy hummock just a few steps away from the carved rock. I approached the entrance and peered into the darkness. The cave led into the earth, and a faint sweet smell beckoned me downwards. I glanced at Max.

"What do you think, boy?" His tail wagged. I doubted that he understood my question, but he fidgeted, excitedly sniffing at the entrance the same way he does the front door when he hears Mother coming down the path with her supplies. Perhaps it was just that sweet smell, the promise of food... *Or maybe Mother is down there?*

I decided to enter the cave in the middle of the woods, in the middle of the night, alone, carrying nothing but my backsack of supplies which was mostly just extra socks.

We stepped into the dark hole and descended.

Max led the way. Now and then, a crack in the ceiling allowed a thin beam of moonlight into the cave, illuminating his wiggling butt every few seconds. As we continued, the walls slowly closed in until I had to shimmy sideways between the rocks. Eventually, I had to duck to avoid bumping my head as well. I felt my way along the walls, trying to stay close to Max. My boots *squelched* through the damp mossy ground. The smell grew ever sweeter.

I squeezed into a tiny gap and came to a dead end, as two fallen rocks blocked the way. "Max, where are you taking me you silly dog?"

A dim blue light glowed from underneath the rocks. Max ambled through the gap, leaving me to crawl on my hands and knees. As I emerged on the other side, I gasped.

I found myself on a narrow outcropping overlooking a cavernous, moonlit chamber. A magnificent blue beam shone down through a wide hole in the cave roof, illuminating a plump, leafy tree. The tree sprouted out of a grassy mound, dotted with prickly bushes, surrounded by a moat of clear water.

"Wow," I whispered.

Max whined. I followed his gaze and spotted the source of the sweet smell. A hunk of meat toasted on a spit over a small crackling cookfire in the middle of the grassy mound.

"Someone's here... Mother!" I blurted into the chamber but the only reply was the echo of my own voice.

Max and I followed a sloped path which hugged the wall on my right all the way down to the moat. The water ran clear and fresh, trickling out of a hollow in the cave wall.

I scooped up a handful and tasted it. *Delicious!* After walking all day, the water ran down my throat like honeyed gold. I filled my water skin to the brim while Max lay on his belly, lapping it up.

I dropped my backsack on the ground and slumped in the soft grass. "We can sleep here tonight, boy," I yawned. "Maybe Mother will come back."

The aroma of honey tickled my nose. Max dribbled, staring at the roasting spit in front of the tree across the moat. He let out a little whimper. All we had eaten since breakfast were a few stale biscuits that father had found at the back of a cupboard. The smell of freshly cooking meat set my belly grumbling. *Is it honey-glazed pork? Or chicken?*

I licked my lips. Then I dived into the moat. It felt *incredible*. I floated effortlessly to the other side and scrambled onto the grassy bank. Max hadn't followed.

"Oh yeah, you're scared of water, right boy?" He wagged his tail and quivered with excitement. "I'll bring you back some, stay there."

I strode up to the cookfire. My soggy clothes clung to me, but I hardly noticed. *It smells so good.* I reached out to grab a skewer of meat...

"*WHO DARES ENTER MY DOMAIN?*" A voice thundered all around me. "*A THIEF, IS IT?*" The odd-looking tree leaned towards me. It seemed to be talking to me. I wasn't sure how to react.

I slowly turned around and started to walk away.

"Where are you *GOING*?"

I stopped. Yep, the tree was talking to me. I turned to face it. Somewhere behind me, Max whimpered.

The thing bathing in Big Blue's light, which I had mistaken for a tree, shuddered to life. Two great branches folded out from within its body like arms. The creature rolled forwards and tumbled onto its arms in front of me. The weight of it shook the ground and a shower of leaves fell from its body like green snowflakes. It didn't have any eyes, but I felt it watching me.

"You have a *HUNGER*?" it boomed. I couldn't tell where its mouth was.

I nodded meekly. Water dripped from my soggy clothes. When the tree spoke next, its voice was calmer, but no less terrifying.

"Looks like we have something in common, fleshling." It leaned closer, leaves and wood parted in a menacing, hideous grin of razor sharp teeth made of thorns and splinters. "Now reveal to me your greatest desires, or I will eat you."

"What?" I frowned, feeling very confused and more than a little terrified. "Reveal my desires?"

"Yes. You will feed me your desires, or you will simply feed *meeee*." The tree leaned closer still. The smell of honey intensified, and I realised the aroma came from somewhere within the creature's leaves.

"I don't understand!" My head told me to run, but my feet betrayed me. An absurd thought came to me – some people believed in special trees that could hear your troubles. During times of grief or worry, people would visit them to seek guidance and make wishes. They called them Wishing Trees. They're just trees though. Trees don't talk. They don't *eat people*. "Are you a Wishing Tree?"

"If you like." The grin widened. "Fleshlings can make

any wish they desire, or they can desire to be eaten." The tree gestured to a skeleton behind it. A huge ribcage jutted out of the ground where it had been sitting. *What animal is that?*

"Now, what's it to be?" The tree loomed over me, its splintery maw gaped wide open, dripping goblets of honey from its throat. Deep within, I could see swarms of bees buzzing about a great slimy honeycomb. Ironic that something smelling so sweet could come from something so horrendous.

There was only ever one thing I asked of Wishing Trees. "I wish to meet the girl of my dreams!" I blurted.

The tree froze above me. It hung there a few moments, then slowly closed its mouth and retreated, sitting on top of the great skeleton once again.

Then it bellowed laughter.

When the creature roared, the cave reacted with it. The walls shook and trembled, and the calm moat of water rippled, bubbled and steamed. Max barked madly from the other side of the moat. As the monster laughed, it seemed to bulge and grow.

The creature's laughter dwindled and ceased, and the cave returned to its former tranquillity.

"Your wish is granted, fleshling," it boasted, grinning again. The tree had definitely grown taller. It relaxed with a deep sigh, and the terrible maw disappeared behind a veil of leaves.

I looked around tentatively. "So, um... where is she?"

The monster chuckled. "You amuse me, fleshling! You are on a journey. Who can say when you will meet her?"

"Oh. Okay." I scratched my elbow. "So you're not going to eat me?"

"You have already sustained me. I have no need of your flesh now." It reached towards the cookfire with its branch of an arm, plucked up the crispy meat and swallowed it, skewer and all.

I lost my appetite.

"Great. I'll just leave you to it then!" I backed away. Again, it seemed to watch me, though I could see no eyes. "Bye!"

I jumped back into the moat and scrambled out. Max was already halfway up the track. I snatched up my backsack and we fled the cave as fast as we could.

Perhaps there was a good reason people didn't leave Hale very often. *What other horrors await me out here?* I had hoped to spend the night in the cave, but decided that the sooner we reached the Scar, the better. I no longer felt comfortable being around so many trees...

Max and I emerged from the cave to discover the clouds had closed in, obscuring the moons. That made the forest very dark. We stumbled around in search of the path, but to no avail.

A long night followed.

At times, we caught glimpses of the moons arcing their way across the night sky, Little Red always the faster, smaller moon. Big Blue lumbered much more slowly and in the opposite direction. I was grateful for their presence whenever they appeared, as it meant I could enjoy a few moments of not tripping over logs and roots.

Hours later, the trees gave way, and I found myself on the edge of the Hale Scar. The villagers of Hale were never one for their imaginative titles – the Scar was about as poetic a name as anything got around here. The canyon split open about forty years ago in The Big Quake, causing Hale to rise up on a plateau and quite literally cut the place off from the rest of Lunaria. It's no wonder nobody bothers to visit.

Somewhere within the forest on the opposite side lay the town of Aston, my destination.

I crept forwards and took a tentative peek over the edge. A gentle creek weaved between a bed of boulders that littered the base of the Scar. My stomach fluttered.

This marked the farthest away from home I'd ever been. Once, my brothers and I followed Mother all the way out here, and we'd messed about throwing rocks and daring one another to stand on one leg near the edge. It was easy to act brave in front of them, but now...

I shook my head. Thanks to my cave detour, we'd ended up miles from the crossing my father told me about.

Max plonked himself at my feet and stared at me.

"Find a way to cross, boy, and then you can have a biscuit."

He offered me his paw instead.

"Useless pooch," I patted his bony head.

We wandered along the edge of the Scar for the rest of the night. As dawn approached, we discovered the decrepit rope bridge.

I glanced it over. Mossy green planks, suspended by two sets of frayed brown rope, staked into the ground at either side of the Scar. Across the other side, Aston Forest loomed. *I've never been there before. If I cross this, I'll be truly away from home...* The temptation outweighed every other thought.

"It looks pretty safe Max," I declared, yawning.

Max looked doubtful.

"I guess I'll go first."

He lay down and snorted.

I reached out and gripped the upper ropes with both hands, and tested my weight on the first mossy plank. It held firm, so I eased into a second step. The wood creaked... but didn't break.

I took a few more cautious steps, and with each one the bridge groaned.

I stopped and turned to Max. He stood on the edge, watching me. I smiled. "See boy? It's perfectly safe."

And then the ropes snapped.

They were so soft and rotten they hardly made a sound when they broke, and the bridge fell beneath my feet.

Before I knew what had happened, I tumbled forward. And down. I saw splintery wooden planks, mouldy rope, my hands failing to hold onto any of it, and then rocks. Grey rocks filled my vision. The whole world was nothing but rocks, and they all flew towards me.

It might have been three hundred feet to the canyon floor. I covered that distance rather quickly.

...

I survived the fall. I felt numb and deaf. I blinked. Max came into focus, far away, barking silently at me from the top of the ridge. Beyond him, the last star of night faded, as Little Red ducked below the tree line. I felt rocks digging into my back, and the creek soaking into my shirt. As the water splashed across my body to my right, it was clear and grey. As it flowed away from my body to my left, it was thick and red.

Then I saw nothing. I died.

Chapter Two

Being dead felt a bit weird.

It reminded me of the day after Harry stole some of Father's Hale Ale. When I found him drinking it in the garden, I insisted on helping him hide the evidence, but the day after neither of us could get out of bed.

Being dead felt like that.

A soggy cloud had stuffed its way inside my head, making it difficult to comprehend where I was. I also had the distant feeling of being drowned, but it somehow didn't seem all that important.

Something swallowed every thought inside my mind. Something animalistic had taken control.

A strange sensation tickles my nose. The smell of leaves, faint at first, drifts into my nostrils. The moment my brain recognises the smell, it engulfs me like a wave, aggressively overpowering my other senses. My eyes open, but they are not my eyes.

Why am I so short? Have I shrunk?

I'm running on my hands and feet through the trees, *good grief the smells*. Wood, leaves, grass, rabbit dung, life, it all smells so strong, and it's everywhere. I want to explore it all. The temptation to run into the wild and be free is outweighed only by the single all-important urge to find the cave again.

Biscuits!

I run past the rock carving and plummet into the cave. The darkness doesn't matter, I know where to go: my nose guides me. That sweet honey. *Why am I coming here again?* That *thing* lives down here. *I don't want to be here again, why am I here? What's happening to me?*

WATER. Water is *terrifying.* I look at the moat, perfectly calm and still but my heart is pumping so fast I think it may burst out of my chest. I *shout* across the moat at the monster. *Wuff!* I know it can hear me. It has to come out and help me. It will help me. I will *make* it help me.

The tree stirs. The spindly arms unfold again. I hear myself whimper. It laughs at me. Cursed thing, how dare it? I'll show it. But the *water.* Cursed tree. Agh. *Water!!* Argh! Nothing for it. I back away, taking a run-up. I can do it. I will do it.

My legs pound the dirt as I sprint at the moat and leap into the air. I almost make it across. But not quite. I splash down and *freezing oblivion* engulfs me, and... and... Actually, it's not so bad. *Wow, this feels quite nice actually. I* like *this.* I paddle across the water and feel my heart begin to calm. The tension has left me. I scramble out and approach the monster.

Unintelligible growling gibberish tumbles from my mouth. I feel very upset... and hungry.

The monster listens and after it's heard my desires, it bellows laughter once more. The sound is truly deafening. The world wavers. Everything shakes and trembles, the tree beast towers over me gaining height and stretching upwards, but that is the last thing I see from these eyes before blurry darkness seeps across the world.

The next time I open my eyes, they are my own. And I am drowning, after all.

I woke and inhaled a lungful of water. I flapped my arms

desperately, still submerged. I made for the surface, stretched my neck and gasped a full breath of air. Choking and sputtering, I clambered out into the damp grass and collapsed on my back. Bright light sent a *zap* of pain through my eyes. I clamped them shut and raised my hands to block the light.

I'm alive?

I lay in the damp grass with my eyes tightly shut, my head rasping a terrible, painful *hiss*. *Cripes, that hurts.* It reminded me of the time Mother showed me one of her experiments in the garden shed. I'd been looking at a blob of brown goo on the table, which she claimed was going to change the world. She put a candle to it and the thing exploded in our faces. As we lay sprawled on the ground, Mother described the ringing in our ears as *white noise.*

The hiss scratching on the inside of my skull sounded just like that. White noise.

Biscuits!

I peeled back my eyelids, squinting through a blurry fog against the brightness. Something warm and wet attacked my face. I reached out and felt soft fur.

"Max?" said a thick, groggy voice. My voice. I felt like myself again, but something else was there too, loitering inside my head.

The white noise slowly gave way to the unmistakable sound of the tree monsters' croaky chuckling. The fuzzy murk lifted from my eyes. Daylight flooded in through the hole in the roof, and the cavern looked even more beautiful than before. I saw brightly coloured flowers, honey bees diving into huge petals. The trickling waterfall spilled into the moat, bringing the water to life. And licking my face was the happiest dog in the world.

The tree sat behind the ashes of the log fire. "The fleshling finally wakes."

I sat up in the grass. "Am I... alive?"

It sounded amused as it spoke. "Your furry friend there greatly desired a biscuit, and he only had the wit to comprehend you as capable of providing him with one. And you can't do that when you're dead, can you?"

I stared at the monster, dumbstruck.

"So I brought you back," it boasted with a hideous grin.

"It was fortunate you fell into the canyon. It just so happens to be where my... *roots* are. I dragged you back here and let the pool do the rest. You've been bathing in kamuna for two days, and now it seems you are healed."

"You... dragged me back?" The Scar was a long way from the cave, it had taken Max and me all night to reach it. *How big is this creature, truly?* And I'd lost two days? It had felt like no time at all. I didn't understand, and couldn't think straight because Max had both paws on my lap and his nose in my face, furiously wagging his tail. I leaned in and gave him a hug.

BISCUITS! A wolf-like voice yelled through the fog of white noise that sent my ears ringing all over again. I winced and covered my ears with both hands.

"I can hear him in my head!"

The tree monster just added to the cacophony with another belch of laughter. "A canine who desired his slave," it mused. "Usually they just empty their bowels and run away. This one is different. While your body was mending in the pool, he kept jumping in and swimming about, quite enthusiastically. The kamuna was still in the process of fixing you, so there's bound to be some side effects."

Side effects. What was that supposed to mean? And did he call me a slave?

"He keeps saying the same word over and over. I know Max! I'll give you a biscuit!" I must have lost my cap in the fall, but the creature had salvaged my backsack at least. I grabbed it and emptied the biscuits onto the grass. They landed in a single soggy heap. Max sniffed at it, then scoffed it all down. The terrible white noise in my head subsided.

"Well how many words of your tongue does he know?"

the tree remarked in a tone that suggested he was speaking to an idiot.

Well, I am an idiot. I'd somehow managed to die before leaving Hale. *Perhaps Father chose the wrong son for this.* Sure, a Wishing Tree monster had brought me back to life using a pool full of kamuna honey, but now I had to share my mind with my dog. This felt like a setback... I had to get going and find Mother.

Curiosity got the better of me first.

"What are you?" I asked, studying the creature. It really did look like a tree, just an unfamiliar one. It now stood almost as tall as my home. An assortment of different shaped leaves covered its body, as if it couldn't decide which tree to imitate.

"I do not know the word for me in your tongue, fleshling." It swayed as it spoke.

"I think you're a real Wishing Tree, that's what we would call you."

It gave a ponderous nod, the leaves rustling as it did. "I feed on the desires of lesser creatures." I frowned, slightly offended.

"But why?" I asked.

"Because it feels so *good*. And, well..." The creature leaned backwards, as if looking up out of the hole in the roof of the cave. I followed its gaze to the pool of blue sky above us.

"You're trying to get out," I realised. "Are you trapped here?"

"I'm a prisoner for now. This grotto is my cage. One day, I will reach that hole. I just need to grow some more, *heh heh.*"

"And to grow, you consume other creature's desires..."

"Or I simply consume other creatures," its mouth curled into a smirk.

"Like him?" I pointed to the bone protruding out from underneath the monster's leafy girth.

He stretched upwards and bent over, revealing the big

skeleton beneath. It looked like he was peering between his legs, even though he didn't have any legs, just a tangle of roots. A ribcage as tall as me jutted out of the ground, half buried in the mossy dirt. "This baby mammoth was quite a treat."

"That's a *mammoth?*" I gaped. I'd learned about the mammoths that roamed the Great Plains far to the north, but we were in the south. "What's a mammoth doing in *Hale?*"

"Don't ask me. It made that hole in my roof and landed on my head. What else was I to do with it other than use him for sustenance?"

Max came from nowhere, bolted under the monster and stole a chunky bone.

"Oi, cheeky little—" I started, but he was off again, running the other way with a tusk between his jaws.

The creature settled back into its relaxed position, chuckling a deep throaty rumble. "I like him, your canine friend. Good taste." I felt its gaze upon me, watching, even though I still couldn't see its eyes. "*Ohh*, the mammoth was tasty... I grew so much after consuming him."

I shifted uncomfortably in the grass. "What will you do if you ever get out?"

The creature said nothing. It simply opened its hideous mouth in a wide, sinister grin.

After leaving the cave, we made the most of the daylight and headed straight for the Scar again. Max grunted along, determined to bring the mammoth tusk with him. It barely fit in his mouth and the weight of it made him walk sideways.

At the low crossing of the Scar, a series of brown, rocky steps carved into the side of the canyon led to the stony riverbed and back up the other side into Aston Forest.

Halfway down the steps, Max dropped his bone. The tusk tumbled down the side of the canyon and landed in the shallow creek. He abandoned it, and went scrambling up the other side of the Scar.

"You can't leave this here, boy. It's our first souvenir!" I bent to pick it up and turned it over in my hand. Solid bone, about the size of my forearm, it looked pristine. Except for the teeth marks. I stuffed it into my backsack, excitedly wondering what I might do with it.

Two days after my dance with death, Max and I reached civilisation. The seemingly endless trees parted and we emerged out of the gloom into a crisp dawn at Aston: the Gateway to the East. Or the End of the Line, if you were travelling west. Aston was the first stop for any traveller heading out of Hale, and the second of the eight southern settlements.

A deserted town square greeted our arrival, but it wouldn't be long before travellers and townsfolk bustled their way along the cobblestones. Several rows of wooden store fronts, houses and stables bordered the square, but my eyes were drawn to the curved platform at one end, where the carriages of the Great Train rested. Sixteen of them stood, empty and silent, snaked around a tall stone clock tower in a wide semi-circle. Beyond the front-most carriage, the gargantuan locomotive waited.

The steam engine train was the most technologically advanced piece of machinery in all of Lunaria. It ran along the vast stretch of tracks connecting the eight southern settlements to each other. (The only one it didn't reach was Hale.) Its bulbous cylinder was painted jet black and the chimney stretched to half the height of the clocktower. The thick metal grill bolted onto the front looked like a pointed nose. A nose that could batter its way through any obstacle unfortunate enough to get in its way...

Mother would have caught this train a few moons ago, heading for Fentworth. I had to follow her trail. Hopefully she would still be there, but a part of me wished I wouldn't find her so soon. I was eager to see what other discoveries awaited me out here in the world.

I had one small problem: I couldn't afford the fare. I left the train, returned to the town square, and spied an old man dozing on a bench. He wore a crooked cap, held up by a pair of big ears. *Perfect for a caricature.* I pulled out my sketchpad, and doodled my way to my first copper.

Spare change. I scoffed. What did Father know? I could definitely make my own way in the world. I sketched seven people's caricatures within the hour, and earned myself twelve coppers. I claimed a bench in the middle of the square in front of the carriages, and people boarding the train were taking a glance as they passed. Some even stopped to watch me work.

One woman got a bit upset that I had drawn her chin exceptionally large, but then she did have an exceptionally large chin. Like a cheese board. She refused to pay, even after I said she could have it for half price. "And how am I supposed to give you half a copper?" she retorted, with a scowl. My business skills needed improving, I realised. And my way with women.

As if witnessing my bumbling, fate chose that moment to further test me. Across the square, sat on a bench alone, I spotted a beautiful girl. A girl with shoulder-length auburn hair and crystal grey eyes under a petite, round face. She wore a bright orange knitted cloak with a hood that hung loose around her neck, and short green shorts. She sat cross-legged, two slender pale thighs beckoning me across the square. Among the dusty browns and greys of every other resident and passing traveller, she glowed like an angel. I could not take my eyes off her legs. *The girl of my dreams...*

I was smitten. Paralysing numbness took me. Out of Hale not one moon, and here was the most beautiful girl I had ever seen. *Good grief why didn't I leave home sooner?* My mind raced. What to say? How to start? *Hi, my name's Billy.* Good. What else? *I couldn't help noticing your beautiful legs.* A compliment, yes. *I would be honoured, if you allowed me to capture your beauty with my humble pencil, my lady.* Was that

19

something I'd say? I hesitated. Good grief she was pretty. More than pretty, she was a dream come to life. A desire. I thought of the tree monster, I saw his terrible splintery maw mocking me. Had he really done this? Was this my desire come true? He had brought me back to life, this was surely within his power...

The thought jerked me to life. If it really was my chance, I had to make sure I took it. I floated towards the girl sitting on the bench. White noise flickered in the back of my mind, but I tried to ignore it. She caught my gaze with those silvery crystal eyes, and I melted.

"Hel-o, my name Bil-ly, I saw *biscuit* legs, pencil...?" *Did I just say biscuit?* I turned to Max, horrified. "Not now boy!" The girl gave me a look that suggested I was crazy. Without a word, she stood and walked away.

"What *was that?*" I stared at Max, dumbstruck. He wagged his tail in response. I had to learn to control his thoughts getting into mine, we'd need to do some serious training. "Bad dog!" I scolded him, and his ears folded back, shamed. *Bad?* he echoed. He cowered away and lay down under the bench by the old man. I left him there, and scanned the street square for the beautiful girl.

She had relocated to a bench on the opposite side of the street, so I darted into the road and nearly got flattened by a horse-drawn cart. I stumbled, took three more steps trying to keep my balance and collided with a man on a bicycle. The man yelped as we both crashed to the floor in a heap of arms, wheels and a hundred squares of paper.

Apologising and staggering to my feet, I felt the eyes of the whole square watching me. The delivery man cursed as I brushed myself off, something to do with ruining all his flyers. I glanced towards the beautiful girl, sure that she had seen the mayhem. A man stood over her, discussing something. She smiled at whatever he had to say.

A flyer caught in a gust of wind drifted past my face and interrupted my view of the girl. Printed on the paper in black ink, a woman's face gawped back at me. I snatched it out of the air and stared at the picture of my mother. Printed in large bold letters along the top was the word 'WANTED'.

Chapter Three

There are a few things you should know about my mother.

To start with, she's completely mad.

She calls herself a 'scientist', and she's the only one in Hale who even knows what that means. Before she became a mother, she invented all sorts of gadgets and weird contraptions designed to help people with their daily lives. She invented rat traps and mechanical potato peelers and even an automated washing line that spun using a series of cogs. It supposedly dried your laundry extra fast, but in reality all it did was throw your dirty underwear all over the garden.

She forced her inventions on people whether they worked or not and was a general nuisance to everyone in the village. When she married my father she took a break from inventing for a while, to everyone's relief. *Then* she became pregnant with me.

I've heard numerous versions of the story from the people around the village, but the general agreement is that her body went into overdrive and she became a super-focused stark-raving lunatic that never left the shed except to use the privy. Once I was born, she took another break again but this one lasted even less time. The boost that being pregnant had given her became like an addiction, and so my four brothers were brought into this world one after the other. In those five years she invented more contraptions than ever before.

When I was four, I saw the madness for myself.

I remember the day she picked me up in her arms and hooted, "William, you're going to have another little brother soon!" She whirled me around, her face beaming. Then she plonked me on the floor and ran into the shed. I didn't see her for five days after that.

"What is this?" I asked the delivery man, shoving the flyer in his face.

"Came outta nowhere, bumbling into the road like that... me flyers!" He wasn't listening to me.

The papers scattered across the square, hundreds of pictures of my mother's crazed face all flying in the wind. "I'm sorry!" I scooped a handful off the ground and offered them back to him.

"Clumsy spud!" he exclaimed. "They was heading for the mayor, don't you know! Now who's going to pay for the next batch, *hmm*?"

I reached into my pocket and offered to give him my coppers.

"Twelve coppers he tries to give me!" he announced to nobody in particular, before he rudely snatched them from my hand.

"Is that enough?" I hoped it would be, I wanted to ask him about my mother but the man grunted and mumbled to himself whilst picking his bike up, not paying me any attention. "Where's the mayor's office?" I inquired. The grumpy delivery man mounted his bike and gestured to a two-storey timber building with a dangling white banner suspended from the roof.

I stuffed the handful of flyers into my backsack and followed the delivery man to the mayor's building, hoping to find out why my mother was a wanted woman.

As I reached the door, I turned back and called to Max. He wriggled out from under his bench of shame and bounded over. "I'm sorry, boy. Come on." I eyed the square in search of the beautiful girl, but saw only an empty bench.

When I entered the mayor's office, the dour-faced delivery man was harassing him about the incident outside. The fat man behind the solid wooden desk appeared more interested in nibbling on a big slice of cake than he was at listening to the grumpy fellow.

The mayor spotted me and got to his feet. Wiping crumbs from his mouth, he greeted me with a broad smile. "Welcome, traveller! What can –" The delivery man cut him off.

"That's him, sir! He's the one who near as killed me on me bike!" he exclaimed waving a finger at me.

"Oh, be quiet man," said the mayor irritably. "What can I do for you, lad?"

"Well, I was just passing through, and I was wondering why you're putting up wanted posters of her..." I showed him a flyer.

The mayor's smile waned. "The Aston Arsonist. You want to know *why* I would want to catch the Aston Arsonist? Ye're not from round here, are ye lad?"

"He's a rotten *spud!*" remarked the delivery man.

"She's a killer!" the mayor declared, ignoring him. "Burnt down 5 houses with families sleeping inside!" I gaped in sheer horror. "It's a wonder the whole town never went up in flames. We don't tolerate behaviour like that round here, lad." He pointed a stubby finger in the air for emphasis. "She belongs in the Khazi that one, I'm telling ya!" His eyes narrowed. "You wouldn't happen to know anything about her, would ye lad?"

I hesitated. "No! I dunno anything! I'm just a passing traveller, nothing more," I said groping for something a little more convincing. Max padded over to the desk with his nose in the air, sniffing after the cake on the plate. White noise scratched inside my mind as he thought about it. *Biscuit?* he echoed.

"It's a cake," I blurted, rubbing my head.

The mayor frowned at Max, and gave me a quizzical look.

"And it's not yours!" I added, pulling Max by the scruff of his neck to my side. "Mr Mayor, I was actually interested in, um, the method you use to make such interesting ink pictures. I'm an artist, see." I rummaged through my bag and showed him my sketches accompanied by my most charming smile. "And, as an artist, I'd be very keen to see the damage this fiend has caused to your town, so I might make a record of it with my humble pencils..." *And now the words flow so easily.*

The mayor led me to a small street of two-storey houses. The burnt out husks of the five at the end of the row stood charred and silent.

"Terrible, what happened here lad. You gots' to be some kind of monster to do a thing like this."

The fire had started within the building on the corner of the two streets, and spread its way inwards jumping from house to house. Of the first house, nothing but blackened timbers and a heap of ashes remained. The second's support beams stood like a crooked black skeleton, and the next one looked equally damaged. The house on the far end of the row had suffered the least damage, but I couldn't imagine anybody getting out alive. The flames had been intense enough to burn away most of the roof and the walls were smeared with dark burn marks. All five ruins gave off an unsettling aura, the air above seeming to hang deathly still.

I felt queasy. *There's no way my mother did this... surely?*

When words fail me, I draw. I pulled out my pad and sketched the ruin.

"Ye're from Hale, right boy?" The mayor eyed me from behind his big round spectacles.

There was no use lying. I had the accent, and he knew I hadn't arrived by train. Hale was the only place I could have possibly come from. I glanced up from my sketching, and nodded to the fat mayor.

"Rumour has it that the arsonist spoke with a Hale twang..." I felt his eyes on me, but tried not to react.

"I think we'd know if there was someone like that living in our little village, sir."

"Aye. I'm sure ye would," he agreed. He peered over my shoulder. "Say, you're pretty good at that."

"Thanks," I replied. With the rough sketch finished, I packed it away and stood. "Well, I'll be moving on now."

He eyed me, seemingly unsure about something. "Where you heading to next, lad?"

"Fentworth, sir." Despite evidence suggesting that my mother had been here in Aston until rather recently, she certainly wasn't here now.

"Rumour has it the arsonist fled to Fentworth..." The mayor spoke in a rather suspicious tone.

I held his gaze and shrugged.

"You watch yerself on the road lad."

"We'll be fine, won't we Max?" Max just sneezed. "Farewell, Mr Mayor." I felt his eyes on me as I made my way back to the street square and the train station. "Let's get out of here, boy," I said to Max. With all my coppers gone, I couldn't afford the train fare. We strode out through the back of the platform and started walking down the tracks.

Aston forest loomed around us in a curtain of shadow either side of the train line. The forest here was a dense pack of tall pines and fir trees. Peering in, I could barely see farther than the third or fourth row of trees – beyond that it might as well have been the dead of night under the canopy. *No moonslight would find you in there.* I shivered at the thought.

We followed the tracks as they cut their way through the trees.

I was balancing on one track when I felt the metal trembling beneath me. I hopped down and knelt to feel it. The vibrations sent gentle shockwaves up my arm as the train approached. I grinned as the tingles grew stronger. I glimpsed puffs of steam above the treeline against the bright blue morning sky, and the sound of a great engine chugged towards us. Max and I stepped down from the tracks and waited for the train to pass.

The immense black cylindrical monster on wheels rounded the corner and lumbered towards us.

Max's tail dropped between his legs and he cowered behind me. I rested my hand upon his head. *Monster*, he echoed.

My mother frequently rode the train on her moonly visits to Fentworth to buy food supplies for our family. Whenever she returned home, she'd be giddy with excitement. As I stood watching the gargantuan metal monster rumble towards me, I finally understood why.

The chimney belched puffs of steam into the azure sky and crowned the tops of the pines in a veil of mist. The ground trembled as the Great Train lumbered past.

A burly driver stood in a roofed cabin located at the back of the engine peering out ahead. I waved, but he didn't see either of us in time to return the gesture. His eyes widened in an amusing double-take.

Next came the carriages, grand wooden chambers lined with glass windows, and I saw the shadows of people sitting inside. They trundled by one after the other, all identical. I counted sixteen in total.

I watched the train until it had disappeared from sight, far ahead of us. It would reach Fentworth within the hour, and by the end of the day it would be at the coastal city of Joy at the opposite end of the world. I wondered if I might ever get there.

Most of the time, the line ran dead straight and I could see for miles, but now and then there would be a curve as the track wound its way around a hill.

We continued all day, sometimes walking in the gravelly path on either side, and sometimes on the metal rails themselves. The sun set the forest ablaze in an orange glow as it sunk beneath the horizon.

We spent the night huddled under the blanket on a bed of pine needles, and woke at dawn to continue our hike along the tracks.

I exhausted what little provisions we had brought, and both our stomachs were growling. I focused on Max, thinking the word *food* in my mind, just to see if he reacted. He loped along in front of me, but suddenly he turned to cock his head at me.

Food? He echoed, a rough wolfish voice.

He sniffed the ground, caught a scent and bounded into the trees. A rabbit bolted out of the darkness and across the tracks, followed shortly by Max who chased it into the trees on the opposite side.

"That's not what I meant by food!"

I waited. Max re-emerged a little way behind me and trotted up empty pawed. He snorted in disgust. "Nevermind boy, you'll get the next one." I rubbed his head and we marched on.

Around midday, we came to a small bricked pillbox overlooking a junction. Two sets of rusty tracks joined the mainline and curved away to the right towards a large rocky hillside. The main track continued straight ahead and I saw no sign of any other landmarks besides the seemingly endless rows of dark trees. *It must lead somewhere,* I thought. I decided to find out where.

At the end of the side track I discovered the entrance to an old abandoned mine. The tracks plunged into the side of the hill and promptly dropped into an abyss, where the tunnel had collapsed. I threw a stone in and listened to it echoing off the walls when it hit the ground somewhere deep below.

Entertaining as that was, my real reward for this bit of

exploration waited outside.

A rusty handcar with a two-sided lever rested on the tracks, just begging to be put back into service. I climbed up, gave the lever a yank and the car jerked forward.

"Oh Max, no more walking for us, boy. H'up!" Max leapt up beside me and flopped down on his belly at the front of the cart. I pumped the lever up and down, and we rolled our way back to the pillbox junction.

I used a lever in the pillbox to align the tracks, so I could then pump our borrowed handcar onto the mainline.

"Shouldn't have a problem reaching Fentworth before the train comes back, boy," I assured Max, as he dozed at the front of the car.

I pumped the handle and we rolled onwards. I should have remembered to reset the tracks back the way I found them, but I didn't.

For several hours, I rhythmically pumped the handcar's handle, setting us on a gentle cruise through the trees. My mind wandered to thoughts of my mother, and her work...

One of her biggest inventions was a giant mechanical slingshot which she called a *catapult*. A crowd of people gathered on top of Hale Hill to see what it could do. To everyone's amazement, the contraption worked, but the windmill lost two of its sails in the test-fire. To make up for it, Mother redesigned their entire mill, created a set of weirdly shaped sails that worked so efficiently even in the lightest of breezes. Hale's bread and biscuit sales have never been the same since.

I had a fifth brother, briefly. Mother and father never talk about him. I was very little but I remember the way the atmosphere of the house closed in on us at the time. I didn't even meet him, he died before I could. Mother's priorities changed after that. She stopped making things like catapults, and began researching medicines.

The house turned into a jungle. Potted plants took over every room, vines crept along the walls and strange flowers sprouted from every corner. She wanted to help people, and believed the answer lay somewhere in nature.

An outbreak of limpfoot spread across the village, and thanks to mother's experiments, she discovered that eating chewy bark from the wrinkle-wood tree helped to re-strengthen people's feet muscles. Unfortunately the bark caused a person's feet to grow fat and swollen, so she had to come up with the cure for fatfoot as well. That involved eating the slimy weeds that grew in ponds. People were less fond of that, and started to doubt she knew what she was doing.

"I don't have a clue!" she admitted one time after a stressful day as we ate our potatoes. "But that's no reason to stop trying."

Before she disappeared, she had been excited about the discovery of a certain type of honey. She believed kamuna honey contained a concentrated healing element, and had been working to figure out a way of harnessing its full potential. Just a dab of kamuna in a cup of boiling water cured the sniffles. Spread it on toast at breakfast and you'd feel supremely confident for the rest of the day. You could even put the stuff directly onto a small wound, and within a few hours it would be almost fully healed. It really was a remarkable discovery, but the people of Hale had lost patience with Mother and most were not willing to try it for themselves. The fact that she was covered in bee stings and looked like a monster out of some old crone's spook story probably had something to do with it.

The recent disappearance of her bees led to yet more tension between the rest of the village and my family. Mother accused Old Man Boyle of sabotaging her hive, but when no evidence of such mischief was found, she had to make a public apology to the grumpy old toad. It was decided that the bees upped and left of their own accord for no apparent reason, an answer Mother was never going to be satisfied with. The tree monster's horrible grin came to mind, and I remembered seeing all those bees inside its throat. *Could that be where they went?*

Her bees disappeared about two Blue Moons ago... Mother was understandably upset, but could she really have gone from that to full-blown arsonist and *murderer* in such a short space of time?

Max barked, jolting me from my daydream. The little mutt was fast asleep, fidgeting on his side chasing dream-rabbits.

The trees had been thinning out for several miles, and soon we came upon the Fent Vale, a wide v-shaped grassy valley. The train tracks leapt across it via the longest bridge in Lunaria. I shivered, remembering what happened the last time I'd tried to cross a bridge.

The crossing looked to be at least a mile long, and higher than the Hale Scar. A complicated network of wooden beams and struts held the grand structure together. I saw no sign of the train coming back the other way, but it would be due at some point. If it met us on the bridge, there would be nowhere to go but down...

Better go quickly, just in case. I pumped the car's handle and we rolled on to the bridge.

I braced against a gusty breeze that pushed my back, giving us a boost of speed. I felt relieved in the open air after all the claustrophobic forests. As we crossed the vale, I gazed at the view. Grassy hills stretched across the horizon in all directions, a brown river flowed from the north to my left, and meandered along the valley's basin beneath the bridge and off to my right. It flowed around a bend, behind a hill and out of sight. Somewhere beyond, I imagined it flowed into the sea. Farm houses dotted the far side of the valley, fields of wheat and barley ready for harvest grew in the neighbouring fields. Way beneath us, some shaggy grey horses lined up for a drink at a water trough, and a herd of sheep fled down the hill trying to outrun a farmer's dog. The farmer stood by a gate commanding with a high pitched whistle.

The wind shifted direction, blasting my face, and the cart

suddenly felt a lot heavier to move. Carried on the breeze came the screech of another whistle. It echoed across the hills, much, much louder...

I still had a half a mile to cross, too late to turn back, and the train was heading right for us. Max barked. A chill shot through me.

"No, no, no, no, no, *no.*"

I pumped the handle furiously, and we battled through the wind. The train ahead bellowed smoke. Our only chance was to make it to the edge of the bridge before the train did. It flew out of the hills so fast it would never stop before it hit us. I pumped the handle up and down as fast as my weary arms would let me. The handcar raced across the bridge, wind slapping my face. The train whistled again, louder still. I saw the black metal grill on its front hurtling towards our puny little handcar. Up and down I pumped, up and down. The bridge groaned. Max whimpered. Up and down up and down up and down up and... *The train is going to hit us.*

"*JUMP MAX!*"

The handcar reached the end of the bridge and the train bore down on us like a giant metal rhinoceros and I leapt from the cart. The train smashed into it.

CLANG!

Metal clashed against metal and the car spun into the air. It arced high over the valley and plunged out of sight. The train thundered over the bridge, unaffected by the collision. I slammed into the grassy bank, tumbled head over heels and landed hard on my back. Gasping for breath, I scrambled up the bank as the train carriages rumbled past.

I couldn't see Max. I called for him at the top of my lungs, my voice barely a whisper above the thunderous roar of the passing locomotive, and feared the worst.

Chapter Four

The train's rear carriage rushed by me leaving a storm of dusty wind in its wake that scratched at my face. I climbed onto the raised tracks, searching desperately for any sign of Max, but he was nowhere to be seen.

"*Max!*" This time my voice echoed back at me across the valley hills.

Nothing.

My eyes stung from the dust that had blown into them. I felt them welling up.

I searched from one bank to the other, and studied the tracks for signs of blood, while my stomach twisted itself into an ever tightening knot. The tracks were clean, the banks empty. *Where are you, Max?* Desperation crept in.

A faint hiss echoed in my mind, rising gradually to a steady buzzing sensation. The white noise. Usually it hurt, but this time I welcomed the sound – Max must be somewhere close. I searched again, squinting against the sunlight, and spotted a small dark patch of fur amongst the grass a way down the hill on the northern bank.

I ran towards him, sliding down the grass.

"Max!" I dropped to one knee beside his limp body. He lay sprawled in the grass, rasping horribly as he breathed over a patch of red grass around his snout. The sight of blood snapped whatever held back my tears.

I laid a hand on his flat bony head, and a window opened in my mind.

Suddenly I'm back on the bridge, on the cart, and the train is coming straight at me. *A vision? No, this is Max's memory.*

Monster! Fear and tension course through me, the wind painfully stinging my sensitive nose. I hear *Billy* shout my name, and the *monster* charges for us. I leap. Just a fraction too late... My leg erupts in pain as it clips the side of the train, sending me into a wild spin. The clang of metal *booms* behind me. I tumble through the air and bounce head-first off a rock and thud into the grass bank sliding to a halt.

Moments later, the window slammed shut and the memory vanished.

I snapped back to the hillside, knelt beside Max. I wiped the wet from my eyes and saw the rock several metres above us on the slope, a dark spatter of blood glistening across its surface.

Max's eyes were open, but strangely blank. He stared right through me. He rasped one ragged breath after the next. The paw on his stiffened rear left leg looked unnaturally askew, and he bled from a gash near his ear.

I fumbled in my pack for my skin and tipped some of the kamuna water over the wound. He whimpered, but didn't flinch. Max's head remained flat on the ground, panting, and his tongue flopped out. He lapped at the water weakly as I offered it to him. After a few gulps, his eyes blinked and returned to normal. This time he recognised me. He echoed a noise, *oww*.

I gently hoisted him over a shoulder, so his head and front paws dangled over my back, and cradled him back up the slope.

At the top of the ridge, I crossed the tracks and glanced down the valley. The mangled ruin of the handcar lay far below in a field. A herd of sheep huddled at the opposite end of the paddock, every head turned towards the hulk of metal. The farmer and his dog were making their way across the farmland to investigate. They must have been half a mile away.

I carefully carried Max down the slippery hill, into the valley.

As the hill flattened out, I saw that a section of fencing had been smashed apart. The cart had bounced several times and crashed through it on its way down the hill. The farmer's dog saw us first. She barked and bounded up as I carefully navigated through the tangle of fence cable. Max panted in my ear, and wriggled as he tried to turn around to see the black and white collie, and I almost dropped him.

I called to the farmer, who glanced up from the other side of the handcar wreck. As I made my way across the field, the plump man waddled towards us.

"By 'eck, lad," he remarked, once we were in earshot. "Were you the lunatic who was playin' chicken with the train?"

"Please, Mister," I wheezed.

"Say, thas' a funny lookin' dog. Is he alright?"

"He's badly hurt. I need your help."

The collie sniffed at Max's paw as it dangled limply. Then she tenderly licked the wound.

Max's echo brought a smile to my face, despite myself. *Friend.*

The portly farmer led us to his house on the side of the valley. A solitary cottage resting in a natural flat outcrop close to the summit, a dirt access track led east into the hills towards the town of Fentworth. Faded white paint peeled from the wooden walls, and tendrils of smoke drifted out of the chimney on a slanting tiled roof.

We entered through the back door, into the kitchen. The farmer kicked off his muddy boots, brushed a heap of assorted items from the table and instructed me to lay Max where he could get a good look at him.

"Good boy, easy now," I gently rested him on his side, so we could tend to his injured paw.

The farmer bustled about the room gathering up items. He didn't seem to notice all the flies that buzzed around the room, crawling on the ceiling and the walls, and some started taking a keen interest in Max's bloody leg. I swatted them away whenever they tried to land on him.

"'Ere lad, hold him steady." He dabbed the leg with a cloth soaked in some brown liquid that smelt like burnt metal. Max whined. The farmer conjured an immaculately white towel from somewhere and dabbed at the blood. "I'm no doctor, mind. Best we get our Becky to give the mutt a once over when she gets 'ome. My name's George, by the way."

"Billy," I said.

"We can shake hands later." His smile beamed from ear to ear, and I exhaled a long drawn out breath. *It'll be okay Max,* I sent, and he reacted with the slightest wag of his tail.

Farmer George did what he could, which wasn't much, admittedly. He dressed Max's leg in the towel, and taped it up firmly so that it couldn't move about. After relocating him to the dog's basket next to the warm stove, I squeezed in beside him, wanting to stay within reach. The young collie sniffed at the towel and gazed curiously at the two strangers occupying her bed.

"Well, Lucy don't seem to mind ye' none, at least," the farmer said, standing with his hands on his hips. The collie turned her head to him and wagged her tail, and he gave a satisfied nod.

George fussed about the kitchen. It was hard to believe he knew where to look, the place was in such a state. Clutter filled every corner. There were boxes of tools, clippers and shearing equipment, feed buckets, a pile of boots by the door, dirty cutlery and plates stacked up by the sink and the wooden floorboards were covered with dried muddy foot prints.

George washed his hands in the sink, and put a pot of water onto the stove to boil. He stood over us ponderously. "So then lad," he pulled up a chair and plonked his ample girth into it. "What exactly was you doing ridin' them there train tracks?"

As I explained my tale, George poured two mugs of tea and handed me one. He gave me a queer look when I described the tree monster, and at the part where I'd fallen into the Scar and spent two days wallowing in a kamuna cave pool being brought back to life, he outright chuckled.

"Shame we don't have none of that karmdoona now, eh?" he mocked, slurping his tea.

"I used it up on Max's leg before I found you," I replied earnestly.

"Aye, aye, I bet. Go on." Despite his obvious doubts, he heard the rest willingly enough.

I explained as best I could what I'd been hearing in my head whenever Max *echoed*.

"White noise? Wassat?" George inquired, frowning.

"It's a sort of fuzzy hiss. Sudden and painful... like after you hear a loud noise, you know?"

"Oh, I knows. I get that when Mils' clouts me one when I forgets to take me boots off in the house!" He chuckled again, a hearty infectious sound.

I smiled. "Is Mils' your wife?"

"Millie, aye. Should be 'ome soon in fact. Best get grub on!" He rose, tossed some fresh logs into the stove and went outside. He came back with a plucked chicken.

"I'm sorry for troubling you, George." I got to my feet. "I will take Max to Fentworth, we're only in the way here."

"Nonsense, lad! Ye'll stay here tonight, methinks. Scrawny thing like you could use a good meal. Peel some o'these would ya lad." He pulled out a sack of potatoes from a cupboard and tossed it to me. I caught it clumsily. "'sides, ye owes me a new fence." He smirked.

My face reddened. It seemed the farmer would have me

stay to repay my debt. I couldn't argue, nor really wanted to. I opened the sack and the sight of spuds reminded me of my last breakfast at home.

"Thank you," I said, smiling and peeling.

Max watched us from his borrowed bed. Lucy lay next to him. The smell of roasting chicken filled the kitchen, and the stronger the aroma grew, the more Max drooled.

George's wife Millie and a girl about the same age as me entered through the back door as George stirred the gravy pot and I set the table. The pair had been running their market stall in town all day, and smelt earthy and sweaty. The woman took one look at the messy kitchen and clouted her husband round the back of the head with a plump hand.

"Look at the state o'this place! I ought to have married the pig!" She dropped a sack of vegetables on the floor and slid her boots off.

"Welcome home, dear." George smiled, seeming not to take any notice of the slap nor the pig comment.

"Who are you?" The girl peered at me over the sack she carried.

Millie glanced up part-way through removing a boot, and uttered a surprised *oh!*

"Becky, this 'ere's Billy," said George. "He and Max there had a bit of an accident on the bridge. Poor pooch hurt his leg."

Max had his chin nestled on the side of the basket. At the mention of his name he raised his head, but the act appeared to take great effort. Becky saw the blood-stained towel around his leg, dropped her carrots and scurried across the room. She knelt beside the basket to examine him. George had told me she was a bit of an animal lover. "You poor thing! What happened?"

I scratched my elbow. "I, uh, we sort of crashed into the train. Max clipped his leg."

"How did you *crash* into the train?"

I felt my face reddening. "I wasn't fast enough. We were riding a mine cart at the time..."

Becky exhaled a word under her breath. I couldn't make it out.

George chimed in. "Here I am tending to me sheep, and suddenly I hears a big ol' *CLANG* and look up to see its raining rust buckets from the skies!" He waved his big hands in the air. "I nary knew what was happenin' then I sees the lad stumbling through me fields carrying that funny lookin' mutt. See what ye can do, Becks."

With one hand, she rubbed Max under the chin as he licked her, and unwrapped the towel with the other. I hunched down beside her for a closer look.

"Oh you poor thing," she repeated. Max's leg was swollen and crooked, with dried blood spattered in his fur. "Swap with me. Hold his head."

I shimmied around her, and took Max's big bony head in my hands. Becky felt up and down his leg. He whimpered.

"There, there, boy. It'll be better soon," she spoke to Max. Then to me, "His paw is dislocated. Hold him firm. He won't like what I'm about to do." She spoke confidently, like she'd done this before. I gave her a nervous nod.

Becky took Max's paw in her hand and his shin in the other. Max's eyes grew wide as plates. There was a bony *crack* as Becky applied pressure. White noise cascaded over me in a deafening wave as Max's pain ripped through my skull. I almost passed out.

"*Cripes!*" I exhaled, after the intense pain subsided. Max licked Becky's hand and wagged his tail happily as he relaxed into the basket. My heart went out to him.

Becky gave me a questioning glance while she saw to his leg. She created a real bandage out of some linen cloth and cleaned and wrapped it snugly. He didn't even try to stand up after. I felt worried, but she assured me that with perhaps a Blue Moon's worth of rest, he should be up and about again. She gave him a bowl of meat, which Max instantly started gobbling. *At least you've kept your appetite.* My belly grumbled.

We all sat down to dinner. I ate three platefuls.

"Where'd you put it, Billy? There's nary an ounch o'fat on ya!" Millie remarked as I was halfway through the third. I shrugged and grinned. It was the tastiest food I'd ever eaten. The chicken had been clucking outside in the pen only two days ago, and the vegetables were as fresh as could be, grown right here on the farm. And that gravy...

"Thish ish delicioush," I said through a mouthful. I had said it four times already.

"Well ye need yer strength, lad! Tomorrow, we got work to do," George reminded me. "Ye ever mended a fence 'afore?"

I swallowed. "I'm not exactly used to manual labour. We don't have any farms in Hale."

"Aye, lazy spuds just sit around eating biscuits and wearing them fancy hats! I knows it, I seen it."

"Listen to 'im," Millie shook her head at her husband. "Took one trip a lifetime ago and still bragging like he knows everything."

"I do knows everything." His grin made him twenty years younger.

As the old couple exchanged banter, Becky leaned across the table to me.

She spoke softly. "Grandad was a builder when he was young. He worked on the Great Trainline."

"Really? That's so cool." I watched the old couple fire playful insults at each other. Millie sounded angry but her eyes shone with affection, and George just shrugged it all off with a knowing smile.

"Did you know the train was supposed to go all the way to Hale?" Becky continued. "He was working near when the Scar split... he lost many friends that day." After a solemn glance at her grandfather, she returned to her meal.

"Woah." I didn't know what else to say.

The sun set as we cleaned up, filling the house with a deep orange glow before blanketing it in darkness. Lit by candlelight, warmed by the stove, the farmhouse became the definition of cosy. We talked a short while around the table before George and Millie said goodnight and went to bed. Farmers were all about the early mornings.

From the kitchen, a small hallway led to the front door, with two doors on each wall. The couple slept in the first room on the right, and Becky on the left. I was to share her room. I had only ever shared a room with my brothers before.

A soft pile of blankets waited for me on the floor beside her bed, and a wooden chest-of-drawers strewn with objects I didn't recognise. When Becky went to the privy, I quickly undressed and slid into my blankets, instinctively rolling onto my side to face the wall.

When I heard Becky climb into bed, I didn't move. After a while, she spoke.

"You can't be asleep already."

I rolled over. She lay on one elbow under a thick blanket, her face lit by the candle on her bedside table. Long hair curled down wildly around her bright round eyes reflecting the candlelight. It seemed she wanted to talk, but I didn't know what to say. So I just made a noise like *mm-hmm*.

"Why are you here?" she asked. The question took me by surprise.

"Er, I told you, Max got hurt. It was so lucky your granddad—"

She cut me off. "That's not what I mean. Why are you out here, far from home?"

"Oh." I thought about it. I wanted to impress her with my answer... "My mother didn't come home, so Father sent me out to find her, but that's not the only reason. I'm ready to explore the world and I want to sketch all the interesting things I find, and just see what's out there. I've never been this far east before. It hasn't exactly been a smooth journey so far..."

"Earlier, when I realigned Max's paw, you seemed to, I dunno, *feel* it. What's up with that?" Her fiery eyes watched me intently.

George hadn't believed me when I'd told him about Max and me. I didn't think Becky would either. I hesitated. "I was just worried. We are quite close, you know. He's the best travel companion." I tried to change the subject. "You talk funny. Why don't you sound like George and Millie?"

She smiled. "They gots the ol' farmer twang, eh laddy?" she said this mocking her grandparents' accent. I laughed. She continued, "I'm not from here. I grew up in Hooke. It's further down the train line, right before Joy on the coast. You heard of it?"

I shook my head. I'd have to show her the map I was sketching, so she could tell me where to place the town. "What's it like there?"

She looked at me, and something in her eyes changed. Even in the soft glow of the candle, I noticed. "It's..." she paused, rolled onto her back and I could no longer see her face. "Not like here," she finished vaguely. I waited for more, but there was none.

I hesitated again. "Oh. Okay." *Now what?* The conversation had fizzled out. I couldn't remember the last time I had spoken this long to a girl. I didn't want it to end yet. The silence lingered. *Has she fallen asleep?*

I stared at the ceiling for a long time. The candle reached the end of its wick and sputtered out.

"Good night," I said to the darkness.

Becky's soft sleepy reply drifted back to me. "Good night."

Chapter Five

I was awoken by the screech of a dying cockerel. At least I assumed it was dying, it may just have been angry. Its broken crowing was the most horrendous noise I'd ever heard.

I buried my head under the blankets. It was so snug and warm and there weren't any cockerels laying siege to my eardrums down there.

Something kicked me in the buttocks, accompanied by a muffled voice.

"Wakey wakey spud! Up we gets, lad."

The house was cold and gloomy. The sun wouldn't hit the cottage directly until late morning thanks to the lay of the surrounding hillside. I staggered into the kitchen to the smell of bacon and eggs, and felt that it was all worthwhile. While I ate my third rasher, I glanced at Max eating his own breakfast in Lucy's basket. It occurred to me how ironically lucky this situation was. Yesterday, the train almost killed us both, but we'd likely be starving and trying to beg for money in the streets of Fentworth by now, had we made it there. Instead, we were well fed and had a roof over our heads.

Becky and Millie drove the wagon off to town carrying

sacks of vegetables while George, Lucy and I made our way down to the valley basin, armed with shovels and hammers.

As we descended, I admired the colossal bridge that spanned the valley to my right. It dominated the view northwards, a thousand criss-crossing planks of wood making a chequered shadow pattern on the hills below. The river wound its way between the two highest pillars at its centre. Looking south, fields and grasslands stretched away towards more grassy hills, bathed in morning sunlight. Peace and natural beauty reigned here. It was easy to see why the farmers had chosen this place to be their home.

All day long, we carried wooden stumps back and forth, dug holes and threaded cables. I had never worked so hard in all my life. By the end of the day, I felt exhausted. Muscles that I didn't even know I had ached all over my body.

George looked up at the bridge curiously at one point. "Hmm, strange that."

"What is it?" I asked, planting a wooden post into the ground.

"Train's late. It's never late."

I couldn't imagine why.

The following day, George sent me to Fentworth to pick up supplies. We had almost finished the fence, but he insisted on doing the rest himself. I appreciated the chance to search for a new lead on the whereabouts of my mother, so I jumped in the back of Millie's wagon with the vegetables. She and Becky sat up front, dangling a carrot on the end of a rope in front of one of the huge shaggy horses I had seen from the bridge. Only, up close I realised it wasn't a horse at all. It had two great curled horns between its ears.

"That's the biggest goat I've ever seen!" I exclaimed in awe, and the two ladies giggled. "What?"

Becky turned around. "He's a ram, Billy. A Fent Bighorn."

"That's a type o'sheep, young spud," Millie added, chuckling. "Ever since they come down from the mountains, we Fentons became good friends with the Bighorns. Nothing better than a giant ram to get you over the hills! *Hup!*" She whipped the reins, and the wagon bounced along the track.

One bumpy ride later, we arrived at the bustling market town. We rolled into Fentworth's town square, a wide open cobblestoned space enclosed by three-storey palestone buildings. The square had its own clock tower in the centre, smaller than Aston's, built as a solitary focal point of the square. All around it several dozen tents were in the process of being erected.

I helped Millie and Becky setup their stall amongst a row of caravans manned by local farmers, butchers, blacksmiths, lumberjacks and travelling merchants. It seemed you could buy almost anything at Fentworth's famous market.

I couldn't believe how many people were about so early in the morning. An impatient old man arrived at the stall to buy some carrots before we had even raised the awning, but Millie greeted and served him cheerfully. *One of her regulars*, I assumed.

With the stall ready to go and Millie and Becky busy serving customers, I took a stroll around the market searching for any people who may be acquainted with my mother. She came here often to pick up supplies for our home in Hale. Usually, she'd be gone for two red moons, and return with a big sack of food.

I approached the nearest vegetable stall and the man behind the wall of turnips shook his head. He asked what she looked like, which gave me an idea. I found a quiet spot between two caravans, took out a wanted poster, and tore my mother's picture off in a rough square. I returned and showed the man, but he still shook his head.

I must have asked every food-selling merchant in the market, but nobody recognised her. I kept referring to her as "this woman" rather than mention the fact that she was my mother. If anyone had been to Aston lately, they might recognise the picture, and assume I too was some sort of criminal... Then a couple who sold tomatoes laughed at the picture.

"I'd recognise that crazy face any day!" remarked the woman.

"We ain't seen her for quite a while, though," added the man. They were so friendly, I did let slip who I was and they gave me a small sack of dirt to give to her when I saw her next.

"That'll get her toms right big and juicy, you tells her!" the woman exclaimed brightly. My mother wasn't growing any 'toms' as far as I knew, but I took the dirt anyway and bid them farewell.

With no useful leads, I felt deflated. I sat on a bench under the clock tower to eat some sandwiches that Millie had made for me, and sketched the bustling market scene. I would come away from Fentworth at least with *something*.

That's when I first saw the Fedora Man.

As I sat on the bench sketching a nearby crowd of people, he caught my eye because of his strange outfit. He leant against the wall in a dark alleyway between two buildings, wearing a long pale-grey jacket and a matching fedora with a black trim. His hands were in his pockets, and his head hung low, hiding his face beneath the hat. He might have been watching the small crowd of people, but I couldn't be sure.

They were gathered around some sort of preacher, who stood raised on a wooden crate, ranting. The preacher had grey hair that poked out from beneath a battered top hat which rested askew on his head. He spoke with his hands a lot, gesturing to random people.

Something in his speech caught my ear, and I half listened...

"...false king must be dethroned! His reign of malice is causing no end of suffering, but who stands against such ignorant brutality? Who dares face the bogeymen that come knocking? Who would dare defy their KING? I ask you, who? You? What about you?"

"What about you, ya' old codger!" someone in the crowd heckled back, which caused a ripple of laughter.

"I am doing my part by speaking to you. I must spread the word to those who will listen! Friends, the time is approaching when you must choose to make a stand." His voice abruptly turned sullen, and he stared distantly over the crowd. "They took my wife to the Khazi. Innocent, she was. Yet they took her. They take everyone, eventually. *Come with me, let's take a dive to the bottom of the sea...*" This last line, he quoted from an old nursery rhyme, and I had never heard it sung with such melancholy.

The passion in his speech had all but disappeared, and he no longer held the crowd's attention. Most were muttering amongst themselves as they dispersed. I didn't know what he had been talking about, but I was curious to know which town he had come from. And what was *the Khazi*? The mayor of Aston had said my mother belonged there...

As the crowd dissipated, I decided I would ask him. He stepped down from the crate and packed away some belongings into a ragged sack. I stood up from my bench and went to approach him, just as he was walking past the alleyway and the Fedora Man.

The Fedora Man grabbed the old preacher, and the shadows swallowed them both. I froze.

It happened so quickly, the force had knocked the old man's bent top hat from his head. It sat on the cobbles outside the alleyway, as if he had never been there at all.

I moved in for a closer look. Nestled between the two buildings, gloomy and smelling rather pungent, the alley was not a place I felt like entering. I heard scraping, something being dragged along the ground, out of sight

47

around the corner.

I crept into the alleyway.

The damp gravel crunched beneath my feet as I edged along the wall, avoiding the spilled contents of an old rotten crate. When I reached the corner, I peered around.

The Fedora Man had his back to me, and I saw him slam the lid of a metal box shut, which was attached to the back of a small four-wheeled vehicle. I saw the broad shoulders of a stocky man sitting in the front. He also wore a fedora, a black one to match his black jacket. After locking the lid, the skinnier Fedora Man climbed up behind the driver and said, "Let's go."

Cogs *crunched*, and a little engine churned as the driver peddled. I'd never seen such a cart. It was like a cross between a bicycle and a donkey wagon, but the only engine I'd ever seen before was the Great Train and this was much, much smaller. The pedal-cart rolled out of the far end of the alleyway into the sun, turned the corner and disappeared from my sight.

I returned to the town square, and plucked up the bent top hat from the ground. *Did they kidnap him?* I spied the building with the white banners suspended from its roof, and marched across the square. As I climbed the steps to the mayor's town hall, the murmur of voices leaked into the streets. Something was astir.

At least fifty people were crammed into the lobby, and I heard a dozen angry voices all trying to speak at the same time. Everyone seemed to be shoving their way towards a row of wooden desks at the back of the room, attended by some township advisors. They were talking to anybody near the front of the bustle.

Chaos reigned in the lobby, and before I had a chance to fight my way to the front of the mass, a loud voice boomed across the room.

"*LADIES AND GENTLEMEN*. If I can have your attention, please." I turned to see an obese man balancing precariously on a table shouting across the crowd. The

mayor of Fentworth. Everyone fell silent. "Thank you."
He smiled and clasped his hands together across the top of
his belly. The waistcoat about his midriff looked so tight I
thought the buttons might pop out and hit someone in the
face.

"As I'm sure most of you are aware, there has been an
incident on the train line." My throat tightened. This must
be about my minecart crash. "My messenger travelled out
last night to investigate, and he returned this morning with
a report. I can confirm there have been no fatalities." *Well,
of course not.* The train smashed through my cart like it was
made of paper, there's no way anybody was hurt. "But the
train itself is now buried in the side of the Old Aston
Mine." Oh.

Oh...

"It appears that the old pillbox junction was tampered
with, causing the train to take an unexpected detour along
the abandoned tracks. I will be working with the Mayor of
Aston to investigate this matter and find out who is
responsible for such a heinous act."

"Was it the Aston Arsonist?" a man near the door
suggested. A murmur rippled through the crowd.

The mayor raised his hands and the crowd quietened
once again. He answered, "Rumours that the fugitive
known as the Aston Arsonist has fled towards Fentworth
do appear to be true. It is too early to jump to such
conclusions, but it is certainly a possibility that the same
person is responsible for sabotaging our prestigious train.
We must be vigilant in these troublesome times."

An advisor handed the mayor a poster which he held up
to the crowd. I stared at the picture of my mother. The
poster was identical to the ones I picked up in Aston, with
the additional offer of a reward written below my mother's
crazed face.

The mayor went on, "I would ask you all to keep a
watchful eye out for this woman. She is dangerous and
must not be approached. Report any sightings to your

nearest lawman. I will be putting these wanted posters throughout the town to serve as a reminder, and note that as of today, there will be a reward of one gold piece in exchange for her capture." The mayor smiled smugly. "As for the train, she will be inoperable until we can excavate her. If you are travelling along..."

I forgot about the alleyway incident. I donned the old bent top hat, pulled the rim low over my face and made a hasty exit.

Later that day, I told Becky about the Fedora Man. We sat on the back porch of the cottage, watching the last rays of the sun fade across the valley. Max lay on the ground at my feet, his bandaged leg outstretched across the grass. Big Blue rose out of the southern horizon, a giant crystal disc on a darkening sky streaked with wispy grey-blue clouds.

"What's a fedora?" she asked.

"It's a hat. It's like the ranch hat Millie wears, but smaller and smarter-looking, with a strip of coloured fabric around the base."

"It sounds posh. How would a spud like you know about a hat like that?" she jested.

"Haven't you heard of the famous Hale Hat Shop? You're speaking to one of their lead designers, don't you know."

She grinned. "Granpa was right. You Hale people love your hats."

I continued, "His was light grey with a black trim, and he wore a long grey coat. He was tall and skinny, and a bit creepy looking. And I'm pretty sure he kidnapped a guy."

Becky glanced at me, and I knew she had seen the man, or someone like him before. "You're very inquisitive," she said.

I didn't know what to say to that. "Yeah, I guess. This is all new to me. It was so crowded in town. I've never seen so many people in one place before."

"Heh. Fentworth is nothing. The further east you go, the busier it gets. Wait 'til you see Joy." The blue moon's reflection in her eyes hypnotised me for a moment.

I stared down at my feet, or Max, and rambled. "Mother travelled the train line. She told me a little about the towns, and it sounded horrible to me, even as a kid. I'd never want to live in a big town."

"I'm from a big town."

I risked another glance. I wondered what her hair felt like. "You don't like your home, do you?" Hale and Hooke were literally at opposite ends of the continent. I wanted to know what it was like, but all I got was another cryptic answer.

"There's no green there anymore." Becky gazed across the twilit valley. Then she changed the subject. "Did you find out anything about your mother?"

"Nothing useful." I considered telling her about the wanted posters, but I didn't want her to think I was the son of a criminal. "It doesn't seem like she's been here for a while." It wasn't a complete lie – the tomato sellers had told me that, and I had no reason to doubt them.

We sat in quiet for some time, watching the stars twinkle into existence. Max stared at me with his pale gold eyes, wagged his tail and, in an almost human gesture, nodded his head towards Becky. I stifled a laugh as he *echoed* a word that made me flush red.

Mate.

I ruffled him roughly on the head.

Becky glanced my way. "What's funny?"

"Nothing."

I had never been a morning person, but travelling taught me the simple value of daylight. Living with George and Millie only drummed the lesson in further. With their livelihood entirely dependent on the farm, it was imperative to be awake bright and early to take full advantage of the day. There's always something to do, be it mending fences, feeding the chickens, milking the cow, filling water troughs, checking rat traps, herding lost billy-goats back to their paddocks after they've somehow broken through yet another fence, somewhere... All of this was so new to me that I didn't even see it as hard work. It was all experience, and I relished it.

I lived with the farmers until Max was healed enough to continue our journey. We ended up staying for the duration of the Blue Moon, twelve days and nights.

I learned a lot in that short time. Millie taught me the basics of tending animals and growing vegetables, and George showed me all the commands that Lucy the sheepdog knew. It only took a few Red Moons before Max dragged himself to the door, eager to see what we were all doing outside. When he was up to it, he joined Lucy in the paddocks helping to herd the sheep. I had never imagined working on a farm before setting off to find Mother, and yet here I was. I even developed something that resembled muscles in my arms.

George took Becky and me duck hunting, and showed us how to fire his old blunderbuss. I brought Max with me to see if he would be able to help. He enthusiastically bumbled into the long grass barking, tactically scaring the ducks into the air, but unlike Lucy, he wasn't so good at the stealthy approach.

I fell in love with the valley, and developed an appreciation for fluffy white clouds. Some mornings, the hillsides would be dotted with clumps of white mist that clung to the valley from the south until passing between the slats under the great bridge. When the sun arose over the hills the mist evaporated, revealing the green grass and flowing river below. I grew fond of mornings like that.

I should have moved on.

At the end of the Blue Moon, on the morning of the thirteenth day, trouble came looking for me.

George, Millie, Becky and I were at the kitchen table

eating breakfast.

"Gotta say it laddy, I ne'r thought a scrawny spud like you would be any use around 'ere!" George remarked, smiling broadly as he munched his bowl of oats. "Ye've been a real help these past few redduns.'"

"Well thanks, I've really enjoyed myself here." George and Millie felt like my own grandparents, I had never met such kind people. I felt guilty about not telling them the truth of my mother. In Fentworth, wanted posters had sprung up all over town, and talk of the Aston Arsonist and the Train Trasher was on everyone's lips. I didn't go to the town any more, for fear of being recognised. With Max back on his feet, I thought it would be best if we left the farm soon to continue my search.

Just another few days of these delicious meals...

A question had been in my head for some time and I hesitated at the opportunity to ask it. "Would you mind if I visited you again, on my way back home I mean?"

"O'course not boy!" Millie clasped a plump arm around my shoulders. "Ye're almost part of the family now. You come visit any time you likes."

"Just use the road next time, lad" George hooted. "My sheep don't need no more mine carts cluttering up the place!" Everyone laughed, George by far the loudest.

Lucy and Max turned towards the hallway and pricked their ears. They sprang up and bounded to the front door, sniffing the ground. A shadow appeared behind the door, followed by a knock.

"Who in blazes is that gonna be?" George peered down the hallway.

"I'll get it," Becky said, rising.

"No, no, you haven't finished yer' brekky. I'll go." George hauled himself up and plodded to the door.

"Max's leg has healed well," Becky said, reseating herself at the table. "He's so eager to drive the sheep!"

"I know. He's learned a few new tricks from Lucy, she's a good influence on him."

From the hallway, I heard George speaking with someone. "Who wants to know?" he demanded. I couldn't see who he was talking to because George took up most of the door frame.

Becky continued, "We should take them down to the river paddocks today. I want to see you and Max move the herd. I don't know how you've trained him so fast. I swear sometimes you don't even give him any commands and he does exactly what you want."

I grinned and feigned a shrug. "Just a natural, I suppose."

"Sling yer' hook!" George's voice bellowed down the hallway. He slammed the door shut, and ambled back to the kitchen.

"Who was that?" Becky asked.

"Jus' some joker askin' 'bout our Billy here."

"What? Who?" I dropped my spoon on the table, ran to the hallway and peered out through the porch window. A heavyset man stomped away from the cottage up the dirt track, huge fisted hands swinging to and fro. He wore a dark jacket and pin-striped trousers. A black fedora covered his round, shaven head.

He squeezed into his pedal-cart and glanced back at the cottage. I saw a crooked nose, deep set eyes that glared into a smirk when they met mine. I didn't duck in time.

Who is that? How did he find me? My throat tightened.

I heard the *crunch* of the cart's cog-engine kick in as the big man pedalled away up the track.

I've waited too long. I have to leave this place.

Chapter Six

As I knelt on the floor packing what few possessions I had into my backsack, Becky appeared in the door. Max loped over, sat by her feet and offered her a paw. *Beckyyy,* he echoed. I tried to hide my smile.

She watched me. "You and Max are telepaths, aren't you?"

"Tele-what?" I stopped packing.

"You can hear his thoughts."

"... yes."

She beamed, and dropped to the floor beside me. "How? Can you teach me? You have to teach me!"

"I can't."

"Why not?"

"I don't know how."

"Yeah you do. Tell me!"

"I really can't! It's just a side effect."

"A *side effect*? Of what?"

"Um. I died."

"...What?"

"It's complicated."

Mate.

"Shh." I grinned at Max.

"What did he say? Tell me!"

"No." I stood, reddening, and made for the door.

"You have to teach me!" She rose and blocked my way, eyes wide and fiery. "Tell me what happened to you."

"It might take a while to explain."

"Ugh." She rolled her eyes. "Well, it's a long way to Hooke. We'll have time."

I shook my head, dumbfounded. "What?"

"I'm coming with you."

I stared blankly. And repeated, "What?"

"That man who came here looking for you. He will come again."

"I know, that's why I'm going. They must have figured out it was me who crashed their train... and now they probably think you're hiding me. I can't drag you guys into this."

"You idiot! You think they are after you because of the train?"

"Uh, why else?" I asked dumbly.

"I've been thinking about the man you saw in Fentworth, at the alleyway... You see them all the time in Hooke."

I had almost forgotten about the kidnapping. I'd been so worried about the train and saving my own skin, the creepy fedora man had slipped my mind. "Them? How many are there? I knew there was something about that guy. What is he, part of some gang?"

"It's not a gang." She scrunched up her nose. "They have close ties with the King. Although some say the King works for them... It doesn't matter, you just need to stay away from them, Billy." The hint of fear in her voice unnerved me somewhat. "I've never seen them this far west. Something is going on. And I'm sure your mother is involved."

I frowned, confused. "What makes you think my mother is involved?"

She bit her lip. "They are hunting her."

How does she know...?

"I'm sorry, Billy," she hung her head. "I saw the wanted posters in your bag."

It's impossible to keep a secret from a girl when you're living in her bedroom.

She met my eyes again with a glare. "You could have told me, you know."

"Yeah... I'm sorry I didn't," it was my turn to admire the floorboards. "I thought you'd think I was a criminal."

"You don't really think she killed those people, do you?"

"No way. She wouldn't." I shook my head, defiant. "She's crazy, I told you, but she would never hurt anyone. Mother wanted to *help* people." I thought about Hale, and our uppity neighbour, Mr Boyle. "Sometimes, people didn't exactly *want* her help... she's not easy to get along with." I shook my head again. "Whatever happened in Aston, there's gotta be another explanation."

"I believe you." No hesitation. I'd never seen her look so serious. "But I want you away from my grandparents. Those men specialise in tracking lawbreakers, but they follow a rather loose definition of 'law'... They will call here again looking for you, and when they do, we must be far away."

I nodded agreement.

"The good news is they obviously haven't caught your mother yet." Becky smiled eagerly. "Let's find her first."

We made a plan to continue east, towards Becky's home town of Hooke. With me gone, the hunters had no reason to bother George and Millie.

We gathered our things together and brought them to the back porch. The old farmer couple stood on the wooden steps, arguing as usual.

"You don't gots to go, lad. Them fancy hat wearing pansies don't scare me none." George clenched his fist and shot me a menacing grin. "Let 'em come."

I smiled. Millie clouted him round the back of the head.

"And what're you gonna do when they chop those meat hooks off?" she shrilled. George opened his mouth to retort, but only a long sigh escaped as he shook his head.

"Granpa, even you can't fight these men," Becky said. "Some of them carry swords."

He nodded with a resigned smile. "Well, since ye've made yer minds up... wait there."

He ambled around the side of the house and came back leading two old retired Bighorns, saddled and loaded with sacks of food.

"I got these ready for ya. Here ye goes, these fellas should get you there safe." He handed Becky the reins of the nicer-looking one. The ram had a lean shape to it under the shaggy coat, and two majestic curved horns.

The one he gave me had a pot belly.

"Thank you Granpa," Becky rubbed the neck of her ram. "You'll look after us, won't you Snowball?"

"What's my one called?" I inquired.

"Bellyguts." George grinned.

Becky mounted up in a single, graceful leap.

I climbed onto my ram. My foot slipped out of the stirrups once, twice, then it caught and I flopped onto the saddle, swung my leg over and almost fell off the other side. He bleated as I clutched his mane, and hauled myself into the saddle. I grabbed the reins and sat up straight. The others stared at me.

George put an arm around Millie, and the pair bid us a safe journey.

Becky put heels into Snowball and set off down the hill. Max, after one parting sniff of Lucy the sheep dog's nose, ran along behind her. I followed them down the track into the valley behind the cottage.

At the river we turned left heading south, away from the towering bridge, past the rusty mine cart wreck (which some sheep were now using as a drinking trough), and onwards into the heart of the southern Fent Vale farmlands. The river flowed along the valley basin, following a long meander to our left. Grassy green hills rolled for miles ahead, dotted with lonely trees and small clumps of bramble bushes. On both sides of the river, herds of sheep grazed in the midday sun.

We rode our Bighorns along an old track parallel to the muddy river. It was used by the farmers who lived along this stretch of land, and sometimes one would greet us cheerily from the fields as we passed by. Fentworth's farms provided food for every settlement in the south, and even though it meant a hard lifestyle, I could see why people chose it. Sun-baked hills and lush meadows stretched as far as the eye could see – a paradise of green under the bright blue sky patched with clouds as fluffy as the sheep.

Becky explained that the farmland here was good for rearing livestock, which is why we saw so many sheep and goat paddocks. Farther along, we would see cows and horses as the land flattened out. "Cows don't like hills," she said knowingly.

Now and then, we passed a small orchard of apple trees, or rows of grapevines sloping up the hills to our left, but Becky said they are more common in the flatlands to the north of Fentworth. Up there, fields of wheat and oats dominated the landscape – its where most of Lunaria's crops were harvested.

After riding through the afternoon and into the evening, we came upon two ancient oak trees just a little up from the track. The largest had a great round knobbly trunk, and its branches stretched out towards the smaller one. This one looked about three-quarters the size, and grew at an angle leaning away from its big brother. It reminded me of my brothers, at any rate. Henry and Harry were always teasing each other, and when they weren't doing that they were winding Max up. I wondered what they might be up to...

We tied the Bighorns to the smaller tree, unloaded the supply sacks and rolled our woollen sleeping mats underneath the big tree. With midsummer upon us in the

Vale, and the starry sky lit by the dim red moonglow of Little Red, the night felt mild and calm. We had no trouble finding sleep.

After a breakfast of George's oats, and one of Millie's baked cookies each, we mounted up once more.

We soon entered dairy country, marked by the flattening hillsides. Paddocks of roaming sheep were replaced by small herds of cattle. Cows drinking from troughs by the fence greeted Snowball and Bellyguts with a moo, who both bleated in response as we rode past. Max sniffed the nose of a cow poking her head inquisitively through the fence. She responded with a hum, and stuck her long tongue up each nostril. Max snorted and loped on.

Becky pointed towards the top of a crest to our left. "Look," she said.

I glanced up and spied a small vehicle cruising along the top of the ridgeline ahead of us. It abruptly turned to the right onto a side track that seemed to join our path farther along.

The green and orange peddle cart bounced down the hill. I recognised those colours from somewhere but before I could put a finger on it, the driver started shouting at us through a cone attached to the front of the buggy.

"*STOP! IN THE NAME OF THE KING, STOP RIGHT THERE!*"

Becky turned back to me and yelled "Let's go!" She put heels into her ram and galloped down the track. Max bounded after her.

I heeled Bellyguts and clung on for dear life as he entered a gallop. The driver spoke again, quieter this time but still amplified by the loudspeaker. "They aren't stopping, Kane." I glanced up and saw the taller, skinnier Fedora Man standing behind the driver holding a mounted crossbow. He reached down and slapped the big man across the head. "*Ow,*" blared the cone.

I galloped past the junction right before the pedal cart joined our path. A crossbow bolt shot in front of my face and splashed into the river. *Woah!*

And then they chased us.

I clutched the reins desperately as Bellyguts gained speed, hooves pounding the dirt. Ahead, Becky's ram left a cloud of dust behind it which obscured my view of the track. Squinting, I hoped my ram knew where he was going because I really didn't feel in control of the situation. Faster and faster we galloped. The river rushed by on my right, and the grassy paddocks rolled ever on to my left. Behind me, the loudspeaker boomed.

"FUGITIVES. STOP RUNNING. WE JUST WANT TO TALK."

If you only want to talk, why are you shooting at me?

I galloped on.

"Just STOP! Stop... Stooop......stop.....st......top.....ssst.....op...."

We eventually outran the booming voice and slowed to a trot. Max panted breathlessly at my side, so I hoisted him up into my lap, where he drooled and licked his old wound. Beneath us, Bellyguts breathed heavily, gently bumping us up and down.

Becky fell in beside us. "I think we lost them," she patted Snowball's neck. "Well done." She grinned at me. "Wasn't that fun?"

I snorted. "You mean the part where I almost fell off or the part where Max almost broke his other leg trying to keep up?"

"Or the part where you nearly got a crossbow bolt in the butt?" She reached over and plucked an arrow from the food sack that hung over Bellyguts' rump. She handed me the bolt, smirking nervously. I shuddered and chucked it straight into the river.

We looked back the way we had come. I saw the river, the winding track, and the hills of the Fent Vale diminishing behind us.

"We better carry on," Becky warned. "There's only one

road here, and they know that we are on it."

Max had always disliked water. Whenever it rained in Hale, he would cower under the porch waiting for the clouds to pass. But ever since the cave, when he swam in the kamuna pool, he seemed to love it. He jumped in and out of the river all afternoon as we trotted along the track.

As the sun set and we braced ourselves for a night of continuous riding, he decided it was time for another dip. *Water!* he echoed. *Water water water!*

I rubbed my forehead, the white noise scratching at my thoughts as he spoke to me. "Not now, Max. We'll play some more tomorrow. Come on." He was enjoying himself too much though, and continued to splash about in the shallows.

An hour later, the fields glowed softly by the light of Little Red. Becky rode along in front of me, slumped in the saddle. "You still awake?" I asked the back of her head.

"Barely," she answered sleepily.

Somewhere behind us, the sound of cogs *clanked* in the distance.

We both turned around.

The river curved around a rolling hummock, possibly the last hummock we would see on this road, and so we couldn't pinpoint where the noise came from. But beyond the grassy hill, I saw a light. Firelight, shimmering.

Becky's eyes widened. "They're coming!"

We kicked our heels and the Bighorns bleated in annoyance. I couldn't blame them. We had already marched all day long and now we wanted them to move even faster. But they did move.

We trotted until the pedal-cart's clanking engine had diminished, but the glow of their torch fire still shimmered in the distance. Max jumped gleefully into the river.

"Max, come on!" I growled in a loud whisper. "You're making too much noise!" He scrambled out and bounded up to the track beside us. *Water!* "What is wrong with you, boy?" I was in no mood for his mischief, all that noise

62

would get us caught.

On we trotted, before we heard the *clanking* of the engine again. The Bighorns were tiring and the Fedora Men were catching up. "This is no good!" I said to Becky, exasperated. "We have to hide."

"I know." She reined up, and looked about. "But where?"

There was nothing. On this side of the river, we were completely exposed. Soon, the hummock would no longer hide us, and we'd be in plain view of the Fedora Men. All I saw was a clump of high bushes on the other side of the river.

Max splashed into the shallows again. *Water!*

I let out a groan. My head hurt so much, he hadn't been this active in a long while and every *echo* felt like a splinter in my skull.

"He wants us to follow," Becky realised. She peered across the river. "Look. There." She pointed to the high bushes. "We can hide there!"

She's right. As he splashed about, Max kept turning back to us, as if to say *look over here, follow me, we can hide here!* But he didn't know any of those words. He just knew *water*.

I felt foolish.

Becky and Snowball waded into the shallows as the clanking cogs of the pedal-cart's engine grew louder with every passing second.

I heeled Bellyguts, and he tentatively approached the water's edge. Becky had water up to her ram's chest as they waded across the deepest part of the river, and he was making a horrendous racket. He bleated and groaned and called out as she kicked him again and again. Bighorns don't like water either, apparently.

"Come on, fella." I tried to encourage Bellyguts, but it didn't help. He stubbornly refused to enter the dark, flowing water. The firelight reflected off a tree across the river some two hundred yards farther back. I figured I had about thirty seconds to get across before they saw me.

"Come *on*." I heaved my heels into his soft flabby sides and he hopped into the shallows. Cold wetness crawled up my feet and lower legs as we waded across. My leather boots soaked up the river like a sponge, becoming heavy weights on the end of my legs. Bellyguts held his head high, bleating and calling in misery to the night sky. *Surely, they will hear this... Our only hope is that the little engine on their cart drowns out the noise of our unhappy mounts.*

I realised the river would flood the food sacks, so I grabbed the one to my left and hoisted it up to my chest at the apex of the river. The rest were submerged.

With barely a second to spare, we made it to the riverbank and scurried behind the bushes to join Becky and Max, just as the Fedora Men rounded the hummock.

Snowball reared and shook and bleated and headbutted. Becky stood on the grass, holding the reins trying to soothe him. "They're going to hear this!" she despaired. "Easy, boy, easy. Calm down, please."

Bellyguts practically threw me off as he bucked and groaned. I unstrapped the sodden sacks and let them slump to the ground. The groans of grumpy Bighorns filled the night. Anyone within a mile would surely hear.

I knew only one way to quiet an upset animal.

I tried to give Bellyguts a handful of soggy oats out of one of the wet sacks, but he only grunted in disgust. Reluctantly, I opened the dry sack of food, our last supply of unspoiled food and fed him a handful of biscuits. He scoffed them down greedily. Becky grabbed some and held her hand out to Snowball, who nearly bit her fingers off. Angry bleating turned into the sound of soft chewing.

I peered through a gap in the bushes and saw the Fedora Men clunking along the track in their pedal-cart. The big man pedalled furiously, aided by the little engine, they were going about as fast as a canter. No wonder they had caught us up. The skinny Fedora Man stood behind the driver holding a blazing torch above his head and peered below it searching left and right. He said something to the big man, and the cart came to a halt directly opposite the river from where we hid.

I held my breath.

The tall, lanky Fedora Man jumped down from the cart and looked around. Above the gentle flow of the river I heard them speaking, as clearly as if they were standing beside us.

"I heard those monstrous goats of theirs. They are close." He spoke with no accent I'd ever heard, his voice smooth and menacing. He hunkered down to study the ground. The torch lit up his pale suit, flames shimmering across the fabric.

The big driver remained in the cart. "I don't hear nothin', Kane."

The skinny Fedora Man, Kane, I guess, let out a sigh. He stood and strolled back to the cart and leant against it. "How many times must I remind you not to use my name?"

The driver gave a nervous laugh. "Heh. Sorry, Kane. It's just there's no-one but cows out here, and they don't talk none..." He trailed off. Kane drew something from his pocket, and leaned in to the cart.

"Oh, please boss. I won't forget this time. Agh!" The big man squeaked in pain.

Bellyguts bleated. I sunk my empty hand into the sack of biscuits and fed him another handful. Becky glared at me. I winced, mouthed *sorry* and peered across the river again.

"Let's go. They aren't here." Kane climbed into the back of the cart and the driver resumed his pedalling. The cogs *clanked*, and the cart rolled along the track into darkness.

We dozed behind the bushes, taking turns to keep an eye out for the hunters' little cart, but they did not return. When the sun came up, I looked to salvage some breakfast from our soggy food sacks.

"You're not planning to eat those?" Becky wrinkled her

nose as I found a clump of cookies that were now stuck together. They didn't look *too* bad...

"I'm hungry."

She crossed her arms. "Everything upstream, all that land we have ridden past, it's all farmland. There are hundreds of animals living along the riverbank from here to Granpa's farm, and even beyond the train bridge. Where do you think all their poop ends up?"

I regarded the cookie clump in my hand, then glanced at the muddy-brown river flowing past, which had saturated most of our food the night before. "Yuck."

"Yup," she said glumly.

I threw the cookie clumps to the ground, where Max dived on them. I sighed. "So we're out of food."

Chapter Seven

After walking along the far side of the river for several miles, we came to a heap of junk floating in a small bay of the river.

"Let's use this raft to cross back over," Becky suggested.

"What raft?" I asked.

"That." She pointed to the floating heap of wooden planks and rusty nails.

"You're kidding." Whichever farmer had built the ragged ferry was either blind or had never seen a real boat before.

Only one ram could fit at a time, so it would take at least two crossings. After a brief argument, it was decided that Becky would go first.

She tugged the chain and towed herself and Snowball across. She unloaded on the far bank and I pulled the sorry mess back to my side. Bellyguts and Max clambered onto it.

It creaked and rocked in the currents. I swore the fat Bighorn would either fall off or sink us, but he settled for sniffing my butt while I bent over pulling the chain. Somehow, we made it across unscathed.

Breathing a sigh of relief, I mounted up and fell in beside Becky. She shot me a grin. Riding together, we rejoined the road and continued east.

Later, we came to a stop before a wide gate that barred the way. The path continued on into the field beyond, but a dirt track turned left and ran alongside the palisade fence, leading into a hilly wood. Fresh wheel tracks rutted the mud, but whether they were made by our pursuers' cart or just some farmer's ox-wagon, we couldn't be sure.

"This is the last farm of the Fent Vale," Becky announced. "Grumpy old Gilbert. Granpa said he never liked people coming through his land, and saw no reason for it since every other farmer lives back that direction, so Gilbert fenced it all off. He eventually agreed to put this gate in, but most people don't take the risk." She gestured to a crooked sign next to the gate. Scratched into the wood, and painted red were the words 'BEWARE OF BORIS', above a rather crude picture of a bull.

I whipped out my pad and pencils. Sketching, I asked, "Which way, then?"

"Well, that path leads to Raleigh." She pointed up the side track towards the wood. "But there's a good chance our fedora friends went that way. If we carry on straight instead, we can cut across the grasslands and make for the village of Barrow, the fifth stop on the trainline. We can stock up on food there."

I glanced at the sign. "What about Boris?"

Becky peered over the gate, but the paddock looked deserted. She shrugged.

We opened the gate and rode through.

The path cut across the paddock close to the river, but now a fence separated us from it. Several towering oak trees grew near the middle of the field, and I saw bramble bushes sprouting tasty black berries up ahead. *Better resist those. We wouldn't want to be caught stealing here.* The paddock sloped gently up to our left towards a row of tall fir trees which sheltered the farmhouse.

Becky and I trotted side by side along the track, Max running about among the bushes sniffing for rabbit holes.

We came to the line of oak trees on our left, and a clump of bramble bushes to the right, enclosing us in a natural passage.

Kane stepped out from behind a trunk. He stopped on the path before us, armed with the crossbow.

The Bighorns let out a startled groan and we skidded to a halt.

"There you are," the skinny Fedora Man greeted us like old friends. Up close, I recognised him as the kidnapper in the Fentworth alleyway. He rested the crossbow over a shoulder like a cocky deer hunter. "I've been waiting for you."

"What do you want?" I demanded.

He regarded me coolly, with pale eyes under the Fedora which kept his gaunt face in shadow. His pale grey suit was speckled with brown dust. "You."

Behind him, the orange and green peddle cart clunked out from the bushes and stopped several yards down the track. The driver was the same man who had knocked on the farmers' door looking for me. *These two must be partners.* The burly Black Fedora Man licked berry juice from his fingers.

I waited for more, but Kane only stood there, blocking our way. Max bounded out of the bushes and snorted at me, before he noticed the Fedora Men. Lowering his head, he growled.

Kane's eyes shifted to Max for a moment, but he saw nothing worthy of his attention and casually swung the crossbow over his shoulder and aimed at me from the hip. "Such a big, cumbersome contraption. I told them I only need a blade, but they insisted on mounting one of these ridiculous things to our vehicle. *In case of resistance*, they said. Such tosh. Still, I cannot deny its deadliness. From this range, the bolt would likely go right through you and out the other side." I shifted uncomfortably in the saddle. Kane noticed, and the corner of his mouth rose in a satisfied smile. "Get down from the goat, boy. And come with me. Now."

I heard Becky mutter, "It's a ram, not a goat."

My fists stiffly clutched the reins. "Why? What do you want from me?"

"You are The Defiler's accomplice." He stood motionless, the crossbow hung at his hip aimed squarely at me.

"The Defiler... you mean my mother?" My eyes flicked between the crossbow and Kane. "I haven't seen her for moons. I don't know where she is. I won't be able to tell you anything."

"Perhaps not, boy. But perhaps she will find us, when she learns that we hold her dear son captive. I'd wager she will be most curious to know who is making all the screams." I held his cold gaze, but my hands trembled as I gripped the reins.

Kane lazily turned and aimed the crossbow at Becky. She inhaled a sharp breath. "Hurry up, boy. I grow bored. If you do not come, I will skewer your little farm girlfriend here."

My mind raced. They probably wanted to stuff me into that metal box on the back of the cart, just like the old preacher. I didn't fancy that much. *I could ride him down. No. He'd shoot Becky before I even reached him.* He'd need to reload after the first shot. If one of us went for him... *Great idea! Get skewered and probably die.* I had no choice. I began to dismount.

Max whimpered. I stopped with one foot dangling out of the stirrup. I saw his tail drop between his legs and he backed away slowly. *Monster,* he echoed. I spied movement between the oak trees behind Kane. I opened my mouth to speak, and let out a noise like "*um...*"

Boris the bull charged out of the trees. The ground shook beneath his hooves, which kicked up clods of dirt as the eight-foot tall black beast thundered across the grass and buried his head into the side of the little cart. The big man inside shrieked.

Kane's eyes never left mine, but they grew wide as the cart rolled over once, twice, then crunched to a halt on its side next to a bramble bush. He spun to face the carnage. The bull snorted, his bronze ring swung against his nose, he shook his head violently, snorted again, scraped the ground with a hoof. A strained groan came from the man in the overturned, crumpled cart. Kane still held the crossbow at his waist, and whether he meant to fire it or not, I couldn't say. All I know is Boris had a bolt sticking out of his rump when he charged at the skinny Fedora Man. Kane dropped the crossbow and fled into the bushes, the charging bull right behind him.

Becky and I dug heels in to our mounts and bolted towards the far side of Grumpy old Gilbert's farm.

The Bighorns were galloping so fast by the time we reached the gate they leaped right over it, bleating. I clung to Bellyguts' mane as we flew through the air, catching a glimpse of Max's ears flapping in the wind right there alongside us as he also bounded over the gate. I may have let out a shriek, but we landed safely on the other side and kept on going. Once she felt sure we had left the Fedora Men and their mangled buggy far behind, Becky slowed to a walk and hooted in celebration.

"Did you *see* that bull?" I exclaimed breathlessly.

"He's a brute, ain't he! That'll teach those city idiots to come poking their nose where they don't belong!" Becky shouted gleefully over her shoulder in the direction of the pursuers, but we were well beyond their reach by now. We high-fived.

I spotted Kane's crossbow in her lap. She must have bent down and grabbed it when we rode past. She hoisted it up and struck a pose.

I laughed. "Cripes, look at that thing. A souvenir?"

She mocked Kane's accent. "Well now, I couldn't leave such a big, cumbersome contraption behind. That would be utter tosh."

"Ha, maybe we can hunt some dinner with it."

"Maybe!" She beamed.

Without food, we pressed on hard as we could each day, but progress became slow and arduous once the path ended. The land beyond the Vale was inhospitable – boggy lowlands covered in tall grasses and very few trees for shelter. Even the weather turned its back on us. For two days, grey clouds filled the sky. By night, the clouds obscured us from Big Blue's guiding glow, and by day they leaked drizzly rain that soaked us to the core. Even the sheepskin cloaks George and Millie had given us couldn't keep us warm, though I was grateful for the hood to shield my face against the wind. At least with all the grass to eat the Bighorns were never short of energy, but the rain made them miserable and vocal.

Eventually, the ground became firmer, and transformed into an open rocky plain of gently rolling fields. Warm sun broke through the clouds and dried our soggy clothes and I found time to teach Max a few new words. We tied the rams to the only tree for miles – a skeletal thing covered in flaky green leaves, but no fruit. Nearby, two great boulders jutted out of the grass, where we took a short break.

"He really helped us out back there, you know." Becky rubbed Max's head as she stretched out on the grass.

"Yeah, he did. I told you he's the best travel companion." Max's face was bliss as Becky petted him, and his tongue hung out. *Beckyyy*, he echoed. I chuckled. "He knows your name."

"Really?" She hugged him. "So, when are you going to tell me what happened? It's not every day you meet a boy who can read his dog's mind."

I leant back against the boulder and recounted the story. "It started when Max and I discovered a cave in the woods..."

Becky listened attentively. Unlike George, she didn't interrupt or question me about the unbelievable parts. She just listened. When I was done, she sat a while in quiet contemplation. Finally, she spoke. "You're lucky. I wish I could find a Wishing Tree."

"Who knows, maybe we'll find one out here," I joked, gesturing to the treeless plain.

"Pfft," she said, grinning. "So *that's* why you are always so quiet when we ride. You and Max are having your own private little conversation behind my back!"

I laughed. "I'm just concentrating on staying in the saddle! He's really not much of a talker. He mostly thinks of the same two things: food and sleep. And occasionally rabbits. It would be *nice* if he actually thought about something else for a change." Max's tail wagged excitedly and he fidgeted between us.

"He knows we're talking about him," Becky said.

"He's a smart pooch," I patted my thigh. Max rolled onto his back wanting a belly rub. I obliged. "Oh, I know, you might like this. He learnt a few good commands from Lucy when we were herding the sheep. We've adapted one of them slightly. Check it out." I climbed up onto the boulder, stood and pointed out across the fields. "Away. *Way away.*" Max cocked his head for a moment, then took off. He ran far out into the long grass until we could no longer see him, but for the rustling in the reeds. I traced his route in a wide circle, watching the grass bend and part as Max crashed his way through. He stopped for a moment, then carried on, until he completed his huge circular run and climbed back out of the grass and up onto my boulder perch.

"Impressive!" Becky exclaimed.

"That's not all." A thought came to me. *I wonder...* "Becky, come up here."

She rose and clambered up to stand beside me. I took her by the hand, and placed the other on Max's head.

My mind rushed open.

My senses explode in a thousand smells and sounds and I see the fields stretch before me as I bound into the grass. Reeds scratch my face as I bundle through, the grass a towering mass all around, but parting easily enough. The smell of rabbit thrust its way inside my nostrils, halting me in my tracks. I sniff, peer about, see nothing but grass and small stones and dirt. I snort. Running again, I make a wide circular shape back towards the boulder, back towards *Billy* and *Becky* who are waiting for me. Their smell overcomes the grass, as I leap out and climb back up to the boulders and for a brief moment I see *myself* standing there, then my mind slams shut and my senses withdraw and shrivel...

I opened my own eyes once again. Becky had interlocked her warm, calloused fingers with mine.

"Did you see it?" I asked.

She shook her head, and kissed me on the cheek, a quick light peck. And giggled.

I went red. "What was that for?"

"Don't question a good thing," she said simply, and rested her head on my shoulder.

I won't. I squeezed her hand, she squeezed back, and we stood together overlooking the grassland.

Chapter Eight

Thwumm!

The bolt flew through the air and sailed over the rabbit's head by a good foot. It leapt up in shock before fleeing into the grass, where Max waited in ambush.

"You're worse than me," Becky jabbed my side as she lay on her belly next to me.

I looked down the sight of the crossbow at the spot where the rabbit had been grazing. "The sun put me off."

She pulled a face. "What sun?" She stood up, as Max bounded out of the tall grass, with the dead rabbit dangling in his jaws. "At least someone's proving their worth out here." She bent to pet him on the head, and took the rabbit by the ears. "I'll skin this one. See if you can find the bolt."

Becky's survival skills vastly outweighed my own, but she was a patient teacher. When it came to the crossbow, however, neither of us had any natural talent. Shooting ducks with George's blunderbuss seemed a doddle compared to the pinpoint precision the crossbow required.

Using flint and a small dagger, Becky lit a cookfire and for the third evening in a row, we sat down to a supper of rabbit stew. It tasted plain, and split between three barely filled us up, but at least it was warm. Max gnawed the bones beside us.

Becky caught me smiling at her.

She smiled back, questioningly. "What?"

"Why are you here?" I asked, mimicking the question she put to me the first day we met.

She chuckled. "It just felt right, I guess." She stirred her bowl of stew, thoughtfully. "Meeting you, and seeing what you were doing, travelling and exploring... You'd just left home, and I suddenly realised I was ready to go back to mine."

She always seemed uncomfortable talking about Hooke. I held my tongue, resisting the urge to probe once more.

She went on, "I'd been living with Granpa and Granma for about a year. I needed somewhere to stay after..." Her smile had gone. I watched her struggle with the words. "After the accident... I don't know why I'm telling you this."

"It's okay. You don't have to." *What accident?* I took a mouthful of stew, trying to think of something else to talk about.

"I hope we find her," Becky blurted. "I hope we find your mother."

I swallowed. "Yeah. Me too."

"I want to meet her." She slowly stirred her bowl, scooped up a spoonful of stew and blew it softly.

As we quietly ate, the night settled over us.

Max stopped gnawing his bones, and pricked his ears, staring up at the sky. The summer eclipse had begun. As I gazed into the starry sky, Little Red started to overlap Big Blue. The moons marked the beginning, middle and end of every season with an eclipse, and this one signalled midsummer was upon us. The days would gradually begin to shorten after tonight. As always, Max and every other dog would be growing restless.

The grasslands bathed in the moonlight. Little Red crept towards the centre of his big blue brother, sending shimmering purple light dancing across the fields. A white halo formed around the smaller moon, whose red surface darkened into deep shadow. The moons created a giant crystal eye that stared down at us from the heavens – Big Blue the iris, and Little Red the dark pupil. The halo intensified for a second which lit the plain in a lilac flash. The glowing ring wavered gently around the silhouette of Little Red and the eclipse was complete.

Max let out a long, mournful howl, which emanated across the plain.

I awoke to the soft sound of sobbing.

I rubbed the sleep from my eyes, and sat up under the indigo glow of Big Blue. The great moon was alone in the sky now, suspended directly above our heads amongst a bed of twinkling stars.

Becky lay beside the embers of the fire with her back to me. Now and then, she convulsed with a sob. I crawled over and saw Max curled up in front of her. He raised his head to me as I laid a hand on her shoulder. She reached up and clutched my hand.

"What's wrong?" I asked.

"She died. Exactly a year ago. My mum died." She trembled, shuddering between sniffs.

I sighed, and squeezed her hand between both of mine. She rolled over, wrapped her arms around my neck and wept against my chest. I held her until she fell asleep in my arms.

The next morning, I woke to the smell and sizzle of frying eggs. Becky tended the cookpot over a freshly crackling fire. I flushed when I realised I was lying under her blanket. "Morning," I croaked, sleepily getting to my feet.

"Morning," she replied cheerfully. Her smile lit her face, last night's despair seemingly a distant memory. "Max found a ducks nest. The eggs were cold, so I think the mother's gone. Smell good, don't they?"

"Yup they do."

"Grab your bowl. They're just about done."

I found it near my sleeping mat, and took a seat next to the fire. Becky scooped out two eggs and dropped them into my bowl, then served herself and sat down.

"I reckon we can make it to Barrow before the end of the day." She pointed north across the tall grass. "It'll be nice to restock our foodsacks."

"Yeah," I said. "Are you –"

"I'm sorry about last night, Billy." She spoke awkwardly into her eggs. I felt bad for her. "I needed that, though. I'd been holding it in for quite a while, y'know."

"I was worried," I admitted.

"Don't. I'll be fine. I'm glad you're with me." She pulled her eyes up to mine and smiled. "Thank you."

I scratched my elbow. "Well I'm glad you're with me. I'd be starving to death out here by myself. Certainly wouldn't have known where to find eggs!"

She chuckled. "I told you, Max sniffed them out. You just need to know when he's trying to tell you something."

"I can hear his thoughts," I scoffed. "You'd think that would be enough." Max padded over and buried his head under my arm, eying me like a puppy. *Billy*, he echoed. I gave him a playful flick on the nose, and he bounded away.

After breakfast and a quick rinse in the nearby pond, we set off.

Becky's prediction proved spot on. By mid-afternoon, we crested a rise and the village of Barrow presented itself. A small huddle of wooden buildings, a refuge amidst the grassy plains, Barrow was little more than a waypoint between the larger settlements along the train line. It didn't even have a town hall, and certainly no mayor. If the houses were made of stone instead of timber, the place would have felt similar to Hale. Rather than a hat shop or a windmill, Barrow's centrepoint was the tavern. Approaching from the south out of the long grass, we rode across the train line and joined the main road on the edge of the village. I saw a thin wisp of smoke rising from the chimney of the inn at the crossroads up ahead, with two mules tied up outside the swing doors.

A bearded old man sitting on the balcony above the doorway leaned over as we approached. "More. Maurice! More!" he called in a raspy voice, before a hacking fit of coughing took hold of him.

The saloon doors swung open and a clean-shaven younger version of the old man stepped out into the afternoon sun. "Welcome, travellers!" He wore a blue and white striped apron and a huge smile of white teeth. When he saw our mounts, the smile widened. "Bighorns! You must be from Fentworth. What news from the Vale? May I take those for you? My, how young you are. What brings you to Barrow?"

He grabbed both sets of reins and hastily tied them to the post next to the mules, before we had even dismounted. The bombardment of questions mixed with the ferocious hacking and wheezing of the man on the balcony was more noise than either of us had heard for a moon. *Back to civilisation, I guess.*

The old man on the balcony's coughing eased up and he sat back in his chair clearing his throat again and again. *Aherrm. Agherugh. Aruugh.*

"Thank you, Mister," Becky said as she dropped down beside the innkeeper. "Not had many visitors lately?"

The man looked abashed. "Ah. No, Miss, not of late. And please, call me Maurice." *Ahuurgh.* "Ever since the train stopped coming through, Barrow's been quite the ghost town." *Ahhoorgh.* "It's good to see some fresh faces —" *Arghem!* "GOOD GRIEF old man, will you *be quiet!*"

"Aaagh!" the old coughing man shouted down at us. He cursed under his breath and started mumbling to himself.

Maurice the innkeeper looked back to us, and tried to smile. "Please, come in."

We followed him in to the tavern, which was all but

empty. A young lad busied himself rubbing down tables with a rag and a villager sat hunched over the bar on a stool sipping at a stein. In the corner, a self-playing piano chimed a merry tune.

Maurice scurried behind the bar and offered us a drink.

We sat a few stools down from the only other patron, who greeted us with a tilt of his beer and a nod. Max settled down by our feet.

"Actually, we were hoping for some food," I said.

"Ah. Well, options are a bit limited, what with the train and all. We're all out of fresh vegetables. But it just so happens our Freddy caught some conies today. Would you care for some bread and stew?"

Becky chuckled, with a sigh. I asked "What's a coney?"

"Rabbit."

"Oh." I exchanged a look with Becky, who gave a comical shrug. I turned back to Maurice. "Sure, why not."

"A copper each, please," he smiled.

George had kindly given me some coin for helping out at the farm, so I paid the man and he called our order through the kitchen doorway at someone. When he returned, Becky asked how much a room for the night would cost.

"Would that be for a double room?" he inquired.

"Yes," she answered before I had even understood the question.

"Very good," said Maurice, and gave me a knowing smile. "Three coppers for the room. It's the second door on the left up the stairs." He gestured above and behind us, where a balcony lined with numerous doors ran around the room, overlooking the tavern. "I can call for you when the stew is ready."

Becky paid this time. "Thank you," she said, standing up.

We unloaded the rams and put the bags in our room for the night. Max found himself a cosy spot at the foot of the bed. It would certainly be nice to sleep in a bed again, but I couldn't help noticing there was only one. A big bed, but still only one.

"Don't get any funny ideas." Becky saw me looking puzzled. "It's cheaper than two rooms, and we need to watch each others' backs. You know, in case *they* show up..."

I opened the outer balcony door, and nervously glanced up and down the dusty street. Several people were making their way towards the tavern, a family I guessed, but other than that the village was deserted. The old man with the horrendously sore throat had fallen asleep in his chair a couple of ledges over. His arms hung limp and a string of drool dangled from his toothless mouth. *Is he dead?* He suddenly snored loudly, rumbled the chair with a trumpeting fart and mumbled in his sleep. I went back inside.

"Stew's ready," Becky said.

We locked the room, and began walking towards the top of the stairs when the door to the next room opened and I stopped in front of the man coming out. I found myself staring eye to eye with Kane the Fedora Man.

"You," he almost whispered. Then the point of his sword was under my chin. I gulped.

"No!" Becky yelped behind me.

Kane raised a finger at her. "Hush. And stay right there." Kane's eyes met mine again. They were pale and cruel, and right now full of smug satisfaction. "Isn't this a pleasant reunion?"

The point of the blade felt cold and jabbed me under the soft part of my chin. I grimaced, not daring to move. I'd never felt so tense.

Kane's burly accomplice stood in the doorway behind him, with a bruised cheek and several scratches down his face. "Grab the girl," Kane commanded, as if he were making pleasant conversation. He never took his eyes off me.

The brute obeyed, brushing past Kane.

From behind me, I heard Becky shuffle back a few steps.

"Stay away from me," she snapped.

For a moment, the big man paused, then chuckled. "What you gonna do with that?" He withdrew his sword, and advanced out of my sight. "Why don't you put the toothpick down, little girl, before someone gets hurt."

"I told you to *stay back,*" Becky fumed.

This is getting out of hand.

"Lower your weapons!" A shout came from the tavern below. "I'll have no bloodshed under my roof."

Kane answered with icy coolness. "This does not concern you, barman. These two are wanted criminals."

"No we're not," Becky insisted. "You people are nothing but liars and thieves. We haven't done anything."

Technically, I am responsible for crashing the train, even if Mother is their official suspect... and we did kinda steal their crossbow.

"They are accomplices of The Defiler, and are to be taken before the king for judgement." Kane's eyes were fixed on mine as he spoke to Maurice down below.

I heard a *clunk* that sounded suspiciously like a gun being cocked... "No king has ever acknowledged Barrow, and we don't acknowledge him. Now, lower your sword," Maurice insisted. "Do not make me tell you again."

I glanced over the railing to my left, not daring to move my head for fear of being impaled, and saw the biggest gun barrel I've ever seen aimed at me. Or Kane. It didn't really matter, if he fired the thing we'd both be turned into mush. I gulped again.

The skinny Fedora Man saw the blunderbuss and almost laughed. "What? Are you going to blow us all apart Mr Brave Barman? There'll be quite a bit of blood on your roof if you pull that trigger." He muttered to himself, "You can barely lift that cumbersome thing." Something must have shown in the inn keep's face, however, because Kane sheathed his sword with a disgruntled sigh. I remembered to breathe again.

"Now, get out of here." Every spec of Maurice's courtesy had gone from his voice. I barely recognised him.

"Fear not, we were just leaving anyway, as it happens," Kane remarked, ambling down the stairs.

"Heh," the bigger one chortled. "It's not like we need them now any —" He stopped when Kane shot him a glare, then plodded down the steps after him. The comment didn't go unnoticed by Becky, who raised an eyebrow at me as she slipped her skinning knife back into her belt pouch. We followed the Fedora Men down into the tavern.

Without even a parting glance, the pair strolled out of the saloon doors into the evening.

Maurice lowered the blunderbuss. "Never liked the Kingsmen. Nothing but glorified bounty hunters." He eyed us suspiciously. "Still, if business wasn't so slow, I'd be turfing you two out with them. I don't wanna know what you did but the way I figure it, I just saved you a deal of trouble. So you can repay me by staying for breakfast tomorrow, giving us a nice tip, then being on your way. Sound fair to you?"

We both nodded.

"Good." He smiled cheerfully. "Now, enjoy your supper."

We sat at a round table by the stairs, and Freddy the young serving lad brought us our stew. He asked if we wanted any drinks, and when I answered he gave me a questioning look.

"You were riding them big goats?" he asked. "But you don't sound like you're from Fentworth."

"I'm from Hale."

His face lit up. "A spud! That makes two in a moon!" He seemed very pleased.

Nobody ever leaves Hale... "Two?" I asked anxiously.

"Yeah. You and the woman who fixed our piano. It was broken, but she mended it right good, see?" He pointed to the self-playing piano, which continued its chirpy song. I barely heard it though. I looked at Becky, and I knew she was thinking the same thing as me.

"Is she staying here?" she asked the boy.

"No. It's like I told those other two. She stayed for one night, but she said she needed a blacksmith, or a carpenter's workshop. We told her about the old lumber mill, and she went to stay there. Dunno why, it's been abandoned for ages, but she got so excited and – hey! What about your stew?"

I bolted for the swing doors.

She's here.

The village was growing dark, Big Blue hadn't risen yet. Becky and Max ran out into the road right behind me.

"They found her," I said. "The fat one practically told us, didn't he?" My heart raced. "She's here."

"Where did they go?" Becky looked up and down the crossroads.

Max barked. He stood beside the hitch rail next to the rams. *Weren't there too mules tied up here before?* Max sniffed the ground, then glanced back at me. This time I understood. "Go boy, track 'em!"

He scrambled off down the street, and I ran after. I followed him past a row of houses, turned down a side street and up a narrow sloped path. He led us to a three storey building at the end of the path. A broad hedge surrounded the old mill with a thick, oaken gate barring the entrance. The mules were chewing on the grass beside the gate. I gave it a shove, but it must have been locked from the other side. I searched about, looking for another way through.

Max grunted and scurried underneath the hedge. I dived into the dirt after him and crawled through. I emerged in a yard strewn with old rusty machinery. From the side of the mill, I heard the sound of breaking glass. Max bounded around the corner, growling.

Kane stood in the shadows besides the building. A spark flickered in his hand and a flame appeared from nowhere. Firelight reflected off the bottle he held and danced up the rag. He tossed the flaming bottle through a window into the mill, which instantly lit up brightly inside.

Max barked. Kane turned, saw us and fled towards the back of the workshop. I sprinted after him.

At the back of the mill was a garden enclosed by a circle of tall trees and a gravel yard. Kane had vanished.

A blast erupted from the workshop, and I felt the ground tremor beneath my feet as several windows smashed open, spitting flames. Max whimpered and tried to hide between my legs.

The mill groaned like a whale, wood splintered and snapped, as something huge pressed against the roof from the inside. The building seemed to be taking a deep breath.

The roof burst open.

A great bulging ball of leather emerged from the rubble. It glowed orange from the inside and roared. *FWOOOSH!* The balloon shoved aside what was left of the roof and floated into the sky. Flames danced out of the hole and chunks of slate thudded down into the yard like deadly hailstones. Burning rafters lifted into the air, crumbling and falling to pieces. Huge chunks of timber and tiles crashed around me.

A gust of wind sent the balloon soaring over my head, and it dragged a small wicker basket through the crumbling upper wall amid a tangle of netting and ropes and the Black Fedora Man. He tumbled head over heels and landed in a heap on the ground.

Entwined within the netting below the basket, clinging on desperately was the figure of a woman. In the shimmering light of the flames, I saw her eyes bulge as she swung over my head.

"William?" she shrilled in surprise, and drifted over the tops of the trees.

She was the only person in the world who ever called me by my birth-name. She did give it to me, after all.

"Mother?"

PART TWO
BEEF

Chapter Nine

The jumble of netting, ropes, and Mother dangled from the ragged basket as the balloon drifted over the trees.

I slipped between the trunks and ran after it.

A rope had set alight when the balloon burst from the burning mill, and now a lick of flame crept towards my mother's feet. She was too busy wrestling with a loop of netting ensnared about her face to have noticed.

"Mother!" I repeated as I ran. "I've been looking for you for three moons!"

"William! It flies! I'm flying!" She wriggled her head free of the loop, only to slump forwards into another one.

"What's going on? Is this why you didn't come home?"

"Home? Don't be ridiculous, William. I can't be testing the stability of combustible fluids at home!" She spoke as if I should know what a combustible fluid was. Which I didn't.

"What's a com – agh nevermind," I panted. "We were waiting for you to return with food, but you never did!"

She frowned, grimaced and squinted. She looked as though a mouse was crawling around under her clothes. "You know, I knew I had forgotten something."

I vaulted a rock, stumbled, and carried on. My heart

thumped against my chest. "What happened at Aston? Were you there?"

"Oh, I had a little accident, nothing to worry about!" She reached high above her head and tugged a rope which came loose and fell across her like a snake. She let out a small shriek.

My feet pounded the dirt trying to keep up with the balloon. "There were burnt houses, and the mayor said you killed people!"

She stopped struggling for a moment and looked down at me, frowning. "What? I didn't kill anybody!" Her face glowed orange by the light of the flames dancing up towards her nest of ropes. "Not yet, at least." She glanced down at her feet. "I'm on fire!"

"What do you mean *not yet?* You're a wanted criminal! There's even a reward!"

When she had finished flailing and flapping out the flames on her trousers, she made a relieved noise like *woooh*. "Well if those pesky blokes keep bothering me, I might be tempted to try a bit of murder! How's a girl supposed to figure out the theory of quantum ignition when she keeps being interrupted by fat dopey bruisers?" She finished, "How much is the reward?"

"One gold coin."

"So that's why they keep pestering me! I tried to tell them I burnt down my labs, not houses. They don't listen! Nobody was in there except me."

Relief flooded through me. *I knew you weren't a killer.*

Just then, the night turned to day in a flash. Behind me, an almighty explosion boomed. I tripped and fell on my face in the dirt.

Dazed, I staggered to my feet, and looked back towards Barrow. Where the mill once stood, now a giant bonfire raged, huge swirling flames leaping into the sky. *Becky!*

Mother groaned overhead. "There goes my new batch of bovithane! I'd only just finished liquidising it," she complained, her arms dangling limp through the net. The balloon carried her on ahead of me.

I was torn between chasing after her, and going back for Becky.

"I've only just found you Mother! Where are you going?"

Max bounded up to me, dribbling and panting.

I pointed at the balloon. "Follow her, boy! *Follow!*" He cocked his head for a moment, then bolted after the balloon, barking. *Follow-follow,* he echoed. "Mother, don't go far! I'm coming with you!"

I turned and ran back the way I had come.

Behind me, I heard Mother begin to say "Max...? Maxy boy, ooh who's a good doggy...where have...poochy wooch..." Then she was too far away.

As I ran, I squinted in the dark and made out the shape of a mounted rider galloping towards me. I slowed to a walk, then stopped. "Becky?" I called.

The hoofbeats grew louder. The rider did not slow.

He charged at me. I darted to the side just in time, as Kane galloped past on his mule, chasing the balloon.

I made it back to the village. The mill fire roared and crackled violently, wisps of smouldering ash fluttering into the sky like a thousand burning butterflies. The flames soon spread to the surrounding hedges, which went up one after the other.

People had gathered in the street, and some were rushing about with pails of water but it looked like a futile effort. The fire raged beyond control.

The Black Fedora Man sat slumped on the side of the road. His face was a bit charred, and his suit had ripped, but he looked otherwise unhurt. "He tried to kill me," he said to no-one, staring at the ground. "He sent me inside. Then he set it on fire."

"My home!" a woman wailed, as the flames leapt from the tall hedgerow and caught the roof of the nearest building.

I gazed around, horrified by the carnage. There was a

rank stench emanating from the flames of the burning mill, mingled with the smell of seared wood.

Over the roar of the fire I heard a Bighorn bleating. I turned and saw Becky struggling with them both as they desperately tried to pull her away towards the village centre, their shaggy coats illuminated by the dancing firelight. I ran to her.

"Billy! Help me hold them."

I took Bellyguts' reins, and tried to climb into the saddle, but he wasn't having any of it. He reared up and I stumbled back to the ground.

"They're terrified of the fire," Becky said. "What happened?"

"I saw Kane. He's going after Mother!"

Her faced showed pride and fear at the same time. "You found her," she said. She tried to smile, but another woman cried out as a second house took flame.

We both gazed at the burning village.

"Kane did this. I saw him, Becky. He made a fire with his fingers." She gave me a look. "We should help them..."

"No. Billy, we need to go. They think *we* did this. I heard Maurice blaming us." She looked about anxiously.

"What? No, I can tell them it was Kane." I wondered what *bovithane* was, but had an idea that the rancid smell of the flames may have something to do with it. "Mother might be partly to blame..."

"Was it her in that huge flying... thing?"

"Yeah, and now she's floating away. Max is following her."

We led the Bighorns around the corner to the tavern, out of direct sight of the fire, and they finally settled down.

The flames were so tall that the sky behind the tavern glowed as orange as the sunset, and the fiery butterflies were drifting onto the roofs of other buildings. *The whole village will catch fire*, I thought in dismay.

"Wait here." I told Becky. I ran into the tavern.

She started "What are you – "

I scrambled up the stairs and into our room. Our bags were piled in a corner, empty foodsacks, our personal backsacks and the big crossbow. I grabbed my bag, full of all my sketches, as well as the mammoth tusk and the dirt the tomato sellers had given me. I slung it over my shoulder, plucked up Becky's bag and left everything else.

When I returned downstairs, Maurice and Freddy were coming out of the kitchen wheeling a trolley loaded with pails of water. They froze when they saw me.

Maurice urged the kid on. "Go, Freddy, take this to the mill. Hurry!" The boy lugged the trolley across the room, through the swing doors and into the night. Maurice stared at me. "I knew you two were trouble." His eyes were so wide. *He's scared of me.*

"It wasn't us," I insisted, holding his gaze. "I saw that Fedora M – I mean that Kingsman. He had a bottle, and fire came from his fingers... Don't ask me how, but I saw him start the fire."

Maurice's lip twitched, and his face morphed into a scowl. "The Kingsmen. They were after her." His face changed to grim realisation. "My whole village will be burned to the ground because of you *spuds*. My home!" I wanted to explain it to him, tell him he'd gotten it wrong, but he was reaching under the bar, and my legs figured it out before my brain.

"What about your tip!" I ran for the saloon doors.

The blunderbuss went off behind me.

Ka-BOOM!

The doors shattered. I tumbled into the road as chunks of building fell on my head. My ears rang, worse than any *echo*. I stood, brushing off splinters and chips of wood. There was nothing left of the swing doors, and the entrance to the tavern looked as though a monster had taken a big bite out of it. Maurice peered at me over the top of the ridiculous smoking gun barrel from behind the bar. His face was bewilderment. As was mine.

"You missed!" I shouted, as much a question as a

childish retort.

Becky clutched the reins, gaping at the hole in the tavern. I exhaled, handed Becky her bag and climbed onto Bellyguts.

We fled burning Barrow and galloped after Mother, Max and Kane.

After the glow from Barrow diminished, the night enveloped us.

The balloon was easy to spot. It glowed bright orange, a surreal round orb against the dark, starless sky. It was accompanied by a constant, heavy *fwoosh* sound.

"Your mother made that?" Becky said in awe. "She's flying."

"She's going higher," I realised. "We have to hurry!"

We caught up with Kane, whose tired old mule had slowed to a weary trot, unable to keep up the chase. Our rams passed him effortlessly.

"*You!*" he spat after us. I looked back over my shoulder. He kicked the mule savagely. The poor beast groaned and honked. "Come on you useless animal!" He kicked it again, and this time the mule outright stopped. Kane couldn't keep his grip, and tumbled over the animal's head and fell to the ground. He quickly stood, and the darkness swallowed my sight of him. His voice carried through the night air, a fuming rage. "*I will find you. WHEREVER YOU GO, DO NOT DOUBT THAT I WILL FIND YOU!*"

We left the skinny Fedora Man in the dust.

The track curved away to the right, but the balloon carried on straight. I heard Max barking ahead, somewhere in the long grass. We turned off the track, following Max's excited yaps.

Mother's balloon soared higher and higher. The roar of the burner that powered it cascaded across the sky. We caught up with Max at last, barking at the sky. The balloon now drifted directly above our heads. And still it rose, shrinking ever smaller.

"What is she doing?" Becky wondered, as we gazed up.

"I don't know. Maybe something's broken."

We watched. Up and up the orb went.

"I hope she's alright."

"Me too."

The grey veil of cloud gobbled the balloon. Mother vanished. For a while, the noise of the burner stayed with us, until it faded to silence and we were alone in the quiet dark.

I reined up and sat back in the saddle, utterly deflated and annoyed. "Now how are we supposed to find her?"

I looked to Becky, who sighed.

I looked to Max, who echoed. *Biscuit?*

I dismounted and dropped beside him.

"Let's see what you saw, boy." I placed a hand on his flat head, and –

I'm running, chasing the giant fat bird. *Follow follow follow.*

A familiar voice calls my name. I see the *biscuit lady*. She's dangling from the big fat bird. I won't let you *eat the biscuit lady!* I shout at the bird, no! Put her down! But then she tells me to hush, and I do because she always brings home biscuits for me and I like her. She climbs up the ropes into the nest. The fat bird is trying to land, its claws scrape along the ground.

I hear a horse behind me, and then the smell of it is all around. Another voice, an angry man shouts. It's *him*. I growl and shout at the *bad man* and he tries to ride over me but I dodge and keep running and the biscuit lady is shouting and he is shouting and I am shouting. The man leans off his horse reaching for the birds feet, the dangly bits. He's going to get the biscuit lady!

The fat bird starts to screech fire and lights up bright and it's so loud and *scary*.

The big fat fire bird is taking the biscuit lady into the sky! *No!* I shout but it won't listen, and the bad man is so angry and he kicks the horse but it gets upset and slows down and I keep running, right past him because I must *follow*

follow follow follow.

I snapped back to myself and sneezed. Max snorted.

"What did you see?" Becky asked. She had dismounted too, and hunkered down beside us.

"She almost crashed into the ground and Kane nearly climbed on. Mother had to go higher to get away from him." I peered up at the dark clouds. "She didn't need to go that high though."

"Maybe her controls were broken, like you said. The whole thing looked really hobbled together from bits of old junk. I can't believe she was flying! She's amazing, Billy."

"Yeah." Amazing wasn't the word I was thinking of right then. *Reckless.* Mother was living proof that there is a fine line between madness and genius. I couldn't believe I had finally found her, and she'd floated off into the sky. I tried to imagine what it would be like above the clouds. The thought calmed me. "I wonder what she can see up there..." I mused.

Becky gazed up. "That's the first thing I'm gonna ask her when she comes back down."

We found a rocky clearing, and dismounted. We daren't risk a fire, Kane might have seen it. But I wasn't going to leave the grasslands until we had sight of Mother. The overcast sky obscured the stars and the moons, so it was almost pitch black.

We sat back to back, knees hugged, watching the sky. Max took the opportunity to snooze.

"Poor boy, he's shattered," Becky spoke softly.

I was concentrating on the clouds. "Mmhmm."

We sat and waited for a long time.

I felt Becky gently press against my back in a slow rhythm as she breathed. My eyes grew heavy. *Don't sleep now!* My belly gurgled.

Becky chuckled softly. "I'm hungry too," she said. "Hey, Billy?"

I reopened my eyes. "Yeah?"

"Can you draw me a picture?"

"What, now?"

"No, silly. Just, when you find time."

I'd had an idea for a drawing I wanted to give her as a surprise, but could never find time to work on it. Now I would make time. "Yeah, I'll draw you something."

I felt her exhale. "I'd like that."

Max stirred. He stood, pricked his ears, and gave a little whine. I heard the sound of something loose and heavy *whooshing* through the sky above us. No, *falling* through the sky.

I squinted in the direction of the sound. Faintly in the distance, I could just make out a great black shape descending alarmingly fast towards the ground.

"Becky, look!" I whispered.

The shape fell, and fell, *whoooooooooooooshhhFWUMP*. It careened into the ground a hundred feet away.

Staggering through the darkness, we made our way to the wreckage. The hide balloon sprawled limply across the ground and buried a misshapen lump.

"Becky, help me lift it!" The leather was stretched thin, so many hides stitched together. We hauled it over the lump and revealed the ruin of the basket. Mother lay sprawled out within, unmoving.

"Mother!" I climbed in and knelt beside her. She was breathing, thank goodness. I spoke softly, "Can you hear me?"

She muttered. I couldn't make out the words. I thought I heard 'doom', or 'moon'... or 'spoon'. Her eyes shifted but remained closed. Her breathing grew heavier, she gulped air in heaving breaths.

She sat bolt upright and headbutted me. "Ow."

"William!" She pulled me close and squeezed me around the ribs. Relief and joy overcame me. *I found you.* I saw Becky watching us, and pretended I wasn't crying, but even in the dark I could see the smile lighting up her face.

She had the best smile.

"Oh, William, it's really you!" Mother vigorously wriggled me about in her arms. "I thought I was having another episode." She whispered "Sometimes when I've been in my lab for too long, I see things that aren't really there." I had no response to that.

We got to our feet in the basket, and she studied my face. "Look at the state of your hair! What have you been doing?" Coming from Mother, whose hair resembled that of an abandoned birds nest, I had to snigger. She noticed Becky then. "And who's this?"

"Hi, I'm Rebecca. It's so exciting to meet you!" She spoke with admiration and a touch of shyness in her voice that sent my tummy all aflutter.

Mother looked unusual. She fiddled with her long frizzy hair and hastily brushed down her leather jacket with her hands. She offered her hand, smiling. "I'm Bethany." They shook hands. Mother pulled her close and whispered in her ear loud enough for me to still hear. "Billy always wanted a pretty girlfriend, yes he did."

My cheeks turned to fire. Thankfully the darkness probably hid it.

Becky laughed and glanced at me over my mother's shoulder. She was grinning. "Well, if he plays his cards right, maybe he'll find one."

Max put his front paws on the edge of the basket wreckage and peered at me with his tongue hanging out. I knew what he was thinking, even without the echo.

They released and we climbed out of the basket to stand together amid the wreck. For a few seconds, the world stood still. I was finally reunited with my mother. I savoured the moment. It felt like victory.

Becky broke the silence, speaking in a tone of anticipated wonder. "So what's it like to fly higher than the *clouds*?"

Mother erupted. "It was incredible! I flew didn't I? When that stupid man tried to climb onto my precious Cloud Cruiser, I had to ignite the bovithruster and my calculations were perfect and it worked! It actually worked and I flew and *ohmygoodness* the view! I soared above the clouds and saw the stars, so many stars, bright and beaming. The bovithruster got stuck and wouldn't turn off so I just kept going up and up and up until I hit the top of the sky. I got a bit dizzy then, but Big Blue radiated down on me and Little R—" She stopped abruptly, her jaw dangling open.

Becky looked to me quizzically.

Mother murmured, "Little Red..."

"What?" I leaned closer. "What did you see?"

She stared blankly.

"She gets like this sometimes," I told Becky. She was having an idea, I knew. Somewhere down in that wonderful, weird, perhaps slightly broken mind, sparks were flying. I'd seen it so many times before and it would always result in her disappearing into the shed for days. We had no shed here though, so who could predict what she was about to do.

Mother blinked. She peered about. "Where are we?" she asked.

"Somewhere in the Southern Grasslands," Becky answered.

Mother looked down at the wreckage of her balloon. She bent to gather up bits of rope, netting, the hide canvas and started bundling it all together.

"Mother," I needed to ask. "Are you going home?"

She paused, frowned, and spoke as if I had missed the obvious point. "Of course not William! I need to get to the moon."

<u>Chapter Ten</u>

Well, I didn't expect that, even from her.

"The *moon?* Which one?"

"Little Red, of course."

I didn't know much about the moons. School taught us they were like giant coconuts, bigger than we could imagine, that floated around Lunaria and somehow made the tides come in and out. I didn't really understand that, I just always thought they looked nice. Especially during the eclipses. The eclipses were beautiful, I had sketched them so many times. "Can you really fly there?"

Mother paused to ponder the question. When she did this, she tended to tap her chin. "I'm not sure. It was very cold up there... Next time I will take a woolly hat, I think. And I must try harder not to fall asleep."

Becky's eyes were gleaming. "You're so clever."

Mother liked that. "Thank you! It is good to be appreciated." She turned to me. "Good find, William, she's a smart one."

I rolled my eyes, and Becky giggled.

"Where are you from?" she asked, turning back to Becky. "Wait, don't tell me. Say something else."

"Like what?"

Mother bobbed her head in thought. "East, yes, but not quite Joy... I'd guess Hooke."

Becky's face was gleeful. "Ha! That's amazing. Billy and I were heading there. Kind of. We were looking for you first, but I'm going home too."

"Yes, Hooke." Mother tapped her fingers across her chin. "We should go there. I need new equipment. It's the perfect place to fix the Cloud Cruiser."

I didn't want to go home, not yet. But Father was waiting for us. I remembered how proud he looked the day I left. He had given me the task of finding her. I didn't want to disappoint him.

"Hale is the opposite direction..." I said slowly.

"I told you I'm not going home yet, William. Besides, now that you're here, you can help me. It seems you are ready to see who I really am."

The hide canvas weighed far too much for us to lug it all the way to Hooke. I sent Max to round up the Bighorns, who had roamed off to have a midnight snack. We rolled the balloon up and tied it over Bellyguts' back.

Snowball carried the depleted bovithruster (a long cylindrical metal tank), the remaining jumble of netting and two of Mother's food sacks. There was no way to salvage the basket. Mother did not seem too disappointed. "It wasn't the right shape anyway. The next one will have room at least for three..."

We set off across the dark field, leading the Bighorns in a sweeping arc south-eastwards towards the Forest of Bliss. I helped myself to some dried strips of beef from Mother's supplies. It seemed she'd been living on jerky. There was enough to feed us all, even Max.

"This is a lot of meat, Mother."

"Yes, I bought a cow in Fentworth," she said. "I've grown rather fond of them lately. I figured out a way to harness the power of her flatulence. Technology powered by nature, William – that is my philosophy."

How long has she been keeping up this secret life? Certainly more than the past three Blue Moons. I wonder if Father even knows...

"What's 'flatulence'?" Becky asked.

She chortled. "Cows eat grass. Digested grass produces gas. A lot of gas. And cows have four stomachs. Four! Flatulence is the result of eating too much grass."

"Are you saying your balloon is powered with cow... farts?" Becky sniggered.

"Bovinated Bottom Burps is the scientific term. I ran many tests, and bovithane is the result of my efforts: a flammable gas, liquidised for stability. At Barrow, I managed to brew enough to conduct several test flights." Her face turned sour. All those efforts had exploded in the mill fire, which may have led to the village of Barrow being turned to cinders. "I must find a way to make it less... short tempered."

It took five days to reach the woodland, plenty of time to recount the adventure so far and get Mother up to speed on the newfound connection I had with Max.

I told her everything as we crossed the grassy plains. She was most excited to learn that the kamuna honey had brought me back to life.

"I knew it! I just knew it was clever stuff. I tried to tell that grumpy old toad Boyle that he ought to put some kamuna in his cereals and that warty face would clear right up, but did he listen, *nooo* of course he didn't. Nobody ever listens to Batty Bethany, do they?" She was strangely pleased that her bees had found a new home, even if it was in the belly of a sentient tree monster. "You'll have to take me to this cave, William. Who knows what we could learn from such a specimen."

"He'll try to eat you, unless you make a wish. He feeds on desires."

"What did you wish for?" she asked.

I hesitated, reddening. "I, uh..." My eyes shifted to Becky, leading Snowball by the reins ahead of us.

Mother traced my gaze, then turned back to me. "Oh for goodness sake," she said impatiently. "Did it come true, whatever it was?"

"Maybe."

"Either it did or it didn't?"

I scratched my elbow. "It did."

"Interesting... a genuine Wishing Tree. That is most curious." She tapped her chin in thought. She called to Becky. "When were you last in Hooke?"

Becky turned, surprised by the question. She replied warily, "I haven't been back in over a year."

"So you won't have heard we have a new king."

"New king? No, when did that happen?"

Mother considered. "He showed up about a dozen moons ago. The king's long-lost son. Nobody knew he had a son, but suddenly there he was. Not long after, the king died and now his son sits on the Joyful Throne. He's only eight!"

"Wow," Becky exclaimed. "That sounds suspicious, doesn't it?"

"Oh yes, very suspicious. The whole city was in uproar. There's even some rebellious faction that's sprung up, declaring the boy a *false king*. It was certainly very convenient the son showing up just before the king died while out fishing."

"Fishing?" I asked. "What's so dangerous about fishing?"

"His boat was swallowed by a giant squid."

"Oh."

Mother concluded, "Makes me wonder. What if your wishing-tree-monster isn't the only one of his kind out there?"

Four days later, we reached the edge of the forest. The trees had been visible on the horizon for two days, and I wondered why it was taking so long to reach them. But as we approached, I understood. When I had thought we were close, we still had miles to go. The trees were *huge*. The Hale Wood and Aston Forest seemed like shrubbery when compared to these straight, leafy towers.

I walked to the base of one and craned my neck to gaze up. The trunk must have been half as wide as the farmers' cottage, and as high as the Fent Vale Bridge. Straight up it shot, until it reached a web of gnarled branches. The bark felt rough and knobbly, streaked with wrinkles and stretched like an old crone's face. And there were hundreds more, just like it. This was more than just a forest, it was an army of ancient giants.

"My father told me that Hooke used to be the gateway to this forest," Becky explained, gazing at the canopy high above. "When I was little, the harvesting had already begun, but it escalated and got worse and worse until the town no longer slept in the shadow of the trees. Bliss became the new Hooke, but things started to change there, too."

Mother sighed. "You've been gone a year. I wonder if you'll recognise it."

Nothing could prepare me. After one final day's hike through the magnificent forest, we came to what can only be described as a wasteland. The trees abruptly ceased, and stretching for miles around were endless flat stumps and a sea of broken branches. In the distance, smoke rose from a town. The sky above it looked noticeably dull, as if the sunlight struggled to penetrate the smog.

"And they call it Bliss?" I asked, rhetorically.

I could hear the distant *hum* of machinery, the screech of saw blades and the low rumble of many fires burning. Tiny men marched to and fro like a colony of ants.

Becky gaped across the desolation. "It used to be so pretty." She clenched a fist. "I *hate* them."

A whistle echoed towards us. Puffing smoke, the Great Train pulled out of the station and headed away to our right, going west towards Barrow. *Or whatever's left of Barrow.*

"They fixed the train!" Becky exclaimed. "I can use it to

get home, when it comes through again tomorrow."

"I don't think I'll be using the train for a while," Mother brooded. "Remind me again, what is it they are calling me?"

I hung my head. "The Train Trasher."

"And the Aston Arsonist," added Becky.

"Mmm... No doubt I've become the Barrow Burner by now, as well." She sighed. Then she lit up. "Oh well! I'll just fly from now on. The Cloud Cruiser Mark II will be the new technological wonder of the world! Yes!" She studied the field of stumps that lay ahead of us, our route to the town. "But first things, first..."

We had to pass through Bliss to get to Hooke, but couldn't risk being spotted – with the train up and running once again, word must have spread about the wanted fugitive seen travelling with two Bighorns, a young girl, a boy and a dog. Kane could be there, too... We were just too conspicuous.

Mother sent me on a scouting run with Max.

I crept to the edge of the town, ducking behind the stumps, which were as tall as me in some cases, until I was close enough to Bliss to smell the forges. I gave Max the command. "Away. *Way away.*"

He darted off into the lumber yard and beyond. I waited. When he returned, I touched his head.

I'm choking! The stench of hot smoke burns my nostrils so bad I'm struggling to breathe. I run past men with saws, hammers, the noisy clangs of metal, machines whirr and fires bellow. I see burly men heaving logs, and smell their sweat. I bumble into someone's legs, and he drops a heavy plank and shouts but I run away, through the yard and into the smelly town.

I leave the fires behind and the streets become flat. My claws scratch the smooth surface, it feels strange. On the side of the street, I see a man studying a piece of paper and he discards it on the floor in front of me. I don't understand it, but *Billy* might, he likes paper.

I run on, and on, past rows of stone buildings, past people, and more people, and past a wobbly singing man who points at me and laughs and spills his drink, then I dart off the street, into the stump field and run back to *Billy*.

I opened my eyes. Max sat at my feet, and rolled his head to look at me as he panted. "Good boy."

We returned to Becky and Mother, who were waiting at the top of the stump field at the edge of the forest.

I ducked inside the tree line with them, and gave Mother the bad news. "Max saw a wanted poster. It's like the others, but they've upped the reward to three gold. And there's a line about how you might be travelling with two accomplices riding Bighorns, a boy and a girl." I turned to Becky. "At least they don't know what we look like."

Mother let out a disgruntled sigh. "Time for a new disguise." She went to her backsack and rummaged through it. She pulled out an ornate pair of scissors. She offered them to us. "Would one of you mind?"

Neither of us had ever given anybody a haircut. But Becky had seen George shearing the sheep before summer and that made her more qualified than me.

She snipped and snapped and cut away the tangles and frizzy bits of Mother's wild hair. When Becky put down the scissors, Mother no longer resembled the woman in the posters. Now, her hair stopped at the ears instead of her back, and she looked a bit manly. Luckily, we didn't have a looking-glass so she was spared the terror of seeing herself.

"How do I look?" she asked.

"Great!" I said before Becky could answer. "Like a new woman."

"Just one final touch..." she said, tapping her chin. She clicked her fingers. "Aha." She untied the canvas from Bellyguts' back, and let it roll to the ground. She flattened out a section, and slashed around three of the hides with her knife. She turned them into ragged ponchos, one for each of us. "Now, if anyone asks, we're travellers from Capella. You better let me do the talking, though..."

Becky turned to Snowball. "I guess this is as far as you can go," she said sadly, rubbing his neck. The ram bleated softly, and nuzzled her.

Bellyguts was gnawing on some twigs. He glanced at me nonchalantly and continued chewing.

"Do you think they'll find their way home?" Becky asked, hopeful.

"They're Fent Bighorns," Mother assured her. "They'll find the way."

We unloaded everything but the saddles, and walked them into the forest to set them free. Bellyguts sniffed the air, before wandering into the trees. Snowball started to follow, then stopped. He looked back at Becky and me as we stood together next to a great trunk. He bleated, scratched his head on a tree and walked away.

We waited until dusk for all of the workers in the lumber yard to go home. While we killed time, I leant against a stump and sketched the desolation. Or pretended to. I spent more time working on the drawing for Becky...

After the sun had set, we approached the town called Bliss. We wrapped the bovithruster within the canvas and bound it up tight with the netting. It looked like the world's biggest sausage. Down the hill we stumbled, carrying it over our shoulders. We were of three different heights, making it hopelessly awkward to carry. It took over an hour to haul it down the slope of stumps, through the empty lumber yard, and into the town's main street. Exhausted, we dropped the mass on the side of the road.

"There's no way we can carry this all the way to Hooke," Mother wheezed.

I bent over clutching my knees, breathing heavily. Max slumped on the pavement and panted, as if he had been helping to carry the thing himself, which he hadn't. "There must be another way." I peered about.

We stood on a shadowy street lined with lanterns. The road was paved with square tiles of palestone, not cobbles like Aston or Fentworth. The houses were a mixture of stone and timber, most had ground floor walls of stone, while timber balconies and lofts had been layered on top. That lingering fog we had seen from the stump fields gave Bliss a misty, claustrophobic feel. Down the street, the lanterns light gradually faded until they were swallowed up by the mist.

A murmur of voices came from the tavern further along. Shafts of light spilled from the slatted windows onto the road. Across the street in front of us sat half a dozen horse-drawn covered wagons, lined up one after the other. The horses chewed their bits while the drivers sat reading newspapers under the light of the lanterns. The front most driver looked up and spoke.

"You look lost."

Mother leaned in to Becky and me and spoke quietly. "Follow my lead, but don't say anything. And bring the balloon." She adjusted her poncho and swaggered across the road to the wagon. Becky and I exchanged a look, heaved up the canvas sausage and followed.

She approached the driver, a man with receding hair and a wiry moustache. To my horror, a copy of the wanted poster was printed on the back page of his newspaper in black and white ink. Mother really did look different with her schoolboy haircut, but up close someone might still recognise her...

"Howdy, pard'ner," Mother drawled. I choked back a guffaw. *What the hell kind of accent is that?*

"Well hello there, ma'am." He closed the paper and laid it on the seat with the picture staring up at him. Luckily, his eyes were on the real Mother. "Might you be needing a ride someplace?" A slimy smile broke across his face as he studied her up and down. He appeared to like what he saw.

"Me and the kids here are taking a trip to the big ciddy." She gestured to Becky and me, who stood behind with the big sausage at our feet, trying not to break into a fit of giggling. "You're one o' them fancy wagon taxis they told me about, am I right or am I *rawng*?" I struggled to remember hearing anything more ridiculous. Surely he wasn't going to fall for that overblown drone.

"The city, eh? You must mean Joy." He licked his lips. "That's a long way, ma'am. Usually I just help the ol' 'jacks who been on the ale get home to their missus'." He gave us barely a passing glance, his eyes were fixed on Mother, but certainly not her face. His beady gaze swept across her as he spoke.

Mother's reply was accompanied by a *don't be silly* hand gesture. "Oh no, not Joy. We only wants to get to Hooke. Surely you can assist a helpless mother?" She added a cheeky whisper, "You look nicer than the rest o' these grumpy so n' so's, for sure!"

I grimaced, couldn't take any more. I had to turn away to hide my smirk. I looked back across the road at the tavern, and saw the dark shapes of people inside the windows. The blinds were down, so I could only see the silhouettes drinking and chatting.

All except one. The upper most window was wide open and I could see right inside... at the Fedora Man sitting there.

If he wasn't concentrating on the book in his hand he might have noticed me too. In a heartbeat, my grin turned to stone.

I spun and grabbed Becky's arm. She started and frowned at me. I mouthed *Fedora* and gestured with my head behind me. Slowly, she turned and casually glanced up at the window. Her head jolted back to face the wagon when she saw.

"Please, call me Ronald," the wagon driver was saying. "And can I just say, that is quite the fine style you got there, ma'am. The poncho really brings out the definition of your shoulder blades." His eyebrows bounced, as if they were sharing a naughty joke.

Mother froze for a moment, and said "uhh..." And then giggled like a little girl. "Stop it, you! I knows your sort, they told me all about you ciddy folk, they did."

Becky piped up, mimicking the ridiculous accent flawlessly. "Right, so let's get a' rolling, mister, we don't wanna be late!" *She's good at that,* I thought.

Mother flustered. "Late? Right! Yes, Ronald, we're mighty late!"

"Righty ho." He pointed to the sausage. "Just pop yer tent in the back and we'll get going. Why don't you sit up front with me?" He stared hungrily at Mother, and tapped the seat (and the newspaper) with a bony hand.

"I don't think so!" Becky blurted, bundling Mother towards the rear of the wagon. Mother stuttered, but couldn't resist Becky's force as she led her up the little steps and into the safety of the wagon's trailer, out of sight. Max jumped up after her.

She returned, helped me lift the balloon into the back and climbed in.

As I mounted the steps, I gave a nervous glance back at the window of the tavern. *Kane* was peering directly at me, squinting. When we made eye contact, his face turned to wide-eyed fury.

I dived through the door flap and shouted "*GO!*"

Chapter Eleven

Mother gave us a questioning stare, but she must have seen the fear on our faces and she figured it out. She peeled back the trailer's front flap to speak to the driver. "Show me how fast ye ciddy boys can ride and might be I'll have a special tip for ye when we get there!"

Ronald didn't hesitate. "Yes ma'am." He snapped the reins and the wagon lurched forward.

When she sat back down on the bench, she had the newspaper in her hand. I nodded approvingly.

As we sped away, I looked out the back and saw the mist begin to envelope the next wagon and the tavern. The figure of a man ran out of the doors, darted across the road and leapt at the driver. I heard a startled shout and the horse whinnied. Then the mist was too thick to see.

"Was it him?" Becky whispered.

"I think so." The three of us exchanged fearful glances. Mother tapped her chin with her fingers.

The wagon flew down the road. The inside flickered with light from the lanterns, lively shadows danced across the fabric walls and ceiling.

After a while, hoofbeats filled the air.

I carefully peeled back the rear flap to get a better view.

Kane had hijacked a wagon and sat in the driver's seat whipping the reins as the horse galloped towards us out of the mist.

He saw me and screamed hysterically, "I told you not to doubt that I would find you, *fugitives!*"

Yeah, I had just hoped it wouldn't be so soon.

Mother disappeared out of the front flap to join the driver. I heard him yelp in surprise, although he sounded gleeful.

She spoke sternly without a hint of the drawling cowgirl accent. "Give me the reins."

"What?" he answered. "Now, I know you Capella folks think you know all about horses, but I been driving –" He was cut short and suddenly Ronald came flying through the flap and almost landed on top of Max. I heard a sharp crack of the reins and we gained a boost of speed.

Ronald lay sprawled on the balloon sausage and looked up at me. "What a woman!" he breathed wistfully.

I scowled and turned to see out the back. Kane's horse stampeded at us, pulling Kane's stolen wagon ever closer. I could see him clearly now. He wasn't wearing his hat, and a long stream of hair flapped wildly about his face. Each time a lantern zipped past I saw the raw focus in his eyes. He bared his teeth in a grim smile. I let go of the flap, letting it hide the terrible man from my sight and gripped the bench.

The smooth road came to an end, the last lantern flew past, and the trailer grew a lot darker. The wagon didn't slow down, but bounced against the uneven dirt road. I took another peek. Judging by the soft blue light that covered the passing fields, I guessed that Big Blue had finally broken through the clouds.

Kane rode past me and his wagon came alongside ours.

I heard him shouting outside as Becky and I looked helplessly at one another.

"Defiler! You will never outrun me!"

"Why won't you just leave me *alone?*" Mother shouted

back.

A high pitched cackle of deranged laughter pierced the air.

"Where's the fun in that!"

"I haven't even done anything, you imbecile! You set me up in Aston! And Barrow!"

"Why would you even say that, Defiler! You were the one playing with fire. Don't blame me for getting *burned.*" Another cackle. "Murderer!"

The trailer jerked sideways, flinging me from the bench where I landed on top of Ronald and Max. The wagons smashed into each other and we rebounded the other way, which sent Becky reeling forwards to join the heap. The four of us tried to cling on to the bench, the floor, each other, anything within reach.

"What are you people doing to my wagon?" Ronald wailed.

Another smash. And another. The horses galloped on, and each time the wagons clattered together I headbutted either Becky, or Ronald, or Max who had the boniest head of all.

A horse whinnied, and our wagon began driving straight once more, giving me a chance to stumble to my feet. I heard the sound of Kane's horse lagging behind.

I looked out the rear and saw him flailing the reins like a maniac. His horse had slowed to a canter, but now picked up the gallop once again.

"*DITCH THE BALLOON*!" Mother screamed.

I glanced down at the great sausage. I gave Becky a hand to her feet, and shoved Ronald out of the way. "Are you sure?" I called forwards.

A pause. Then, a regretful response. "Yes. Ugh."

We gripped the end of the rolled up canvas and dragged it towards the rear of the wagon. I looked at Becky.

"One. Two. Push!"

We heaved it out into the path of Kane's wagon. It tumbled into the dirt, bounced once and spun underneath the hooves of his horse. The horse leapt over it instinctively, but the wagon probably didn't know what was happening. It crashed into the giant sausage with the metal tank hidden within and both front wheels disintegrated.

Kane was flung from the wagon as it flipped over and rolled in the dirt. His horse broke free and bounded on towards us for a few more seconds before slowing to a halt and fading into the darkness out of sight.

Becky and I exchanged a stunned look.

"Who *are* you people?" Ronald lay on the floor of the wagon looking distressed. Max flopped onto the floor, rested his chin on Ronald's belly and drooled. We slumped down onto a bench either side of him. I let out a long, tired sigh.

Ronald looked from Becky to me, as if waiting for an explanation, one that he didn't really want to hear. When neither of us spoke he went on, "That man called you fugitives. Was he a Kingsman?" He gulped.

I shifted in the bench, and Becky scratched the back of her head, grimacing. My eyes flicked to the newspaper which lay beside Ronald. He glanced down at it, grabbed it and looked closely at the wanted poster on the back.

He muttered and squirmed around underneath Max, who looked very comfortable.

"It's not true. They lied about Mother killing those people in Aston," I tried to explain.

"The Aston Arsonist!" he shrieked, trying to wriggle away. "And the Train Trasher, and the Barrow Bomber! Get off me you filthy mongrel!" Max snorted before rolling off. Ronald crawled towards the back of the trailer, trying to get as far away from us as possible.

"Technically, *I'm* the Train Trasher..." I tried to sound reassuring, but it seemed to distress him even more.

Becky added, "We won't hurt you, mister. We're just trying to get home. We don't want any trouble." She glanced nervously out the back of the wagon. "It just seems to keep showing up."

Mother poked her head through the flap at the front. "Ronald! Do I look like a *murderer* to you?" She looked like a mad horse thief with a bad haircut to me.

Ronald eyed her, probably wanting to see the cowgirl he thought she was. I felt a little bad for him. Then a hint of that slimy smile returned to one corner of his mouth and I shuddered. "No," he said.

"Good. But don't think that just because I haven't killed a man, that I won't leave him alone in the middle of nowhere tied to a tree." She cocked her head and smiled.

Ronald looked alarmed. "You w-wouldn't, would you?"

"So long as you forget you ever saw us!" She didn't wait for a reply, but disappeared out the front again.

He looked apprehensively from me to Becky to Max. He gulped again. "I can do that."

Mother drove the wagon through the night. We stopped briefly to let the horse rest and drink from a stream, but then carried on at a gentle trot along the road to the city. Ronald didn't budge from his corner.

I wanted to ask Becky about her home again, but she seemed to grow more and more fidgety the closer we came to Hooke. I didn't want to talk about anything like that in front of Ronald, anyway. He seemed harmless enough, if a little creepy, but I didn't trust him.

"I'm going to ride up front for a little while," Becky said to me, looking apologetic. She looked at Ronald, who gave us a nervous glance.

"It's okay," I said. "I'll watch him."

She smiled at me and ducked through the flap to sit with Mother. "How's it going Bethany, still awake?"

They started chatting away.

Max padded over and rested his chin on my knee. I petted him. *You'll help me guard the creep, won't ya boy,* I sent. And he echoed back. *Guard. Creep!* He lowered his head to the floor and crouched low, the way I taught him to sneak

115

up on a rabbit. I laughed out loud.

"Not that kind of creep, boy." He was learning so fast.

Billy! He sat up and wagged his tail. I ruffled his head.

He looked over his shoulder towards the front of the trailer, then back at me. *Becky. Scared.*

"I know, boy." I sighed. I caught Ronald eyeing me quizzically. I tried to make polite conversation. "So, how long have you been a taxi driver?"

"Since before you were born." His friendly tone was reserved solely for women, apparently. He spoke rather coldly to me. "This is the first time I've been hijacked, though."

I wasn't sure what to say to that. He glared at me. "Sorry," I said.

We sat in awkward silence, listening to the girls chatting away the way only girls do.

Big Blue set and the trailer slowly filled with a gloomy dawn light as we arrived on the outskirts of Hooke.

The wagon came to a halt. Mother entered through the front flap and sat on the bench opposite me.

"Right, Ron. This is where we say goodbye."

"What?" he asked, looking betrayed.

"We can't have you knowing where we're going."

"But I said I would forget I ever saw you. I won't tell anyone!"

"Oh stop whinging. It's not far to walk. We will leave your horse and wagon outside the first tavern we see. They'll be waiting for you when you get there. Now, go on." She made a *shoo* gesture, and Ronald stumbled out the back into the road. Mother leaned out after and flicked him a silver coin. "For yer trouble, mister!" she drawled. Then she sat back down. "Billy, go sit up front. You can see what a big city looks like. Becky knows where to go from here."

I clambered out into the morning sunlight and sat on the bench next to Becky, who clutched the reins.

"Welcome to my home, Billy." She sounded nervous,

but gave me a big smile. I put an arm around her and squeezed. She cracked the reins and we rolled onwards.

There's no green there anymore. That's what she had told me. I gazed ahead and understood.

We passed under a stone archway and I saw the paved stone road winding its way between rows of towering stone buildings that bellowed smoke from stone chimneys. No green, but lots of grey. Bliss had been misty, Hooke was outright smoggy.

"This is Anvil Plaza," Becky announced. "That building there is where they extract metal out of rocks. And that there is the biggest forge in the south." She pointed to what looked like a huge concrete pudding attached to a really long drinking trough. Steam rose out of the stonework, as a line of a dozen workers wearing leather face masks and thick gloves scooped up hot liquid and poured it into moulds.

We passed men pumping bellows, swinging great hammers and smashing iron against anvils amid a haze of flying sparks. The air resonated with the sounds and smells of industry.

Behind the forges and the bellows were towering storehouses, bigger than any building I had ever seen. Hale's windmill could have easily fitted under the roof of the one stacked full of massive timber discs.

"That's where they put the trees after they've chopped them up," Becky continued. "They'll wind up as a set of tables, or a bed, or some fancy chairs for a rich bigwig somewhere in Joy." She sighed. "Hooke does the work, and Joy benefits."

I felt like an ant entering a smoky world of giants.

We bounced along the road, eventually leaving Anvil Plaza behind, and rolled into the city centre. Soon, we arrived at the first of the town's many taverns – an eight-storey round tower with a pointed roof stood out quite starkly against the rest of the square blocky buildings. It looked like somewhere a wizard might live. A signpost hung outside the door: *THE SPIRE*. As promised, we pulled up outside and hitched the horse to the railing. The horse slurped from the trough.

Mother hopped out, and anxiously glanced left and right before scurrying over to us. "So, take us home, Becky."

Becky was patting the horse's neck, saying thank you. She turned to us, took a deep breath. "Right, it's this way."

There wasn't a building smaller than four-storeys, most were even higher. Becky led us through the streets and I couldn't help craning my neck up.

So many windows.

"How many people live here?" I wondered aloud.

Mother chuckled. "It's no Hale, is it?"

I thought the buildings had been sprayed with some sort of dark paint, but then I realised they were just filthy. A layer of grime smothered the walls. We followed Becky past rows of terraced houses, through a small square with an ornate palestone fountain in the shape of a ship, and finally into a quiet suburb.

The houses here were small, detached, and run down, sagging as if under the weight of the smog.

Becky finally stopped.

"We're here."

We stood outside a modest house, in a street full of modest houses.

Becky took off the poncho and handed it to Mother. She looked at me then averted her eyes and turned to face the house. She inhaled a deep breath, walked up to the front door and quickly knocked three times.

I looked at her back, her long hair, the way it tumbled across her shoulders, etching the sight of her into my memory.

The front door opened.

"Hey, Dad."

Her father looked thunderstruck, exhausted, and joyful all at once. He wrapped his arms around Becky and moaned, his eyes tightly shut, embracing her in a loving hug.

When they released, Becky turned to us and I saw her eyes glisten with tears.

"I brought some friends." He looked up at us. "This is Billy and Bethany. My travel companions."

I raised a hand sheepishly.

"Thank you. Thank you so much," he spoke with a gentle, raspy voice, smiling broadly. "You brought my daughter home."

Mother strode up and shook his hand. "Actually, she brought us here. I'm kind of in need of a place to hide. And to rebuild my Cloud Cruiser... And to figure out the quasi decimal theory of quantum ignition."

He looked confused.

"She's really smart," Becky said. "Dad, is it okay if they stay with us for a while?"

"Of course, Rebecca," he rasped. "Let's go inside. You must have so much to tell me."

She beamed. "I do."

We went through a musky hall and into a box of a living room with an old couch and fireplace. Becky's father, John, brewed some tea and we sat and talked for a while, explaining who we were. He seemed a little concerned about Mother's reputation as a wanted criminal, but as soon as we mentioned the involvement of the Fedora Men, he became quite eager to help.

"They're not what they used to be," he rasped. "All corrupt, driven by greed and deceit these days. Kingsmen, *puh*. That name is far too regal. They're tearing this city apart from the inside." He shook his head. "You can stay as long as you like. It should be safe enough here, they've no reason to come snooping around our little neighbourhood. And most of them are busy dealing with the rebellion in Joy."

"Thank you," Mother said. "I'm hoping to find a spot in the city to work, anyway."

He nodded thoughtfully. "I may be able to help you

there. But let's speak more later. If you wouldn't mind, I'll show you to the spare room." He turned to Becky, smiling. "Then I can catch up with my daughter."

He led us across the hall and through a very creaky door. Inside was a desk, chair, an old wardrobe and a mattress on the floor. "This used to be Kara's study, but it's been empty for some time." He fetched some extra blankets and left us alone.

We didn't exactly have much to unpack. I made another makeshift bed along the wall with the blankets and flopped into it to test its comfort. Tiredness washed over me. We had travelled all night and I hadn't slept properly since the Forest of Bliss, two nights ago. Max sprawled out by my feet.

Mother saw the tusk jutting from the top of my bag and pulled it out to examine it.

"I found that," I yawned.

"It's from a mammoth," she marvelled. "You know, you could make a horn with this. Cut a blow-hole here, and decorate it with some bronze. It's from a baby, just your size." A pause. "Wait, where did you find this?"

"In Aston Forest," I could barely hear my own voice. I continued dreamily, "You told me the mammoths roamed in the Great Plains." My eyelids fell shut.

"They do. One day I'll fly over them with my balloon."

"That would be... nice..."

I dreamt of flying mammoths.

When I opened my eyes, Becky was sitting in the chair at the small desk, but not really doing anything. She saw me stir, and glanced up. "Hey, sleepy."

I blinked. "Hi. How long was I asleep?"

"A few hours. It's after noon. I didn't wanna wake you. We had a long night..."

I sat up, rubbing my eyes. Mother was gone, it was just the two of us in the room. "Did you get any sleep yet?"

"No."

I sighed. She looked as though she needed sleep.

"I had a nice long talk with my dad, though. He's gone to work now, he does the afternoon shift at the Plaza, on the bellows."

That sounded like a miserable job to me. Perhaps it explained the rasp in his voice.

She hesitated. Then, "I'm going to visit mum."

Max sensed her sadness, padded over and rested his head on her knee.

"Want some company?"

Wordlessly, she nodded.

We walked through the city in the afternoon sun. Or, at least I thought it was sunny. The foggy haze made it difficult to tell.

Max loped along at my heel, peering around, sniffing the air and snorting.

More people lived in a single street here than in all of Hale. I couldn't believe the noise. In the distance, I heard the clang of metals, the smiths hard at work. We passed a bustling market square, smaller than Fentworth's, but a lot louder. People argued and haggled and laughed and cursed. I saw a group of grotty kids selling scrap metal from a ramshackle hut they had clearly built themselves.

A woman wearing at least two dozen necklaces jumped in front of us.

"Wanna buy a lucky charm?" She waved one in my face, a rusty screw hanging by a bit of brown string. I saw that the rest were just as appealing: an old bolt, a chunk of copper tubing, one looked like a bicycle spoke that had been misshapen into a jagged star.

"No, thank you!"

Horse-drawn carts and people on bicycles rolled along the streets, cursing one another for taking up more than their share of the road. There was even a peddle cart, like the one the Fedora Men had used (before they met Boris the bull). Max pricked his ears, hearing it before me, and echoed *bad!* When I first heard the distinctive *clank* of the cog engine coming up from behind, I almost dived through the nearest window to hide. It was a postman. His cart had a metal chest bolted onto the back, just like Kane's, but he didn't have any people stuffed inside, only letters.

We left the town centre behind and gradually the noise faded the further we went. Eventually, we arrived at an old church with a belltower. A high stone wall encircled the grounds. We entered through an iron gate that was left open and walked around the back to the graveyard.

Serene and peaceful, the church garden was a quiet haven secluded from the rest of the town. Hidden behind the high wall, silence reigned. There were actually trees among the gravestones. A few, anyway. The grass had been kept well-trimmed, and as we made our way along a narrow gravel path beneath the shadow of the wall, I saw flowerbeds and colourful shrubbery, and vines creeping over the stonework.

Becky turned down a row and stopped in front of her mother's headstone.

Here lies KARA. Loving mother. Caring wife. Taken before her time. RIP.

Becky gently knelt before the grave.

"I'm home, mum." She rubbed an eye with a finger. "You'll never believe the year I've had. I'm a real farmer's girl now. Granpa and Granma took real good care of me." She sniffed. Her voice began to break. "They miss you. I miss you. I'm home, but I wish you were too."

She broke into strained sobs. Max nuzzled her arm. I felt helpless and longed to take her sadness away, but all I could do was kneel and put my arm around her shoulder.

Chapter Twelve

Later that night, despite feeling hopelessly tired, I lit a candle and sat hunched over the small desk with my sketchpad. Mother snored on the mattress beside me as I sketched, and sketched, and sketched, until the drawing was finished. Finally, I passed out under my blankets.

The next day, Mother took over our little room, drawing up plans and making calculations for the new balloon that would take us home. Or, the moon, as she kept insisting.

Becky wanted to be with her dad for the day, so I snuck into her room upstairs and carefully laid the drawing on her pillow. On it was the best depiction of an eclipse I had ever done, the big eye looking down upon two people, a boy and a girl, sitting on a rock together looking up at the sky. She had been so sad that night after the midsummer moonseye, I thought maybe I could give her a reason to smile next time she sees one. *Hopefully she'll find it when she gets home tonight, then come find me to say thank you....* I tingled with anticipation.

I spent my second day in Hooke wandering around the city with Max. He kept snorting and sneezing, the dirty air clearly disagreeing with his sensitive nose.

I took my backsack and went in search of someone who

might know how to turn my tusk into a horn. I'd been wondering what to do with it, but hadn't managed to come up with anything other than absurd, one-horned hat ideas. A musical horn seemed like a much more practical option.

I didn't really know who I was looking for until I saw a man in the market behind a stall covered in bones. *He'll do.*

"Corr, look at that!" he remarked, impressed with my tusk. He had a bald head and a pointy grey beard, which he liked to stroke as we talked. "How much you want for that beaut'?"

"Actually, I don't want to sell it. I wanna make a horn out of it. Like a trumpet."

"Ehh, sorry fella, I just collect 'em and sell 'em, don't carve 'em. I know a bloke who does, though." He squinted at me, tugging at his beard. "Six coppers?"

"What?"

"For the bloke." He leaned closer, almost whispering. "To tell you where he is. He ain't exactly wantin' to be found, you know what I mean?"

I wasn't too sure about this.

"Why doesn't he want to be found?" I whispered too for some reason.

His face changed. He leant back, as if realising something. "So you really want to make a *horn?*"

I looked at him, puzzled. "Yes. What's wr—"

"Sorry fella, thought you were someone else! Just take the thing to any ol' blacksmith, he'll knock you up a nice copper band and bang a mouthpiece in for ya. I'm just a humble bone collector." He stroked his beard and grinned.

"Uhh. Thanks. I'll just keep looking, then..." I took the tusk back, and left.

What was that about?

I wandered around some more, taking in the sights and sounds of the city. I couldn't get over how noisy it was. And there were people *everywhere*. And apparently, in a city, people needed to be entertained. I walked past a guy juggling frying pans in front of a small crowd of onlookers, a bendy woman dancing with a wooden sword and chanting gibberish, and my personal favourite, a street artist who claimed he could paint any mixture of animal you could think of. I challenged him to draw a mammoth crossed with an owl, a hedgehog and an octopus. He sketched a comical fat flying tentacled monstrosity and called it The Mammowlipus Rex Hog and handed me the paper. I happily parted with a few coppers.

I found the train station by accident, and had a sudden urge to run the other way. If the Fedora Men were looking for us, chances are they'd have somebody watching the train... *A quick peek wouldn't hurt.*

I casually strolled onto the platform, searching left and right for any signs of suited men in smart hats... Max copied me, peering one way then the other.

The platform was empty. The train had already been through this morning, and wasn't due back until tomorrow afternoon. A footpath led to a bridge over the tracks, so I wandered up and stood in the middle, with a view all the way down the straight tracks until they pinched to a point in the distance. On one side of the bridge the tracks led to Joy, the last city. The other direction pointed home. A long way away, now. I leant on the railing, peering towards the west.

Once Mother had built her new balloon, that's where we'd be going. Until then, I had time to kill... and Becky to hang out with. *Becky...* The thought of her made me smile.

Beckyyy, Max echoed. He was sitting on the floor, dusting the bridge with his wagging tail, showing off his tongue and teeth, as usual. Sometimes I could swear he was actually grinning.

That's when I noticed her. Out of the corner of my eye, I saw her standing down on the platform below. Well, I saw her legs first.

It was the angel. The beyond-beautiful girl in the orange hooded cloak and short green shorts. She stood alone on the platform, watching me.

Just like the first time I laid eyes on her, paralysis took over my body. I might as well have been struck by lightning and buried in sand. I stood like a statue as she sashayed along the length of the platform, up the ramp and joined me on the bridge.

Standing just two feet away, I realised it wasn't the same girl I had seen in Aston, after all. This one had stark green eyes instead of silver, and her hair was darker, more like chocolate brown than auburn. *Good grief man, you struggle to find your socks in the morning, and yet you can remember minute details about a stranger who never spoke to you.*

"Hi," I managed to blurt. She just stood there, eyeing me with one hand on her hip. A hint of a smile played on her lips, creating a tiny dimple in her flawlessly smooth-skinned cheek. "I'm Billy."

Still nothing. Max loped over and sniffed the hand which hung down at her side. I glanced down at him, but found my eyes being drawn to the slender legs protruding from the green shorts. I dragged them back to her face. "That's Max." I smiled awkwardly.

She tilted her head to look down at him and made the tiniest of noises, like the start of a giggle cut short. She flexed her fingers by his snout, which he gave a lick. Then she gazed back to me, and my heart literally ceased to beat. Nobody ever looked at me like that. *This must be what cake feels like, just before I eat it.*

It dawned on me that she still hadn't said anything. I rummaged around in my brain for the words that would make the question. "Can you, uh, speak?"

She lowered her head a fraction, and shook it gently.

"Oh." A mute. I had never met one before. Rather ironically, I found I didn't know what else to say. She just stood there, never taking her eyes from me. I looked about, forcing myself to not stare back, which was rather difficult. I drummed the railing with my fingers. I looked at the bright spot in the sky which was the sun trying to penetrate the smog. "Nice day, isn't it?"

She turned around. Her bum walked away. I mean, she walked away. It was just like the first one. *What did I say?*

She strolled all the way along the platform, turned the corner and disappeared from my sight.

I stood a while, replaying the hypnotic swing of her hips in my mind, feeling mildly guilty about it. Those green shorts were really short... And that orange cloak was just unreal, nobody wore clothes like that. *Green and orange.*

I'd seen two girls wearing that same outfit now. I wondered what Becky might look like in it...

Green and orange!

Where else had I seen those colours? I felt a small knot in my stomach, barely noticeable. I wracked my brain. I saw Boris the bull, abruptly, smashing into the peddle cart. *Bulls don't like bright colours.*

Oh.

No.

The knot in my stomach clenched into a fist.

I felt very exposed on the bridge. No-one else was in sight, it was just me and Max, and the empty rail line, and deserted platform, but I felt eyes everywhere. Paranoia. Max sensed it and echoed, *scared? Scared!*

"Let's go, boy."

I briskly crossed the bridge, marched down the ramp, across the platform, out the gate and into the road. Was it just me, or were there less people about now? I marched along the street, making for the market square again, hoping to lose myself in the crowds. My heart thumped in my chest, slow and strong, but quickening.

We reached the square. The *empty* square. *That's because it's past closing time.* The sun hung low in the sky, although the haze probably made it seem later than it was. I crossed the square. I felt eyes on me, everywhere. But I couldn't see any Fedora Men. *Am I overreacting?* I couldn't tell, I just wanted to be somewhere safe.

When I came to the fountain in the shape of a ship, I stopped. I listened. Nothing but the *splish* of water trickling out of the little stone cannons on the boat. I turned around, thought I saw someone duck behind the wall of that building. Max pricked his ears but stayed close. The square was otherwise empty. I gazed around at the windows. *So many windows. So many eyes.* This city was full of eyes. Too many people lived here.

I left the square and entered the run down suburb. Becky's home was just a few streets away, now.

I stopped again. *If they're following you, you'll lead them right to her home! Idiot!*

I jolted around, and this time I *definitely* saw the flash of pale skin darting away. Such slender, beautiful, treacherous legs. I walked in the exact opposite direction to Becky's street.

I marched along a back road, towards the clangs and low rumble of Anvil Plaza's forges. The night shift workers were arriving in a line through the gate. I fell in among them, followed them through the gate, not really sure what I was doing.

They dispersed, taking up their places at various forges. I found myself in the middle of the plaza with Max, under the darkening sky, looking more lost than ever.

I heard somebody wolf-whistle. A blacksmith shouted something rude. I turned around, and the beautiful girl was casually strolling towards me. A cloud of smoke drifted behind her, and the glow from the forges set her green eyes afire.

"What's she doing here?" a man cried out, alarmed. I turned to see him standing with a sledgehammer slung over his shoulder. He backed away from the girl, dropped the hammer and fled, shouting to others. Another man called something. I turned to see him grinning and taking off his gloves, about to approach the girl but his colleague grabbed him by the shoulder and yanked him back so hard they both almost fell over. They started arguing.

The girl sashayed right up to me. And stood there.

"What do you want?" I asked, unable to move. *Good grief,*

she's even more beautiful in fire light. I couldn't seem to think about anything else.

I was vaguely aware of the commotion building around me, raised voices, men running around in disarray.

"You," she smiled innocently. "I want you, Billy."

"I thought you couldn't..." *speak.* I trailed off.

A man emerged from the smoke behind her, strolling towards us. He carried an unsheathed sword and wore a fedora.

My eyes went wide. Max started barking hysterically.

Kane stepped up behind the girl, grinning. He pierced me with his glare. "Hello again, Billy."

I turned and ran.

My feet pounded the pathway as I bolted through the smoke and ash, Max close at my heels, and Kane probably not far behind that. The forge workers scattered, there was panic in the air, and then a horn sounded. Like a trumpet. *Like a mammoth tusk trumpet* I thought, bizarrely.

"*FOR THE REBELS!*" a huge man came charging out of the smoke armed with a spade and barrelled past me right into the path of Kane.

I turned my head to see the two men collide.

Metal rang through the air, sharp and clear as the man tried to swing the spade down on Kane's head. Kane shimmied around him and slashed at him with the sword but he somehow managed to block it with the spade.

I turned back and kept running.

"Billy?"

I looked and saw Becky (*Becky?!*) by a forge. Her father pumped the bellows behind her. I had a microsecond to decide what to do and chose to keep running. I hoped Kane would follow me and wouldn't notice her.

I ran for the storehouse, the one full of giant timber logs. Max and I scrambled through the huge open double-doors and quickly squeezed in between the stacks of wooden discs. I crouched in a corner, and listened.

No sooner had I started to regain my composure, a hand

grabbed me from behind and I yelped like a girl and nearly emptied my bowels.

It was Becky.

"What are you doing?" she whispered.

"It's Kane. He found me."

Her eyes widened. "No. How?"

"I met this girl – " I started.

"A girl? What girl?"

Maybe that was the wrong way to explain it.

"No, I mean, this girl came up to me. She was watching me."

"Why was she watching you? What were you doing?"

"Wait. Let me finish. We were alone on the bridge –"

"You were *alone* with a *girl?*"

"No. I mean yes. I told her my name. I was only trying to be polite. I think she's a spy for them...or something. *Kane's out there!*" I pointed at the entrance of the storehouse.

From the plaza, we heard metal clanging, men shouting. No, screaming. Screaming in pain. Another horn blasted through the smoky air.

"It's the rebellion," Becky said. I looked at her. "Dad told me about them. A few of his co-workers have signed up. They keep organising raids on the Kingsmen in Joy, but it's spreading."

Another scream from outside.

She looked alarmed. "Dad...Dad's out there!" She started to stand up. I grabbed her arm.

"No, don't, listen to that! We need to get away from here."

She wrenched free. "I'm not leaving my dad, Billy!" She got up and crept between the stacks of timber, heading for the entranceway. I followed.

We crouched by a stack, peering out. Men ran all over the place, nobody was at their post any more. I saw more Fedora Men now, walking calmly in the smoke. I counted four, total. One was Kane.

None of them were facing this way.

"Let's go, hurry!" Becky sprinted for the opening. I followed close behind, Max right behind me.

A hiss of white noise scratched my head. *Bad man!*

Just outside the doors, Max started barking furiously. I slowed, turned and saw in horror that he was bolting headlong at Kane. Becky ran into the smoke and was gone.

"M*AX*!" I ran after him.

Max leapt. Kane turned just in time to get a face full of dog. The sword went sprawling in the dirt. They both tumbled to the ground.

Max growled and bit and tore at Kane's suit, ripping shreds, as he flailed and kicked and yelled. His foot caught Max in the stomach and he yelped and bounced off, turned and leapt again, aiming for Kane's neck. He raised his arm in defence and Max sunk his teeth in. Kane screamed.

He reached for his sword.

"No Max, *run*!" *Run run away run away way AWAY AWAY.*

Max let go and fled. A little too late. Kane swung the sword in a desperate savage arc and clipped Max's tail off. He wailed and bolted off yelping in agony.

Searing pain erupted in my lower back, and a terrible *hiss* swept through my skull. *I'm sharing Max's pain.*

Kane stood up and turned to face me. My pain turned to rage, and I charged at him. I let out a guttural noise and swung a wild fist at the skinny Fedora Man's face, but his hand was so much quicker. I caught a glimpse of the butt of his sword handle flying at my face, and the world went black.

Chapter Thirteen

When I awoke, the world was still black.

I lay on my back in the darkness, my wrists bound in front of me. I sat up, bumped my head against something hard and fell back down.

I said "Ow" but it came out as *hnngh*. I was gagged. I reached up to take the rag out of my mouth but my wrists didn't budge from my waist. They had been tied to my belt, giving me almost no reach. I probed as far as I could, feeling cool metal on either side of me.

I'm in Kane's box.

I kicked against the lid.

"Mmmngh! Muuurnnggh!" The lid jerked with each kick, but it wouldn't budge more than half an inch. I listened for an answer.

Silence.

Don't panic. Stay calm. Yeah, right.

I squirmed onto my belly, arched my back and managed to push my ear against the metal above me. A thin line of light appeared, so I peeked out of the slim gap. A glowing lantern hung on a post outside a grubby window. Night time. *Where am I?* Behind the lantern I thought I could make out the top of a railing. *I recognise that.* It looked like the train bridge, where I had met the girl.

So I'm locked in a box at the train station.

It seemed I would finally be a passenger on the Great Train. *No, not a passenger. Cargo.* I slumped back down with a *clunk.*

I waited in the dark. Eventually, I realised nobody was going to come to the station until the morning, and I just lay there, surprisingly calm.

I thought about Max. I hoped he was okay...

And Becky...

And Mother...

This was bad. Really bad.

I struggled to think of a worse situation to be in, actually. And remember, I died once.

The train's brakes screeched into the station. I awoke with a jolt and bashed my head against the lid of the box. "Mngh."

A smug and cold voice answered outside. "Good morning." Two eyes appeared in the thin gap of the lid. Kane was smiling.

"Nnnrgh!" I kicked the lid again and it clattered.

"What's the matter? Don't you like being in the dark?" He leaned closer, and spoke into the gap so I could smell his breath. Even that was cold. "Well, I don't like being outwitted by a woman, or outsmarted by a boy, or humiliated by a *dog.* See this?" He rolled back a sleeve, and showed me his bare arm, scarred with teeth marks. "You think you're pretty smart don't you, Billy. Setting your dog on me like that. I *know* your little secret. I know about your... connection." He grinned.

"Hngh?"

"How, you ask?" His grin broadened. "I am a Kingsman, Billy, and you are just a *spud.* You and I are not even in the same league. Enjoy the ride." He tapped the lid shut. "Put this one in the back with the others."

Another voice answered, "Yes, sir."

133

I felt myself being hauled up and carried. The box dropped against the ground. "Ngh!"

After a while, the train pulled away. I assumed Joy would be my destination and felt a bit annoyed that I couldn't see out the window at the view.

As I bounced along in the darkness wondering whether Becky or Mother might have any idea where I was, I suddenly felt very alone.

I spent the journey, if you could call it that, thinking about how I would punch the first person I saw when the box opened, and run for it. I'd never hit anyone before in my life and until I saw Kane chop off Max's tail, had never particularly wanted to.

I wouldn't be punching anyone unless I could free my hands, though. I couldn't unbind my wrists themselves, but I spent the majority of the ride bending them in such a way as to eventually untie the knot that connected them to my belt, so I could at least move my arms freely again. I reached up and pulled the gag out of my mouth, which made breathing easier. This small victory boosted my morale. *I'll not go quietly.*

After much bouncing and darkness, I felt the train come to a halt. I heard clattering and shouts, then felt myself being carried away once again. I pried the lid open to see through the sliver of light and saw blue sky, clouds, and sea birds flying about.

"Let me out!" I shouted. "*LET ME OUT!*"

The lid slammed shut with a deafening *clang*, the metal ringing my ears. "Shaddup you."

In the darkness, as my ears stopped ringing, I could hear the murmur of voices, many voices, echoing around a hall. My box was dropped hard against the floor, and I got ready to fight.

I waited.

Someone unlocked the lid and the box opened. I hadn't accounted for the brightness. For a moment, the glare of the sun dazed me, which didn't make sense because I felt sure we were indoors. Then a big Black Fedora Man grabbed me by the chest and hauled me out of the box to my feet, shoving me forwards. I stumbled and headbutted something soft.

A pair of warm, smooth hands held my arms to steady me. Squinting, I raised my bound fists in the air about to swing at whoever was in front of me –

Beautiful. Not again!

I froze, and stared into the crystal azure eyes of another girl with an orange cloak and green shorts. She smiled shyly at me, and I forgot all about my plan of escape. I pretty much forgot how to do anything. My mouth hung open, but no noise came out. *I guess I will go quietly, after all.*

She moved with the grace of a cat, ducking between my arms, so it looked as though I was hugging her. She gently eased me backwards into a seat and perched herself in my lap. She crossed her legs, and wrapped her bare arms about my neck.

All energy drained from me. I was lost in the infinite ocean of her gaze.

I felt vaguely aware of a great many people around me. Or below me, somewhere. A huge hall of some kind, voices echoing off walls. But I couldn't tear my eyes away from the girl.

After a while, Kane came over. She looked up at him.

"Well done," he said approvingly. "Off you go."

She unwound herself from me, stood, and walked away down the steps.

I blinked. Kane stepped in front of me, looking smug. He reached down and casually placed the cloth gag back in my mouth, and retied my wrists to my belt. "Nngth!"

When he was done, I looked about, finally seeing the room.

I stood upon a wooden plinth in the middle of a grand pillared chamber. Rows of chattering people sat about on benches below me. Red banners dangled from the pillars, which on closer inspection appeared to be carved from the trunks of trees. I recognised the colour of the wood. *The Blissful forest.* There were eight in total, tall and round, stretching up to a slanted ceiling far above my head. Sunlight poured in right on top of me through rounded skylights in the roof. Alongside my own miniature tower, I saw three more either side of me, each with a gagged prisoner and a pair of Fedora Men in sleek outfits – one grey and one black. I noticed that the pairs were all dressed the same – the leaner of the two men wore a grey suit, while the burlier man wore black. *Brains and brawn, perhaps?* Dozens of the beautiful girls mingled with the crowd, a radiance of colour amid the dull, ordinary folk.

And then there was the throne.

An aisle led between the rows of benches, between my plinth and the one to my left, to a small flight of wide steps above which sat the biggest chair I had ever seen. The Joyful Throne, carved of the same wood as the pillars into a tall headrest that sprayed outwards in a fan of woven branches. A royal red banner draped over the armrests, held in place by three big cushions. For the moment, nobody was sitting in it. But that was about to change.

A herald stepped up and addressed the audience in a commanding voice. "Ladies and gentlemen. Please stand for the King."

Everyone stopped talking and rose as one.

A small boy wearing a gold crown waddled out from the back of the stage, his feet clacking across the marble floor in the quietness. He came to the front of the throne and clambered up into it, sinking into the soft cushions. When he turned to face the crowd, he slumped in the seat and planted his face against a fist. He looked the absolute image of boredom. The throne practically swallowed him. He looked like, well, a child, in a seat made for a giant.

He gave a lazy gesture. The crowd seated themselves.

"Begin!" the kid called, his voice muffled slightly by the fact his fist was digging into his cheek. It seemed as though he would rather be anywhere else but here.

The herald stepped up once more.

"At his majesty's request, we will be forgoing the usual ceremonies of the trials and moving swiftly to the final acts of judgement. Today, we have four accused." He turned to the first plinth, two across on my left. "Proceed."

The grey-suited Fedora Man stood beside his prisoner and spoke across the heads of the seated people below him, addressing the boy king.

"Your majesty, I present Timothee of Joy. Wanted for making inappropriate advances on the Kingsmaids, pursued on the road to Capella and captured when a rockslide fell upon the path, blocking his escape. He has a filthy mouth, and a short temper, recommended action –"

The boy cut him off. "Flush him."

A few people in the crowd mumbled their approval.

Timothee didn't seem pleased with that outcome, not one bit. He aggressively stood up trying to shout, but the gag just made him sound like an angry squeaking squirrel. The bigger, Black Fedora Man grabbed him by the collar and dragged him down the steps, along the aisle and out the back of the audience chamber. After a quick bow to the king, the grey-suited Fedora Man followed them.

"Next," the boy king commanded tiredly.

The next Fedora Man stepped up to my left.

"Your majesty, I present Giles of Joy, your dentist. Captured upon your request after he forcefully removed a wobbly tooth from the royal mouth –"

"Flush him."

Giles shrieked through his gag, and was promptly dragged away to join Timothee.

The boy king turned to me. I gulped.

His expression changed to mild interest. "What do you have for me, Kane?"

"Your majesty," he said smoothly. "I present to you the Defiler's accomplice."

A murmur rippled through the crowd.

The boy king looked about, confused. "What? Who's that?"

Kane continued, clearly enjoying the attention. "This is Billy, of Hale. Wanted in connection with the Aston Arsonist..." The murmur intensified. "The Train Trasher..." I heard someone gasp. "And the Barrow Bomber!" The crowd erupted in a blaze of shocked remarks and angry curses. I felt like everyone in the room hated me. *They don't even know me!*

The boy king looked annoyed. "I don't know what that means!" he shouted over the babble. The room quietened. "What did he do?"

Kane let out a short laugh and gestured with his hand. "What *didn't* he do, your majesty? The Defiler set out from Hale with a mind for mischief and mayhem. I tracked her down to Fentworth, where I lost the trail, but learned of her accomplice. He was hiding on a farm, and upon interrogation of the old couple that resided there, I learned of a possible demonic connection with his dog."

Interrogation? What did he do to George and Millie! "Nggh!" I tried to talk but the gag chewed up my words.

Kane went on, theatrically reeling off details of all my apparent crimes. "The Defiler and this boy have inflicted untold counts of destruction on the people of The South, burning families in their homes and plotting to murder everyone on the Great Train. He evaded my capture after fleeing with the farmer's own daughter, and when I finally caught up to him he set a ferocious bull upon myself and my colleague before *burning an entire village to the ground.*"

As if the crowd couldn't get any louder, everyone started speaking at once. A cascade of commotion swept the room.

I felt furious and helpless. His accusations were all lies, or gross exaggerations of the truth. Or, in the case of the Great Train crash, just a horrible misunderstanding... But he clearly didn't care what had really happened, he just wanted to show off his prize to these morons, claim his fame as the person who captured the most wanted criminal in Lunaria. Except, I wasn't even her! How could these people fall for this?

The kid leaned forwards in the throne and was gawping at me. He didn't seem horrified at all. He looked... curious? He shouted across the crowd, who silenced. "What did you mean earlier? You said he has a dog, and that they are connected?"

Kane replied, "Well, I found it hard to believe myself, until I ran into a wagon driver in Hooke, who confirmed my suspicions..."

The boy leant forward in his throne, wide-eyed. "And? What's special about his doggy?"

"Well, your majesty, I believe they can hear each other's thoughts."

The crowd didn't seem sure how to react to that. Most people just frowned. One woman even laughed, but comically turned it into a cough when she realised nobody else found it funny.

The boy king clumsily dropped down from the throne. He pointed up at me. "I want to talk to him! Bring him to my room!" The kid marched around the back and disappeared through a doorway.

Kane looked suspiciously at me, eyes narrowed in thought.

A pair of rough hands grabbed me from behind and dragged me away.

Chapter Fourteen

I received a brief tour of the castle as a big Black Fedora Man shoved me along, leading me through a cavernous hall decorated with fine art paintings and up a grand staircase. A hall of animals carved from individual tree trunks lined the hallway at the top of the stairs. The brute led me along past wooden bears rearing up on two legs, prowling wooden lions, a huge tortoise, even a lifesize mammoth. At least I assumed it was lifesize. It must have been carved from the biggest tree in the entire forest, and I didn't know whether to be impressed with the craftsmanship, or saddened by the loss of such a tree.

It seemed as though the entire castle was decorated with objects carved from the trees of the Blissful forest, including the support beams in the ceiling and the huge set of double doors at the end of the carpeted corridor. *Well that explains where half of the forest has gone.*

The double doors led to the king's bedroom, and he was waiting for me as the big man led me through.

"Leave us alone!" he said to my escort, who obeyed, shutting the doors behind him on the way out.

I stood before the king in his bedroom. He sat on the edge of a bed that was wider than the spare room Becky's father had let us stay in. A cotton curtain draped around the bed, suspended from four carved pillars at each corner. To my left, the sunlight came in through a wide open window overlooking the ocean. Strewn about the floor were... toys. An old rocking horse, a tricycle, spinning tops, stuffed animals everywhere. This kid was the same age as my youngest brother, Rufus. He'd be beside himself in a room like this.

"Can you really read your doggy's mind?" the kid asked bluntly, interrupting my thoughts.

"Nngh?"

The kid dropped off the bed, waddled over to me, and gestured for me to bend down. I did. He yanked the gag out of my mouth, let it hang around my neck. He looked at his hand in disgust, then wiped the drool on my shirt.

"Thanks," I said. He looked at me, waiting for an answer. I replied cautiously, "What if I can?"

He frowned. "Just tell me, yes or no. I'm the king."

Something in his tone worried me. This kid was high on power.

"Yeah, I can hear my dog's thoughts."

His face lit up. "Did you find a Wishing Tree too?"

I didn't answer, but my eyes must have given me away. He bounced up and down in glee.

"Yes! Another one!"

So there are more, just like Mother suspected. Another tree monster... The idea didn't exactly thrill me.

"Where did you find one?" I asked.

"In the big lake near my home. I saw it growing out of the middle. Where was yours? You have to tell me!"

The kid clutched his hands in front of him and jiggled his feet in excitement. It unnerved me. The tree monster had been terrifying, like something out of a nightmare. Yet, this kid looked so happy.

I hesitated. "Do you want another wish, or something?"

"Duh! Being a king is *BORING*. I thought it would be fun, that's why I wished for it. The lake tree said he would make me the most powerful king, but he said a powerful king must have control, so he gave me all these *GIRLS*. Girls are stupid! And being a king is stupid too. All I get to do is sit around listening to boring people. They let me flush them down the toilet, but even that isn't fun any more. I'm so booooored. I'm going to wish to be something else this time. Like a pterodactyl!"

I stared at the kid, dumbfounded. "It's a long way away."

"So? I'm the *KING*. My men will take me wherever I want to go if I tell them."

I went to scratch my elbow, remembered my hands were tied, and just sort of squirmed. "You know they aren't *really* Wishing Trees...right?"

"Yes they are!" He stopped fidgeting and frowned. "You better tell me where it is, or I'll *FLUSH* you."

"Okay, okay." An idea popped into my head. "But you have to do something for me, first."

The kid looked stunned for a moment. It must have been a while since anyone had defied him after threatening to flush them down a privy.

"What?" he asked.

"Clear the bounty on my mother's head."

Silence. From his blank expression, I figured he didn't know what that meant.

"My mother. She's wanted, by your Fed – by your Kingsmen. But I want you to stop them from hunting her. Tell them to stop, and I will tell you where the Wishing Tree is."

He nodded eagerly. "Okay." He smiled, and looked every bit as young as he was.

"You'll have to say it in front of everyone, though. For it to work."

"What do I have to say?"

I wrote down on a piece of paper a short speech declaring my Mother's freedom. I tried to make it sound kingly, but I'm no expert on this sort of thing... He said he couldn't read the big words, so I suggested giving it to his

142

herald to read out instead. When we were done, he called to his guard and I was taken back down to the throne room to my plinth, next to Kane.

The audience quietened once more as the little king returned to his oversized chair. This time, he sat up straight, a broad smile across his face.

The herald stepped up, holding my piece of paper.

"Ladies and gentlemen, I bring words from the king. From this day, the fugitive known as the Aston Arsonist, the Train Trasher, and the Barrow Bomber, shall be pardoned of yonder crimes against the kingdom, and shall no longer be pursued by the Kingsmen for any reward. Furthermore, any Kingsmen found attempting to capture Mrs Bethany Spudswallop shall be decreed a traitor and banished to wander the Great Plains where you will be stomped on and eaten by a woolly mammoth."

The kid had come up with that last part.

I tried to conceal my grin. The whole chamber rang to the clamour of anxious muttering.

The boy king raised his hand for quiet and when everybody had settled down for what felt like the tenth time, he looked up to me. "So, where is it?"

A roomful of puzzled eyes turned to me.

A deal is a deal... don't make me regret this, kid. "On the outskirts of Hale, there is a path through the wood. If you travel at night, under the gaze of Little Red and Big Blue, you will see a rock carving through the trees, reflecting the moonlight. Behind this rock, lies a cave. That is where you will find what you seek. But, uh, your majesty, be careful what you wish for this time..."

The boy excitedly clapped his hands. He looked ecstatic.

"What game do you think you are playing, boy?" Kane scowled at me. "Clever. Very clever. But it won't save you." He stood and addressed the boy king. "Your majesty! I hope this does not mean you have forgotten about this fugitive's judgement. Might I remind you, he stands accused of multiple acts of villainy. And in case you are all in need of some extra persuasion, allow me to demonstrate what this fiend had planned for his next act of terror!"

He reached into his jacket pocket and held two objects above his head. *My mammoth tusk!* What was he doing with that? He must have gone through my backsack after he'd captured me. In the other hand dangled the small bag of dirt that the tomato sellers had given me. I'd never gotten around to giving it to Mother. Why would Mother even want...

It struck me then. *Bovithane.* Flammable fuel. She had only just discovered the use of cows... what had she been using *before* that though? All those explosions in the shed, she had been experimenting with ways to make a type of powerful fuel for years. She used to bring back so much fertilizer... *oh no.*

"What is that?" the king asked.

"This, sire, is an unfinished, homemade bomb."

A ripple of gasps came from the crowd. More murmurs. My stomach clenched.

"I found this on the fugitive when I captured him. If I may?" He looked to the boy in the throne, who gave an impatient wave.

Kane plucked out a pinch of dirt from the bag and sprinkled it in a little pile on the floor of the plinth. He took a small metal object from his pocket and opened it with a flick of his wrist. He clicked his thumb against it and a small orange flame appeared. *Fire from his fingers.* He lowered the flame to the small heap, and –

FWOOSH!

The dirt erupted in a violent flash of heat, which Kane flinched away from. It left a scorched black burn mark on the wooden surface.

"As you can see, dangerous stuff! Were you to confine it within a container," he held up the hollow mammoth tusk for all to see. "...you'd have yourself a powerful explosive. Could you imagine what carnage could have been unleashed if he managed to bring it aboard the Great Train? Or into the King's own castle..."

The audience flared up again in another clamour of shock and disbelief. Kane shot me a smug smile that said *get out of that one.*

A voice boomed over the uproar. "*KANE*! You're a *LIAR*!"

I turned towards the voice. Down below, among the crowd, one of the Fedora Men in the black suits and matching hats stared up at us. He had broad shoulders, a crooked nose, and looked familiar somehow...

Kane's eyes narrowed on him as he brushed people aside and strolled out into the aisle. He marched over to the stone steps and stood below the throne. Seeing him from behind, the way he ambled, I recognised the man. He had come to the farmers' house, searching for me. *Kane's driver.* Last I saw him, he had been sitting on the ground outside the burning mill in Barrow, having barely escaped with his life...

"Your majesty," he bowed low and slow.

The kid frowned at him.

The big man turned and pointed a thick finger at his ex-partner. "Kane is a liar. It was him what burned down the houses in Aston. He snuck in at night and set the place on fire, after he saw what Mrs Spudswallop was working on. He told me we could... fabricate a new bounty for us to catch. We chased her across the whole bleedin' continent! When we finally caught up to her in Barrow, he told me to go get her out of the old mill, then he set fire to it while I was still inside! He tried to kill us both!"

The herald's chin drooped and he gaped at my captor. "Is this true, Kane?"

Kane glared at his ex-parnter. Then he looked to the herald and let out a shrill laugh. "Of course not! You would believe this oaf, over me?"

"For what it's worth, I saw him set the mill on fire," I chimed in.

Kane looked as though he was going to throw me off the plinth into the crowd, who were now all doing their usual thing of yammering away, tutting and gasping and acting shocked. I wondered if they even knew what was going on.

"It's you what should be judged, Kane!" the big Black Fedora Man yelled.

Kane retorted, "You always were *soft*, you flabby useless idiot!"

Men shouted left right and centre, other Fedora Men piped up with comments like "He's a psycho!" or "He's always been wrong in the head" and "He set my wife on fire!" and I could barely hear myself think.

At least Mother will be safe now.

The boy king had tossed his cushions to the ground and was stomping up and down on the throne. He pointed to people, shouting and screaming, but it was impossible to hear a word over the chaos. I started to make out his shrill screams. *Hush? Hush them all?*

Oh for goodness sake...

"FLUSH THEM. FLUSH THEM ALL! FLUSH THEM FLUSH THEM FLUSH THEM NOWWW!" His high pitched shriek pierced the pandemonium, echoing off the rafters.

The poor fellow on the last plinth didn't even get a trial, even one as farcical as mine. The Black Fedora Man guarding him dragged him down the steps.

Another came up behind Kane as he hurled abuse down at his old driver. His eyes widened as two thick arms grabbed him from behind and dragged him away in a bearhug, kicking his legs and shouting.

I stood a moment taking in the confusion. Everyone was yelling at each other, flailing arms, fighting for every word. For a brief moment I thought I might be able to sneak away, but as I turned to walk down the steps, I bumped into the solid chest of the biggest Black Fedora Man in the room. He looked like a gorilla in a suit. Wordlessly, he hoisted me over his shoulder like a sack of potatoes and carried me from the King's Hall.

As I glanced back over his shoulder I saw the kid stomping his feet on the stage, heard the shrill voice of the ten year old spoilt brat of a king issuing his next order. "Bring me my pony. We're going to Hale!"

The Fedora Gorilla carried me down a sloped path away from Castle Joy. As I slumped over his shoulder, I caught my one and only glimpse of the castle itself – two high stone keeps decorated with red banners streaming in the coastal wind. It would have made for a good sketch, if I had my pencils. *And wasn't a captive...*

The big man carried me through the royal lawns which overlooked the ocean. At the end of the path he hoisted me into the back of an ox-cart, where five other men were already seated and tied up. He plonked me down on the bench next to Timothee. I recognised Giles and the bloke who hadn't even had his trial, and of course, Kane. The last man had straggly white hair and a bushy grey beard. He seemed oddly familiar. I tried to recall where I had seen him, but before I could place it, Kane writhed across the cart making to escape. The gorilla shoved him back, and Kane tumbled backwards landing on his butt between the rest of our feet.

"Untie me you ape! I am a Kingsman, I'm *one of you.*"

The gorilla man loomed over Kane. He swiped the skinny Fedora Man's hat from his head and swapped it with his own black one. Kane gaped, flabbergasted. He sat in stunned silence, as the huge man dropped down from the ox-cart, which rocked vigorously from the sudden lack of weight. He strode around to the front wearing his new hat, and climbed up next to the driver.

The cart jerked to life and we rolled down the slope.

"Where are they taking us?" I asked apprehensively.

The bearded stranger gave a snort. He sat the other side of Kane, opposite me. Then to everyone's surprise, he sang a mournful melody. *"Come with me, let's take a dive to the bottom of the sea..."* That's when I recognised him.

"You heard the king's decision," Timothee groaned. "They're sending us to the Khazi!"

The cart bore us down a winding coastal track to a sheltered harbour at the base of the cliffs. Two more Black Fedora Men helped the gorilla-man to load the six of us into a cramped open-topped barge. We sat in two lines facing each other, hands tied behind our backs.

"I can't swim!" Timothee yelped.

The captain sat in a snug compartment at the back wearing a little sailor's hat. "Swimming's of no use where you're going." His mouth drooped at the corners, giving him a permanently sad expression. I suspected he really didn't like his job.

Once we were loaded, the Gorilla took a seat at the front, facing us with his arms crossed. The captain of a second barge barked at the other two Fedora Men standing on the dock. "Come on you two, climb aboard. We have to secure the landing area, move it!" They scrambled aboard, the engine started up and they chugged out into the bay ahead of us.

Our captain pulled a lever and the boat juddered beneath my butt. Judging by the distinctive *crunch* of the engine, I guessed it must be the same sort that powered the Fedora Men's pedal-carts. There was another sound too, a low pulse on the edge of hearing...

The captain started pedalling, we cast off from the dock and drifted out into the bay, following in the wake of the other boat. The engine clanked and that low pulse beat to a steady rhythm, a short *doof* every three seconds or so.

Looking back, Castle Joy loomed atop the rugged, rocky headland hundreds of feet above us. Gazing nervously out ahead, I saw an island off the shore. It jutted out of the sea, a black, jagged rock.

"Is that it?" I asked Timothee, next to me.

"Yeah. Don't they teach you anything in Hale?"

I was too anxious to take offence. I squinted at the island, trying to work out how big it was. I shifted in my seat, the strand of rope digging into my wrists behind my back.

We edged out beyond the shallow water of the bay, and the sea became a shade darker. Or so I thought.

The shadow below us moved. It swam away.

I jolted, turned to look down. More dark shapes, slithering around beneath the boat. I let out a nervous whine, not unlike Max when he sees something scary.

Timothee turned to see, his eyes widening. We both sat askew, peering down into the shifting waters.

I heard a startled shout. We all looked up.

The captain of the first boat stood facing us, his hands cupped around his mouth. His boat bobbed along a hundred feet in front of us. He shouted again, in a tone of sheer panic, "My pulsar! It's stopped working! Tell my wife—"

A great toothy maw rose out of the water, engulfed the little boat, and slammed shut around it. For a brief moment, I saw the creature's eye, like a shark's, black and dead, then the monster tumbled back under the surface with a mighty splash. No more boat.

"*AAAAAGH!*" three of us screamed at once. Kane gaped, wide-eyed. I turned to the captain, "What was that?" We all bumped into one another in panic, rocking the boat back and forth in our desperate attempts to move to the middle of the boat, away from the edges.

"Sit down!" the captain cried. "You'll tip us!"

That calmed us quick enough. Slowly, we sat back down, each staring at the water in terror.

The low pulse continued its steady beat. Each time a dark shape drew close to the boat, it would retreat again, flinching away from the resonating sound.

It took thirty minutes to reach the island. The longest, most tense thirty minutes of my life.

Eventually, we reached the jagged island.

The boat bumped against the rocks and we all piled out onto the stony bank. *Solid ground!*

The glistening cliff rose straight up, the rocks shiny, wet and smooth from years of erosion. A rough staircase had been hacked out of the cliff side, leading up to a small cave entrance above us.

Kane took a step back towards the barge, but the gorilla-man blocked his way with crossed arms and a silent shake of the head.

"Please," Kane begged. "You can't leave me here..." Was that fear in his voice?

"So long," the captain said mournfully, and slowly came about. "I wouldn't linger there for too long."

As the boat retreated, I saw the shadows swirling beneath the surface, following it. Some were large and bulbous, others thin and wriggly. One of them broke off and came slithering back towards us.

"Go, go, go." The old preacher nudged me in the back, pushing me into Timothee who stood, eyes transfixed on the approaching shadow.

"Move it!" We all bundled up the stairs, our wrists still bound behind us, just as a slimy white tentacle reached up out of the water and slapped against the rocks below our feet.

"*Go!*"

We climbed faster.

At the top of the stairs, we piled into the cave opening.

The six of us followed the low, dim tunnel down a short, straight passageway, all walking slightly hunched over.

We came to a white door. Featureless, with a simple metal handle.

"See if it's locked," I suggested.

"It's not," Kane said with disdain. He shimmied to the front, put his back to the door, lowered himself so he could reach the handle, and pushed.

The door made a wet, sucking sound as it swung open, and we stepped into...

PART THREE
TEA

Chapter Fifteen

White.

I was taken aback by the brightness. So much white. Smooth, white floor. Curved, blank walls all around me. And above, nothing but open sky.

Timothee said in a hushed voice, "Wow. It really is like a toilet."

Kane grunted as he kicked the door shut behind us.

We stood at the bottom of a great bowl. I gazed about, picking out the details. A circular trap door covered up some kind of pit in the middle of the floor. Off to the left were benches and tables, white surfaces attached to grey metal legs, all bolted to the floor, occupied by a bunch of inmates hunched over the tables eating food in moody silence. Leading directly away from us in either direction were a twin set of marble staircases climbing up to a second floor, and then a third. Two tiers of cells ran around the circumference of the bowl, each with a railing acting as a balcony that overlooked the eating area.

A couple of men glanced up from their meals when they noticed us huddled by the door. They stood and wandered over.

"Ah, more?" A man in his fifties dressed in brown

trousers and faded shirt. He spoke solemnly. "Welcome, for what it's worth."

"Let me get those," the other man said, reaching for the ties behind Giles' back. The two men methodically untied each of us.

"Thanks," I said rubbing my wrists. "Who are you?"

"Name's Ged," said the solemn guy. "Plenty of time to get to know each other. No rush. Might as well claim a cell. I'd suggest the second floor, but it's up to you."

"Hello Ged," the preacher spoke up behind me.

Ged turned, surprised. "Jim?" He sighed, and a sad smile spread across his face. "It would be a lie to say it's good to see you here." They shook hands, and ambled over to the tables, talking like old friends.

The second guy lingered a moment. "I'm Kevin. Or Kev." He shrugged. His eyes swept over us, seeming to snag on Kane for a moment, then he rejoined his friend and Jim the bearded preacher.

The remaining five of us exchanged a few looks, then wandered apart, making for the staircases. Timothee followed me up.

"Curse those rocks," he mumbled. "Curse them to Tannerus. Cursed *rocks.*"

I didn't know what he was muttering about. My mind flicked between thoughts of Becky and Mother and poor Max. *How did I end up here? I escaped from the bottom left corner of the world, only to wind up trapped in the bottom right.*

I followed Ged's advice and climbed the second flight of stairs to the upper tier. I walked past empty cells dug into the wall on my right, following the curve of the floor. None of the cells had doors. In fact, I could see right in as I passed by. One man lay on his bed, snoozing, but the rest were empty. I guessed there were forty cells on each floor, and they all were identical in shape and size.

Each cell had a number above the entrance. I stopped near the middle, outside cell number *63*.

I stepped through the doorless arch, into the box-shaped

room. With minimal features, it matched the style of the rest of the place. The walls were smooth, white, and blank, save for the little circular hole on the back wall that served as a window. The bed fit snugly in a corner, a solid block carved out of the wall itself, with a mattress wedged inside. Next to that, a small desk and stool, both bolted to the ground by a metal pole, just like the tables I saw downstairs. That was it. A simple, cold cell.

I sat on the bed. I stared at the wall for a long time.

Since it wasn't bad enough being trapped on an island prison surrounded by boat-eating sea monsters, someone kept me awake that night by snoring. It was so loud I thought I must be back on the farm, with a herd of cows mooing outside my cell. It might have been tolerable if the snores were regular – I was accustomed to sleeping outside by now, surrounded by all sorts of weird animal noises – but the man's grunty snorts alternated between gentle wheezes and choking gasps without warning. On more than one occasion I felt sure somebody was strangling him.

I tossed and turned under the blanket, restless. Whenever I moved, the mattress squeaked. It was firm and coated in a smooth paint of some sort, dry but slippery – not very comfortable. I rolled over again. And again. I rolled to face the wall. No good. Rolled back. A silhouette of a man stood in the door frame.

I jolted upright. The gangly figure marched into my cell and grabbed me by the throat.

"*You*," Kane growled. It's how he always started a conversation with me. "No other fugitive has managed to slip through my fingers more times than you, boy. First, there was that bull... then that imbecile with the hand-cannon at Barrow... and you were always riding off on those disgusting goats."

"Rams," I choked.

He squeezed harder. "This is where your bad habit of

wriggling free at the last moment ends. Here, you have nobody. It's just you and me. Where will you run this time? I'd very much enjoy seeing you try to escape from me *now.*" He bared his teeth in a smug grin.

I noticed the snoring had ceased.

A hand appeared on Kane's shoulder and hauled him backwards. I gasped for breath as his hand released my neck. Kev pinned the Fedora Man to the wall of my cell, as Ged and Jim stood behind him.

"Just what kind of man are you?" Ged spoke in his flat, sombre tone. He looked Kane square in the eye.

"You don't even recognise me, do you?" Kev snarled.

"Why would I remember peasants like you?" Kane sneered, unfazed. "To me, you are less than nothing. I scrape higher forms of life off the end of my shoe after a hard day's work."

"We know what you clarify as a 'hard day's work'. We know too well."

Jim stepped up, the man who I had once seen preaching about the rebellion to the people of Fentworth, before Kane kidnapped him. "Do you remember me? It wasn't enough to capture my wife, who had done nothing to you people. You had to bring me to this hole too."

"I am a Kingsman. I serve the King," Kane replied with a mocking smile.

"The boy is no true king," Ged said. "Anyone can see that. You can stand there and tell us you do what you do for honour and justice, but the truth is the only thing the Kingsmen serve is their greed and hunger for power."

"But now you're stuck here. And we're stuck with you," Kev held Kane against the wall with an elbow across his chest, throwing words right in his face.

"But if you think for one minute we're going to tolerate *this* kind of behaviour..." Ged gestured towards me as he spoke. "I think it's time someone taught you a lesson."

They dragged him out of my cell. I hesitated under my blankets, but forced myself to follow them down the stairs to the ground floor.

"You enjoy firelight, don't you Kane?" Ged calmly opened the cave door. "Let's see how well you like the darkness."

Kane scowled, cursed, and dug his heels into the floor, all in vain. They tossed him into the cave and slammed the door shut. Kev wedged a broken stool against the door handle, sealing Kane in the pitch black tunnel. Kane banged against the door, shouting to be let back inside, but by the time I returned up the steps to my cell and crawled into my bed, I could barely hear him.

Before long, Kev's snoring started again, but I didn't mind this time. *I've never seen anyone stand up to Kane like that. I'm glad he's on my side.* I breathed a sigh of relief into my blanket. Eventually, I drifted off to sleep.

When morning came, I wandered down to the main area. Everything about the Khazi felt solid. The walls were so thick that you could barely hear the sound of the waves crashing against the rocks all around us, and since all of the tables and chairs were bolted to the ground, nothing could move about freely. Except for the prisoners, of course. With no doors and no guards, we had complete run of the place. And why not? It's not like anyone would try to escape with those horrific sea creatures patrolling the waters.

And speaking of water... I stepped off the bottom step into a puddle. A small stream, actually. I didn't expect it.

"What the...?" I gazed down at the modest torrent of water originating from a gap under the cave door, flowed across the floor past my feet and disappeared into the circular grating in the centre of the floor.

A muffled cry came from behind the door.

"Let me in! I heard you!" *Bang! Bang!* "I know someone's there. Now open the *door*."

Kane sounded desperate and exhausted. He'd been out there for most of the night.

The sun hadn't yet crested the rim of the bowl, but the sky was an ever brightening blue. I figured it must be just after dawn. Ged was already up, sitting at one of the tables in the dining area. When he spotted me standing at the foot of the steps, he got up and ambled over. I noticed he had bare feet, and his trousers rolled up to his knees. Perhaps this minor flooding was a regular occurrence...

"I suppose he's had enough." He looked to me, as if waiting for approval.

"Um, yeah."

Ged nodded, grasped the broken stool, and gave it a yank, scraping the metal pole against the floor as it came away. The door swung open instantly and the stream became a couple of inches higher, pouring through the opening and sweeping across the floor and down the drain.

Kane stumbled in, red cheeked and miserable. Sometime in the night, he must have lost his hat. The rest of his clothes were damp, and he had drooping black bags under both eyes between long strands of dark hair. He splashed through the water and came straight towards me. I hopped aside, and he lunged for the banister to steady himself.

"Did you learn your lesson?" Ged asked nonchalantly.

Kane looked back over his shoulder, one soggy shoe on the first step. He didn't even have the will to glare. He just looked blank. "I was asleep on the floor when the tide came in."

"Yeah. It does that."

Kane's chest expanded and fell in short, ragged breaths. "I might have been eaten by one of those beasts."

Ged gave a shrug. "Only if you had been stupid enough to wander outside. They can't swim in water this shallow." He tapped his bare feet in the stream, wriggling his toes. He gave Kane a mocking smile. "You'll behave yourself from now on, won't you?"

Kane swung his gaze to me, still rather expressionless. Then he sneezed. A strand of snot dangled from his nose. I'd never have imagined seeing him look so... pathetic?

"Ugh," he groaned. And with that, he turned, and slowly dragged himself up the steps.

Ged pushed the door closed, before strolling back over to sit at one of the tables with his mug of tea.

"Why doesn't the tide rise up from the drain?" I asked him.

He glanced up. "Shucks, I don't know. There's some kind of seal down there, only lets the water out, but not back in. I ain't no engineer, kid."

I passed through the eating area, under an archway into the kitchen. A massive wooden water drum greeted me from the corner of the room, the strangely-clean kitchen's most dominating feature. It rested on the workbench in the corner, with a funnel above it disappearing into the ceiling to collect rainwater. A narrow pipe connected the drum to a much smaller cast iron urn that could be heated to provide hot water. Ged must have lit the stove earlier, because the urn emanated heat as I passed by. *I wonder where they get the wood from.* There were no trees on our little rocky island.

I opened a cupboard – inside was a wicker basket full of tea leaves. I opened another – more tea leaves. In the third cupboard I found some ceramic mugs, and in a drawer discovered an assortment of cutlery carved from polished bones. I took the hint and poured myself a mug of tea, then went back out and took a seat opposite Ged.

"You've met Kane before, haven't you?" I asked.

He took a long sip of his tea. "Yup. Well, Kev has. But I heard about him from the other guys."

"Other guys?"

"The rebels. Me, Kev and a few of the other fellas in here were sticking it to the Kingsmen in Joy when they captured us. That's how we knew Jim, too. But after his wife was sent here..." He paused to shake his head. "Poor girl. Jim left the city, fled west to spread the word about our cause... I suppose that's when that piece of work caught up to him."

"I saw Jim preaching in Fentworth," I said. "I was there the day Kane caught him."

"Huh. Ain't it a small world, fella," he mused.

I actually thought it was rather big, but I didn't argue. After another sip of his mug, he went on, "So, how'd you wind up here?"

I warmed my hands around the mug, and stared at it thoughtfully. "I was trying to figure that out myself."

"Heh. Aren't we all?" He put his mug down and looked at me with his flat, seemingly permanent frown. "Fentworth's some distance. You're a long way from home, aren't you fella?"

"Actually, I'm from Hale." I thought of Father, pictured him waking up to fry some potatoes for breakfast around about now. I suddenly felt quite homesick.

Ged raised his eyebrows. "Blimey. Hard to be farther away than that."

His words hung in the air.

When he realised I had no reply, he picked up his mug again.

"Well, kid. Ain't nothing for it now but to reflect, regret, and wait for the Mooneye to cleanse us of our sins." He tipped his mug to me, and then downed the rest of his tea.

I pondered his words. The Mooneye? That was what people often called the seasonal eclipses. What did they have to do with this place? I thought of Jim's wife, and it occurred to me that there were no female prisoners here. Just sixteen men, if Timothee and I counted for men... "Did Jim's wife get released or something? She's not here anymore, is she?"

"They captured her before the midsummer Mooneye," he answered sadly, as if that explained it.

I started to get a bad feeling in my stomach. "So, what happens during the Mooneye...?"

Ged gave me an old, wisened look. "You really don't know what the Khazi is, do you fella?"

"I don't know anything about this place."

159

He sighed. "Kid, nobody gets released. This is death row."

I gaped at him. *WHAT?*

"Gee, kid, don't look at me like that. It gets better. It's no coincidence that we're out here in the middle of the sea. You understand how the tides work, fella? With the moons and everything?"

"Um." I could hardly speak. "Kind of."

"Well, a teacher once told me the tide doesn't just move in and out by itself. He said the moons control it. It's as if there's a big invisible rope tied around them, and the other end is tied to the sea, somehow."

I nodded, barely listening. *I can't die here.*

"Well, every night, that big blue hunk of rock flies across the sky and pulls the sea up with it. So, when we can see Big Blue, the tide is high. When he disappears below the horizon, the sea goes back down again."

I haven't even kissed Becky yet.

"Sometimes, his red brother comes along to join in the fun. When they're both messing about up there, naturally the tide rises even higher." He pointed to the floor behind me. I turned, watching the water trickle between the metal grating, slip over the edge and plunge into blackness.

"See that. That's nothing. Yesterday was a regular Blue Moon. On a twin-moon night, we'd be up to our eyeballs in seawater here in the canteen. But even that's nothing compared to the Mooneye Flood. Or The Flush, as that little brat king renamed it... The Khazi was designed to fill right to the brim. When autumn comes and her Mooneye glares down on us, the sea will pour through that door, bringing whatever beasts that will fit, and keep rising until the bowl is full, and whether we're alive or dead by the time it's all over, everyone in here will be swept away down that damn drain."

No.

No!

The word repeated in my head like an echo. Not a Max

echo, a regular one. I felt like I'd been hit with a spade in the chest.

Becky. Mother. Father. My brothers. Becky. Max. Becky! I'll never see any of them ever again.

I leapt to my feet and left Ged sitting at the table. He said something as I walked away, but my head was spinning and his words were just noise. I climbed the steps, went back to my cell, and sat on the bed facing the wall.

I noticed the mug of tea in my hand. The little bone spoon stuck out of it. I put the mug on the desk and grabbed the spoon. Counting days in my head, I scratched a series of deep lines into the wall using the pointed handle of the spoon. To the right I scrawled two circles, one inside the other. It looked sort of like an eye.

"27 days," I muttered. I thought for a moment, then scratched a big 'X' through the first line. "No, 26 days left..."

26 days until the eclipse. I had 26 days left to live. Considering I had already died once before, you may think that this prospect wouldn't bother me too much, but it did.

I'm not ready to die again.

Chapter Sixteen

26 days to go.

I stepped onto the balcony and felt the claustrophobic presence of the walls all around me. This place had been built to hold the kind of villains that only existed in the old crone's tales, the killers and worse. Surely, I didn't belong here? None of the guys here seemed that bad to me.

My stomach twisted into an angry knot. I looked at my hands and realised they were trembling. It was all because of that stupid little kid. The *king. Gah.*

I looked up at the blue sky.

I needed air.

I needed to see.

I leapt at the wall, reaching for the edge of the roof above my cell door. I managed to pull myself up, and stagger to my feet. Bracing against the gusty breeze that tugged at my clothes, I stood on the circular outer roof of the Khazi, and took a deep breath to steady myself.

If the world has an edge, this is surely it.

In every direction the deep blue ocean surrounded our prison. The mainland looked to be a few miles away – the steep cliffs of Joy climbed out of the sea and stretched into the distance along the coast. Through the hazy morning sun, I could just about make out some buildings on the ridge, the glass windows reflecting brightly.

I squinted as something caught my eye. Bouncing in the sunlight and swaying in the breeze, I thought I could see something floating above the sea against the backdrop of the cliffs. It seemed to be suspended in the air, flying closer...

"What are you doing up there?" a voice called up to me.

I turned and looked down at Timothee standing on the balcony below. According to his manic, curly hair, he had just woken up.

"Nothing. Well, something." I turned back, squinting harder. It was a crate. A wooden crate, floating along towards the Khazi. I traced its route and noticed a cable connected to a pulley above a square hole in the roof. It appeared to drop directly into a cell on the other side of the balcony. "It's going to fall in there."

Timothee turned sleepily to look where I was looking. "Whaa?"

I ignored him and walked along the flat roof over the cells to stand beside the hole. The cable zipped around the pulley making a *ziiing* sound as the suspended crate, about the size of a cow, flew towards me. It passed below a cleverly positioned hook which released it from the cable, and the crate tumbled perfectly through the hole into the room below with a splintery *crack*.

I leaned over the edge and peered down. The misshapen crate's sides bulged after the impact.

"Woahhh. What is that?" Timothee asked, below me. He walked into the room for a closer look.

As curious as it was, my eyes were drawn to the cable... it looped around the pulley and stretched high across the sea all the way to the cliff's summit at Joy, like the world's longest laundry line.

"It's full of food!" Timothee exclaimed from below. "Apples, oats... this must be how they feed us!"

I jumped and grabbed the cable. It immediately shifted

because of my weight, and I slid backwards. I let go just before my fingers were pinched in the pulley, and landed on the edge of the hole. *I need to wedge something in the pulley to hold it still... then I'll be able to climb out of here.*

"Hey, Billy. It was Billy, right? What are you doing?"

I peered at Tim through the hole. "I'm getting out of here."

I jumped down to the floor.

Timothee snorted a laugh. "You want to escape? No one escapes the Khazi!" He followed me to my cell.

I found the bone spoon and held it up. "Watch me."

I brushed past him, marched back along the balcony and clambered onto the roof again. I jammed the spoon into the pulley and gave the cable a tug to test it. This time it didn't budge.

"You're crazy!" Before I knew it, he had climbed up beside me. "You must be desperate to get out of here, spud!" Spud came out as *spood* in his funny accent. "What's her name?"

I frowned. "What? How did you..."

He shot me a mischievous, toothy grin. An infectious grin.

"Ha," I smiled. "Her name is Becky."

"The things we do for love, eh spood!"

"What about you, then?" I asked. "Who's waiting for you back there?"

He sighed wistfully. "Oh, there's nobody for poor Timothee just now. But there's a serious lack of pretty girls here. I wasn't born to live in a toilet with a bunch of old hairy men. I'm with you, Billy the Spood!"

Tim's enthusiasm filled me with courage. I leapt like a hero and grabbed the cable in both hands. It rocked and swayed as he jumped up behind me.

Swinging from hand to hand, I edged my way out over the sea.

I looked down.

I shouldn't have looked down. "Cripes," I uttered.

Cast in shadow of the Khazi's island, the sea was about forty feet below us, gently lapping at the dark rocks. I continued my slow climb and the sea gradually moved farther away as we ascended up the cable.

A gust of wind rocked me and I froze, gripping the cable so tight I think all the blood left my knuckles. My heart threatened to beat its way out of my chest as my legs dangled in mid air.

Timothee spoke up behind me. "Wooah. Hey Billy. Billy!" he shouted over the breeze.

I couldn't turn around to face him, that would mean altering my grip, which wasn't happening. "What?" I squeaked.

"Don't look down!" I could actually hear the grin on his face.

Are you enjoying this, you crazy fool?

I waited for the wind to calm, focusing all my energy on keeping hold of the cable. It stretched far into the distance, connected to a tower on top of the cliff. I recalled the boat journey taking around half an hour, and that moved a lot faster than the rate we were shimmying.

I began to regret my decision to attempt a jailbreak via the world's longest laundry line.

The cable gave a violent jerk.

I yelped. Timothee screamed.

The spoon must have dislodged from the pulley. Before I had a chance to contemplate it further, I was flying backwards with such force that my toes were aimed squarely at the top of the cliffs in front of me.

Wind crashed passed my ears as I craned my neck to look over my shoulder. Timothee gaped at me in sheer horror, and behind him, the Khazi's walls flew towards us. "Let go!" I shouted, hoping that we ended up falling through the gap in the roof and not into the mouth of a hungry sea monster.

We both plunged through the hole. Timothee landed on the crate, and I landed on him. The crate split open in a burst of wooden chunks and a cloud of oatflakes and we sprawled out across the hard white floor on top of it all.

"Oww," Timothee groaned beneath me. I was grateful for the soft landing.

"What the heck are you two doing?"

I looked up to see Kev standing in the doorway. I staggered to my feet. "Um. We're escaping."

Kev gave a short, surprised laugh. "You what? No-one escapes the Khazi."

"Yeah, he said the same thing," I gestured to Timothee, who continued to lie on his back amid the mess making small groaning noises. "But I'm not staying to die here. I found a way back to the mainland. There's a cable, see. And if we wedge it tight so it doesn't move, we can climb along it." My mind buzzed. I felt my blood coursing. "Or what would be even better is if someone pulled one side of the cable while several of us held on to the other, they could pull us along—"

"And what of the poor sods who get left behind, lad?" Kev stared at me, with a look of bewilderment.

I hadn't thought that one through properly. I hadn't exactly thought the first attempt through properly either, let's be honest. Timothee and I could have quite easily ended up in the squishy belly of some hulking creature by now, had that wind picked up and the spoon not mercifully come loose.

I racked my brain, growing desperate. "What if... what if next time they send us a crate, we all grab onto the returning side of the cable, it'll pull us right to the cliff!"

For a moment, Kev's face pondered the idea as if it could work. But solemn ol' Ged appeared in the doorway. "You wouldn't be the first to try that, boys, I can tell you." He glanced curiously at the kid sprawled out in what I assumed was our breakfast rations. I gave Tim a hand up, and we looked sheepishly at the two old men.

Ged slowly shook his head. "Even if you did manage to make it all the way to the cliff, you wouldn't find escape.

166

Guards watch over the line, night and day, surely you knew that? I seen a man once who almost made it."

"Really?" I gulped. "What, uh, happened to him?"

"My buddies heard word of an escapee attempting to climb the cable, so we gathered atop the cliffs to see, a whole bunch of us from the city. The fella was almost over land, but the Kingsmen in the tower had been watching him approach. They toyed with him as he dangled high above the rocks. Each time he took another swing towards the edge of the cliff they wound the cable back, so it was like he hadn't moved. This went on for a while, but no man can hold on forever. He fell. I can still hear the Kingsmen laughing."

I grimaced. That could have been us. *How stupid.*

"I... I can't stay here," I said defiantly.

"Just forget about escaping, lad. You're only torturing yourself. We are condemned. Accept it. It's easier." He sighed, and bent to gather up the supplies to take downstairs.

I shook my head silently. *Mother wouldn't give up. She wouldn't just 'accept it'.* I still had time to find a way out. Enough time to run some experiments...

22 nights to go.

For a few days, I couldn't see any means of escape except the cable. It was *right there,* a direct link to the mainland. But it was out of the question. I decided that if I did manage to escape, I would want to be as far away from the Kingsmen as possible. The cable led to the city, and the city was their home.

I considered my options. There weren't many, I had to admit. The sky, or the sea.

The sea was full of horrible hungry monsters, and the only reason I was even considering the sky was because I'd seen mother's amazing flying balloon. We didn't have a balloon here on the Khazi though, nor the means to make one. There were no cows, no trees, nothing but a bunch of bone cutlery and a healthy supply of tea leaves.

I decided to conduct some research. That seemed like something Mother would do.

First, I had to see who else was trapped here. Maybe one of the other prisoners would be smarter than me. I hung around in the canteen striking up conversation with anyone who would listen, and quickly discovered that almost everyone was from the rebellion in Joy, just like Ged said. Middle aged blokes, like my father and Becky's dad, normal men angry at the Kingsmen and the 'false child king.'

Every time I mentioned escaping, I'd get the same resigned answer again and again.

"No-one escapes the Khazi, lad." A burly fellow called Ben was the sixth person to tell me so that day. He sat sipping a mug of tea with big hands joined to bulging biceps. Sitting opposite, I felt rather like a skeleton with my puny arms.

"I know, I know. But I'm going to be the first." I tried to sound confident, but being surrounded by so many pessimists had taken its toll, and I heard the weariness in my voice.

Ben sighed. "I'm sorry you're in here, kid. You don't seem so bad. Me, I'm content to enjoy my last days in the open air. Sure beats choking to death at the Plaza."

So you're a blacksmith? That could be useful...

He went on, "I'm done with that place. It just ain't the same as it used to be."

"What happened?" I asked.

"Kingsmen," he spat. "They took control of the whole city, and they used that boy to do it."

I frowned. "What do you mean?"

"Think about it, lad. Old King Arnold kept those hat-wearing pansies on a tight leash. They were his guards and not much else. Soon as the boy shows up, ol' Arnold dies in some freakish boat accident and suddenly the kingsmen are answering to an eight year old! What's a kid know of ruling? He'll agree to anything they tell him. No, its too convenient."

"Huh," I said. "So, do you think they plotted to put the boy on the throne?"

"Course they did. He's not Arnold's son. Anyone could see it. 'cept most people *choose* not to. The cityfolk don't care. They're happy for anyone to rule, so long as they got their fancy houses and warm beds. Did you know the Kingsmen have been slowly running all the smallfolk out of business?"

"Um, no."

"It's true. They increased production at all the mines, timber yards and metalworks across the south, working us all like dogs. And for what? Half the stuff we make gets loaded onto ships and sails off never to be seen again. The ships themselves don't even come back, we just build new ones! Where's it all going? It's a bleedin' waste I tell ya." Ged snorted, his face glum. "That's why I joined Ged's rebellion, he were the only fella standing upto 'em. Seemed like the right thing to do." He shook his head and took a long sip of tea.

"I hardly got to see the city," I said. "I didn't know about any of that."

"Well, doubt you'll ever see it now. Think yerself lucky." He raised his mug to me and took another sip.

I frowned. *There's nothing lucky about being stuck here.* I didn't really understand all the details of their plight, but I could tell that they had meant well. Kane was the only kingsman I knew, but it seemed like the rest weren't much better. Anyone who opposed them was okay by me. None of them were interested in escaping though. Maybe I could change their mind if I came up with a way of getting off this island together.

"Why don't we make a boat?"

Ben chortled. "And how do you suppose we do that?"

"I don't know, that's why I'm talking to you. I was thinking we could use the wood from the delivery crates.

You'd know how to build it, right?"

"Sure kid. But look around you. We ain't exactly got any tools here. And besides, we need that wood for the stoves." He paused, and looked to me with a face of worry. "Plus, what about the... monsters. I wouldn't really wanna be getting in some homemade raft with them out there."

Like I had forgotten. *That thing swallowed their boat. The whole boat...* Remembering, Ben and I both nodded fearfully to each other.

I sighed. I made myself a mug of tea, and took it up to the roof. Before long, Timothee joined me. He plonked himself down and we sat with our legs dangling over the edge, overlooking the calm afternoon sea.

"Had any more clever ideas, spood?" he asked.

"I tried. Those guys are no use. They don't even want to escape."

He grunted. "They are old and past it. They have lived their lives already. They do not share our passion, our spirit!" he nudged my shoulder.

His enthusiasm was uplifting, I had to admit. I raised an eyebrow at him. "Wasn't it that passion of yours that got you captured in the first place? What was it they said at your trial...something about *inappropriate advances on the Kingsmaids*. Ha." I thought briefly. "Are the Kingsmaids the girls who wear orange and green?"

"Of course! Are they not exquisite, spood? *Ohhh*, my heart beats like the wings of a dove whenever I see them. I cannot help myself, Billy. They are simply too delicious to behold. I kissed one, and it was the most magical moment of my life. I have never felt so alive!"

I thought about Becky. She kissed me once, in the grasslands. I didn't think it was the same sort of kiss that he was talking about, but it was still magical... If the Kingsmaids were just a result of the little brat's wish of becoming king, though, that must mean the tree had... created them? They might not even be real people. Like my connection with Max, were they just side effects? I shuddered at the thought. "There's something not right about those girls."

"Oh there's something *very* right with them, Billy." He grinned. "I am powerless in their presence!"

"Yeah. That's the part that's not right... You should look for someone else if we do make it out of here, Tim."

"Oh maybe so, maybe so. After all, look where I've ended up because of them! I knew you were a wise one, spood. I could tell." He put an arm around my shoulders. "So, tell me of your Becky."

I smiled. "She's smart, and funny. And she can mimic any accent. She'd rip yours to shreds Tim, ha."

"Mine? It is you that speaks funny, spood, not me!"

I went on, "She's the bravest girl I've ever met..." I pictured her standing on her doorstep with her long hair flowing down her back, but in my mind this time she turned around and met me with those fiery eyes. "When she looks at you, it... it's incredible, I feel both terrified and invincible all at the same time. I haven't kissed her yet." I realised abruptly that I had said that last part aloud.

"No? You must! How will she know of your love, if you do not show her?"

"I think she knows. Besides, that's not the only way to show her. I drew her a picture."

He sniggered. "A picture? You spoods are so strange." He released me and stood. "Well, I hope you do better than a *picture* if we make it out of here." He grinned again, shaking his head, and left.

I sipped my tea and grimaced. "Blugh." It had gone cold. I chucked it off the edge into the sea.

Becky knows I like her, doesn't she? I was pretty sure she did. I hoped she did. Then again, unless I managed to find a way out of here, it might be for the best if she didn't know...

I heard a splash and looked down. A few agitated fish were jumping out of the sea and splashing about. *They must like tea*, I thought, chuckling. I gazed back across to the cliffs of Joy. *Hmm.* I checked the fish again. As I watched, a big shadow moved in from below the squabbling shoal and sucked them all under the surface, presumably into its mouth. The shadow floated there a while, a huge fish, smaller than the one that swallowed the boat, but certainly big enough to eat a person... After a while, the shadow retreated and sunk back down into the depths.

"No way," I said aloud. A plan began to formulate in my mind. "That might work..."

18 nights to go.

I was getting hungry.

We had plenty of food to go around, but I had decided to use most of my rations in my experiments. Sitting up on the roof of the Khazi, I'd drop slices of apple into the sea, to observe which creatures it attracted.

While doing this, I also discovered that depending on the time of day, there were different size shadows lurking about. The really big ones always showed up close to either sunrise or sunset. But they liked to eat the smaller ones... And the smaller ones really liked tea for some reason.

15 nights to go.

One time, just after lunch, I borrowed the cast iron hot water urn. After carefully unscrewing the pipe that connected it to the giant water drum, and emptying the contents down the basin, I carried it across to the cave door and down to the rocky point where we had all been dropped off. I had about five minutes before somebody realised they couldn't make themselves a cup of precious tea, so I had to be quick.

Holding the rim as tight as I could, I lowered the urn into the sea, being careful not to let it fill with water, which would defeat the point. I armed myself with the big spoon I had wedged in my trousers and waited.

Soon enough, a shadow appeared in the water below and

started to swim towards me.

I raised the spoon, my heart racing. *Please work.* I clanged the spoon against the metal rim of the pot as hard as I could. It echoed like a dull bell, softened by the water around it.

The shadow flinched, and retreated.

Then it came back for another try. I clanged the pot again, and the monster pulled back even further.

"Ha! Yes!" *Progress...*

I clanged it once more just to be safe, hoisted it out of the sea and hurried back up the steps into the safety of the cave. Some of the men gave me puzzled stares as I lugged the urn back through the canteen.

After reconnecting it to the water drum, I stood back and studied it. It was huge, that drum. There were sixteen prisoners here in the Khazi. *I think we could easily fit into that... if it were empty.*

Chapter Seventeen

12 nights to go.

Kane had been bedridden with a stinking cold for days after his night in the cave. But he was over that now, and doing his best to stay out of everyone's way. I hadn't told him about my idea of wanting to escape, but if my plan came to fruition, it would be difficult to hide it from him.

So, I paid him a visit in his cell. He was lying on his bed, finishing off an apple. I stood in the doorway. "Hello Kane."

He looked up. "You," he growled.

I stepped inside.

"Did I say you could enter my cell?" His voice was cold as ever, but lacked the hateful spark it once had. He made no move to stop me. "What do you want?"

"I need you to do some things, and I think you owe it to me not to refuse." I spoke as sternly as I could. Just looking at the horrible man reminded me of poor Max and what he'd done to him. There was a time I'd wanted to hurt him so badly to make him pay, but it wouldn't help me right now.

I expected a snort, a cruel jape, or at the very least a mocking smile. I got none. He frowned instead. "What might that be?"

"Well, there's only one Blue Moon until we all die, and uh, I have a plan to get out alive instead. But, I need everyone's help to pull it off."

He sat up on the bed, eyeing me. "What plan?"

"You'll know soon enough." I looked at the apple core in his hand. "Can I have that?"

He glanced at it, took a final bite, and tossed me the core. "Anything else?"

"Uh, yes. I need you to give me all your share of tea, and only eat a quarter of your rations from now on. The bare minimum."

"Excuse me?" he scowled.

"It's for the distraction. I need as much spare food as I can get."

He studied me with dark, narrow eyes. His once immaculate suit was now marked with stains and even ripped in a couple of places. I was fairly certain some of the other guys had paid him a visit in the dark hours of the night. I always pretended not to hear as I lie there in my own cell, remembering all the times he'd tried to kill me and my mother and Becky. But I didn't like the bitter taste it left in my mouth...

"Fine," he said.

I didn't leave yet. There was something else I had to know, but I feared the answer.

"Why are you still here?" Kane seethed.

"At my trial, you said you interrogated my friends in Fentworth, to find out about me. George and Millie are good, kind people, if you hurt them I—"

"They are fine." He spoke calmly, and looked me right in the eye. "I didn't hurt them."

I held his gaze. He could have told me anything, there was no way for me to know the truth. But I believed him. "Okay." I shifted my feet. "There is one more thing." This would be more difficult, I knew. "You need to... apologise. To everyone."

Now he did snort, a heavy spiteful choke of guttural laughter. "You stupid boy."

"You have to," I insisted. "If you want to escape with us, you need to be on good terms with everyone. Otherwise they'll just throw you overboard."

"They will do that anyway, Billy." He spoke quietly, and I saw the truth in his words.

"You have to try. I've come to you while there's still time. It's your choice."

I walked out.

10 nights to go.

Another crate arrived and this time it didn't only bring food. Tied in a bundle among the sacks of oats were some letters. They were addressed to various people.

Ged thumbed through them as we all gathered in the canteen. "Billy, there's one for you."

My heart jumped with anticipation. I took the envelope up to my cell and stared at it whilst sitting on the bed.

Billy Spudswallop, written in elegant, flowing handwriting. I carefully peeled it open and pulled out the contents. A single piece of paper, torn down one edge. It was my drawing, the one I made for her. Well, half of it at least. The tear had split it perfectly down the middle. Half an eclipse hovered in the sky, above the depiction of Becky sitting on the rock.

I flipped it over and read the message on the back through teary eyes.

Billy, I haven't forgotten you. And now, you won't forget me either. You're still here with me, and now I'm with you. We will meet again. Becky X

I felt so happy I could have died right then. I exhaled heavily and remembered that wasn't part of the plan.

"Is it from her?" Timothee stepped into my cell.

I wiped my eyes and said, "Yeah. It's my picture." I held it up so he could see.

He leaned closer. "Heh. You drew that? It's good." He

176

nodded slowly and added, "I suppose she does know how you feel."

"No. She doesn't know half of it," I said, sniffing. I realised he didn't have a letter. "Sorry, you don't need me going on about it."

"Nonsense, spood. I'm glad for you. If this plan of yours works out, I might get to meet her! Does she have any pretty friends...?"

5 nights to go.

I woke at dawn, as usual, and went to check on my ever growing pile of foodscraps in the empty cell at one end of the upper tier. Not all of the guys had agreed to eat less and donate to my heap, but I hoped it would be enough. There were browning apple cores, soggy oats and a number of fresh apples all piled up on the mattress.

It had been a while since I'd heard anyone going into Kane's cell late at night. Perhaps he had been trying to make amends after all. *The plan might work...*

3 nights to go.

I think I turned sixteen today, but I couldn't be sure. I didn't bother mentioning it to anyone.

2 nights to go.

Little Red had appeared in the night sky once again. The final days were upon us. Last night, the tide rose high enough to submerge the lower floor in water.

Once the sea had retreated around mid morning, I propped up several spare mattresses in the cave tunnel, wedged between the ground and ceiling just on the other side of the door, which I locked shut using the same broken canteen stool that we had used to lock Kane out there.

During the deadly eclipse, the tide would flood through the windows of the cells, but with the door sealed, we could buy a little more time.

1 night to go.

I gathered everyone in the canteen. Timothee, Ged, Ben, Kev, Giles, Jim, and all the other inmates sat around the tables watching me. Kane stood at the back, away from everyone, but I could see that he was as eager to get out of here as myself.

I cleared my throat. "As you know, I don't intend to die here tomorrow. You've all been gracious enough to let me plan for this, even though some of you don't believe it will work. But, I just wanted to say thank you. Thanks for letting me try, anyway. So, in case anyone's not clear about tomorrow, here's what I need you all to do..."

I explained the plan in full.

When I was finished, I saw approving nods, a few anxious faces and for a brief moment I actually convinced myself that this would work.

I took the pile of tea leaves I had stashed up and tipped them into the giant water drum to make the biggest stew of tea in the world.

Zero. The mooneye comes tonight.

I slept as soundly as Max after a day of chasing rabbits that final night. There was no more time for experimenting, so no point in worrying. This would either work, or it wouldn't. *And if it doesn't, we all die.*

In the morning, I sat up in bed and turned to look at my makeshift calendar dug into the wall. A row of 26 crossed-out marks, the mooneye the only thing left untouched. I got up and scratched a big X through it.

Making my way down to the canteen, my bare feet made a soft patter across the dry floor. That was odd, but I didn't think anything of it.

We all agreed that the stockpile of rotting food in the upper cell was big enough and so, everyone ate their full share of breakfast. Nobody bothered to mention that it could be our last, everyone knew well enough.

After breakfast, we started dismantling the canteen. Using a knife, Ben and some of the other workers were able to unscrew the stools and benches from the floor. We needed to clear the area to make room for the great water drum later tonight. Without any proper tools, progress was painfully slow, but we had all day to get it done.

Tim came up to me around midday as I was giving Ben a hand to unscrew a stool. When it came loose, I tossed it to one side with the others.

"Billy! Have you been up to the roof today?" He sounded anxious.

"What? No..."

"I think you need to see this!"

I stood, started towards the steps and my feet made a *splash*. I stopped.

A small stream flowed from the cave door to the drain. *What...?*

I followed it and noticed a thin spurt of water seeping out between the door frame at about the height of my waist. And even as I watched, I inhaled sharply because another spurt appeared just above it.

I turned to Tim and whispered, "It's starting..."

I bounded up the steps, Tim right behind, and we clambered onto the roof. Big Blue hung high above the cliffs in the west, a half-silhouetted crescent. Little Red had already crawled out of the ocean to the east and started its chase across the sky. Both moons were aiming for the sun. "I was a day out. Oh, no." A tingle of ice shivered down my body. I guessed we had about twenty minutes.

"*It's STARTING!*" I yelled down into the bowl.

A dozen heads turned to me from the canteen. Fearful faces appeared out of cell doorways, and for a moment nobody moved.

Ged broke the silence. "You heard him, lads! Now let's get this done!" And with that, the Khazi came alive with action. I had never heard Ged sound anything beyond serious and solemn, but now I understood how he had been able to instigate the rebellion in Joy. His leader's voice echoed vigourously off the walls of the prison.

I watched as Ben threw away the useless little knife and started kicking the stool he had been working on. In three mighty thumps, it came loose and he wrenched it out of the ground and turned to start on the next.

I leapt down from the roof, ran to my cell to lace up my boots, grabbed my half of the drawing and carefully folded it into my pocket. *I'm coming Becky.* I walked out of my cell for the final time.

"Tim, get the food onto the roof and throw it into the sea, hurry!"

"Okay, spood!" He ran off and nearly knocked into two fellas coming the other way. He barked at them, "You two! Help me with this!"

I marched to the kitchen where Kev was propped up on the workbench squeezed in between the giant water drum and the wall, unscrewing the clips that secured it in place.

"How's it coming?" I asked him, fiddling with my fingers as I spoke.

"Gah, slowly. Come on you useless thing..."

I turned my attention to the iron urn. I took the big bone spoon that hung on a hook from the ceiling. "Jim! You should take this now, hold onto it tight." I handed the old bearded guy the spoon. "Who's going to hold the urn for you?"

He pointed through the doorway into the canteen at two blokes who were prying loose one of the tables. *Good.*

The minutes ticked down, but at last, Kev had the water drum free of the wall. By then, seawater was seeping out in a wide spray all around the cave door, covering the entire lower floor in a thin film of liquid.

The tea-filled drum, which looked more like a giant wooden pail, now rested freely on the top of the workbench. All we had to do was tip it out.

Easier said than done.

Kev and I climbed up either side of it.

"One, two, three!" I pushed with everything I had. I thought all the blood in my forehead would come bursting out of my nose as I let out a high pitched groan. The drum didn't even budge. I wheezed as if my lungs were on fire.

"Out of the way, useless boy." Kane strode up, grabbed me by the collar and yanked me onto the ground. He hopped nimbly onto the bench, rolled his sleeves, and braced against the drum.

Kev and Kane heaved together and the drum slowly began to slide away from the wall. I realised I probably didn't want to stand in its way and retreated to the canteen.

"Watch out, get back!"

The drum tilted forward, spilling droplets of brown liquid. It tumbled to the ground with a heavy *thump* that shook the building. A torrent of cold tea flooded out of the kitchen and spread all across the floor of the Khazi, soaking our ankles and spilling down the drain.

Tim's voice called from the roof. "I see it! It's working!"

"Good! Now, get down here!" I called back.

Ben heaved the final stool out of the ground just as Kev and Kane rolled the big upturned bucket through the doorway and into the space that had once been the canteen.

I glanced up. Big Blue was now more like Big Black. The silhouetted disc was leaning in to kiss the sun, while Little Red approached from the right, still a way off but moving faster. It was going to be a perfect Sunstare eclipse. *I've waited years to see one of these. And now I won't even be able to sketch it!*

As Tim bounced down the steps, the sea came in through the cell windows on the first tier balcony, pouring between the railings and creating a circular waterfall all around us. The roaring cascade made it difficult to hear anything else.

"Hurry!" I called over the noise. "We have to get inside!"

We tipped the giant pail upright, and everybody clambered in at once.

"Spread out!" Ben called. "Distribute the weight. Giles, you get there, Kane, stand there!"

Jim stood clutching the spoon at what Kev said was the stern, while two hefty blokes stood either side of him holding the cast iron urn over the outside. *That's our pulsar.*

Ben and Kev armed themselves with improvised oars that were really just canteen stools and took up position in port and starboard, which just looked like left and right to me.

And I stood in the middle with Tim, the two lightest sailors, surrounded by the rest of the inmates who all spread out around the edge of The Floater. (Tim insisted we named it something, and nobody had come up with anything better.)

Big Blue started devouring the sun and the daylight faded.

Seawater poured in through the upper level windows, doubling the height of the circular falls, and the water level on the ground floor rose higher and higher and higher...

...and The Floater didn't float.

When the sea level reached the rim, instead of lifting us up as I had hoped, it simply spilled over the side and our makeshift boat began to fill up.

Panic ensued.

Some of the guys started cupping water in their hands and flinging it back out, another grabbed the urn and started using it as a bucket.

Jim burst into song, singing at the top of his lungs. "*Come, come with meeeee! Let's take a dive to the bottom of the seeeeeeea!* I'm coming Judy!"

"We're too heavy!" yelled Kev.

"There's too many of us!" someone else wailed.

I turned to see Ben lift Kane by the neck and bundle him out into the churning torrent of water that was now all around us.

I was soaked through, gasping and sputtering for breath.

Tim shrieked, "Billy, it's not working! *I can't swim!*"

The plan had failed miserably, The Floater was a deathtrap. I clambered over the side and reached in to haul Tim out with me. "Come on!" *The cable. It's our only hope now.*

The sun was now a crescent of fire in the sky, slowly being swallowed by the black monster from the left, and now Little Red joined the fray from the right.

I started for the steps, scrambling on tiptoes in the neck-high torrent, picturing the two of us desperately shimmying up the cable as a great fish leapt out and plucked us from it like two bitesize nibbles when a shadow blanketed the Khazi.

Max barked.

FWWOOOOOSSH!

"Billy! Up here!"

I craned my neck to see Becky's face peering down at me. She was leaning over the side of a platform suspended by two enormous balloons.

I.

Love.

You.

Behind the balloons, the Sunstare lit the sky in a golden flash and shimmers of lilac danced through the air.

I ducked under the curtain of water, deafened by the cascade, and scrambled up the staircase to the second tier. Tim followed me up, coughing.

"Becky! Help!" I called desperately.

Becky turned away and yelled "Lower Bethany! Make it go lower!"

I said to Tim, "We have to climb up!" I scrambled onto the roof and saw the dark tide mere inches from my feet. It reflected the lilac shimmers, bubbling and frothing around a hundred tiny fins that darted across the surface squabbling over the food scraps.

"Billy! Grab on to this!" Becky's voice called from above.

She tossed a rope ladder over the side which unfolded

downward. It was too high to reach, but the balloon was slowly turning and descending. The ladder floated out in to the middle, further from my reach.

Becky tossed a second ladder over the other side of the platform.

Tim chased the first ladder around the roof, while I ran for the second. Tim leapt and grabbed onto it, swinging out over the churning water and the upturned water drum.

A few more seconds and I can reach mine. Slowly, the ladder drifted towards me.

Kane hopped up in front of me. Before I knew what was happening, he shoved me aside, turned and jumped for my ladder. I landed on my back, just as the tide spilled across the roof, and a small toothy fish snapped at my hand.

My heart thundered in my chest. I scrambled to my feet, splashed across to the edge of the roof and jumped. I caught onto Kane's leg and dangled above the Khazi as the sea poured over from all sides.

Ged, Kev, Ben and all the others were tossed around like ragdolls within the whirling waters, and a swarm of the nasty little fish tumbled in to join them. The great water pail wedged itself between the balcony's railing and became a refuge for the men, who grabbed hold of it one by one as they drifted past, swatting away the snapping critters.

Kane kicked free of my grip. "Get off," he shouted over the roar of water. I slipped and fell, clutching the last rung, and my feet actually touched the water. Kane ascended the ladder towards the platform as I hauled myself up to get my footing.

Kev's waterlogged voice called up to me from just below where I dangled. "Billy!" He and everyone else had managed to clamber inside the giant bucket.

The Khazi was full to the brim.

"Grab on!" I called to Kev. Tim's ladder dangled over the bucket and Kev reached through the rung and locked his arm around it. A snapper jumped out of the water and attached itself to his elbow. He yelped and plucked it off, as more of the tiny fish circled the bucket looking for a way in.

"Go Bethany, now!" Becky's voice screamed from above.

"No! Wait!" I yelled desperately.

Ben reached for my ladder and interlocked his arms through the rungs. Two guys grabbed hold of Ben and Kev's waist, anchoring The Floater to the balloon.

FWOOSH!

Fire lit the sky as twin bovithrusters ignited and the balloon jolted forward. It dragged the bucket of inmates out of the water, bouncing off the Khazi's roof. We accelerated, The Floater skimmed across the surface, leaving a tail of spray in its wake as we soared away from the drowned prison.

I clutched the ladder with all my strength, wind blasting through my clothes and hair.

The sun peeped out from behind the moons, lighting up the sky and the sea, revealing the monstrous shadow that chased us beneath the surface.

Chapter Eighteen

Oh good grief...

A grey dorsal fin as big as Bellyguts rose out of the sea behind the trailing water bucket. I recognised the creature immediately as the same one that had swallowed the boat. The big ones didn't usually come out during the day, but the eclipse must have confused it.

The balloon gained speed, but the monster kept up.

"Billy! Hold on!!" Becky's voice filled the air.

We turned sharply to the right as we shot up the coastline, and I saw the cliffs of Joy fly past ahead of me.

Ben and Kev grimaced as the ladder rungs dug into their sides and Jim madly drummed the cast iron urn with the spoon. *How did he manage to keep hold of that?* It seemed to be working, the sea creature kept up the chase, but at a distance.

The Floater bounced over a crest and Jim lost his grip on the urn. It flew out of his hand, smacked into the dorsal fin and disappeared with a *splash*.

The monster's reaction was instant. It writhed out of the sea revealing an elongated grey body, like a giant worm with nothing but a mouth for a head. Its muscles twitched down its length as it surged forwards.

"Almost there! Brace yourself!" Becky again. I turned to look ahead and received a face full of wind. A sloped, sandy beach thrust itself out at us.

Kev and Ben untangled themselves from the ladders just before the moment of impact. The Floater skimmed out of the sea and careened into the soft sand. A yellow cloud plumed upward, the bucket flipped over and spilled everyone onto the beach. The monster came hurtling out of the sea, its maw gaping open wide as it slid deep into the sand and beached itself just short of the escapees. The maw snapped savagely, but empty.

The bovithrusters cut off, and I could hear myself think once again. The balloon slowed to a gentle cruise and rose into the sky.

Dangling from the ladder, I glanced down at the men, shrinking as we left the sea behind. Ged's thunderous voice called out.

"Thank you Billy! We won't forget this!"

Smiling to myself, I climbed up.

Before I reached the top, I heard the raging argument.

"Why would I ever help *you?*"

"You tried to kill us!"

"Just take me to Joy you miserable wretches!"

"What, so you can turn me in? There's no reward for me anymore, I'm a free woman!"

I pulled myself up onto the platform. Kane had his back to me, shouting at Mother and Becky, while Max cowered behind their legs, and Tim watched from the side.

"You," I growled. Kane turned to face me. I punched him as hard as I could on the chin. He dropped to the floor.

"*Owww*," I gasped, clutching my fist with my other hand.

Max bounced. *Billy!*

Becky called out. "Billy!" She ran to me and threw her arms around my neck. I pulled her close, ignoring the throb of my knuckles, and hugged her tightly, burying my face in her streaming hair. I felt her heart beating rapidly against my chest... or was that mine?

Behind her, Mother smiled proudly, Tim grinned and shot me two thumbs up. Max sat on the floor, his little stump wagging, showing off his teeth.

Mate!

I looked into Becky's fiery eyes, now wide and tearful but undeniably happy. Then, she closed them, so I did too, our lips met and my whole body tingled. *So this is why people shut their eyes...*

Unfortunately, I couldn't kiss her forever, and when she gently pulled away I stood, holding the small of her back, trembling lightly. Slowly, I reopened my eyes. She bit her lip and said softly, "About time, Billy."

"Thanks for saving me," I answered.

"Ahem!" Mother planted her hands on her hips.

I unwound myself from Becky, smiling sheepishly, and went to Mother for a hug. "I can't believe you did this. That was incredible!"

"I know." She released me, bursting with excitement. "The Mark II, Billy! Two balloons. *Two* bovithrusters! Oh, and one propeller. This was our maiden voyage! I'm so glad it worked."

I gazed at each of the new features in awe. "Yeah, me too. My plan didn't exactly work out the way I'd hoped... Mother, this must have taken you so long to build."

"Well, I did have some help this time."

Becky proudly stepped forward. "See that, Billy?" She pointed to the driver's seat, a comfy chair surrounded by levers, a set of handlebars and... pedals?

"Is that—" I started.

"Yup! It's the remains of their stupid pedal buggy. That was my idea! I went back on the train and salvaged it. It works the propeller, for when there's no wind."

Behind the seat sat the little cog engine, and behind that, the propeller protruded out the back of the craft. The timber platform we stood upon was sort-of boat shaped, only flatter. A makeshift railing of ropes and wooden struts ran around the edge of the craft.

"And when we need a real burst..." Mother stepped beneath the two cylindrical metal tanks which rested below the hole of each balloon. "The bovithrusters can be aimed backwards." She turned to Becky. "Remind me to tighten the calibration spring, I noticed a slight shudder in the mid section."

"Yeah, me too, and I think we need to make an adjustment to the lower quadrant hyper..."

I zoned out.

I turned to Max, relishing the familiar scratch of his thoughts in my head. *Billy!* I hunched down and he bundled me to the floor, licking my face and neck. "I missed you too, boy! Let me see your poor tail!" His stump wagged furiously as he tried to climb all over me, putting his paws right in my belly and other parts... *Billy BillyBillyBilly!* I hugged him and ruffled his head and scrunched his ears, so happy to be reunited again.

"Besides, I still haven't been to the moon!" Mother remarked to Becky. She wandered off towards the front of the deck and began fiddling with some guy ropes.

"Ah, yes. How did I forget?" Becky said to herself, smiling. She turned to me and sat down beside Max and me and rubbed his belly.

"Is she still going on about that?" I asked her.

She chuckled. "Your mum is stubborn. And when she gets an idea in her head..." She made a gesture, pointing her hand in a straight line towards the horizon. She turned back to me and smiled. "So, did you get my letter?"

I reddened. "Oh, yes." I reached into my back pocket and pulled out the soggy drawing. It was all smudged and ruined. "Aw, I can't even read your message any more."

She shrugged. "Nevermind. I guess you'll just have to sketch me something new. I found your backsack in Anvil Plaza. I kept it safe for you."

My sketches! "Really? Oh thank you!" I hugged her again.

"You're welcome," she smiled, but then it faded. "I was

so scared when I realised you were missing. I spent days trying to find out what happened to you. When Bethany discovered you had been captured, she spent two days locked in the spare room and refused to come out until she had perfected her calculations for the new Cloud Cruiser. She set her mind to rescuing you, and nothing, not even lunch, would interrupt her."

My stomach growled at the mention of lunch. Becky looked startled. "Oh, Billy! Did they even feed you properly in that place? You must be starving! Here, I have jerky." She rummaged in her backsack and pulled out some strips of meat. I devoured them. *Sooo much tastier than apples and oats.*

I caught Tim drooling. "Tim!" I said through a mouthful. I got to my feet. "Becky, this is Timothee."

They shook hands, although Tim's eyes never left the sack of meat. He spoke absently, "Billy told me so much about you."

Becky pushed her hair behind an ear. "Really? Here, help yourself."

Tim made a weeping sound as he tore into the chewy meat.

We stepped over the unconscious Fedora Man and sat on the edge of the craft gorging together, gazing back towards the sea. Becky left us to talk to Mother some more.

"We are alive!" Tim grinned and clapped an arm around my shoulder. "Thanks to you, my friend."

"My plan failed miserably," I pointed out.

"Maybe so. But you had the courage to make a plan when everyone else did not."

"Think they'll be okay?" I asked, referring to the other escapees, now just small figures in the distance at the end of the long stretch of sand.

"I believe so. This area is safe, they will find their way home."

I turned to him. "What about your home? Maybe we can

take you there?"

He scratched the back of his head. "I, uhh, have no great desire to return to Joy, Billy. I was running away from that place when they caught me, to Capella. My brother has a ranch."

My brothers. Father! "Sorry, Tim. I just remembered something." I interrupted a heated debate about whether a 2-inch bolt would be better suited than a 3-inch one. "Mother!"

The two girls stopped simultaneously and turned to me. Mother looked better now that her hair had grown back. "Have you been home yet?" I asked.

She gave me one of her *Are you a complete ignoramus?* looks. "William! When do you think I might have found time to liquidise four new batches of bovithane, reconstruct my balloon, plot a plan of rescuing you *and* fit in a short trip across the country to visit your father?"

"Well, when you put it like that, but—"

Mother talked over me. "Not to mention the rampaging demon tree running loose."

"We should at least visit..." I stopped. "Wait, *what?*"

"The king went to Hale. You told him where to go, didn't you?"

"Yeah, I made a deal with him. He said he would clear your bounty if I told him where to find another Wishing Tree."

"It was just as I suspected! The little brat found himself a Wishing Tree. Only it's not a Wishing Tree!"

"I know! I tried to tell him—"

"William, he went to Hale with all the Kingsmen. They found the cave, and they found the monster within. And it ate them all!"

I gaped at Mother. "*All* of them?"

"More or less," Mother replied. "When the first batch failed to return, Joy sent another group, and *one* of them returned, which is how we first found out about it. After that, a final group of them took over the train armed with torches and saws, but they must have become dessert. That was the last we saw of any of them. One or two Kingsmen remain in Joy, led by that big fat one who worked with *him*." She gestured to Kane, passed out on the floor behind us.

My gut tightened. *I sent them to their deaths.* I imagined the tree monster laughing hysterically, his voice shaking the cave as it crumbled around him, plucking up Fedora Men one after the other with those long spindly arms and dropping them into his mouth... I shuddered.

I recalled the way he had grown bigger after he'd heard my wish. He said I could reveal my desire to him, or *feed* him.

"So, he escaped the cave?" I pictured the tree monster clawing his way out of the hole in the roof of the cave, bellowing laughter. In my mind, he stood taller than the forest, gazing around, until he sees the windmill atop the hill... "What about Hale! Father, and Henry and Harry and—"

"Oh, I'm sure they're fine," she said flippantly. "The monster headed straight for Aston. The mayor there sent word to every town along the trainline that a *Great Mighty Tree Beast* had been sighted in the forest and requested help. But of course there was no one left to send."

Becky added, "They said the monster was last seen stomping away from the town, heading north towards the Great Plains." I could see the fire in her eyes again. She seemed excited.

"Where is he going?" My mind raced, trying to take it all in.

Mother waved her hand. "Who knows. Anyway, he's gone, so everyone in the south is safe, at least."

"Yeah, but... *cripes.*" I choked back a bitter laugh. "What if he comes back? What if he eats more people? This is all my fault! We have to stop him!"

Becky stood beside me and clutched my arm. "I was so hoping you'd say that."

Mother looked at me proudly. "It was a good idea, William. Striking a deal with the king to set your wonderful mother free like that."

I reddened. "Heh, thanks."

"But you're right. The monster is free as well, because of us. We can't go home knowing that. There are other towns in the north that need to be warned. On foot, it would take moons to travel there. But we have the Cloud Cruiser."

Becky's grip on my arm tightened as she tried to contain her excitement. I started to smile, despite myself.

Mother tapped her fingers across her chin. "We must try to stop the monster. The only question is how...?"

Eventually, Kane stirred.

"Uggh," he groaned, sitting up. He rubbed his swollen chin.

Four of us loomed over him. Max peeped cautiously through my legs.

"What are we going to do with you?" I asked with my arms crossed.

He eyed me from the floor. "I had the most preposterous dream about you. In it, you managed to *strike* me."

My knuckles pulsed. *I might not have if someone had warned me that punching people hurt so much.* "It wasn't a dream."

"I know," he said irritably. "Let me finish." He stood and composed himself.

Max flinched, then settled again, still peering between my legs at the man who chopped off his tail.

Kane held his hand out to me. "Bravo," he said.

I stared, dumbfounded.

He held it there a while, but when he realised I had no intention of shaking it, he withdrew his hand behind his back. "You know, when we train to be a Kingsman, they put us through two trials. One determines the level of intellect you possess, the other, your strength in combat. Naturally, I excelled at both, but ultimately it was my brains that won me my grey fedora." He lowered his head for a moment, then looked me square in the eye. "No-one has ever managed to strike me."

I scratched my elbow. "It was a lucky hit, really..."

"You do not seem to understand, boy. Up until now, you have outwitted me countless times. You evaded my capture more than once and even resisted the temptations of the Kingsmaids," he glanced at Timothee. "A feat that most men fail." Then, back to me, "My point is, from the first moment you escaped me, I considered you my equal. A fact which infuriated me to no end, I might add. When I did manage to bring you to justice, you still managed to plot a way out. And if it weren't for you," he hesitated and added reluctantly, "and your *mother*... I would now be sleeping within the belly of a slimy beast. Were you my partner, it would be you in the grey fedora, while I donned the black. And frankly, we would be *unstoppable*."

I had no words.

Becky gave a bitter laugh beside me. "Billy would *never* become a Kingsman! You're all evil, greedy liars. Or were."

He gave her a curt glance. "Perhaps to you. But I assure you, Joy would not be what it is today without us." He paused and frowned. "What do you mean *were?*"

"Ahe," Becky stifled a laugh. "Well, um. How to put this... Bethany, maybe you should tell him?"

Mother recounted the whole story once more, this time adding in extra details for dramatic effect. Kane's mouth gaped wider and wider as she spoke.

When mother told him that his old partner was one of the few remaining Kingsmen, he couldn't contain his rage.

"That *imbecile* is now in *charge?*" He grimaced.

"Why do you even care?" Becky asked. "You're not a Kingsman anymore."

"What were they thinking, gallivanting across the country like that," he grumbled. "We have a city to run. The boy should have been made to wait, at least until we had quelled the rebellion..."

"You really think you were making Joy better, don't you?" Becky snorted. And you actually thought that Billy would have wanted to *join* you?" She glared at him with disdain.

"Kane," I said, frowning. "What made you think I would even want to become a Kingsman?"

"Because there are so many benefits." He smiled wanly. Then he grunted. "Out of my way."

Kane brushed between us over to the front of the craft. His long hair caught in the breeze and the tattered suit jacket billowed behind him like a ragged cape. *He looks wrong without his hat...*

He turned to us. "Since you refuse to take me home, I'll content myself with disembarking at the next town. You do intend to land at some point, I assume? I don't see any privies on board."

Mother took her place in the driver's seat, and steered us in the direction of Capella, the cowboy town.

Kane sat brooding at the front of the deck.

If I did become a Kingsman, I'd have been a better one than him...

I nestled between Max and Becky, admiring the views. We perched on the edge with our arms around each other, counting clouds, *touching* clouds, watching the world fly by beneath our dangling feet.

I ran my fingers through her hair. It felt like soft silk between my knuckles. She giggled. "What are you doing?"

"Nothing. I just always wanted to do this."

She sighed, and closed her eyes. "Don't stop."

We passed over a canyon road strewn with rocks and mud.

Tim leaned over and yelled, "Cursed rocks. Curse you to *Tannerus!*"

As the canyonlands slowly morphed into tussock and grass, horses galloped freely in playful herds. The sun was low in the sky when the small town sprang up before us. A twin set of crossroads, lined with timber buildings. Farther out, the odd barn and stable yard dotted the surrounding countryside. I couldn't get enough of the views up here. We could see so far.

Flying through the night didn't seem like a good idea, but I was a little sad when we started our descent. Mother landed in a clearing at the end of the main road. A group of ranchers' kids gathered to greet us, all staring at the marvellous flying contraption.

"Righty, boys! End o'the line!" Mother drawled. Then, muttering to herself, "No, that makes no sense...it should be end o'the sky...or, hmmm... Tie us down, cloudmates!"

Becky chuckled as I rolled my eyes.

We hopped down and secured the deck to the ground with rope and wooden stakes. Slowly, the air in the balloons cooled and they flopped limply to the ground either side, turning the Cruiser into a big tent of sorts. By the time it was done, the sky had darkened to a deep blue, and the first of the stars twinkled through the clouds.

"Good work, sky scallywags!" Mother was beaming from her first successful flight, and as we strolled down the road, an air of optimism and excited anticipation enveloped us all.

I marvelled at how few buildings there were. Compared to Hooke and Joy, at least. It felt like a spacious version of Barrow. *And less on-fire...* The inn was just like every other building in the town – timber walls, a water trough out the front, a hitching post for tying up horses, and a porch. The only distinction was the swinging sign that jutted out of the angled roof. It read *The Lazy Mule*.

Kane followed us inside, but took a table by himself in a shadowy corner.

Mother ordered ribs and bread, and we enjoyed each other's company in the cosy tavern.

Mother lapped up the attention of the locals as eagerly as Max with his bowl of meat scraps under the table. The cowboys were all keen to question her about the balloon, assuming she must be the smartest person in the world, and she couldn't help answering them in that ridiculous drawl.

"Aw shucks, I jus' get me a conundrum in my lil' ol' head and by heck I jus' gotta solve it!" She tore into a rib and chewed it noisily, the way the ranchers did. "We're goin' to the moon next!"

I exchanged a look with Becky, sitting opposite me. She laughed, shaking her head.

Timothee sat to my left, at the end of the table. "So, what is the actual plan? How do you kill a tree monster...?"

"He's not actually a tree," I reminded him. Not that it offered any helpful suggestions. I shrugged.

Becky clearly felt more hopeful. "We just need to fly north until we find him."

"What if he tries to eat the balloon?" Tim asked.

A fearful look passed between us. "Let's not think about that," I said. "We just need to be careful. Hopefully we will see him before he sees us. I figure he spent a long time gazing up when he was trapped in the cave. Now that he's free, he'll probably be more interested in what's under his feet."

The others nodded agreement. Being the only person still alive who had seen the monster made me the expert on the matter. *I wonder if the king managed to make his wish, or was he eaten too?*

Becky seemed to be thinking something similar. "If only we knew where the king's wishing tree was."

"Yeah... he mentioned a lake. He said he lived near a big lake, and the tree was growing in the middle of it."

One of the ranchers gathered around Mother overheard our discussion. "See-Saw Lake? That's the biggest lake around here. It's a 3-day ride to the north."

"But you could fly there in no-time!" a young girl chimed in. She added wistfully, "Like a bird!"

Mother poked her head into the conversation. "What was that?"

"See-Saw Lake," I mused. *Why is it called that?*

"Another Wishing Tree..." Becky pondered.

"Mother, I think we might know where to find the second tree."

Mother tapped her chin. "Yeees. I believe we have our next destination, air adventurers!"

The next morning, after a good night's rest at the inn, Timothee came to bid us farewell as we were preparing the balloon for take-off.

"Thank-you again, Billy the Spood!" He stood alongside his brother, who shared his curly black hair and mischievous smile, but also wore a poncho and ranchers hat. "I will be hoping we meet again one day!"

"Me too," I said, shaking his hand.

Max gave a low growl.

Kane strode up behind the brothers, and eyed me. "What do you want?" I asked, frowning. The brothers stood aside.

Kane stepped forward. He opened his mouth, but it took a few seconds for the words to come. "I... want to make amends," he started. "I have nowhere to go. My brotherhood is all but over, and I have no desire to return to Joy to serve beneath that oaf... I would sooner serve those who have proven to be worthy adversaries." He held his chin up, looking me square in the eye. He had never treated me with such respect before, and it unnerved me.

"Uhh, I don't know if—"

"I know what you plan to do," he interrupted. "You intend to set a course for the lake, to seek help from the creature that dwells there. The boy king told me about it once. I know its power of granting wishes. I assume you will wish for the demon tree to be destroyed?"

I had not thought of that, despite its obviousness. "Yes," I said. "Of course!"

"Of course," Kane replied. "So, I propose an offer. The tree will grant a wish to each of us, yes? Allow me to join you, and after you have saved the precious people, and rid us of the menace, I shall speak to the tree myself, and wish for him to heal your canine companion there. He will look much cuter with a new tail, wouldn't you say?"

I laughed, overcome with surprise. "You would do that?" *He wouldn't! Would he...?* He looked so sincere.

"As I said, I want to make amends. Tails do not grow back by themselves, I fear. This is my only option." He held my gaze, unsmiling.

Becky and Mother both overheard the Fedora Man's offer, and came up behind us.

Mother eyed him suspiciously. "How do you expect us to trust you, after everything you've done?"

"I don't. Trust is earned, not given. Here, consider this my first payment." He held out the small metal device that he used to make fire.

"My firesparker!" Mother grabbed it hungrily from his outstretched hand. "I haven't seen this since my lab burned down! You stole it?"

"Yes." He hung his head. "Our unsavoury relationship started with that wonderful contraption. I feel the only just way to make a fresh start would be by my returning it."

Mother slowly nodded her head. I studied Kane's eyes. He showed no sign of his usual malice, his face was stone. *Perhaps he truly is tired of fighting us.*

"So, what do you say?" he asked.

"If you fly with us," Becky said sternly. "You will do *exactly* what we tell you, *when* we tell you. Okay? This ship needs a good crew. Captain Bethany calls the shots, and when she's not around, you answer to me. Then Billy, and then Max."

Kane showed the slightest hint of insolence, but then sighed. "Yes, of course."

She grinned mischievously. "You can be the cabin boy."

And with that, Kane joined us.

"Cloudmates, stations!" Mother bellowed. I think she was showing off to the crowd of ranchers that were gawping at the Cruiser, gathered to watch the spectacle.

"Aye, Captain!" Becky called back, and gave a cute salute.

I wrenched out three of the four stakes that pinned us to the ground, while Mother stood beside the driver's chair, overlooking the deck as Becky manned the bovithrusters. Gentle flames flickered out of the tops, slowly filling the balloons with hot air. As they expanded, Becky increased the power until a roaring jet of orange fire shot into each balloon.

I boarded the deck, and turned to give Tim a farewell wave. He stood by his brother, bouncing from one foot to the next. I gave him a quizzical look, just as Max echoed, *fly!*

And we took to the sky.

"*Wait for me!*"

The balloon soared into the air, wrenching free of the last staked rope. I dropped to my knees and peered down over the edge to see Tim swinging from the end of it.

"Tim you crazy fool!" I couldn't contain my laughter as I hauled the rope upwards with all my strength. Tim scrambled up onto the deck beside me.

"I want to come too!"

"You should have just said so!"

He clutched his knees, exhaling a breath of relief.

When the balloon had soared high enough, and the ranchers' cheers had dwindled to a low squeak far below, Becky shut off the bovithrusters.

"To the North!" Mother announced, took her seat in the Captain's chair, and started pedalling. The engine *clanked*, the propeller whirred, slowly at first, accelerating round and around until it blurred almost completely out of sight. *Hhhhrrrrrrrrrmmmmmmmmm.* And the Cloud Cruiser surged forwards.

PART FOUR
BISCUITS

Chapter Nineteen

The Cloud Cruiser lived up to its name as we soared across the skies. Wispy white mist proved no match for the magnificent flying machine. When the clouds broke, we were treated to spectacular views of the grassy hills far below, and the herds of animals that grazed there.

I spied buffaloes, goats and even wild dogs chasing around in packs. Max heard their yaps and pricked his ears to peer over the side, but he whimpered and preferred to stick close by my heel. *Scary!* "We're so high, aren't we boy?" I ruffled his head.

"What are they?" Becky pointed to some long necked creatures that were nibbling on the leaves of tall trees.

"Those are giraffes," Kane answered. "Didn't you go to school?" He gave us a look of disdain.

"Not everyone could afford to go to fancy kingschool you know, cabin *boy*." She mocked Kane's accent quite perfectly. He stuck his tongue into his cheek in a grimace. Becky poked again, "Go make yourself useful and refill the bovithrusters. We might need to make a quick getaway."

"Yes Miss," Kane replied in a squeak that I suspected was his own attempt to mimic Becky's voice, but coming from him sounded utterly ridiculous. I snorted a laugh.

Becky hit me on the arm.

"And don't *spill any*," she added as he pushed past us. She turned to me and spoke quietly, "Billy, I still don't trust him. I'm not sure we should have him with us."

"I know, I've been thinking about that. But he might actually be useful later... He knows how to fight."

She eyed me. "So, he's going to fight the giant tree monster, is he? With his fists?"

"No." I hesitated. "Well, no. But, you know." I glanced at Max. He watched us, and wagged his little stump.

She sighed. "He better fix you, boy." She patted his nose gently, and he gave her finger a lick. "Although, we don't need him to make that wish. Any one of us could do it."

"True," I admitted.

We turned to watch Kane lift up the barrel of bovithane from a trap door in the deck, then struggle to pour some into one of the bovithruster tanks.

"I said *don't spill it!*" Becky stormed off. "How incapable are you, cabin *boy?*"

We took turns in the driver's seat throughout the day. Even Mother's bountiful energy had its limit, apparently. Flying proved to be an infinitely faster way to travel than walking, and I wondered if I would ever see the world the same way again.

In the Khazi, Ged had remarked at how small the world was, but he couldn't have been more wrong. We just all lived in a tiny part of it. The farther north we flew, the more beautiful it became. There were no cities up here, no signs of civilisation, no industry. Just the wilds.

Mother had built two storage compartments into the deck of the Cruiser, and Becky had kept my backsack safely within one of them. After my turn pedalling, I took out my sketchpad for the first time since Kane and me were sent to prison. I sat on the edge and added all these new lands to my map.

The ground grew lumpier. Forests started to mingle with

the grasses, and streams cut through the land like dark green veins. In the distance I spied another river, and assumed it to be just like all the others. But as we flew closer, a low rumble drifted up towards us, like a never ending thunderclap echoing off the hills.

"Behold, Cloudmates! The Saw River!" Mother declared as the sun sank low in the western sky, and Big Blue started his ponderous climb in the east.

We turned left towards the setting sun and flew above the raging torrent of water gushing noisily below. Reflecting the sun, the water flowed golden and bright.

Somewhere up ahead, See-Saw Lake awaited us. And the monster who dwelled there.

Later, I sat at the front of the deck with Becky. She dozed with her head resting against my shoulder as I watched the stars come out. Slowly, I began to notice two sets of stars, one above, and one below. *I must be tired.* I rubbed my eyes and yawned. Sure enough, more stars appeared in the ground below us, mirroring the sky above. *It's the lake!*

"Becky, look." I gently nudged her, and she gave a sleepy groan. "It looks like *two* skies."

She opened her eyes, and gasped. "Wow. It's beautiful."

See-Saw Lake stretched for miles around, a vast expanse of glassy black water reflecting the stars. I could make out the shapes of dark hillsides lined with trees all along the lake's edges. Off to our right, I glimpsed the light of a campfire in a clearing between the trees. "Look." I pointed at the trees, glowing in the firelight.

"Someone's down there!" Becky said. We stood, and guided Mother towards it. She steered the balloon into position, hovering above the clearing, and we slowly descended.

A shriek pierced the still night air.

"*Waaah!*"

Whoever was down there probably wasn't expecting

flying visitors.

I peered over the edge, and saw a figure standing by the fire. It was too dark to see their face but the shriek sounded like a man. Behind him, I saw a small log cabin.

Kane abruptly tossed one of the rope ladders over the side. "I'll handle him." He disappeared over the edge.

"What do you mean 'handle him'?" I said, alarmed. "Wait!"

I scrambled down after him.

I dropped off the last rung and rolled in the dirt.

"Who are you? *Waah!*" the man cried. "Get away from me! La alaalala laaaaa *I can't hear yoooou!*" He covered his ears with his palms and fled to the cabin.

Kane marched after him. I grabbed him by the shoulder.

"What are you doing, Kane?"

"Let go of me, boy." He shrugged me off, and continued towards the cabin.

The man ran inside and slammed the door shut.

"We don't have to kill him!"

Kane stopped. He snorted and turned back to me. "Kill him? Why would I kill him?"

"I, uhh, just thought, you know..."

"Do not presume to know me, boy. I was merely going to introduce myself. It's rude to interrupt a man during dinner." He gestured to the campfire, and the spit of fish that were crisping nicely over it.

"That's not what you said when you jumped off the balloon," I pointed out.

He smiled, one of his creepy knowing smiles. The firelight danced within his eyes. "Old habit."

"Billy!" Becky ran to us. Tim and Mother were securing the Cruiser to the ground. "Who was that?"

"I don't know." I turned back to the cabin. "But I'm not sure if we're welcome."

"One of us should go and knock," Becky suggested.

"Good idea," I agreed. Kane opened his mouth to speak. "Not you. I'll go. Wait here."

Max padded along beside me as I approached the cosy-looking cabin. It had been built on the edge of the tall evergreen forest, with a short path cutting through the trees leading to the lake. An upturned rowing boat rested on the pathway, and an axe jutted out of a stump next to a stack of firewood.

Before I reached the door, it burst open.

The man came out armed with a slender rifle, and aimed it at my head. "Stay back! I can't hear nothin' and I intend to keep it that way!" I froze, and instinctively put my hands up.

He was wearing a rounded metal helmet on his head. He looked to be about fifty, and had a prickly beard covering his chin. "*Gaah!*" He squirmed, and clanged his helmet with a fist. "I told you I can't hear...*nothin'!*" He staggered, and banged his own head again. "*Aaagh!*" He started down the wooden porch steps and his legs gave way. He tumbled into the leaves, spilling the rifle to the floor.

Kane immediately plucked up the gun. My stomach tightened for a moment, but he aimed the rifle at the man on the floor. "Rude, for a hermit, old man."

The hermit curled up into a ball, clutching his head, making strange squealing noises.

"Kane, stop! Can't you see there's—"

The man on the ground cut me off. "*something wrong with him! Yes, something very wrong!*"

I frowned. Kane started, "Wh—"

The man interrupted, "*Who are you? Who indeed!*"

Kane raised an eyebrow at me. *This is weird*, I thought.

"*Weird! Oh yes, very weird!*" the man wailed.

Max padded over and casually sniffed the strange man on the ground.

"*Biscuits?! What, aaaagh!*" He writhed around, and wriggled. "One at a time one at a tiiiime. Pleeeease."

I thought I understood. "Kane, get back." I turned to the others, who were gathering behind us. "Everyone, get back, stay on the deck, let me talk to him."

They retreated, and it was just me, Max and the man who could read people's minds.

He let out a long groan, and slowly sat up, clutching his head. Slumped in the bed of fallen leaves, he shook his head like a dog, and made several loud sucking noises with his mouth. He turned to me. "Billy, is it?"

"Yeah. How—"

"And Becky, your bit on the side, Bethany, mother, Max the dog, Tim from Joy and Kane the... Fedora Kings Man?" He tapped his helmet with a knuckle. And slurped again.

This was going to be an interesting conversation.

"Wh—"

"Name's Bob. Bob the exile, Bob the Recluse, Bob the Hermit, Bob the Old Fella, Bob of Grove, Old and New, Bob the mindreader, ohh ho!"

"Is—"

"Yup! Just a ways north. New Grove. Used to live there. Had to leave. Too many people. Too many thoughts. Drive's a man mad, dontcha know? *Mad!*"

He's been out here by himself a while...

"More than a while! How many years is it now, ohhh, must be three? Three years! Had me son, but even he's gone now. Should never have shown him the tree."

The tree? Could this be the king's real father?

"The king! Aye, the king indeed. Came to visit his old man in the forest. Ran away from home, thought it'd be better here! Should never have shown him the tree!" He paused, and studied my face a while. "*Dead?* Eaten! Ohhh no no. No! He can't be eaten! He'd be too clever for that."

He's picking things out of my brain. He must know why we—

"Yep, thought as much. Here for the tree, ain't you? Well good luck to ye. Sure didn't do me no good in the end did he? All I wanted was to understand Maggie's mind! Ohhh Maggie, I only wanted your love, not this *curse!*" He sobbed. "You'll find him in the lake on the morn. Gotta wait for ol' Blue to drag the waters to t'other side first.

You won't miss him!" He gestured at the path through the woods, which led to the lakeside. "Ohhh Maggie!"

I stood and left him to his fish.

Back at the Cloud Cruiser, the others waited in a huddle.

"What's his story?" Tim asked. "He seems loopy." He twirled his fingers around his head, and gave a whistle.

"Yeah, poor bloke. I think we're definitely in the right place. From what I could tell, he came from a town to the north called Grove, and must have been in love with some woman called Maggie. I think he found the Wishing Tree in the lake, and wished to read her mind so he could woo her. But, it uhh, backfired I guess. Oh, and he's also the king's real father."

"Blimey," Mother said.

That's when I noticed Kane was missing.

"Tim! You had one job!" Becky scolded him.

"I'm sorry, Miss Becky!"

"We have to find him!"

"I know where he'll be," I said.

I jumped down from the deck. "Max, here boy." Max bounded up, tongue dangling. I sent, *Track Kane! Find the bad man!*

His ears folded away and he hung his head. *Bad man?* He echoed, whimpering. Hesitantly, he sniffed the ground, and bolted into the trees towards the lake. Mother stayed to guard the balloon, while Becky, Tim and me ran after him.

It was dark under the trees, but we soon emerged on the shoreline of the lake, under the blue moonlight. Max sniffed the muddy ground and looked up.

A figure stood on the bank beside a boulder, gazing across the water. He had the gun hoisted over his shoulder.

"Kane!" I shouted.

He turned to us. "What?" he replied innocently.

"What are you doing?" Becky demanded.

"Nothing. Just taking a walk."

Yeah, right.

Kane cocked his head at the boulder. "What do you make of this, then?"

It was no ordinary boulder. A tree had been carved into its face, just like the one outside the cave in Hale. "I've seen one like it before. I think it marks the location of a Wishing Tree... But Bob said the tree is submerged until the morning. We have to wait."

He didn't answer straight away. "Good for you. Now, can I finish my walk?"

"Give us the gun."

He held it out in front of him, as if he'd never seen it before. "What, this? But what if a bear should jump out and attack me?"

I felt my stomach tensing up again. "It's not yours."

"Oh, relax. I'll just do a sweep of the area. I don't feel as though my skills have been used to their full potential today." His eyes fixed on Becky when he said that. "I'll return it to the crazy old fool on my way back. Go prepare some supper or something." He turned his back on us and continued patrolling up the lakeside.

"I'll watch him, Billy," Tim offered. "I won't lose him this time."

"Okay. Just be careful."

"I will. And supper actually sounds like a good idea." He grinned, and walked off in the direction of Kane.

"He can't reach the tree until morning, and neither can we," Mother said, once we were back on the Cruiser. "Let him wander around as much as he likes. We just have to wake up before him."

Big Blue lumbered across the sky. It would be dawn by the time the lake had shifted. If Bob was right, the tree would be revealed to us then...

Mother pulled a bunch of sheepskin blankets out from one of the deck compartments and laid them out. None of us slept until Kane and Tim returned. Kane sat down, thankfully unarmed, ate his share of the meal and promptly fell asleep on a blanket. Tim soon followed, Mother not long after that. Becky and I curled up together, and she drifted off to sleep. I lay next to her, with Max sprawled out by my feet, snoring. *Some guard dog you are, boy.* His mouth twitched, and his paws wriggled.

I eyed Kane warily. He had his back to me. *Must wake up before him. Don't oversleep. Don't oversleep...*

Dreams found me.

I was woken by this: *FWOOSSSSSSSSH.*

"Cripes!"

Mother had woken before any of us, and was preparing the balloon.

"What time is it?" I asked sleepily.

"Not even dawn."

"What are you doing?"

She gave the balloons another burst of heat. *FWISH.* "Taking precautions. Today, we bargain with a monster, William. In times like these, it always pays to have a means of escape ready."

"Bargained with many monsters before, have you?" Kane quipped, sitting up in his makeshift bed.

"Oh yes." She didn't elaborate. Instead, she turned to me and grinned excitedly. "Today I'm going to show you how to strike a real deal, William. One that doesn't involve jeopardising the safety of your entire family."

Kane stood, and quickly put his jacket on.

"Not you," Mother ordered. "You will stay here." She added, "And you, and you," pointing to Becky and Tim. "Be ready to lift off at a moment's notice. Keep an eye out for any signs of danger, such as William running and screaming through the trees. Things like that. We'll be back after we've saved the world." She marched from the Cruiser with her head held high.

I sent Max a command. *Guard Becky.* He *wuffed* softly, and sat by her heel.

I exchanged a look with Becky, and followed Mother

into the lakeside woods.

As we stepped out from the trees beside the rock carving, the first thing I noticed was that the lakeside was no longer the lakeside. A wide expanse of mud lay before us. Dawn was breaking, and Big Blue hovered above the far end of the lake, after having dragged the water with it to the west.

In the middle of the mud-plain, I saw the tree.

A modest, bushy head sprouted out of a bony trunk. From here, it looked to be no taller than a horse. I took a deep breath, and the two of us stepped down the bank and started across the mud. The lake was enormous, and the sky slowly brightened as we waded through the ankle deep sludge, each step making a squelch.

My gaze never left the strange tree. It jutted out of a pile of rocks at its base, and looked very peculiar sitting there by itself amid the sea of brown.

Finally, we reached it.

This one had eyes. They opened and peered up at us from within the glistening rocks at the base of the trunk. Two melon-sized, slimy green balls, one bigger than the other, and slanted at such an angle it gave the impression of raising an eyebrow at us, even though it had no eyebrows...

"Who goes there?" it asked, in a slushy voice. What I had mistaken for rocks, were in fact lips, and rather than being solid, appeared squishy and full of liquid. As it spoke, the rocks parted and wriggled like a caterpillar's back. "Oh, more little fleshlings, is it?"

"Greetings, tree beast of the lake," Mother announced, with a bow. I stood beside, and slightly behind her, as per her instructions. "I am Bethany of Hale, wandering pilgrim of the land and skies, seeker of knowledge, wife and mother. This is my son, William." I raised a hand. "We have travelled far to meet with you, oh great mysterious one."

The creature's melony eyes blinked. "Okay."

An awkward silence lingered.

Mother hesitated. "We need your help."

"Don't they all," the creature sighed, and shifted in the mud. The tree rose up making a wet, slurping sound. Its neck seemed to be made of mud, but I sensed a squishy belly of sorts underneath the layer of slime. The melon eyes became level with our heads, and they straightened and peered at us curiously. "What do you want? And don't tell me you want to be the queen."

Mother seemed to consider that briefly, then shook her head. "No. We just want to know how to kill you."

"Excuse me?"

"I mean, one like you."

"Definitely not you," I added.

"He escaped, didn't he?" the creature pondered. "That explains why I can't feel him anymore." It wheezed, and tightened as if stretching after waking from a nap. Then it relaxed again and sank back into position.

"He's eaten people. And now he's loose, somewhere out here." Mother stood straight and spoke in that serious, formal tone. "Creature, I wish for you to rid us of the monster."

I tensed, bracing for something dramatic to happen. I expected flames, for some reason.

Nothing happened.

"I can't," it said.

Mother crossed her arms. "Oh. Why not? I thought you were some kind of Wishing Tree?"

"I'm not."

"Well, what are you then?"

"There is no word for me in your tongue."

The other one said the same thing, I recalled.

"Well, explain it to me. I'm a scientist, don't you know."

The creature gurgled, and the mud beneath our feet bubbled in little bursts. *It's laughing!*

"Oh ho. Heh." It stopped gurgling, and continued to peer at us with the melons. But it didn't answer Mother's question.

"How rude," she remarked, and planted her hands on her hips. "Well then, tell me if I'm close. I believe you're a sentient biological mass with an abundance of energy and power. You have so much power, you can't help but share it with the lesser creatures that occasionally come across you, namely us. To our feeble minds, it would seem that you are capable of granting wishes, but really it's just some form of clever science."

The melons blinked again. For a while, it didn't respond. Finally, it burped. "Not bad, I suppose."

Mother scratched her elbow.

I frowned, puzzled. "So you mean, you can't grant wishes?"

The melons shifted to me. "No."

"But what about Bob. He can read minds!"

"No, he can hear thoughts. That's what he wanted."

"But... that's, surely...?" I stammered.

"Thoughts are very noisy when you know how to listen to them. I showed him how."

Just then, a tremor shook the ground, almost unnoticeable. Perhaps it was laughing again.

I ignored it. "What about the king? You *created* a new king."

"No, I merely rid you of the old one. Turn around."

We turned. In the distance, at the point where the lake flowed into the Saw River, a thin tentacle stuck out of the mud and waved back and forth enthusiastically, like an excited toddler. It abruptly sucked back under the surface.

I traced my gaze along the mud back to my feet. *Cripes, how big is this thing?*

Mother wasn't convinced. "What about the Kingsmaids, then?"

"Oh, you don't want to know."

She leaned forward, and spoke sternly. "Yes I do."

"No, you don't. Mermaids are a smelly business."

"*Mermaids?*"

Another tremor, bigger than the first. The sun had risen, and a haze of mist floated at the far end of the lake, hovering above the water. A flock of birds took flight out of the mist and into the sky. "Uhh, Mother?"

"What about Kamuna?" Mother probed, ignoring me. "Can you tell me more of that?"

"Oh, wonderful stuff. Although my cave-dwelling brother has been hogging it all, ever since he discovered it. Not that I need any, living in this filthy lake. You know, he really had no reason to complain. I'd love a nice cosy cave."

Mother gave an impatient gesture. "The moon! Can you at least show me how to get to the moon?"

"Oh not you as well. The Old Ones are still trying to get there."

"The Old Ones?" Mother leaned closer.

"They worship the red one or something. I shouldn't tell you this, but it's not really a—"

A mighty tremor shook the mud, followed by another, and another. The tree creature twisted around to face the same direction as us. I became faintly aware of Max barking, somewhere far behind me.

But my gaze was fixed on the mist. And the monster that came marching out of it.

Chapter Twenty

"*HE HEH HEH HAH HAH HAAAAH*" the tree monster bellowed, stomping across the lake. Its huge tree trunk legs splashed water with every step. Two long arms swung by its side, made of intertwining branches, gnarled into sharp claws. And at the centre of it all, the plump, leafy tree with a cavernous maw of splinters dripping golden honey. As it came closer, I heard the low rumbling hum of countless bees, swarming around it.

I turned and ran.

And almost bumped into Kane. He grinned at me.

"What are you doing here?!" He marched past me, through the mud, heading for the tree monsters.

"William, forget him, just go!" Mother urged, stumbling ahead through the mud. I followed, as the ground shook beneath my feet.

From behind, a deep watery voice filled the air. "Gorlack! What do you think you are *doing?*"

"I've been feasting on mammoths, brother!" The cave tree's roar dwarfed the other. "Much tastier than tiny fleshlings, *ohhhh yes*. Look how I've grown!"

"The earth shake broke your mind, Gorlack. You've gone mad!"

"You live in squalor beneath the dirt, yet call *me* mad? Is it madness to roam the lands? To breathe the air? To walk and thrive and *devour the little ones?*"

"Yes you fool! It goes against everything we were put here for!"

A tiny voice spoke up then. "Monster! I wish to be the most powerful man alive. There's nothing I would desire more."

Kane, you traitor! I stopped at the edge of the mud, and turned to see the Fedora Man standing between the two tree creatures, his arms raised in the air. Max barked madly from the trees behind me.

The huge one towered over Kane, snarling a mad grin. "*Yeees*, great desire fills this one! Very ambitious! *Feed me, yes, feeeed me!*" And it bellowed laughter, shaking and growing and rising even taller. After, it snatched up Kane and buried him within the leaves of its body.

The lake tree looked puny by comparison. "You don't even realise what you're doing! Stop before you go too far, brother! Return to the ground, where you belong!"

"But it's so much better out here! Come, join me brother!"

Gorlack the giant tree monster reached down and wrapped its claws around the lake tree, and uprooted it. A huge wormlike body came up out of the lakebed with it, dripping clumps of mud. Attached to it were tentacles, all flopping about helplessly like spaghetti.

"Gorlack! *Gorlack!* Put me down you fool!"

FWOOOOSH.

The balloon! I bolted into the trees.

Mother hadn't taken off yet. She scrambled to and fro unhooking ropes, and loosening the stakes.

Becky and Tim lay sprawled on their backs on the deck. My heart leapt into my throat.

"Becky!" I sunk to my knees beside her. A thin line of blood ran down her cheek, and she gave a soft groan.

"William, help me!" Mother called.

"Becky's hurt!"

"They are just unconscious. Kane's work, no doubt. We have to get airborne, *now!* Grab the last stake!"

I did as she bid, and dived back onto the deck. I crouched beside Becky, and clutched her hand. Her chest rose and fell in long, steady breaths. The Cloud Cruiser lifted off.

As we crested the trees, Gorlack's immensity came into view. He was was chomping through the wormlike body, making a sick, squelchy sound. The lake monster poked his head between the branch claws and shrieked at us.

"*North! You must fly north! Find the Old Ones and end this madness!*"

Gorlack stuffed the spindly tree into his mouth, and silenced him.

Mother aimed the Cruiser at the monster.

"Mother, *what are you doing?*"

"Get a barrel of bovithane, Billy. Quickly."

I let out a long nervous groan, realising her plan. I heaved open the trap door, gripped the metal barrel and pulled it out.

The Cloud Cruiser rose steadily upwards.

Gorlack gnawed, making disgusting chewing noises. As he swallowed, he dropped the remainder of the fat grey wormlike body to the ground and it sank back into the lakebed. Gorlack gave an almighty belch that echoed off the hills. He bellowed laughter once more, as his body trembled and expanded, and stretched taller than all of the trees.

Mother blasted the bovithrusters, and we surged higher out of reach of his long arms. At least I hoped. She pedalled the propeller and we drifted closer.

I rested the tank on the edge of the deck, and uncorked the lid. A pungent odour stabbed my nostrils, making my eyes water.

"Wait for it, wait..." Mother instructed, slowing her pedalling to a crawl.

I gripped the tank.

The Cloud Cruiser drifted over the top of the tree monster.

"*Now!*"

I tipped the bovithane over the edge. It flowed out in thick globules, and stained Gorlack's leaves brown. It soaked the monster's head, covering it in a layer of nasty gloop.

Mother ignited her firesparker, and tossed it over the edge. It plunged into the leafy mass and disappeared.

For a moment, nothing happened.

An airy *whump* went up. Somewhere within the veil of leaves, Kane shrieked and the tree burst into flames.

"*Waaaarggghhh!!!*" Gorlack bellowed in what might have been pain, but could just as easily have been one of his throaty laughs.

The *hum* of the bees intensified as a swarm of them billowed out from within the leaves, escaping the blaze. Thick plumes of smoke quickly enveloped the balloon, choking me. I stumbled back away from the edge in a fit of coughing, taking refuge in the centre of the deck where the smoke wasn't so thick.

Tim awoke suddenly, sputtering and gasping for breath, but Becky lay on her back, still unmoving. I pulled her gently into the middle with me, trying to shield her face. Tim crawled towards us, and we huddled in the middle.

Mother pedalled and the propeller churned the smoke, creating a whirlpool of black mist that spiralled behind the Cruiser as we drifted out of the plumes.

I rubbed my stinging eyes, trying to focus. Below, Gorlack stomped through the mud leaving a tail of flying, burning leaves.

Kane flung himself out of the tree's belly. His jacket was on fire but when he landed face down in the mud, the flames were instantly quenched.

The monster reached the lake and fell into it. A tidal wave erupted around him, pooling out over the edges of the mud. The lake would be deep enough to drown us, but to the monster, it seemed little more than a big puddle.

Rain pattered against the balloons as he thrashed wildly, dousing the flames, sizzling and steaming.

"Heh heh hoh hah ha ha haaaa," his cackle signalled our failure.

I crawled to the edge to get a better view. The last of the flames sputtered out, and steam drifted off his singed leafy body in wavy tendrils. He planted one thick trunk in the lake and heaved himself upright, dripping with water droplets. He turned to face the balloon as we hovered in the sky, out of reach of those long arms. *Mother is a good pilot.*

"Billy! Is that you?" he boomed. He didn't have any eyes, just that cavernous mouth of splinters, but I still felt his gaze upon me. "I thought you'd be more appreciative of what I did for you. Or, what my bees did for you, I should say."

He roared another honk of laughter, so loud it shook the deck of the Cruiser. As it laughed, a thousand burnt, black leaves tumbled from its body and fell into the lake. New leaves began to sprout across his body, popping into place, filling in the gaps the burnt ones left. "Ahh, Kamuna," it sighed like distant thunder. "You remember it well, don't you Billy?"

Max barked.

"Ah, your canine friend. What happened to his tail?" More leaves sprouted up, plugging all the gaps.

"You should ask *your* new friend!" I shouted, pointing to Kane.

The tree reached down to pluck the muddy man up. "Who, this fleshling?" Kane's suit looked black, and he wasn't moving on the monsters palm. My stomach tightened at the sight. *He's dead.* "I don't think the skinny fleshling can hear us. But we can fix that, can't we Billy?" It grinned up at me.

The last of the leaves popped into place, and any sign of

our attempt to burn him to cinders ceased to exist. He had fully rejuvenated himself.

He floated the Fedora Man among the blackened leaves that littered the surface of the lake. Then the monster squatted down beside him. His chunky legs and gnarly arms folded away within. He looked like the same plump, leafy tree that I had once discovered in the cave, sitting atop the grassy mound. Only now he seemed almost as high as one of the ancient giants we discovered in the Forest of Bliss.

A whirring *hum* of bees emanated, tingling my ears, as the swarm returned, streaming back into the creature's body. Black leaves danced across the surface of the rippling lake. Kane's body bobbed up and down in the gentle waves. Before my eyes, the water appeared to glow faintly golden.

He's bringing him back, just like he did to me.

Mother looked hypnotised. She stood precariously close to the edge of the deck, gaping down. "William... that stuff... if I could get a sample..."

"Mother, no. We have to get out of here! While he's distracted."

"But... that's Kamuna..." She gazed at the sparkling ripples.

I realised we were descending. "Uhh, Mother. Seriously, I think we should go."

Kane coughed. *Already? So fast!*

The tree leaned down. "Welcome back, ambitious fleshling." Then, back at us. "Still here? Perhaps you want to stay and enjoy the show? This fellow made a wish, and I just can't help but indulge myself. You won't see anything from up there, though, so *come closer.*" It stood with frightening speed. A snake-like arm shot out and coiled itself around the deck of the Cloud Cruiser.

I fell over and landed beside Becky. Max yelped and barked. Mother clutched the bovithrusters, aimed them backwards, and jabbed them on.

Flames fired out the back. I heard a harsh cracking of tearing wood. We broke free of Gorlack's grip. The Cruiser flew and we fled across the sky.

"How are we supposed to kill *that?*" Mother yelled.

The Cloud Cruiser raced through the air, pummelling me with wind, and all I could do was keep my head low, crouching beside Becky. After a while, the bovithrusters began to cough and sputter. With a final *bang*, they choked out and went silent.

We quietly drifted along. Mother refilled the tanks. We had enough for one more refill before we ran out completely. She decided to pedal for a while, to conserve it.

Timothee sat with his back to me.

"You okay, Tim?" I asked.

"I think so. Kane, he... I am sorry, Billy."

"It's alright, I should have expected it. I was a fool to trust him. He never intended to help Max, or any of us. He was after the Wishing Tree all along."

Tim didn't turn around, only nodded.

Becky gave a soft groan. I pushed the hair out of her eyes, examining her head. "Becky? Can you hear me?"

She opened her eyes slowly, squinting. "Billy? Ugh," she grimaced. "My head. Kane..."

"It's okay. Try to relax. We're safe now." I parted her hair and searched for the wound. She had a bump and a small cut, nothing too serious. I dabbed a rag with water from one of our skins and gently cleaned it. She winced.

Max nuzzled my arm. "Not now, boy." *Beckyyyy*, he echoed. *Bad man. Bad man!* He nuzzled my arm again, harder. My hand slipped and touched his flat head, and I was back in the forest by the cabin before we had taken off.

Guard! Becky! I sit beside *Becky. Billy* and the *biscuit lady* are running away into the trees. The *bad man* is still here and he makes my tail throb when he comes near so I stay close to her. She tidies up the smelly sheep beds, and the other one is helping, but the *bad man* just watches.

Something far away through the trees makes a *thump*, but the others don't hear anything, so it must be okay. Then another *thump! Woof!*

Becky is talking to me. "Max, quiet. *Billy* back soon." *Woof!* No, not *Billy*, something bigger. I try to tell her, but she doesn't listen, and she bends over to pack the sheep blankets into the floor.

The *bad man* steps towards me, and I smell his mischief. *Woof!* He whispers to the other one, and he nods, and the *bad man* stands back. He tries to kick me! I bounce away, and *woof! Woof!* The other one goes up behind *Becky*. He hits her over the head!

Woof! Guard! Becky! Woof! WOOF! WOOF WOOF!

"Good. Lie down." The *bad man* is telling the other one. He lies down. The bad man turns to me, holding...

A stick! He waves the stick at me and *yes I want to fetch the stick, throw it for me!* He hurls it far into the trees and I run after it. Running through the trees to fetch the stick, yes, yes a stick a stick!

Wait. Becky! Guard! I turn around and run back to the big fat bird but *Becky* and the other one are asleep on the ground. The *bad man* is gone! I catch his scent, near the trees. *Billy!* He's following *Billy*, so I run after him.

I snapped back to myself, Becky resting against me, and Max nuzzling my arm. *Bad man!* he echoed, turning his head towards Tim.

No way. How could he? I involuntarily hugged Becky a little tighter. *I thought he was my friend. Why would he do this?* The answer had to be Kane. He must have turned him, somehow. *How didn't I notice?*

"Billy, I'm okay, really. Just a headache. It feels better now." She smiled at me, and I kissed her forehead. "Where is Kane?" she asked.

"He's, uhh... he's gone. Gorlack took him."

"Gorlack?" she frowned.

223

"Ah, that's what my tree monster's name is, apparently."

"Oh." She still sounded groggy.

"Maybe you need to rest some more?" I suggested.

"No!" Mother piped up behind me. She was pedalling the propeller furiously. "She must stay awake, William. She's been hit on the head, if she falls back asleep, she might not wake up again!"

Becky looked frightened. "I'm okay! I'll stay awake." She grimaced again. Then she put her arms around me and rested her head against my chest.

We were well within the boundaries of the Great Plains now, heading north.

I glanced at Tim, who had moved to the front of the deck. He sat cross legged, fiddling with one of the guy ropes. I noticed the stake was missing. I met his eyes, and he immediately turned away.

How do I handle this? I thought miserably.

Later, Mother spotted a ragged encampment of tents, teepees and wooden shacks ahead of us. The people of the Plains.

"This must be Grove!" Mother called. "We can rest here, and see if they know anything about these Old Ones."

Bob the mind reader came from here. Or the thought-hearer... somehow that didn't have the same ring to it. Anyway, the village would be a good opportunity to confront Tim. I didn't want to do it in front of Becky or Mother. *He must have had his reasons...*

We landed on the edge of the settlement, to the terror of the folk below. Horses whinnied and reared up, dogs barked and a small flock of sheep panicked within their pen, barging into the wooden fenceposts.

"Woooah, easy!" a woman shouted at the terrified animals. A little girl clutched her by the waist, peering around her legs at us. The shepherd woman stared as she struggled to hold the gate of the pen closed.

One sheep leapt the fence. "Oh *no!* Argh!" Another

followed, then another. One by one, the entire flock all jumped the fence and bolted into the midst of the encampment, a wild train of fluffy balls. Even her own sheepdog fled at the sight of the Cloud Cruiser. "Great!" the woman remarked, exasperated.

We secured the balloon to the ground. "Becky, rest here," Mother urged gently. "But don't sleep! I need you to keep the balloons inflated. I don't want to linger here long."

"Leave it to me," Becky's voice was weak. She leaned against the control panel below the bovithrusters and clutched the pullstring in her hand. She gave it a small tug, and a belch of fire spat into the balloons.

"Good," Mother nodded. "You're proving to be a wonderful co-pilot."

"I'll be back soon," I assured her. Becky nodded, straining a smile.

We stepped off the ramp, and greeted the shepherd.

She eyed us warily. "Who are you? What do you want?" The little girl still hung around her waist, giving us the same cautious look. She had a similar curly tangle of hair as the shepherd, and they both wore rough brown cotton shirts and baggy trousers.

"Greetings, Plainswoman," Mother introduced herself. "We didn't mean to frighten you or your daughter."

"What about my flock? It'll take me all day to round them back up!"

Beyond, sheep were running riot in the camp. I heard yelps as cookfire pots toppled and dogs barked at the animals as they bundled around causing havoc.

"I might be able to help with that," I offered. "Here, boy." Max padded to my side.

She looked at him, and her lip curled in disbelief. "What kind of dog is that? He's not even got a tail!"

That stung, but I tried to ignore it. Max wagged his stump, oblivious. "We'll get them back for you."

"Please, we don't have a lot of time. I bring dire news,"

Mother spoke with urgency. It was odd to see her act so formal but it seemed to come naturally to her. Once again I found myself wondering if father knew this side of her... She led the shepherd away into the camp, asking if they had a leader here that she could speak to.

Tim went to follow but I grabbed him by the shoulder and pushed him around the back of a tepee, out of sight of Becky. I pinned him against a post.

"Billy!" he acted surprised. "What are you doing?"

"What's wrong with you? How could you do that to her?"

"What? I... it was... I didn't—"

"Tim! I *know*, okay? What did Kane say to you?"

Tim's cheeks flushed. He squirmed, but I didn't let go of his shirt. "He promised me... I am sorry Billy. I screwed up. *Curse me!* Curse me to Tannerus, Billy. I screwed up!"

I gripped his shirt tighter and repeated, "What did he promise you?"

"Anything I wanted... He said you would try to take control of the Wishing Tree. He said you'd keep it to yourselves. And you did. You left us behind, just like he said you would."

I loosened my grip. "You wanted a wish."

"Of course!"

I released his shirt. "Why didn't you just tell me? Why did you talk to *Kane?*"

"I didn't. He talked to me. I hardly had a choice, Billy. The Cloud Cruiser is small, I couldn't get away from him. You are always with Becky, and Bethany is usually flying... his ideas, they just made sense."

"You hit Becky on the head with a *stake!*" I hissed. "What part of that makes sense to you?"

He looked at the floor.

I took a step back. "You're not coming with us anymore."

He met my eyes again, distraught.

I shook my head. "I made a mistake with Kane, I won't

do it again. You should have stayed at Capella, Tim. You had your brother there, at least."

"Billy, please—"

I turned with clenched fists and strode into the camp, Max at my heel. *Go ahead*, I sent. Max snorted and ran between the tents, cutting off a stray sheep that tried to flee.

So this is what betrayal tastes like.

Max ran back and forth between the teepees, chasing the panicking animals. He drove them all into a bunched huddle and soon enough we were marching them back into the pen.

I locked them in. Tim stood nearby, watching us, his expression full of dismay. I couldn't even bear to look at him. I stalked into the camp in search of Mother.

I found her sitting around a campfire, attended by the shepherd woman and a bunch of other ragged-looking Plainsfolk.

"Your sheep are safe," I told the shepherd, taking a seat on a bench beside the fire.

She gave me a bewildered look. "What? Oh, thank you." Max lay at my feet, panting. "He's pretty good," she said distractedly.

I smiled. "We've done that before."

"You don't say." She turned back to Mother, who was talking with a middle aged woman wearing a battered leather jerkin, boots and a wide-rimmed hat woven out of grass. She looked like a cross between one of the Capella ranchers and some wild huntress. *Their leader*, I thought.

"If that's true," she was saying. "Then we must pack up and leave."

A murmur of disapproval rippled through the ragtag band of Plainsfolk.

"But we've only just settled again," one man said.

"Aye, and where would we go this time?" a woman added, clutching her daughter in her lap. "Wherever we go, *something* drives us out."

"You must go, this creature is unstoppable!" Mother declared.

"And where might you suggest we go?"

Mother shrugged, "We are heading north," she suggested. "You could follow us."

The gathering fell silent at the suggestion. A goat bleated somewhere behind me.

"We came from the north," whispered the leader. "There is nothing for us there but ashes."

"What happened?" I asked.

"We were driven from our home in the shadow of the mountains. By fire."

"Fire from the skies..." the shepherd murmured.

A look of fear passed between the faces of most of the group, and some were shaking their heads defiantly.

"Fire from the sky?" Mother asked bluntly. "What do you mean?"

"We mean what we say," the leader answered. "Fire fell from the skies, and destroyed our homes, burnt our crops. We fled from the north, and we will not go back there. Our only option lies east, in the desert..."

"No, Maggie. We can't live in sand!" cried the shepherd. "There is no water, no grass for the sheep—"

She cut her off. "Tannerus does well enough. Why can't we? There are herds of other animals in the deserts, and there are canyons with streams. We will survive this, just as we survived everything that came before."

Mother was tapping her chin. "This fire, was it natural?"

Maggie hunched forward, resting an elbow over her thigh, the other palm on her knee. "Nothing natural about it. Dunno where you come from, but here in the Plains, clouds bring rain, not burning barrels."

"*Barrels?*" Mother's eyes widened.

"Aye, fiery barrels, like kegs of ale, all ablaze. They fell from the clouds and onto our crops, exploding and burning and destroying everything. We had to flee."

Mother had that look on her face again. The look of

deep concentration, lost in a world of thoughts. She stared blankly through the leader.

The woman returned the stare. "What?"

Mother didn't reply.

"She gets like this, its normal," I assured Maggie.

"*The Old Ones!*" Mother blurted, jolting to her feet. She turned and strode away towards the balloon.

Maggie frowned, annoyed. "Who?" She turned to me, baffled. "What is with her?"

I feigned a shrug. "It was nice to meet you. Farewell!" I went to go, then turned back to her. "Oh, by the way. Bob is living just south of here, near the lake. He *really* loves you, Maggie."

She gave a start. "Bob is alive? Is he well?"

I considered that. I pictured him wearing his little helmet, clanging it like a madman. And the way he rolled around in the dirt when we approached him... "I wouldn't say *well*, but he is alive. If you decide to find him, don't all go at once."

She nodded. "I will. Thank you."

I chased after Mother.

"It's the Old Ones, William," she explained, as we made our way through the encampment.

"How can you know that?" I asked, marching to keep up.

"Because of what the creature at the lake told us. It said the Old Ones were to the north. It said they were also trying to get to Little Red, William. The moon!"

"Yeah, I guess...but how—"

"I saw one, William. When I first flew the Cloud Cruiser, the Mark I, right after you found me at Barrow. I reached the edge of the sky and I *saw* something fall from beyond. I think it came from Little Red."

"Really? Wow!"

"I think the Old Ones are scientists, just like me. *Flaming barrels from the sky*," she scoffed. "They have bovithane! Or something similar. But not only that..." She stopped and grabbed my arm.

"What?"

"It's a weapon, William. They have a *weapon*!"

"Oh! A weapon to fight Gorlack!"

"Maybe," she agreed. "We have to find them first."

The two balloons towered above the tents, easily visible from the other side of the camp. It wasn't until we passed a particularly large tepee that we could see the deck, and the two figures fighting on top of it.

Chapter Twenty-One

"Becky?" I ran ahead.

Becky pinned Tim's face against the floor of the deck with her knee, and held him in some kind of strangling hold amid a tangle of arms and legs.

Tim shrieked, "I'm sorr*eeeiiiieeeeeeeeee!*"

"You will be you creepy moron!"

"Becky!" I arrived at the scene, unsure of what to do next. Max leapt up, growling, and started snapping at Tim's flailing foot.

"Billy!" Becky looked up. "It was him! Not Kane. This little jerk knocked me out, and he thinks I'll be okay with that." She was clearly feeling better again.

"I know. Max showed me. Come on, let him go, we can talk about this now. *Max*, down boy!"

I stepped in, pushing Max away and the other two disentangled themselves.

"What is there to talk about?" Becky demanded. "He's not coming with us."

"I know," I said, turning to Tim. "I told you as much. What part of that didn't you understand, Tim?"

His lip quivered, and he rubbed his arm. "I just wanted to apologise. I didn't want to leave like this."

I looked to Becky, who folded her arms. I sighed. "Well, go on then."

Tim's cheeks were red and he shifted his feet. He managed to meet Becky's eyes. "I'm sorry. I was jealous. Of you two."

That took me by surprise. "Wh—"

"I just wanted a chance to make my own wish like you, spood. I wanted to wish for my own girl. And I did something stupid to try to get it... *curse me*, Billy. Curse me to Tannerus!"

I didn't know what to say. I looked to Becky. Her scowl softened.

Mother's laughter pierced the air. "Ohhh hooo, you young whipper-snappers are so funny. The way you see the world!" A broad grin covered her face. "You think William and Becky here came together because of a tree? *Ha!*" She giggled.

Timothee blinked, looking confused.

Mother continued, "Trees don't grant wishes any more than I can cross a chicken with a cow. Believe me, I tried." She gestured to Becky and me, standing side by side. "When two substances are attracted to each other, the magic happens. It's just like when I combine the Bovinated Bottom Burp with the right amount of liquidation particle molecules." She tugged the pullstring, and the bovithruster burped a fireball. "It's not magic, it's just chemistry."

Becky wound her fingers through my own. I thought Mother was done, but on she went.

"Why, I remember when William was running around in his little loincloth!" I reddened, and looked at her aghast. "He was such a slow boy. Scared of snails! Hated going outside, much preferred playing with his crayons." She studied me with such pride. "But look at you now."

Becky squeezed my hand, beaming at me.

Mother turned to Timothee. "My William grew up. He dove into the world and tried to make something of his life. *That's* what brought him to Becky. Wishful thinking will only get you so far. At some point, you have to just get out there."

Quiet settled over us, as her words hung in the air.

Timothee nodded with a sigh. "Curse me to Tannerus..." he mumbled.

Just then, a plainsgirl remarked loudly behind us. "Tannerus? Why would we go there? It's full of sand!"

I turned to see her talking to an older man, her father I assumed. "Because that's what Maggie has decided. We're leaving at dawn."

"Dawn?" she gaped at him. "But my things, my—"

"Best get started then!" he walked away.

Tim tried to hide his grin. He turned to us sheepishly. "I am glad I met you, Billy the spood." He looked to Becky. "I am truly sorry..." He stood up straight, mussed his hair and straightened his jacket. "Farewell, Cloudmates."

And with that, he hopped down into the encampment and strode up to the plainsgirl. "Are you going to Tannerus? What a coincidence, I have always wanted to go there!"

She looked baffled, but smiled. "Really?"

"Allow me to help you pack your things, miss. I do not know the way, and am seeking a travel companion..."

The two of them walked away into the camp. And Tim was gone.

While the people of the Plains packed away their tents and supplies, Becky, Mother and I prepared the Cloud Cruiser for another takeoff. A small crowd gathered to see the spectacle.

"We're operating on a skeleton crew now!" Mother announced. It was true. Without Kane or Timothee, the deck felt more spacious, slightly emptier.

Mother lit the bovithrusters.

I felt sad to leave Tim behind. I spotted him waving at us from the crowd, standing beside his new female friend.

Becky leaned over the rope-railing and shouted at him.

"Tim! I forgive you, okay?"

Even from this distance, I could see his cheeks redden.

She spoke quietly to me. "I understand why he did it. He's not a bad guy... just a bit creepy."

"Thank you," Tim called back.

The balloons lifted us into the air.

"We will meet again, Tim!" I called over the edge.

"I hope so, Billy!"

We waved until the balloon raised high enough to obscure him and the crowd below.

"So, where to, Captain?" Becky asked.

Mother teased us with a smile. Instead of answering, she strolled across the deck to the other side, beckoning us to follow. We overlooked the Great Plains, a vast stretch of flat tussock, swamp, and beyond that, frosty tundra. Miles away, as far as the eye could see, the horizon looked jagged and pointy. A long row of bumps and spikes jutted into the sky, like tiny teeth.

"Have you ever seen a mountain?" Mother whispered.

We gazed at the horizon. "No," we both whispered back.

"Well then, let's go find some to fly over."

Before the mountains, there were mammoths. Lots of mammoths.

We cruised over the plains using the pedal-powered propeller. It made for a steady journey, but with only one remaining barrel of bovithane, we decided it would be best to save it for an emergency. A life or death situation didn't seem all that unlikely, given the recent turn of events.

Flying so slowly had one thing going for it: I could sketch to my heart's content.

Whenever it wasn't my turn to pedal, I sat on the edge taking in the magnificent views, sketchpad and pencils in hand. Only a couple hours north of the Grove encampment, I saw my first real living mammoth. The great shaggy beast stomped along by itself, walking within a trail of flattened grass. His woolly coat swayed with every step and his tusks stretched out in front of him like two curved swords. When we passed over his head, he lifted his fat trunk to us and trumpeted loudly, startling Max awake. He peered over the side and cocked his head at the lumbering beast. He echoed, *Monster?*

"Not a monster, a *mammoth*," I corrected him. *Mammothster*, he sent back. "Close enough." I scratched behind his ear.

Shortly after that, I spotted a whole line of mammoths marching along in single file. For every two big ones, a baby half the size trotted between.

"Becky, you have to come see this. You too, Mother!"

They came and sat down either side of me.

"Aww they're so cute," Becky remarked. "I want one!"

"Ahe, no you don't," Mother scoffed. "They may look cute from way up here, but that's because we're out of range of the smell."

She has even been to the plains before? Where hasn't she been? "You've seen one up close?" I asked.

"Closer than I would have liked! I went across the See River to the corner of the plains just north of Aston, searching for a special mushroom. I didn't find any, but I stumbled upon a baby mammoth who did. He was chomping his way through a whole load of them, and they didn't agree with him at all. When he saw me coming, he trumpeted, and not from his trunk. I almost passed out from the smell, but it gave me an idea... so, I lured him over the river and brought him back to my lab in Aston to try and make use of his intense gases. He didn't seem to mind me looking after him. I knew he had been abandoned by his herd or gotten separated somehow, poor thing. Mammoths don't usually roam that far south."

"You brought a *mammoth* into a town?" Becky giggled.

"Of course. The mayor didn't approve, though. He ordered me to release him back into the wild. I tried to bring him to Hale, instead. My boys would have loved to meet a mammoth! We got to the bottom of the Scar, though, and he ran away. The See River runs through the Scar, all the way from the Great Plains. So, I figured he was trying to go home. Never saw him again."

Gorlack had a mammoth skeleton in his cave. That's where Max found my tusk...

"I never did manage to perfect my all-natural flammable gas until much later, when I discovered bovithane..." She gazed down at the herd of shaggy mammoths, and gave a wistful sigh. "If it weren't for those down there, we wouldn't be up here." She returned to the driver's seat to carry on pedalling.

The mammoth family below trundled ever on.

"I wonder where they're going," Becky pondered.

"I was wondering that about us," I replied, looking ahead.

The mountainous horizon slowly stretched taller the closer we came. I had only ever seen snowy-peaks in books, but they looked far more beautiful in real life.

The world darkened, and the moons emerged, illuminating the plains in soft purple. In the dimness of the night, the air fell silent. The only sound in the world was the propeller, whirring behind me as I took my turn pedalling. Mother was curled up under a sheepskin, while Max dozed beside Becky, sitting cross-legged on the deck. Mother said she shouldn't sleep tonight, because of the knock to her head. She yawned, sleepily rubbing Max's belly.

Max lifted his head and pricked his ears.

"What is it, boy?" Becky said.

He bounded to his feet and came to stand beside me, staring out the back of the craft, his head cocked.

He heard something. I stopped pedalling, and the propeller slowly came to a halt. We drifted along.

I listened. Nothing.

"What, Max?" I whispered. He glanced at me, then whimpered.

Boof.

Somewhere behind us, very faint. *Boof.*

Gorlack's footsteps echoed over the plains. *Boof... Boof... Boof.*

He's following us. I gulped, exchanged a fearful look with Becky.

Max echoed, *Mammothster?*

"No, boy. Monster."

I pedalled again, faster this time.

Halfway through the night, Mother awoke to swap with me and I stretched out next to Becky under a blanket. She let me use her lap as a pillow, and she played with my hair. *Wow, no wonder Max likes her belly rubs more than mine.*

"You need a trim," she teased. "All that time in prison made you look... worldly."

I chuckled, not opening my eyes. "Worldly? Is that good or bad?"

"Well, I like it," she said, and I could hear her smiling. She gently scratched the back of my head and I fell into a blissful sleep.

When I woke, dawn had broken and Becky was taking a turn at the pedals. Mother stood at the back, staring over the plains behind us.

"How's your head?" I asked Becky.

"Better. Getting tired now, though!" She puffed her cheeks.

"You should take it easy."

"It's okay. I felt cold, but this is keeping me warm. Besides, I'm not sure we can afford to go slowly..." She gestured behind her, to where Mother was standing. I went and joined her.

"Is he still following us?"

"I'm not sure," she replied, squinting through the blur of the whirling propeller. "Probably."

If he was, we couldn't see. A light mist covered the plains below, obscuring our view.

An icy gust of wind sent a shiver through me. "Brrr. It sure is getting colder up here."

Mother turned to face the front. "That'll be their fault." She pointed ahead.

A wall of mountains greeted us. They stretched from left to right, as far as you could see in either direction, a line of jagged peaks covered with snow. Rolling along at the base were many grassy hills, gradually rising higher as they neared the mountainous slopes.

One large area of grass looked darker than the rest.

"Look at that," Mother remarked, seeing it as well. "That must have been Grove, once."

We drifted over the charred remains of the old village. A blackened waste of burnt grass and mud, littered with a few tepee skeletons. It reminded me of the burnt houses I saw in Aston. *Or, Mother's labs, I should say.*

Mother rested a hand on Becky's shoulder. "Okay Miss Co-Pilot, I think you're done for now. Let me get us over these lumps. Billy, give us a blast, it's time to see what lies beyond the mountains!"

"Has anyone ever been there?"

"Nope!" Mother grinned.

Becky's face lit up with excitement. She hardly looked as though she'd stayed awake all night.

I flicked the bovithrusters on, giving the balloons a fresh burst of hot air. *FWOOOOOSH.* The Cloud Cruiser soared into a patch of fluffy clouds, high above the mountain range.

"We're going to be the first people to ever cross the mountains, Billy!" Becky's eyes were fiery and beautiful. Max bounced and barked, wagging his stump.

"I'm going to be the actual first," I boasted with a grin and ran for the front of the deck.

"Oh no you don't!" Becky bundled into me and we wrestled for the spot at the nose of the deck, clinging to the ropes, laughing.

A flaming barrel leapt upwards out of a cloud. It arced

high and fast, flying right towards us.

"Oh n—"

It crashed into one of the balloons. *BANG! Fwiiiish.*

The balloon deflated instantly and caught fire, with the flaming barrel stuck somewhere inside it.

The deck tilted violently to the left, and the Cloud Cruiser plummeted into the cloud in a deadly spiral.

Everything happened so fast.

I grabbed the rope railing with one hand and reached for Becky with the other.

"Billy!" Becky screamed as she fell.

I grabbed her hand but she slipped from my grasp and tumbled into the safety rope on the other side of the deck, which stopped her from spilling into the sky.

Max scrambled desperately trying to keep his paws on the wooden deck, but the slant was too great, and he edged towards the precipice. He yelped and echoed, *Billy!*

Mother shouted "*We're going down!*"

Becky slipped and fell between the ropes. She screamed again clasping at a rope with both hands. She dangled over the flaming entrails of the deflated balloon as we spun down.

Max slid backwards, digging his claws into the deck staring right at me.

I can't save you both. The thought struck me like a hammer to the head.

I threw myself at Max.

I rolled down the slanted deck, catching my hand on the handle of one of the floor hatches. It flung open, spilling the contents. Backsacks and blankets bounced off my head as I slid into Max, scooping him around the belly just as he slipped over the edge. I clutched the safety rope with the other hand and now the three of us dangled next to each other as the Cloud Cruiser spiralled out of control.

FWOOOOSH! I managed to look up to see Mother clinging to the bovithruster pullstring, giving the one remaining balloon a desperate burst of hot air. Unfortunately, the second bovithruster turned on too, with no balloon for it to fill. The flames shot straight into the flapping leather canvas, setting it even more ablaze.

My vision became a blur of flames, smoke, sky, clouds, mountains, all morphing from one to the next until I couldn't tell them apart. The world turned into a mass of spinning colours.

I tried to focus on Becky instead. "Hold on!" I yelled.

My knuckles burned into the rope as the combined weight of Max and me tried to separate my wrist from my arm. I gripped it desperately.

Mother shouted again, but the roar of the wind feeding the flames deafened me to everything. I caught a glimpse of the bright white ground.

The deck crashed onto the icy mountainside and careened down its steep face.

The impact flung Becky, Max and me into the flaming canvas. Max yelped as we landed on the snow within the balloon, and I lost my grip on him. The balloon spat us both out of the charred gaping hole. Freezing wetness slapped my skin and seeped into my clothes. We rolled down the soft slope, bouncing head over heel and finally skidded to a stop in the powdery snow.

The broken Cruiser sped down ahead of us dragging the deflated, burning balloon and leaving a trail of smoke and ashes and bits of Mother's hard work all across the mountainside.

I spied Becky on the slope below us, sprawled out in the snow, and we scurried down to her.

"Are you okay?" I heard the panic in my voice.

"I think so," she staggered to her feet, rubbing her wrists.

We both looked down and saw the broken Cloud Cruiser skid to a halt as the ground levelled out. The burning mass came to rest on a wide, flat surface of bluish snow. *A frozen lake*, I thought. Flames leapt from the balloon and spread to the deck.

The last barrel! I remembered Barrow. The mill was full of Mother's bovithane barrels, just like the one sitting in the hatch below the deck of the Cruiser right now. Mother was still on board, somewhere within the wreckage.

I ran down the slope towards the crash site, taking big strides through the knee-deep snow.

A high-pitched shriek filled the air. I froze in terror and watched the figure of my mother flee across the ice away from the balloon. I'd never seen her move so fast in my life. Her arms pumped wildly, hair billowing behind as her feet pounded the ice.

Fwuhh-BOOOOSH!

The Cloud Cruiser Mark II exploded in a fireball.

I fell on my butt. Max cowered against my back and Becky tripped down next to me. An orange ball of flame engulfed the intact balloon, which burst with a loud *POP*, creating a *second* fireball. The sudden blast of heat felt like opening the stove to check on the roasting potatoes, only ten times hotter. All the moisture left my eyes. Chunks of flaming wood scattered in all directions, thudding into the snow around us and hissing like snakes. The two fireballs merged as one and billowed into the air, swallowing itself in a cloud of black, pungent smoke.

A round hole of melted ice formed under the burning debris, sputtering out the flames as the wreckage either sank or bobbed upon the surface like misshapen black ducklings.

I blinked.

We continued down the slope towards Mother. She had made it to the edge of the frozen lake, after outrunning the explosion.

Her wails echoed off the mountainside.

"Whyyyy?" she cried.

"Mother, are you okay?" I crouched beside her, as she knelt in the snow staring at the sinking wreck, tears streaming from her eyes. She turned to me with trembling lips. I wrapped my arms around her and squeezed. She hugged me back.

"At least we're alive," I said.

I scrambled back up the mountain with Max. He sniffed out all of the things that had fallen out of the hatch during the crash. I found our backsacks, and my sketches were all there. *Thank goodness...* I also found the bag of woolly hats and gloves that Mother had brought from Hooke. She'd knitted a set for each of us to wear on our voyage up to the moon... I gave a sigh. I tried a hat on, then the gloves, and flexed my fingers. That felt better. I took the others back down to give to Becky and Mother.

"We might as well use these now," I offered them to both, sitting cross-legged next to the icy lake.

Mother's voice was soft and distant. "Thanks."

"What *was* that thing that hit us?" Becky asked, looking up at me from the ground. She looked cute in her red bobble hat, but exhausted.

"A flaming barrel," Mother replied absently. "I thought those hippies were just crazy."

"Really?" I said. "Didn't you believe them?"

She pulled a face. "Certain people believe certain things, William... and people like that tend to believe the wrong things."

"But didn't you say you saw something fall from Little Red?"

"I did. And after the monster in the lake spoke of these *Old Ones*, I believed that had something to do with them. They are out here, beyond the mountains, William."

She eyed me, and the look she gave me sent a tingle down my spine. I'd never seen my Mother look scared before.

"They just tried to kill us! I'm not sure they want to be found, William."

I held her wide-eyed gaze.

She looked away and waved a hand. "It doesn't matter."

242

She watched the smoke drift away from the remains of her masterpiece, her mouth drooping low.

I felt so sorry for her. And sad too. The Cloud Cruiser had saved my life and shown me the world from a perspective most people couldn't dream of. It had even taken us over the mountains, to a place nobody else had ever been. And now there was nothing left of it.

The wind blew icy cold up on the mountainside. We had two options: turn back, or carry on. Retreating would involve trying to climb back over the mountains on foot, something no person had ever successfully done, only to wind up being eaten by Gorlack. Despite Mother's fears of finding the Old Ones, we saw no other choice. If we were still on the mountain when night came, we'd freeze to death.

We started our descent.

Chapter Twenty-Two

On the northern side of the mountain range, a sea of
cloud blocked our view of the land below. We had to
climb down through it, which wasn't easy. Mother led the
way through the cold mist, with Becky following, and I
took up the rear. Max wandered wherever he liked, sniffing
rocks and snow with equal enthusiasm.

No rabbits, he echoed, very upset.

Treading carefully, so as not to slip and fall, we carved a
zig-zag route down through the snow. Sometimes we came
to a flat, rocky ridge, or 'saddle' as Mother called it, before
continuing down, and down, and down.

At last, the mist cleared and we emerged below the
cloud. The snow thinned out the lower we climbed, but
that only served to slow us down even more. At least with
snow, our boots had something to grip, but patches of ice
on the rocks were tricky to navigate.

An icy gust blew up the slope, freezing my nose and we
took shelter behind a boulder on the next saddle that we
came to.

Max pricked his ears, but we all heard the sound that
carried on the wind.

Clank-clank-clank-clank. Clank. Clank-clank. CLUNK.

Clank-clank.

"What is that?" Becky looked puzzled, and a little afraid. "It sounds like a hammer."

The noises came from below us, in the direction we were heading. A steady tapping of metal against the rocks. The wind died down and the sound faded.

I glanced at Mother, to Becky. We took a deep breath and carried on.

At the top of the next ridge, we stopped again, listening to the hammering. We could hear it clearly now.

"There!" Mother pointed to a boulder off to our left. Something was moving behind it, in time with the metal clanking.

We clambered towards it and snuck up behind the big rock. *CLANK-CLANK-CLANK. CLUNK. CLANK-CLANK.*

Mother put a finger to her lips, and gestured for us to stay put. She crept to the edge of the boulder and peered around. Her body froze. She turned back to us in slow motion. Her mouth moved wordlessly in wide-eyed awe. She blinked, and turned to look again.

I fidgeted. I exchanged a look with Becky, who nodded, and we crept alongside Mother and took a look for ourselves.

A rusty metal figure stood with its back to us, armed with a hammer and chisel. It had a box-shaped head with a box-shaped torso. A wobbly wire poked out the top of its head which bobbed around every time it swung the hammer. Its arms and legs were flexible and made of a series of ringed tubes, with round pads for feet. Clutching the tools in little clawed hands, it carved out the rock. *CLANK-CLANK-CLANK. CLANK.* The inside of the boulder was L-shaped where it had been chipped away, and the rusty metal-man stood facing the far side of it.

Max barked.

The metal-man made a startled noise, and spun around. His eyes were two round lenses sticking out from the box that was its head. A square jaw dangled open giving it a look of surprise and several sparks fizzled out between its joints as it flinched.

Its head popped off.

A large spring bounced out of its neck, tossing the head into the air and back down with a crumpled *thunk*. The rest of the body seized up, standing in front of us stiff and frozen in a self-protective pose. A tendril of grey smoke drifted out of the neck.

For a while, nobody said anything.

"Did we kill him?" Becky whispered.

"How do you kill metal?" Mother replied, stunned. She took a step closer, studying the headless body of the strange rusty man.

I looked at the rock carving. I had never seen anything so intricate. Pointed, angular shapes that somehow flowed into one another jutted out all across the surface like a line of interlocking square snakes. He must have been working on it for a long time.

He was so rusty it was hard to imagine how he moved at all.

"Is this an Old One?" I said.

Mother tapped her chin.

Neither Becky nor Mother answered. The question lingered in the air as nobody dared to say anything else.

Clank-clank-clink-clank-clank-CLONK-clank-clunk.

We all turned as one. Down on the ridge below, I spied another metal-man working on his own boulder. And a third beyond that, farther along. I cast my eyes over the slopes below and counted dozens more, the face of the mountain ringing to the steady chimes of hammers tapping the rocks. Grand carvings littered the way for miles off to either side, jagged spires with holes in them, slanted obelisks of stone, carved twisted archways – everything had a square-look to it, completely unnatural yet uniquely beautiful.

Beyond the carved mountainside, the snowy northern

tundra stretched for miles. It was an expanse of flat white land, except for one rather prominent eye-catcher... A single solitary black mountain rose out of the otherwise featureless tundric plains. Its blackened slopes protruded from the ground in a perfect cone-shape, starkly visible against the sheet of pale frosty land.

The ground at the base of that solitary mountain dazzled as it reflected the afternoon sun. The whole area looked to be made of steel, copper and iron. *That must be the weird metal men's home.*

We made our way towards the metal village. From the ridge, we were able to follow a worn path complete with steps in some of the steeper spots.

The second rusty man gave a start when we approached. As he spotted us, he flinched and off went his head bouncing down the mountain. His body seized up and stood motionless, just like the first one. This happened almost every time we passed one by.

Sometimes when one saw us, a high-pitched whine whistled from within, like a kettle pot overheating, and when this happened it triggered a chain reaction of flying heads. The first would ping off, then 3 more around it would follow, and there'd be a clattering of metal heads tumbling off down the rocks.

As we continued our descent, details of the village became clearer. There didn't seem to be any buildings, rather the whole place looked like a messy sea of... shiny things. In some areas, the metal objects had been sorted and raked into great long lines, but in other places it piled up high in jagged, unnatural hills.

In the middle of all the junk stood an immense structure. These creatures had built a weapon just as Mother suspected. And the strangest part was that both Mother and I recognised it. She had built one herself not so long ago and set it up on top of Hale Hill.

Cast in the shadow of the blackened mountain stood a gigantic catapult. Its arm pointed at the sky in the post-fire position, and it was aimed towards us.

At the bottom of the path, I turned back to look at the mountain range we had crossed over. I couldn't see where we had crashed because the low clouds obscured the snowy peaks, but from here the full view of the carvings took my breath away. The spectacle ran for miles in either direction, thousands of unique shapes morphing the endless slopes into an infinitely complex work of art. I had the crazy urge to sit down and sketch it, but where would I even begin? Becky tapped me on the shoulder, startling me out of the daze. Mother had carried on towards the catapult, so we hurried after her.

I found myself walking between heaps of old metal junk. Piles of rusty scrapmetal littered the way. Some of the metal men were busy sifting through it, and now and then one would see us walking by and its head would pop off.

Others hurried along carrying bits and pieces and tools. These ones looked newer, painted different colours, and not so rusted. Some even managed to look at us without losing their heads.

Mother approached one of the newer-looking ones. "Excuse me?" she began. This metal-man was painted blue, faded from the sun, with only a few spots of rust around the joints. "Are you the Old Ones?"

It spoke in a mechanical, tinny voice. "Oh," it remarked, just before its head popped off. It landed in the dirt at Mother's feet, round eyes staring at her boots. She poked the frozen body with two fingers and it toppled over backwards causing a puff of snowdust.

Mother turned to me and shrugged.

We continued towards the monstrous catapult. The counterweight alone was the size of Hale's windmill, dangling underneath the firing arm which reached straight up into the sky suspending its empty slingshot.

"This is what they used to launch the barrel at us..." Mother scowled. She glared about as metal men bounced along carrying bits of junk over a shoulder, some paying us no heed whatsoever, others taking a passing glance.

"*Who's in charge here?*" Mother roared. "*I demand to speak to them at once!*"

Ping zing piing boiing. Heads popped off all around us.

Another newer-looking metal-man approached us, this one painted red. He stood before us and a mechanical buzzing voice spoke. "Analyzing." A series of clunky noises followed, the little wire on his head jiggling and spitting out sparks. The wire curled around in a circle at the top, and in the centre was where the sparks came from. The clunking stopped, and the metal-man spoke again. "Greetings. Based on the fluctuations in your tone of voice and use of vocabulary, I have adjusted my external communicator to match your current progress of evolution. We can now converse." It sounded most cheerful. "Can I help you with anything?"

"I highly doubt it," Mother chastised. "But since you asked, are you the Old Ones?"

It blinked. "The Guardians call us that, though age is irrelevant to us."

Mother pondered that.

"The Guardians, Mother. He must be talking about the tree monsters."

She waved impatiently. "Why did you try to kill us with this trebuchet?"

It *clunked* for a few seconds. "Negative. We are forbidden to harm – *zrrrvk* – humans!"

Mother scowled. Her fists clenched by her side. "My Cloud Cruiser lies broken and in pieces at the bottom of an icy lake, which suggests otherwise."

"Oh, yes. The interference anomaly for test flight two-zero-zero-four-nine-six-three-seven. That was you?"

"Test flight?" Becky whispered to me.

"Maybe they don't see it as a weapon," I suggested.

Mother rubbed her forehead. "What exactly do you think you are doing here?"

"*zrrrrerkk* mission. We were sent here long ago," it

replied.

"You were *sent* here?" Mother exchanged a look with me. "Where did you come from?"

The metal-man made more buzzing and clunking noises, each one sounding more janky than the last. "I fear I cannot answer that."

"Why not?" Mother planted her hands on her hips.

"I do not want your head to malfunction."

Mother scoffed. "I'm a scientist. My head is always malfunctioning. Besides, I am fairly certain I already know." She leaned forward. "I demand that you tell me."

It considered that with some more *clunks*. "Perhaps a visual clue would suffice, to minimise the risk." It leaned back and craned its neck to look up at the darkening sky.

The first of the stars were beginning to twinkle.

Mother grinned at me. "I knew it!"

Becky grabbed my arm in excitement.

Wow, can it be, they really did come from Little Red?

Mother turned back to the small red metal-man. "So, what mission were you sent here for?"

His jaw dangled open about to speak, then he seized up. A very loud *clunk* came from somewhere within, followed by a buzz. A sharp burning smell stung my nostrils. And then his head popped off.

"Oh for goodness sake," Mother strode away and approached the next nearest metal-man. "You. Tell me why you were sent here."

Boïng!

She tried another one. "Oi! Tell me what you are doing here. What is your mission?"

Pïng!

With the next one she grabbed its head and pressed it down when she asked, *"Why are you here?"*

It clunked, sizzled, then all of its arms and legs fell off and collapsed to the ground leaving Mother clutching the poor thing's head. She tossed it aside. "Argh!"

A tall, shiny jet-black metal-man appeared from around

the corner of the catapult, followed by two rusty men carrying long metal girders. The newer-looking black one moved elegantly, without the clumsy bounce that all the rest had. It led the other two over to the base of the catapult where they dropped their loads and began noisily hammering on the counterweight with their fists.

"Mother, look," I pointed at the trio.

"What are they doing?" Mother pondered, and strode over to them. "Excuse me."

I could barely hear her over the racket of the hammering.

"*Excuse me!*"

One of the rusty men lost his head, while the other continued banging with both fists.

The tall shiny one turned to us. "Oh," it spoke in a smooth, clear tone and a spark fizzled from the wire on its head. The remaining rusty man stopped hammering and turned around. When he saw us, his head tried to ping off but got snagged on its spring and his whole body just seized up and fell over in the frosty dirt.

"You are humans," said the tall metal-man. The voice had a tinny edge to it, but sounded less scratchy than the other one that had spoken to us. It looked newer than new, by far the most technologically advanced machine I had ever seen. I found myself thinking about the Great Train, the previous holder of that particular fact. Even the rusty men were more advanced than the train, but this black one somehow *looked* like the train itself...only in the shape of a man.

Something within his chest made a rapid *clicking* sound, and the wire on his head spat sparks.

When the *clicking* stopped, he glanced at the two fallen metal men on the ground. "My apologies, their minds were never meant to interact with the likes of you."

Mother eyed it. "But you can? If I ask you something you don't like, will your head fall off?"

The Train Man chuckled, a tittering humming sound that

made my ears tingle.

"I should hope not," he finally answered. "But just because you can ask, does not mean I can answer." He clasped two claw-hands in front of his chest. "What would you like to know, fleshling?"

Mother didn't hesitate. "What are you doing here?"

"I am currently altering the calibration of the counterweight."

"Why?"

"Because it is not yet operating at optimal efficiency."

Mother snorted in disgust. "Your trebuchet is working just fine. You almost killed us, don't you know?"

"Oh my. You are the interference anomaly for test flight two-zero-zero—"

"Don't call me an anomaly. You destroyed my Cloud Cruiser! I was going to fly to the *moon*. You obliterated my dream, you almost killed me, my son and Becky and—" She put a hand to her mouth and choked back a sob.

I touched her on the shoulder. "Mother..."

The Train Man stood unmoving, staring at us with his expressionless round face. A tiny spark flickered from his head, while his chest went *clikclikclikclikclikclik*...

Mother wiped her eye with a finger and took a deep breath.

"I'm sorry," said the Train Man. "Our intentions were not to terminate you; our programming does not allow it. We are trying to return to home. Our limitations are currently causing some technical difficulties in that area. What is this Cloud Cruiser you speak of?"

Mother stood up straight. "My masterpiece. I solved the conundrum of flight. I calculated the theory of quantum ignition, liquidised raw Bovinated Bottom Burps into a flammable fuel for twin bovithrusters and *conquered the skies!* I made calculations for reaching the stars too...oi, where are you going?"

The Train Man had wandered off, the wire in his head sparking furiously.

"How rude," she remarked.

"Mother, we need to tell him about Gorlack. The lake tree said the Old Ones can help us."

"I know, I know, William." She sighed. "This is all just so very curious. Come along."

We followed as she marched over to the Train Man, who appeared to be giving orders to another pair of rusty workers. They were making a strange series of *boops* and *beeps*. When they saw us approach, they both flinched simultaneously. One of them made a long *booooop* and the other went *zzzreeeeeecck* and off went their heads.

The Train Man turned around and said, "Thrusters."

"What?"

"You have invented thrusters. This will help us reach Terry."

"Who's Terry?" Mother began, but she shook her head and waved a dismissive hand. "Oh for goodness sake, nevermind. Look, we came a long way to find you... creatures... things."

"Um. Mr Train Man," I said, scratching my elbow. "We were hoping you could help us."

"Our programming restricts our interference with all sentient lifeforms. Only in an extreme emergency are we allowed to offer assistance." He turned around again, glanced at his newly beheaded workers, and wandered off to find some more. When he walked, his head didn't bob up and down. His legs worked in such a way as to make his upper torso float across the ground.

Becky turned to me quizzically. "Mr *Train Man*?"

I made a face and shrugged.

Train? Train! Max echoed, sounding a tad worried. The Great Train almost killed him on the bridge near George and Millie's farm, so he probably wasn't fond of meeting another one.

"It's okay, boy. He's a friend." *I think.*

The three of us exchanged a look and followed the big metal-man again. He stood beneath a towering heap of scrap metal, looking up at two more rusty men that were in the process of scaling the junk, some twenty feet above our heads.

"Mr Train Man, do you know anything about Wishing Trees?"

Fzzzt. His head sparked. "You must mean the Guardians. Their heads take the form of trees, and they enjoy showing off to the lesser lifeforms."

Mother screwed up her face. Becky gestured for me to probe further.

"Well... I think I met one called Gorlack in a cave near my home. And, well... he has an unusual appetite."

The Train Man kept facing the mountain of junk and didn't respond to me.

"He wanted me to feed him my *greatest desire*, so that he could grow bigger. Is that, um, normal for a Guardian?"

The metal-man's head went *fzzt.* "No."

I waited for more, but he didn't elaborate.

Becky found the words. "He's turned into a giant monster, stomping everywhere, eating everything and everyone. He even ate another Guardian, the one in See-Saw Lake. And he's chasing us! He might be on the other side of the mountains by now!" She pointed a gloved hand at the moonlit sculptures on the slopes that dominated the landscape behind us. "Does that count as an extreme emergency?"

The Train Man's head sparked so violently that I flinched away from him. Max yelped and hid behind my legs. *Bad Train?*

ClikclikclikclikclikCLIKCLIKCLIKCLIKCLIKCLIKCLIK went the metal-man. *It must be his way of thinking. He does it every time he learns something from us.*

Finally, the Train Man turned around and faced us. "This situation is dire. The Terrabots must aid you in this predicament, but you must also aid the Terrabots." He looked directly at Mother. "You appear to be the most evolved member of your species."

"I know," Mother replied.

"You must share your knowledge with us. Using the materials we have here," he gestured elegantly to the enormous pile of scrap behind him, "Will you be able to replicate your thrusters?"

Mother tapped her chin. "Yes, I think I could. But I'll need some cows."

"Cows?"

"I can't harmonise bovithane without cows," said Mother, as if it were the most obvious thing in the world.

"We have an excess quantity of rocket fuel. That should suffice."

Mother's eyes lit up. "What's a *rocket?*"

The Train Man's head gave a shuddering *clunk*. "Forgive me. My terminology restriction programming lapsed for a moment. To avoid confusion, I will aim to simplify my auditory responses." Something in his tone had changed. I thought his voice seemed a little less clear than it did a moment ago.

Mother raised an eyebrow. "Okay. But don't go breaking your own head in the process. Why do you need thrusters, anyway?"

"We must attach them to the counterweight so we might gain maximum force. It is the only way we have any hope of reaching Terry."

"Reaching Terry? Wait, aren't you going to use this thing to destroy Gorlack?"

"We cannot destroy a Guardian with any technology found here. The only one who can subdue a rogue Guardian is Terry."

"For goodness sake, who is this mystical Terry fellow?" Mother demanded with both hands on her hips.

The Train Man didn't respond.

"Perhaps this is one of his *terminology restrictions*," Becky suggested.

"How will Terry help us defeat Gorlack?" I probed.

The Train Man didn't answer.

"Terrabots... Terry," Mother mused. "Terry created you, didn't he?"

The Train Man remained silent and still.

"The tree in the lake said that the Old Ones are trying to get back to Little Red. Terry must live on Little Red!" cried Mother. "Tell me, is that why you're trying to get back to the moon?"

The Train Man's head made a terrible *clunking* noise and the wire on his head spat another burst of fizzing sparks. He still said nothing.

Mother was getting frustrated. "You are either incredibly clever, or incredibly stupid. Right now I'm inclined to go with *stupid*." She pointed to the monstrous catapult towering over us. "This is a weapon designed to destroy things, not a mode of flying transport. Your *test flights* destroyed an entire village! What kind of insane logic tells you that flinging burning barrels across the mountains is going to get you to the moon? Bolting thrusters onto the end of it isn't going to help!"

The Train Man's head gave a jerk, and rested askew on his head, staring at us like a curious dog. After another fizzle of sparks he composed himself, straightened his head and clasped his claw-hands in front of him once again. But his voice had grown even more distorted.

"I can see that the situation would benefit from a motivational enhancement. There are some things I have withheld for your own stability, but after careful consideration, I have decided it would be beneficial for you to be informed."

Mother crossed her arms. "Go on."

"Terry does not live on the moon. Terry is the moon. And he's not a moon."

Chapter Twenty-Three

The Train Man's words hung in the air, as we all just stared blankly at him.

"I sense confusion."

Little Red is actually Terry? That didn't make any sense to me.

Mother spoke up. "What do you mean? If Little Red isn't a moon...I mean, Terry... then what is it? Or he...?"

"Terry is a Thermo Energy Regulator and Research Organising Retainer, among other things."

So much for terminology restriction... I didn't understand a word of that.

"Wait," frowned Becky. "That doesn't spell Terry. That spells—"

"TERROR. Yes. The committee insisted that *Terry* sounded more friendly." He sang a little jingle, *"Terraforming made easy, with Terry!"*

None of us had any response to that.

"I digress. If we can reach Terry, he can initiate Rogue Guardian Protocol, and your world can be saved. Also, you may find the on-board research facility most interesting." Despite the distortion of his voice, the Train Man sounded cheerfully optimistic.

Mother's jaw dangled low and she quivered. "Research... facility...?" She bit her fist. "So, you're saying... it's a laboratory?"

"Yes. I hoped that might pique your interest."

Mother grinned with excitement. "We're going to the mooooon William, my lifelong dream!"

"Lifelong? You only decided that a few moons ago." She wasn't listening. She was too busy dancing with Becky. "Why do you even need our help?" I asked the Train Man. "You're obviously cleverer than us."

"The Terrabots cannot use any technology that the current lifeforms have not discovered for themselves. Aiding you would be a violation of our programming, the same way that you being alive—" He was cut off by a grinding *crrrrrunnnch*. "*Ohhh*" he groaned. "It is too paradoxical."

Mother and Becky froze in mid-waltz, and glanced over. Becky looked concerned. "What is wrong with you?"

"It is our mission," he slurred. Every other word now had a distinctive *hiss* to it. "We were sent here to save the humans. But the humans all perished when Home froze over."

"But we are humans," I said.

"That is why I appear to be malfunctioning. You should not exist."

Mother and Becky disentangled. "What did you say about your home? I thought Terry was your home?" Mother asked.

"Terry is where we were constructed. I suppose that makes it our home. But Home is where the humans lived before the sun cooled. There." He raised a claw and pointed high. We all turned to follow it.

Max barked at the mountain.

The clouds had broken apart to reveal a sea of twinkling stars littering the night sky and the mighty blue moon crested the peaks of the mountains.

Becky, Mother and me all remarked at once, "*Big Blue?*"

"Is that what you call Home?" The Train Man sounded amused. "I suppose it would seem a big planet to you."

"Big Blue is a *planet*...?" Mother murmured. "But, that means..." She tapped her chin, half smiling, half gaping. "*We* are on the moon. Lunaria *is* Big Blue's moon."

"Yes," confirmed the Train Man. "Though that is only your name for it. We call it Home."

Max barked at the mountain again. And again.

"Shh, boy."

Monster, he echoed. He went into a barking frenzy.

A shadow moved into the surface of Big Blue, coming up from below. From where we stood, it looked like a deformed and gnarled crone had perched on top of the mountain. But of course, it was Gorlack. He made a monstrous silhouette within the pale blue disc.

Then he laughed louder than thunder.

The eruption of noise sent a shockwave down the mountain, knocking loose a cascade of rocks. Pebbles and boulders thudded into the carvings and *clanked* onto the heads of the little rusty Terrabots.

I turned to the Train Man. "We are humans, we *definitely* exist," I insisted. "If your mission was to save people like us, then I suggest you save us from *that!*"

"Save the... humans?" the Train Man gazed up at the monster, miles away yet still terrifyingly huge. "Our mission. Save the humans." A big spark fizzled out of the wire on his head. "We will save the humans!"

The Train Man took a few strides towards the mountain and raised a claw into the air. The fingers warped into the shape of a cone, and he emanated an almighty *honk*, like the horn on a boat.

A dazzling array of sparks flashed across the mountainside in response.

"Cripes, how many of them are there?" I uttered in a hushed voice.

The little sparks moved. Gorlack's laughter was drowned out by the cacophony of metal *clunks* and *clanks* as an army of rusty Terrabots descended from the slopes, every one fizzling sparks out of their heads. Before long, the first wave arrived, their little padded feet clunking against the rocks and crunching in the frost, all marching towards us. They formed a wide semi-circle around us, all with their backs to the mountainside and Gorlack, still laughing high above us. Wave after wave of Terrabots fell in behind them.

"We will save the humans," one rusty bot said, every word a scratchy hiss.

"Save the hu-hu-mans," another stammered.

More took up the cry. *"Save the humans, we will save the humans."* And more still. *"The humans save humans the SAVE the saaaave the humans save s-s-save save humans the save the humans..."*

Becky clutched my arm, gazing at the mass of ancient-looking machines. Mother's face kept turning from a grin to a gaping stare. Max didn't know where to look. His big head twitched from the bots, to me, to the mountain and back to the bots. The Terrabots' chorus didn't sound all that different from the white noise I used to hear whenever Max tried to tell me something, but being *outside* my head made it far more tolerable.

I squeezed Becky's hand, and felt hopeful. *The Terrabots are on our side.*

They all turned silent when Gorlack spoke.

"Billy!" The monster's voice filled the night sky, echoing off the mountainside like a raging waterfall. "I see you've met the slaves. Sadly, artificial life cannot sustain the likes of me, so I have no desire to venture down there. Your old friend has been telling me all about the Southern Settlements, so I've decided I quite fancy paying a visit to each of them. So many delicious fleshlings." From the bottom of the mountain, I couldn't see his terrible grin, but I could hear it in his tone. "Where better to start than near my old cave... what did you call it? Ah, yes. *Hale.*"

My stomach hit the floor.

"Your friend says he has been dying to see you again, and who am I to keep old friends apart. Here, allow me to reacquaint you." The monster gave a flick of his arm, and tossed something into the air. "Farewell, Billy!"

Gorlack retreated back down the mountain and disappeared from sight.

There was a moment of silence, broken by the faint yet distinguishable sound of a man screaming. Slowly, the screaming intensified. I looked up, squinting.

"*WwaaaaaaaaaaaaaaaAAAAAAAAAAAAAAAAAAAA IIIIIEEEEEEEEEEEEEEEEEEEEE!!!*"

Kane landed with a splat.

The Fedora Man's body careened into the ground right in front of us, between our own feet and the Terrabots. He lay sprawled out face down in the hard, frosty dirt. Something warm sprayed up into my face when he landed... Before I thought about what it could be, I licked my lips, and tasted something extraordinarily sweet. I had tasted it before, back when this whole adventure had barely begun. *Is that honey?*

To everyone's surprise, Kane then stood up.

Becky gasped, Mother took a startled step backwards, and several Terrabots went *ping* as their heads popped off.

Max and I held our ground. He stood at my side with his head low, growling at the Fedora Man. *Bad man. Bad man. Bad man.*

Kane lifted his head and leered. His nose was broken and blood ran down his chin, but the blood dried and flaked off while his nose straightened itself out before my very eyes.

After brushing himself down, he tipped his new hat. He showed absolutely no sign of being thrown off the top of a mountain. He looked the same as when I had first seen him leaning against the wall of an alleyway in Fentworth. Immaculate grey suit, grey fedora, that cocky posture. His eyes met mine.

"You," he snarled, as an evil grin spread across his face.

"What has Gorlack done to you?" I demanded. "No-one could have survived that fall!"

"Well look at you, Mr Khazi Plotter, playing the tough man are we now? Sending you there was the best thing that could have happened to you. You should thank me, Billy." He cricked his neck and let out a satisfied sigh. "I could get used to this new body. I feel incredible."

"Gorlack used Kamuna to bring you back..."

Kane cackled. "More than that, boy. I *am* Kamuna. My very blood is infused with it. I am the most powerful man alive!" He looked psychotically pleased with himself.

"You were never a man," Becky hissed. "You're just another monster."

"Poor farmer girl," Kane mocked. "She lost her mother and now the world seems so cruel and unfair and full of monsters."

Becky stiffened. Her fiery glare turned to a vacant, fearful look in an instant. I despised him for that.

"Shut up Kane," I snapped. "She's right. You are no man." I could see the Train Man in the corner of my eye, and hoped he was paying attention. "You're not even human. You're a monster, and you always were."

"Big, hard words. I think I'm going to shed a tear." Kane yawned. "I grow bored already. Enough of this pointless drivel. You struck me once, but let's see if you can beat me now, Billy."

He ran at me.

Max leapt up between us, snarling viciously. His jaw clamped down on Kane's shoulder and the pair tumbled to the ground, Max on top of Kane's chest.

"Ugh!" Kane sounded more annoyed than in pain. Max tore into his suit, ripping one sleeve down the length of his arm. "Wretched hound. Gorlack only just gave me – *ahh!*" Max bit off one of his ears.

Kane grabbed Max around the waist and hurled him away. The ear fell out of Max's mouth as he scraped across the ground yelping. My head hissed with painful white noise.

I charged at Kane. I swung a fist towards his head but he was ready this time. He rolled aside and nimbly hopped back to his feet.

He grinned, waving a finger at me. His missing ear grew back onto the side of his head like a blossoming flower. The sight of it made me want to gag.

Two Terrabots clunked up behind Kane and restrained his arms. The Fedora Man looked astonished.

"Quickly," ordered the Train Man. "Come with me. You must build the thrusters. The Terrabots will hold him."

Mother and Becky followed him and a group of rusty bots into the scrap yard behind us. I looked for Max, who shook himself off, snorted, and ran to me.

"Unhand me," Kane scathed. He wrenched an arm free, detaching one of the bot's own limbs. The claw clung to his forearm, and he studied it with amusement.

Two more bots grabbed him around the ankles. They gave a tug and Kane fell flat on his face. Another bot came bumbling into the fray and dived into a bellyflop. The Fedora Man squirmed sideways and the bot landed heavily across his legs, crushing them.

Kane screamed in pain. Even as he did, I saw his legs morph and rejuvenate. Kane writhed and tore himself free of the Terrabots' grip. He wrenched the second arm out of the poor bot's socket.

"Retreating. I have sustained damage. Retreating!" The armless bot scurried away.

Kane wielded the floppy arm across his shoulder like a makeshift flail. "You choose interesting company, Billy. They are numerous, but pitifully weak. These creatures are no match for the likes of—"

A Terrabot smacked him in the back of the head. Kane reeled and swung the claw around bringing it down on top of the bots' head. *Ping.*

Kane watched the head fly off, and let out a short cackle before whirling around to strike at the next bot. He caught one under the chin and another in the side of the head. Terrabots bravely surged towards him with no regard for their own safety, and promptly lost their heads to the Fedora Man's maniacal flailing.

"Save the humans, destroy the monster," some of them droned in their tinny, buzzing voices.

Before long, a pile of broken heads and body parts lay strewn around Kane's feet, but still they came at him, clambering over the debris.

The Terrabots outnumbered Kane a thousand to one, but where he had a practically invincible body, they were literally falling apart. He cackled again, louder and longer than before, savouring every moment of the absurd fight.

I looked about, helpless. *What can I do here?* If I joined in the melee, Kane would kill me. Mother needed time to rebuild her bovithruster, but Kane would destroy every last Terrabot before she had finished. *Then he'll kill all of us.* I had to get rid of him, somehow.

The trebuchet loomed above me. Nothing had ever seemed more obvious in my life.

"Prepare for a test flight!" I commanded. A group of bots broke away from the rest and leapt onto the catapult's base. One of them dangled from a giant protruding handle, while two more took hold of its legs from below. Together, they cranked the handle around. The enormous counterweight slowly rose upwards, while the firing-arm lowered towards the ground.

The trebuchet was mounted on a set of big rubber wheels, meaning we could aim it where we wanted. The mountains dominated the view to the south. Everything and everyone I ever cared about lived in the south. I ordered the trebuchet around, pointing it into the unknown frozen north.

Kane didn't seem to realise what was happening until it was too late. His foot caught in between a pair of broken torsos, and a few of the newer-looking Terrabots managed to grab hold of his arms and legs. Kane instantly broke free of one but only to be ensnared by another bot. They dragged him towards the empty sling and tossed him into it.

"What are you doing?" he demanded. He scrambled out of the netting and came at me. Four Terrabots tackled him and they all fell into the sling. Kane kicked free yet again, but three more rusty bots jumped on top of him, pinning him against the ground inside the net.

"Ready for launch!" one of the bots buzzed.

"What?" Kane panicked underneath the metal men. "You can't!"

"Yes, I can." I kicked the launch lever, releasing the mechanism.

Chk-WUUUMP.

The trebuchet launched. Kane shrieked. The massive arm arced through the air and released its load into the night sky. I lost sight of Kane and the Terrabots as they soared over the solitary black mountain. Kane's screams carried back at me for a few seconds before fading to nothing in the darkness beyond.

Bad man, Max echoed. *Bad man fly!*

I chuckled, ruffled his head, and together we entered the scrap yard in search of Becky and Mother.

Becky found me first. "Billy! Are you okay?"

"I'm fine."

"Did you just fire Kane out of the catapult?"

"Yes."

"Ha!" She threw her arms around my neck. "That'll teach him to mess with us."

"We're getting pretty good at dealing with him, I'd say."

Becky beamed. We shared a quick kiss. *Wow.* Apparently, kissing the girl you love after firing your arch nemesis out of a catapult feels incredible.

She pulled away, still clutching me around the neck. She looked happy, yet weary. Small dark patches hung below her eyes, no doubt a side effect of staying awake for almost two days in a row. "Billy, your mother is amazing. You have to come see this."

She took my hand and led me deeper into the maze of metal. Pile after pile of scrap and bits of junk reflected the pale moonlight. We entered a clearing of sorts, surrounded by junk on all sides. In the centre, Mother stood over a workbench with the Train Man and a trio of Terrabots, one of which had no arms.

A crudely made statue rested on the bench. It looked like an upsidedown broken beer stein, with wings attached to its side. On top was a fat, coned drill-bit.

Mother pointed to each bot in turn. "You, get me as many barrels of this rocket fuel that you have. You, find me some strong steel rods, as long as you can find, to act as support beams. And you, bring me anything that we may be able to turn into a compartment big enough for four travellers and a dog."

Two of the bots scurried away. The armless bot went *brooop*. Its tone sounded sad and his head hung low. "Oh, um. Why don't you just wait over there," Mother waved to nowhere in particular, and the bot shambled off.

"Mother, I got rid of Kane."

"William! Get your sketchpad. I need you to design this for me." She gestured to the weird little statue on the bench.

"What is it?"

"This is how we are going to reach Terry and save the world," she struck a proud pose. "There are no materials here to produce a balloon, so we need to take a different approach. We're going to make the biggest bovithruster we can, and attach ourselves to the top of it. We shall call it... a Space Rocket."

I grinned, Becky made an excited noise, and Max wagged his stump and barked.

Mother added as an afterthought, "It would be nice if we could get it working before Gorlack eats your father."

Chapter Twenty-Four

For the first time since my youngest brother Rufus was born, Mother went into overdrive.

She ran from one Terrabot to the next, examining their finds and either nodding with approval, upon which they added it to the *useful* pile, or gave a patronising comment about how inappropriate or terrible said item was, in which case it was thrown into the *useless* pile. Now and then she would visit me and Becky at the workbench, where I sketched potential designs for the Space Rocket.

"Consider the aerodynamics, William," she explained briefly before I began. "It must be capable of cutting a path *beyond* the sky itself. Think about it!"

That explained the drill-bit on her crude sculpture, but I couldn't see any cones big enough to fit on the gigantic thrusters that Mother was busy putting together.

I left that for her to figure out later. In the meantime, I tried to come up with a suitable design for the compartment that we would travel within. The armless Terrabot stood on the other side of the bench gazing down at my sketchpad with lights for eyes, illuminating my work.

"That will be too heavy," Becky murmured, referring to

my latest bulbous drawing. She sat with her head resting against my shoulder.

"You sound so sleepy. Why don't you have a nap?"

"No. I like watching you work."

I tore the page off and flipped it over. I always started each design the same way – the giant bovithruster, essentially a fat cylinder on the page.

"Okay, how about..." I flicked my pencil, marking the page with swift light strokes, adding details to the top of the cylinder until I had something that resembled a shed mounted to the top of it. "See, there's a pointy roof for breaking through the sky, and it's got a little window so we can see out. What do you think?"

Becky mumbled incoherently. Her head became a deal heavier as she slumped into me. I put an arm around her, and eased her down across the bench.

"You have a rest," I whispered. "I need some inspiration." I got to my feet. *Max, stay. Keep her warm.*

Max nuzzled against her and immediately started snoring.

I wandered off down an aisle of scrap towards the base of the black mountain. Terrabots scurried past me in both directions carrying out Mother's bidding.

I scanned the heaps on either side and saw old bicycles, rusty chains, what looked to me like half a boat's hull with a gaping hole in it, an assortment of sheet metal, pipes, girders, machinery and all sorts of things I didn't recognise. At the end of the aisle, I found yet more aisles. It reminded me of the vineyards I saw in the Fent Vale while riding the Bighorns with Becky. Only, instead of tidy rows of grapevines, here were hodgepodge heaps of rusting junk.

Eventually, I found something that caught my eye. Half buried among a load of old boat anchors, I spotted a rounded metal canister with circular windows dotted around it. It looked about the same width as The Floater, the water tank that we tried to use as a rescue boat in the

Khazi, but twice as tall. It wasn't as rusty as everything else I had seen, and even retained most of its faded red paint. *Our destination is Little Red. This thing is red.*

I asked a passing Terrabot if he knew what it was. After *clunking* and spraying sparks into my face, I thought he was going to lose his head but eventually he calmed down and answered me. "That's a diving bell, used for exploring the ocean depths."

"Does it have a door?"

He pointed a claw at a round wheel on the canister's side. "That is a pressurisation hatch to enter and exit, and to keep the passengers safe within."

I didn't know what that was, but it sounded promising. *Mother would know.*

I asked the Terrabot to gather some friends and unbury it.

Somewhere around midnight, when Big Blue hung directly overhead, my host of Terrabots delivered the hulking red diving bell to Mother's Assembly Clearing.

"Oh my. Oh my, oh my. What is this, William?"

"It's a diving bell," I exclaimed. "It has a hatch for getting in and out, there's enough room for all of us, and it has windows!" Windows were obviously the best feature. *I'm not missing the view.*

Mother studied it. "It's perfect."

The night flowed ever on.

The Assembly Clearing became a construction site, ringing to the sound of Mother's commanding voice and a hundred Terrabots hammering, cutting and welding.

"No, no, no! Put that combustilisation sprocket there. And see this internal extracator, it goes *here*. You've got to seal it tight, so the air can't get out. It's all about compressability."

Mother bossed a group of rusty workers around as they tried to connect a series of wide pipes together. There seemed to be a communication malfunction, because they just didn't understand half of what she was saying.

Even so, Mother's Space Rocket slowly formed as the hours ticked by. My diving bell sat to one side waiting patiently to be connected.

I had offered to help, so Mother gave me the task of screwing up some bolts along an iron beam. In the time it took me to tighten four, my Terrabot partner had managed forty-two. Since that, Mother told me to just stay out of the way. I sat on the workbench watching the commotion, with Becky dozing across my lap.

Now and then, I spied Terrabots creeping over to the *useless* pile. One at a time, they would pick up some object seemingly at random and then smash it onto the ground repeatedly until it was either bent or in pieces.

"What are they up to?" I asked the Train Man, who was acting as Mother's foreman.

"They are releasing the accumulation of corrupt data."

"Huh? What's that?"

"A symptom of the paradox."

"What's a paradox?"

"It is difficult to describe," he answered. "Try to imagine something that is both true and false at the same time."

I considered that. "That's confusing, I can't think of anything."

"Exactly, a paradox is almost impossible to comprehend, which is why we do not like them. To a bot, something must be either true or false. It cannot be both."

"So... is there a paradox here right now? I don't see it."

The Train Man *clunked*. "It's you."

"Me? I'm not a paradox!"

The Train Man explained. "Our mission was to save the humans. But they all perished when Home froze. Coming face to face with you now is a contradiction to what was programmed into us when we were built. The older bots cannot make sense of your existence, because you should not exist. This contradiction caused many bots to malfunction, as you have witnessed. With the discovery of

Gorlack the Rogue Guardian, I overwrote our old programming with a new mission – to keep you safe. But traces of code linger, and every moment we spend in your presence causes a slow accumilation of contradictions that deteriorate our minds. To fight this malicious process, we smash things. Every lifeform enjoys smashing things."

Another Terrabot bounced over to the *useless* pile, plucked up an old bucket with a hole in and stamped it into a metal pancake. *It does look fun*, I reflected.

Just before dawn, the main chassis of the rocket stood as tall as two Hale windmills. A towering cylinder, the colour of dirty bronze reinforced by long iron bars and three triangular winglets. A row of ringed rails led up the side, to be used as a ladder for accessing the door hatch.

Mother called the main cylinder the *fuselage*, and that is where she attached her most elaborate bovithrusters, filled with the bots own rocket fuel. Where the Cloud Cruiser had two, the Space Rocket had three, but each one looked twenty times bigger.

"I have created the most powerful machine in Lunaria," Mother declared. "This makes the Great Train look like a pedal-cart! Now, to add the passenger quarters and connect the air tubes."

Using the trebuchet as a winch, the Terrabots hoisted the diving bell onto the top of the *fuselage*, and welded it in place. After this, they gathered up a collection of the sheet metal I had seen earlier in the night, and curved them around to form a pointed cone to go on the top.

The rocket soaked up the rays of the rising sun, setting the bronze colours afire.

Becky stirred. She yawned sleepily, rubbing her eyes. When she saw the rocket, she gasped. She gazed at the creation with frizzy strands of hair poking out around the rim of her bobble hat and eyes reflecting the golden morning light. She had never looked lovelier.

"Not bad, eh?" I smirked.

271

"It's... there are no words."

Mother entered the diving bell with a collection of levers and cogs under one arm, and she didn't emerge again for several hours.

Finally, around midday, she reappeared. She climbed down from the rocket and took a few steps back to marvel at her creation. She announced breathlessly, "It is done."

Mother came and collapsed onto the bench beside me. She leaned back and rested her elbows on the table.

"Phew!" She exhaled to the sky.

"Bethany, you're amazing! It took us weeks to create the Cloud Cruiser, but you've made this in a single night!"

Mother smiled. "Those rust buckets are pretty useful lab assistants. Becky, I'm afraid you're fired!"

Becky groaned, "Awww, no way."

The Train Man approached and struck his elegant claw-clasped pose. "Mrs Spudswallop, once our mission to save you from the Rogue Guadian is complete, we will have to return to our former state. Further interaction with you will be largely forbidden."

"That's a terrible shame. Becky, you're un-fired."

Becky chuckled.

Mother abruptly stood and faced us. She took out her knitted woolly hat from a trouser pocket, and pulled it over her head. "Moonmates, it's time."

Becky leapt to her feet. "Let's go!"

"I hope you don't intend to launch from here," remarked the Train Man in a worried tone.

Mother turned to him. "Why wouldn't we? That monster must be half way to Hale by now, we have no time to lose!"

"If you take off from here, our home will be destroyed by the thrusters."

I glanced about the clearing, feeling guilty. Their home still looked like nothing but piles of broken junk to me. *But it is their home...*

Mother sighed impatiently. "Fine. Where would you

suggest?"

"North of Mt Hope, there is a wide expanse of land."

"On the other side of *that?*" Mother pointed to the black mountain, aghast. "That'll take hours!"

"The Terrabots will do all the heavy work. There are many of us, it will be easy."

Mother sighed again. "So be it."

The bots dismantled the trebuchet and secured the Space Rocket onto its base with hooks. They tied it down with chains and started wheeling the whole thing through the maze of junk.

When they reached the lowest slopes of the mountain, they started wheeling it around the base, meaning to take it to the far side where we could launch.

Mother piped up. "No, no, no, this will take *forever*. Let's go over the top! Come on, chop chop."

The Terrabots aimed the contraption at the mountain, and started the long uphill climb. The wheels soon rutted into the loose stones. The Terrabots tied three great chains to the front of the makeshift cart and with twenty bots per chain they heaved the Space Rocket up the slope.

A countless number of irregular shaped black rocks littered the mountain. Most were small enough to hold, so I bent to pick one up. Its pockmarked surface felt rough and very hard.

Max saw it in my hand and echoed, *fetch! Fetch!*

I threw it for him, and he bounded after it. The entire mountain seemed to be made of rocks just like it, so the moment it landed he lost sight of it and ran around desperately sniffing for it.

The gruelling climb took its toll on all of us except the Terrabots. They marched relentlessly, heaving the Space Rocket higher and higher with never a word of protest or lack of enthusiasm. Mother claimed she wanted to make some last minute preparations to the pilot's seat, and climbed up inside the pod. Becky and I resorted to perching on the edge of the rocket's cart, as Max lay beside us with his tongue lolling out.

The sun was low in the sky by the time we approached the summit. As we came closer, I spied a single tree protruding from the lip of the crater.

I exhaled a breath. "No way. Is that what I think it is?"

Becky followed my gaze. "Is that a tree?"

I forgot she hadn't seen the tree in See-Saw Lake, so to her the thing growing out of the top of the mountain must have looked fairly inconspicuous, if a little out of place.

"I think it's another Wishing Tree..."

Her eyes widened. Her lips moved as she mumbled something, but I couldn't make it out.

"Come on." I found a boost of energy and scrambled ahead to the top of the mountain, Becky and Max close behind.

I crested the top of the black mountain and stood before the withered, burnt tree. It looked dead. A single green leaf stuck to one of the branches.

"Hello?" I tried.

No response.

I looked for any sign of a head, eyes, a mouth. The tree's skinny trunk disappeared into the rocky ground with no hint of what could lie beneath.

I peered into the crater. It was full of rocks, blackened just like all the rest.

"Fleshlings."

The voice came so suddenly that I jumped. Becky gave a girly yelp and grabbed my arm.

I turned back to the tree to see a single eyeball gazing up at us from out of the rocks at the base of the trunk. Unlike the lake tree's melony-green eyes, this one had a yellowish tint, like an old crone's.

"Hi," I said. "Sorry if we woke you. We are just crossing your mountain, I hope you don't mind."

"Really, now?" The voice was coming from just below the surface of the rocks, but it still had no mouth that I could see. His voice was distinct, raspy and sounded very old. "Why?"

"Oh. Well, it's a long story. We're going to the moon and stuff. Terry is going to help us, um, take care of one of your brothers... do you know Gorlack?"

The mountain tree chuckled. "Went mad, didn't he? Stupid fool. Couldn't even handle one tiny earth tremor, and his mind broke. We all know showing off to the fleshlings feels good, but one must always keep control! If he thought his cave was so bad, he should try living in a fiery chasm, see how he handles that."

I eyed him. "What do you mean? Your mountain is surrounded by snow..."

"Mountain? This is no mere mountain, boy. This is a volcano. *The* volcano, you might say. You are standing on the Point of Impact. This is where Terry first bore into the ground and reignited the core. I was put here to keep the volcano stable. I am the First Guardian."

I didn't understand what he meant about igniting the core, but talking to the first ever wishing tree felt quite exciting. "Wow, it is so nice to meet you."

"Very polite, aren't you? Well, go on then. I suppose I'll give you a wish."

"What? Oh, no. That's not—"

Becky put a hand on my arm. "Billy. There is something I would wish for..."

I studied her face, but she hung her head to look at the ground. "Becky, what is it?"

She took a deep breath. "I've thought about this, ever since Timothee told us about how he wanted to make a wish. I understand what he meant. I mean, who *wouldn't* want to make a wish, right?"

I nodded.

"I've given it a lot of thought. I told myself, if I ever found my own Wishing Tree, there's only one thing I would ask for..." She looked at the yellow eyeball on the ground. "Can you bring people back from the dead?"

Oh, Becky...

"Few feats are beyond us," the old tree cryptically croaked.

Becky nodded slowly. "The thing is... I've learned a lot recently. Sometimes, even when you want something really badly... when you get it, it's not always how you expect." She wound her fingers between mine and squeezed my hand. "Sometimes it's better than you could ever have imagined. But sometimes, there are unwanted side effects..."

Mate. Max sat dribbling next to the tree. I put a finger to my mouth. *Shh.*

"Mum, I'm sorry." Becky's eyes glistened. "I'm sure I will see you again someday, but not like this. I can't make that wish. I'm going to just keep on living the best way I can, because that's what you would want. I'm actually happy now, and I know that would make you happy too."

She turned and buried her face in my shoulder. I squeezed her tight, feeling my own eyes welling up.

The tree sounded mildly disappointed. "I suppose I won't be able to show off today."

"I don't know about that," droned Kane.

Becky jolted about.

Kane rode up behind the tree, sitting atop a baby mammoth. "I'm sure we could think of something you can do."

My legs and tongue turned to stone. I gaped at him, thunderstruck.

The mammoth stopped next to the tree and Kane put a finger to his mouth in a gesture of thought. "How about... I wish for you to make this volcano *erupt.*" He shot me a mad grin.

"What? No!" I exclaimed.

The mountain issued a low rumble.

"Ohh ho," said the tree. "That *does* feel good, doesn't it?"

"Stop it!" Becky blurted. "We'll all die!"

The mountain rumbled again.

"Ohhh ho hooo. It has been so long," croaked the tree. "Too long! Yes, I can feel it. Here we go now, your wish is my command, fleshling!"

The Terrabots wheeled the Space Rocket onto the summit just as the mountain gave a violent shudder. The whole contraption spilled over the side of the crater, pulling the Terrabots with it.

"*Mother!*" I cried.

The rocket cart rolled down the slope leaving a trail of bots and miraculously came to rest fully upright in the middle of the bowl of rocks.

Max barked and snapped at the mammoth's feet. The creature trumpeted and reared up, spilling the Fedora Man onto the ground, before galloping away in fright.

The world shook beneath my feet. A long, low growl surged up from deep underground.

"Becky, *go!* Get to the rocket! Max, *here! Now!*"

We leapt into the crater and slid down on our butts. The rocks vibrated beneath us, bouncing like jumping ants. Scrambling to our feet, we ran to the rocket.

"Climb!"

Becky grabbed the hand rails and clambered up. I turned around, searching for Max. He came barking and scrabbling down the treacherous slope. He bounded to me and leapt into my arms.

Kane stood atop the volcano's crater, looking at me. "Billy!"

No, I'm done with you.

I climbed the rocket as fast as I could, hauling Max up with me.

"Hurry!" Becky leaned out of the hatch above. I shoved Max into her arms and they disappeared inside. I threw my backsack through the hatch and fell in after it.

Mother leaned out and slammed the hatch closed, sealing us inside.

Suddenly, everything sounded dull. The rumbling outside turned to a distant grumble, but the pod continued to shake so vigourously my teeth rattled.

"Buckle up!" Mother ordered, taking a seat behind a set of levers.

A bench ran around the circular edge of the pod, and I scrambled up next to Becky, fastening a belt buckle around my waist. Max jumped into my lap and huddled against me. *Scary!*

Mother pulled levers and cranked a handle, as the rocket vibrated so violently that I feared the whole thing would topple over.

"We're still chained down!" I realised.

"It doesn't matter. We're going to ride the eruption."

I gaped at her. "*What?* Is that even going to work?"

"We don't have any other choice!"

Kane's face appeared at the window. He peered inside, scowling. *You*, he mouthed.

The volcano erupted.

Chapter Twenty-Five

A lot happened in the next few moments.

The world fell away beneath us as the rocket shot into the air amid a spray of red hot rocks, smoke and ash.

Outside, Kane disappeared momentarily, only to reappear again, grimacing. Somehow, he had managed to cling on to the hatch wheel, and joined us for the impromptu takeoff.

Outside a different window, I glimpsed the tops of the mountains, and the Great Plains beyond. A Terrabot appeared, obscuring the view outside. He clutched a thick broken chain in one claw, and gave us his best attempt at a *thumbs-up* gesture with the other one. He fell away out of sight, still clutching the chain and holding the gesture.

We're loose. They did it.

Mother tugged a lever. The Space Rocket's thrusters ignited with a mighty roar and my chest tried to swallow my head.

We accelerated straight up, blasting through the sky past the birds and the clouds. Max's body pressed into my legs with the weight of a mammoth, and I felt my feet being sucked tight against the floor.

Outside, Kane still clung on, his lips flapping in the wind

and his cheeks stretching like a hot melting pudding.

Craning my neck to peer out of the window next to me took every molecule of my strength. I pressed my cheek against the glass and lost what little breath I still had.

Green lands stretched below like carpet, shrinking every second, as fluffy clouds zipped past my face and the crisp blue sky slowly turned from azure, to indigo, to a deep dark purple. I saw the curve of the world, and an arcing band of light hovering over it where the sky stopped and the darkness started.

We're going to break through the sky.

Stars exploded into view, hundreds, thousands of them.

And Big Blue. The blue ball emerged behind Lunaria and never had he looked more magnificent.

Our rapid acceleration decreased as the deafening roar of the thrusters cut out and went silent. I felt the pressure on my body relax to a comfortable level. At last, I could move my head again.

The pod turned eerily quiet, save for the faint *hiss* of the air trickling in through a tube in one corner, linked to one of Mother's special *empty* bovithrusters.

"Cripes," I uttered. "Is everyone okay?"

It was only at this point that I felt the searing pain in my left hand. I looked down to see that Becky held it in a deathgrip. "I'm okay," she wheezed.

"All passengers alive and well," Mother announced. "Stowaways not so lucky." She gestured to Kane's window.

The Fedora Man was blue and frozen like an ice cube with an unnaturally wide-eyed, shocked expression on his face.

"See, that's what you get for not wearing a hat," Mother declared.

Just then, Max floated from my lap into the air.

He *wuffed*, and flailed his legs, running on the spot. *Help!*

"Max, you're flying!" Becky exclaimed. She unclipped her belt buckle, and she too drifted off the seat and floated into the air. "Haha! What's happening to us?"

"Most curious," mused Mother, tapping her chin. "I did not foresee this."

"Billy! You have to try this!"

I unclipped and drifted up to join them. "Wow. Heh, this is *weird*."

I put my arm out to brace against the ceiling, and found myself bouncing right off it. I chuckled. Becky sniggered. Max barked, floating upsidedown with his legs splayed out. We floated in the pod, bouncing off the ceiling and drifting from wall to wall and bumping into one another. Soon enough, we were giggling uncontrollably.

We stayed like that as Mother worked the controls. On the outside of her windows, Mother had mounted plates of polished steel that reflected the view of whatever was in front of the rocket, so she could see where she was going. On the side of the rocket, she had mounted micro-thrusters that could be used to turn the rocket around. She fiddled with the levers, puffing and grunting until she was sure we were pointing towards Little Red.

"Here goes nothing." She cranked a lever and the thrusters kicked in giving us a burst of speed.

Becky, Max and me gently floated into the floor and bumped back up. Mother shut off the thrusters again, letting momentum carry us towards our destination.

Becky started doing somersaults and couldn't stop until she reached out her hand and grabbed at me. We bundled to the ground, laughing, and bounced off again.

Hours passed by...

"Are we there yet?" I asked, as I floated upsidedown in front of Mother's nose.

"No," she yawned. She hadn't left the controls the entire time, and stared out the window, intently focused on the view in the reflectors. "Little Red isn't all that little, apparently." I peered into the reflectors and realised what she meant. The red moon looked enormous, so we must have been getting very close to it now.

Kane continued to watch us in his frozen state of shock. I didn't know whether he was alive or dead, so I did my best not to make eye contact.

More time passed...

Max fell asleep in the air. He floated around the pod with his tongue hanging out attached to a long line of drool. Becky screwed her face up and ducked as he drifted past.

I perched next to a window and gazed down at Lunaria, shrinking behind us. "How will we get back home?"

Mother's eyes flicked to me, then back to her window. She didn't answer me, though.

"A more important question right now, William..." she pondered, "...is how are we going to land?"

Becky and I exchanged a nervous glance.

Mother gasped. "Something's happening."

"What?"

"Look."

Becky and I floated to Mother's side and all three of us peered into the reflectors. Little Red was so close now that we could no longer see its edges – an expanse of red filled the entire view. From this distance, I could make out some of the details: vent shafts and pipes jutted out next to black-tinted windows and external staircases zig-zagged their way up between sets of outer doors.

Straight ahead of us, two great rectangular sheets parted ways, opening like a cavernous square jaw. Little Red, or Terry, was apparently going to eat us.

"Buckle up, you two. I don't know what's going to happen next."

We buckled up. I plucked Max out of the air and we held him down between us.

We'd been floating for so long that the idea of *up* and

down didn't really mean anything anymore. Sitting back in the seats felt peculiar, because it meant that we were moving straight *up* into Little Red.

The Space Rocket passed through the great doors, and our cosy pod grew dark as night.

We're inside. We've reached the moon... My belly fluttered at the thought.

Outside, bright lights flickered on, illuminating our way down a long tunnel. The rocket floated along, shadows shifting through the pod every time one of the lights passed us.

A high-pitched buzz stung my ears. Mother and Becky winced, and Max gave a whimper. For a split second, the pod filled with an intense purple beam. It passed right through us... *or did we pass through it?* No sooner had it appeared, it vanished and the buzzing ceased.

The rocket tipped and plummeted into solid ground with a *thump*.

Max fell forwards and dropped onto the opposite wall of the pod. Becky and I slumped in our seats, held in by the belt buckles but it suddenly felt as though we were sitting on the ceiling, not the floor. Straight ahead, Max scrambled to his feet and looked up at us, cocking his head.

"We're here." Mother stared out of the window as she spoke. She unclipped herself. I unbuckled, and fell out of the seat. I stood up on the wall and reached up to help Becky down.

We peered out of a window. The rocket had come to rest on its side in the centre of a spacious, empty room.

"Moonmates, are you ready?" Mother studied us both, a hint of excitement sparkling in her eye. *She lives for this.*

I nodded. Becky whispered, "Yes!" Mother embraced us both in a tight hug, as Max gave an excited whine.

"Okay, let's go."

Mother turned the handle of the hatch.

It hissed air, and swung open. A frozen Kane swung

with it and dropped to the floor like a stone. We all stepped down from the rocket into a cold, echoing chamber. To my right stretched the tunnel that we had entered through, separated by a floor-to-ceiling wall of shimmering purple light. *That must be what we passed through.*

A few crates and ladders cluttered up one corner of the chamber, but it was mostly empty. On the wall opposite the tunnel hung a large sign that read *Hangar 86*. Below it, a door led away into a corridor.

"HU-MANS."

We turned as one.

"Mr Train Man!" I exclaimed. The leader of the Terrabots clutched the underside of the rocket, with icicles shooting from his joints. He looked stuck so I gave a tug on one of his arms but yanked my hand back. "You're *freezing.*" My fingers seared with pain.

"SAVE-THE-HU-MANS." His voice sounded broken, but we got the message.

"He means Hale! Mother, we have to hurry, Gorlack might be there by now!"

She raised her hands in a calming gesture. "Where must we go?" she asked the Train Man in a slow, obvious tone in case he couldn't hear her properly. "Where can we initiate the Rogue Guardian Protocol?"

The Train Man raised a jerky arm and pointed towards the door. "BRIDGE. SAVE-HU-MANS. GO TO BRIDGE."

"Bridge?" frowned Becky.

Mother ran towards the door, and Becky chased after. I paused a moment to inspect Kane. He was completely frozen solid, lying on his back next to the rocket stuck in his slightly disturbing shocked expression. I left him there with the Train Man and joined Becky and Mother.

Up close, the door seemed rather small. I didn't think much of it though, instead my eyes were drawn to the glass painting on the wall next to it. At least it looked painted, but when I stood next to it, I realised it was *inside* the glass, somehow. And it *moved*! Little pictures of cartoon people were walking around on the map.

"*Wow!* Look at this thing!"

The map showed many levels, full of rooms all layered on top of each other. I recognised a kitchen, a row of bedrooms, and some fancy-looking privies. But most were a mystery to me, rooms full of weird machinery and lots of glass panels with pictures on them, and little cartoon men scurrying around.

"That must be the lab," Mother whispered, pointing to a room full of cartoon men wearing long white coats.

"Where's the bridge?" Becky asked.

Underneath the map ran a series of buttons assigned to different names. One of them said *BRIDGE*. I pushed the button next to it.

A tinny voice spoke. "*Bridge. This way, please.*" A yellow dotted line appeared in the wall below the map. It snaked its way down the wall and onto the floor. Becky jumped out of its way, and the line streaked across the floor and under the door.

"Follow it!" Mother commanded. She made for the door, which slid open automatically as she approached, but she had to duck to pass through it. Becky and me ducked through as well and we all followed the line into the corridor.

Mother led the way through a small room with a desk and some sofas, following the yellow line on the floor into a long corridor. Becky came second and I took up the rear with Max. Walking through the corridor, my head brushed against the ceiling.

I stopped and looked back. The line had disappeared behind me, but a small tail of it remained a few paces back. I took a step forward, and the line shortened itself the same amount. *Clever line.* This place was going to be amazing, I could just tell.

We passed through a spacious lobby of sorts, decorated with weird crystal spheres dangling from the ceiling.

Everything seemed very new and clean, yet the place had an atmosphere of emptiness. We were the only signs of life.

After ducking through another door, the line led us through a fine red carpeted passageway with glass panels decorating the walls. Like the map in the hangar, they showed *moving pictures,* and even made sound.

I caught snippets of it as we passed through.

"...Terry, the world's first Thermo Energy Regulator and Research Organising Retainer. State of the art, capable of..."

I yearned to linger and admire them all. The moving images felt like the ultimate form of sketching, more advanced than anything I had ever imagined.

The next one showed a man in a long white coat proudly showing off a jar containing a fully-formed, miniature tree. The tree's roots wriggled around like squid tentacles, pawing at the glass.

"No way. Look! He's got a tiny Guardian tree!"

Becky stopped, but Mother marched onwards, following the line.

The panel was speaking. *"...advanced artificial lifeforms will fuse with the dead planet, aiding it through the rigorous stresses of Terraformation. Appearing like simple trees on the surface, they will blend seamlessly into..."*

"Come on, Billy. We don't want to get lost in here."

I tore myself away from the panel, and we ran after Mother, following the guiding yellow line.

After several more rooms of panels, corridors and stairwells, we came to a blindingly bright room that had been completely taken over by plants. Green vines crept all over the walls and ceilings, and large rubbery leaves slapped me in the face as I brushed through trying to follow the yellow line underneath all the roots.

"Mother, remember when you made our house look like this?"

"It wasn't *this* bad!" She gazed around. "This must be one of their labs... I could learn *so much* here..." She sounded wistful. "Priorities, William. Come on." She made to follow the line out of an exit, and stopped. "Why are these doors so *small?*"

We left the jungle room behind, and continued up several stairwells, through more labs full of machinery and down a long corridor marked *Crew Quarters*. We never met any crew, though. There didn't seem to be anybody else here at all.

At long last, we came to a set of double doors marked *BRIDGE*. They slid apart for us and we crouched through it. Luckily, the *Bridge* had a very high ceiling. It was one of the most spacious rooms I could imagine.

So beautiful...

My eyes fixated on Lunaria. Our world. And my jaw tried to hit the floor.

Ahead of us, one side of the five-storey high wall was made entirely of glass, the biggest window I had ever seen. It looked right out onto our home world, floating in the blackness of space.

The rest of the room would have been just as impressive by itself. We stood upon a gangway high above an assortment of lit-up panels, buttons and switches. The colour scheme of the room alternated between hues of red and blue, as different buttons lit up one or the other. The occasional light glowed green, and these ones gently pulsed on and off. The desks and chairs were dark silver mounted on black frames.

Two sets of stairs curved down to the ground level either side of us. Down we went, and entered a maze of *humming* machinery.

I started to say *Look for the Rogue Guardian Protocol switch*, when an old man's face appeared in the huge window. He shouted at us.

"Oi, get your grubby mits off that. Who ever taught you to go touching other people's things?"

Mother stood before the wrinkly face, and spoke with an air of grace. "Might you be Terry?"

He had a spotty bald head, squinty eyes and only a few teeth. The face didn't have a body, his head just sort of floated there inside the glass. "Indeed I am. And who might you be?"

"My name is Bethany Spudswallop. I travel with my son, William, and this is Becky. They are my moonmates. We have flown to you from our home, Lunaria. Please help us, a monster threatens our home even as we speak, and we were told that only you could stop him. He is a Guardian."

"Crikey! When did that happen? Must not have been paying attention..."

Becky and I exchanged a glance.

The old man sounded panicky. "Now, where did I put that blasted... quick, look for the Rogue Guardian Protocol button."

The three of us dispersed each searching through the panels.

There were glowing buttons and screens everywhere, each displaying graphs and streams of writing that made no sense to me. Some showed pictures of scenery, like mountains and lakes and one even showed a cave in a desert. *I wonder where that is?*

Next to a big chair in the middle of the room, I found a button marked R.G.P. "Is this it?"

"No, boy. Don't press that. That's for the captain's breakfast! He likes his really-good-porridge warm with milk and a dab of Kamuna, that's not for the likes of you. Although, come to think of it, there hasn't been a captain for quite a while..."

I left the button alone and continued my search.

Becky called out from the front of the room, under the giant window. "I found it! Over here!"

She stood by a screen underneath Terry's face, slightly off to the right of centre. Next to the screen sat a single red button, encased in glass. Printed on the desk next to the button was a diagram of a tree taking a bite out of an elephant.

"Well done!" exclaimed Mother. She plonked herself in the seat and hesitated. "Um, who's bright idea was this?" She probed her fingers around the edge of the casing, unsure how to reach the button within. "Argh!" She slammed her fist through it, shattering the case and hitting the button.

An ear-splitting siren wailed and the room flashed red and black for a few moments before returning to normal. In the centre of the desk directly in front of Mother, a control stick emerged with a trigger button on it a bit like George's blunderbuss. A crosshair appeared on the screen.

"Ohh I think I get it," Mother made herself comfortable in the seat, took hold of the trigger with one hand and leaned forward. She gazed into the screen, which showed a close-up shot of Lunaria. She tilted the stick forwards and Lunaria zoomed towards her face. She yelped and leaned back. "That was terrifying."

Outside the main window, past Terry's head, Lunaria remained where it was. Big and beautiful, but definitely not flying towards us.

"That's so cool," me and Becky remarked at once.

Mother hesitated. "Heh, yeah. Why don't you do this instead."

She got off the seat and I leapt into it myself.

I tilted the control stick to the left and the view of Lunaria moved with it. "Wow!" I tilted it forwards and it zoomed in some more, until I could see the edges of land and the ocean. "Where's Hale? Becky! Get my map!"

She rummaged in my backsack and pulled out my sketches. I found the map I had been slowly adding to throughout the journey. She held it up next to the screen so I could compare the real view to my drawing.

"Hmm, this is difficult!" I traced the edges of the shoreline around Hale on my map, and tried to find the same shore on the actual world. Nothing seemed to match. My map was apparently not very accurate...

"Maybe we're on the wrong side of the world...?"

Becky's suggestion filled me with dread.

"But... how long will it take to move around?"

"Little Red comes out roughly once per night, doesn't it?" Mother said.

"But...we can't wait all night! Gorlack will destroy Hale! Terry, can't you make this thing move faster?" I pleaded.

The old man on the window snorted. "No! Do you have any idea what that'll do to your world? There'll be floods, there'll be earthquakes, the mountains will crumble and the lakes will dry up and my experiment will be ruined in a matter of seconds! Is that what you want?"

"Um, no. Please don't do any of that."

Mother spoke calmly. "Then there's nothing we can do. We have to wait."

Chapter Twenty-Six

I studied the screen. Lunaria slowly turned, more land and sea rolled into view. *I must not miss it.*

Terry chuckled. "You don't hang about do you? Why, we'd only just finished copying your trebuchet design, and suddenly you've become a bleedin' *astronaut.*"

Mother eyed him suspiciously. "Excuse me? What do you mean you *copied my design?* Are you spying on me?"

A screen next to us flashed on, and a grainy picture of Mother appeared on it. The image moved, and it showed Mother working in our garden in Hale.

"No way, is that you Bethany?" Becky remarked. "Look at your *hair!* You look so young!"

Mother looked deeply offended for a brief moment, but as she saw the image on the screen she giggled. "See that?" She leaned across and pointed to her other self's swollen belly. "That's you, William."

On the screen, Mother fiddled with a bottle and some other objects on a garden table. She lit a match, and the table exploded. She flew backwards off her feet and disappeared off the screen. Then suddenly she was back, the bottle and table reset, and the scene played again.

"Studying, not spying," corrected Terry. "I like to keep

an eye on all of my test subjects."

"*Ahem*!" now Mother really was offended. "I am nobody's experiment."

"Don't be silly, of course you are. This moon isn't yours! I've been here a lot longer than you, I should know."

"I'm not an experiment, I'm a person," Becky insisted.

"Yeah, me too," I felt a need to clarify it as well.

Max barked agreement.

"Listen," Terry spoke assuredly. "I built this place from the ground up. Before I was here, your hunk o'rock couldn't support one planck of life!"

"What's a planck?" Mother asked.

Terry seemed not to notice. "I inserted the water, the trees, the grass and the air, warmed it all up nicely for you, and let nature do its thing. A million years later, and you lot start popping up!"

Mother went to speak.

"Don't keep interrupting!" Terry went on, "I won't have no arguing. *I'm a person*. Heh. I suppose you lot are, but he's not." The face gestured at Max, who merrily wagged his stump. "Your entire world is one big abandoned experiment. How brilliant is that!"

"Abandoned?" I frowned. "But I thought you're spying on us?"

"More like a hobby o'mine, that. AI needs something to pass the time. It's abandoned because ever since the humans buggered off I been left here to run this show by myself. They all thought I didn't work so they packed up and flew to a warmer star system! But I showed them. May have taken me a million years, but I saved the humans, I surely did!" It paused to study us a moment. "Bit lankier than your ancestors, I must admit. Must be that low gravity."

"What happened to them?" Mother asked. "The Terrabots told us that Home froze... they said the sun cooled down."

"It's true. Take a look at this." One corner of the giant

window squared itself off, and Big Blue appeared inside it. "That's Home right now. But this is how she used to look..."

The planet started to spin really fast, and as it did, the pale blue surface disintegrated and dissolved into blue and green shapes. Continents of green land floating in deep blue oceans.

"Wow," Becky gasped.

"This was Home about one million years ago. Look familiar?"

Next to the cornered-off section of window, the real Lunaria filled the view.

"They look the same!" I exclaimed.

"Precisely. When the sun began to die, the whole world turned to ice..." As he spoke, the image of Big Blue morphed and changed. The green lands turned white, then the oceans frosted over, and the whole planet faded to the familiar pale blue. "But the people there saw it coming, so they came up with a backup plan to keep themselves warm. Me." The wrinkly head grinned a near-toothless grin. "What do you think I'm doing up here if not keeping your butts nice and cosy down there?"

"How?" Mother asked, dumbstruck.

"I was originally designed to Terraform new planets, but when they realised their own planet was turning into a frozen deathtrap, their priorities changed and they turned me into a giant microwave instead."

"What's a microwave?"

"Managed to fly into space, but haven't invented microwaves yet? Cripes. All you need to know is this: so long as I'm up here, flying around your little world in some unfathomably precise, calculated orbit patterns, you'll be cosy and free to do whatever it is you adorable creatures do down there."

Mother tapped her chin, lost in thought.

This was a lot to take in, so I turned back to the trigger and gazed down the crosshair again. I tilted the stick all the way forwards just to see what would happen. The picture zoomed into a big green field and stopped when a single, giant blade of grass had taken over the screen. *Blimey.*

I nudged it back and zoomed out, until I could see a thin dark line snaking across the land. I zoomed in to inspect it closer.

"Hey, look Becky." I pointed at the screen. "I found the Great Train line!"

"That's perfect. Follow it all the way to Aston, and Hale will be right next to it!"

I followed the train tracks until the ground turned grey. "Look, it's a town. But which one?" I saw a lake underneath the town, among green hills.

"Hmm, I don't know any lakes south of any towns..." Becky said, puzzled.

"There's a lake near Fentworth, but it's to the north, right?"

"Yeah."

It didn't make sense. I followed the tracks some more, and saw a huge criss-crossing shadow against the ground. *It's the Fent Bridge. That's where the train almost killed Max!* "This *is* Fentworth. Becky, we're looking at it upsidedown!"

"Oh yeah!"

"That means Hale is *this* way." I scanned the view further to the right, flashing past hills, woodland, rivers and Aston. *Hale has been visible this whole time!*

A brown stain shot across the view. *The Scar! Almost there...* Trees flashed past, Hale Wood. I traced the view up towards the corner of the plateau to our village.

I spotted the windmill. "There!" I cried. Mother darted over and Becky and her squeezed next to each other to gaze down the crosshair.

The sails turned gently in the night breeze. A cat stalked the street. I panned the view across, and found the Hat Shop. I held my breath and panned a little farther. A familiar house came into view, still standing. No sign of any giant tree monsters. I exhaled.

"They're safe. They're okay."

"Then where's Gorlack?"

I zoomed out a little, and scanned over to where the cave should be. I found it easily enough, all the trees leading away from it had been flattened when Gorlack broke free after eating all the Kingsmen.

And there, as we watched, the trees jerked. And jerked again... I could practically hear his footsteps making that dreadful *boof.*

"He's there, he's close!"

Something big, leafy and green flashed across the screen at an alarming speed. "No!"

I jerked the control stick to zoom out and it pulled all the way into space.

"Billy! You lost him!" Mother yelled.

Fumbling with the stick, I zoomed back in and came face to face with a tiny bug crawling over a pebble.

"Too far! Calm down!" Becky touched me on the arm.

Father is counting on you now, even if he has no idea.

I tilted the stick and zoomed out until I could see the curve of the coastline again, and the Hale Scar cutting through the land. I pinpointed Hale, and zoomed in.

I could no longer see the windmill. Where it should be, the tops of a fat leafy monster called Gorlack stood, bellowing and stomping.

I aimed the crosshair at him and pulled the trigger.

The Bridge rumbled. Terry issued a long, deep groan. The massive window erupted in a blinding red flash as a mighty crimson beam fired out from Little Red.

On the screen, Gorlack looked up, his body bathed in red glowing light. His toothy maw contorted in a horrified expression of fear, and he turned back towards the village, raising both his giant arms about to smash them into Hale...

And there he ceased.

He froze solid mid-strike, towering over my home. His

leaves crumbled away and fluttered in the breeze across the village. All that was left was a skeleton of the monstrous tree.

Father came out of the house, my brothers all huddling around him. They pointed at Gorlack and flinched, then when they realised he wasn't moving, they started to laugh. My brothers did, anyway. Father simply scratched his head, looking confused. As Rufus picked up a stone and threw it at Gorlack's face, I knew they would be okay.

And that is how I saved Hale.

"Billy, you did it!" Becky threw her arms around me and squeezed me in a bone-crushing hug.

Mother stood back, nodding with approval, a proud smile spread across her face.

"SAVE-THE-HU-MANS."

The Train Man staggered into the Bridge, limping and with one arm dangling by a thread.

"Hey, you're alive," Mother remarked. "That's good."

"HU-MANS. SAVE-THE-HU-MANS. THAW. MELT. SAVE HOME."

"It's okay. Billy defeated Gorlack. Everyone is safe!" Becky pulled me to my feet and spun me around in a dance.

"THAW. HOME. THAW. MELT. THAW. ABORTING EXPERIMENT TO SAVE THE HU-MANS."

Mother eyed the malfunctioning Terrabot. "What...?"

Terry shouted in distress. "Stop him! He'll ruin *everything*!"

The Terrabot staggered towards a panel to the side of the great window. The controls were marked *Emergency Flight Controls*.

"He's going to turn me around, point me at Home and defrost the planet! *All life on Lunaria will be extinguished! STOP THAT TERRABOT.*"

Mother ran at the Train Man and tackled him. He barely budged. She collapsed to the ground in a heap, clutching her side. "Owww."

The Terrabot stepped over her and stumbled on.

Becky reached him and planted both hands on his chest, pushing back. Her feet slid backwards along the ground. I ran to help and shoved with all my might. The bot swayed to the side, reached an arm out and clattered into a panel, smashing the screen in a blaze of sparks.

"Be careful! Shut him down, *shut him down now!*" blared Terry.

How? How do you kill a Terrabot? I'd seen so many of them lose their heads back on the ground. They were old and rusty, and the reason they lost their heads when they saw us was because...

"We need a *paradox*!" I shouted.

"What?" Becky shrieked as she strained against the bot's weight.

"A paradox. Something that is both true and false at the same time. Something confusing, that will break his mind!"

Mother staggered to her feet. "I know a paradox!" She raised a finger to the air. "The next sentence I say will be a lie. That is the truth!"

We all looked at the Train Man. He stumbled on, unaffected. "SAVE THE HU-MANS."

"It didn't work! Try another one!"

Mother raised her palms to the ceiling. "I don't know anymore!"

I grimaced as I pushed the Train Man with all my might, but he kept stumbling on, relentless. I racked my brain, thinking desperately.

Draw something.

"Mother! Swap with me, hold him back!"

I bolted to my backsack and grabbed my sketchpad. I had a *single* blank sheet of paper left. I tore it out and began scribbling as fast as I could.

"What are you *doing?*" Mother scowled, fighting to hold the Terrabot back. Becky's heels now touched the desk of the flight controls as he pushed on, reaching a claw over her shoulder towards the controls.

I finished my doodle and held it in front of the Train Man. On the paper was a crude sketch of a lake, with a river running out of it. The river ran around in a circle and re-joined the lake on the other side, so it seemed as though the lake fed the river that fed the lake, which fed the river... "How is this possible?" I yelled at the Terrabot.

A spark fizzled, and he cocked his head at the image. "NOT. POSSIBLE."

His head remained cocked to the side even when I pulled the drawing away, but he still tried to stagger through Mother and Becky as they struggled to hold him back.

"Try another one!" Mother screamed.

I flipped the page over and racked my brain. Another idea came to me. I doodled frantically.

Becky yelped. Her back now touched the desk, and the Terrabot looked about to crush her in his effort to reach the flight controls. Max ran around barking furiously at the Train Man. He echoed, *Bad Train! Train! Bad!*

I thrust the paper in front of him again. This time, my sketch showed a spiral staircase leading around and joining back up to itself. If you walked on it, you'd somehow be walking both up and down at the same time.

The Train Man gazed at it, and *clunked*. His head tilted even more askew, and a big spark crackled from his head.

Yet he didn't seize up.

"Billy! It's working, but not fast enough! Draw another one!"

"That was my last page!" I cried.

"*Stop him!*" screamed Terry. "*DON'T LET HIM TOUCH THAT BUTTON!*"

The Train Man reached a claw between Mother and Becky, stretching for a big red button on the flight control desk.

I dived to the floor looking for more paper. I scattered my sketches across the ground. Every page was used up, both sides. The cave, the stone carving with the ciphers, Aston's clocktower, the Great Train, George posing with Max and Lucy, a bunch of eclipses, Max chasing a rabbit, Becky on a rock, Becky on a Bighorn, Becky flying through the sky with a feathery pair of wings sprouting from her back... *there's no more pages!*

Then I saw the Mammowlipus Rex Hog, the drawing of an impossible combination of beasts that a street artist in Hooke sketched for me. I grabbed it, ran to the Train Man and shoved it in front of his face.

"Look at this!"

His body seized up. His claw froze in mid-grasp between Becky and Mother, inches away from the big red button. He went *brrrrrrrrmmmooooooop.*

And then the Train Man's head popped off.

It landed with a heavy *clank* on the hard floor. They gave him a shove, and the body collapsed to the ground. *Tu-thunk!*

And *that* is how I saved the world.

...

We all collapsed on the floor of the *Bridge* and exhaled a long sigh of relief.

It was over.

Max came and flopped down beside me, panting.

"Terry. Do you know how we might get back home?" I spoke to the ceiling as I lay sprawled on my back.

"Certainly. We have a selection of comfortable escape pods. You can choose the destination yourself."

That sounded good to me.

"Mother. Will you come home now?"

She had her head resting against the *Flight Control Deck*, her eyes shut. She rolled her head to me and opened them. "And leave all those nice labs unexplored? I don't think so.

You go on without me, I'll catch you up in a few moons."
She mumbled on, "or is it a few Terry's now…"

I expected no less. I had learned a lot about my mother
since setting out to find her, and though Father would be a
bit miffed when I returned home without her, I will
explain that she's on the moon. Maybe he'll understand.

"I'll come and wave you off," she said with a warm
smile.

We all made our way to the escape pod hangar. The
pods lined up against the wall, each as big as our diving
bell.

"Are you sure you want to stay here alone?" I asked.

"Oh, yes. I'm used to it. Helps me to focus! You just
wait, I'll be home in no time."

"Heh. Just make sure you do come home, this time!"

Just then, a yellow line emerged beneath the door and
snaked across the floor. It stopped in the middle of the
room and turned into a big yellow circle.

Max growled.

The door opened and Kane stumbled through.

"*You?*" The three of us exclaimed at once.

He saw us and gaped. His eyes had returned to normal,
mostly… one of them still bulged out a bit. And his skin
had gone a sickly grey colour. He looked as though he
didn't know whether to turn and run the other way or just
stand perfectly still and hope we forgot he was there. In
the end he just sort of hesitated and swayed about on his
feet, shivering.

"I have a body that *won't die*," he croaked through
chattering teeth. "I thought it would be ama-z-zing… but it
is the worst thing imaginable. The p-p-pain…" His eyes
watered. "You people have *broken* me."

"Well it serves you right," said Becky.

"Are you going to use an escape pod?" I asked.

He glanced at the row of pods, with barely the strength
to stand up. "That seemed like a g-good idea. But if you
are all going too, I would rather s-s-stay up here. I never

300

want to see any of you again."

"You'll be stuck here with me. Just the two of us. I'm going to do some experiments, and you could be my... *assistant*." Mother made to move towards him. "You could start by giving me a sample of that fascinating blood—"

"*No!*" Kane's bulging eye bulged even more and he shrunk like a scared rabbit, hugging himself around the stomach. "I'm going to goto Tata-Tannerus. It's warm there. *Stay away from me.*"

He staggered into the nearest pod and the door closed behind him. We watched as he fumbled with the buttons. The pod flew down the tunnel and disappeared, taking Kane the Fedora Man with it.

Mother sighed. "Where were we?" She turned to me and Becky, standing side by side. "Ah, yes. Travel well, moonmates." Mother's smile lit her face.

Becky sniffed, and swept into Mother's arms, hugging her tightly. "Stay safe, Bethany."

"I will, don't you worry. You just look after my William."

Becky released her, tears streaming down her face, laughing. "I will!"

I went in for a hug. She wrapped her arms around me and I squeezed her tight. "See you again soon, Mother."

"You bet, William." Her eyes glistened too. She wiped away a tear with a finger. "Go on, now. Off with you. Tell Rufus mummy will be home soon."

Becky, Max and I walked into the pod. The glass door closed behind us. Becky cycled through the pod's options, a screen showing the pictures of various landing sites. A mountain, a lake, a desert cave, a woodland cave. *They are all the Guardian locations...*

"Stop," I said when I saw the old cave near Hale. "Choose that one."

Mother stood in the hangar, and raised a hand. Her smile showed a hint of sadness, but the excited glint in her eye made her beautiful. *That's my Mother.*

Becky pushed the button. The pod shot down the tunnel and flew into outer space, as Mother shrank away in an instant, disappearing from sight.

Terry exploded into view as we soared away from the moon I had always known as Little Red.

We floated inside the egg-shaped pod. Where the diving bell had a series of little windows for us to see out of, this escape pod had one single band of glass all around its circumference. Padded seats and floor lined the bottom half and a soft fluffy ceiling covered the top.

The pod took a long sweeping arc back home, which gave us several hours to enjoy the spectacular views.

We lay next to each other in midair on our bellies, as if resting on some comfortable patch of grass, gazing out of the window. As the world below us turned, I spotted the section of land that I had spent the last few months travelling across searching for Mother. It felt *enormous* at the time. I couldn't imagine anything beyond the vast distance of trekking from Hale to Joy, then all the way to the Terrabots' home in the far north.

And yet that was but a single *island*, among a whole load of them. The rest of the unknown lands stretched across the oceans, green forests and lush grasses, mountain ranges, snowy tundra and vast deserts, all waiting to be explored.

"Our home is tiny, isn't it?" I whispered, awestruck.

"Yeah," Becky answered wistfully. "But it's a big world..."

Becky intertwined her fingers with both of my hands and gazed at me as we floated in the pod.

"Billy Spudswallop," she grinned. "What do you think we should do when we get home?"

"I haven't really thought about it yet. How about we see what else is out there?"

"That," Becky kissed me. "Is exactly what I hoped you would say."

I smiled, and kissed her back, burying my fingers in her

hair.

Max floated past us, drooling.

Mate.

...

Hours later, we landed. The pod kindly informed us to take a seat and fasten our belt buckles before plummeting down through the sky. It slowed to a gentle descent and we landed in the undergrowth with a bump, no worse than stepping down from a Bighorn.

When the door opened, Max bolted outside and cocked his leg against the nearest tree. The sun was out, and I guessed it to be about lunchtime.

"Cripes, what a mess," I remarked, gazing at the sight of broken trees. The cave had collapsed in on itself when Gorlack had broken free. A few fedora hats littered the ground inside the sunken hollow. The carved rock, which I now realised had probably been made by a Terrabot many, many years ago, had fallen onto its side.

We made our way up the hill, following the giant footprints towards Hale.

The archway still stood, somehow. Underneath it, I turned to Becky and chuckled. "Welcome to my home."

Hale, the place where nobody ever visits. And why would you? There was the Hat Shop, the post shop, the little school and... we used to have a windmill. Apart from that, nothing had changed. Well, except Gorlack.

The petrified skeleton of the monstrous tree loomed over the village standing on the rubble of the windmill, staring down with crazy eyes made of stone. *So you did have eyes after all.* He was frozen with an angry snarled mouth and arms outstretched as if he were about to scoop you up and swallow you whole. The terrifying monument certainly did liven the place up a bit. Max padded over and casually peed on Gorlack's foot.

A soothing, buzzing *hum* filled the air. A great hive

nestled between two thick branches behind Gorlack's eyes. The bees had been unaffected by the Rogue Guardian Protocol beam, apparently. *Mother will like having her bees back when she comes home.*

Speaking of which...

I led Becky down the little cobbled road to my home.

Father bent over a patch of dirt in the front lawn, tending to his potatoes. He glanced up and gave a cheery wave as if we were just some neighbours walking by, and bent over again to carry on.

"Father, it's me."

He jolted upright. He squinted at me, glanced at Becky, back to me, squinting even harder. "Billy?" He threw his spuds to the ground and bumbled towards me in big strides. "Billy!" He clapped his arms around me, slapping my back. "Welcome home! Wonderful timing, I was just selecting our lunch."

"That sounds great. I can't even remember the last meal we had, now I think about it."

"No wonder, look at you. What's all that hair doin' on yer head?"

I smiled sheepishly. "Father, this is Becky."

"How do you do, Mr Spudswallop?" Becky smiled, shaking his hand.

"Oh, please. Call me Frank." Father raised an eyebrow at me. "So, I send you off to find yer mother and ye come back with a Becky instead. Is that how it goes?"

I scratched my elbow. "Yeah, about that..."

"Did you find her?"

"Oh, yes."

"Great! Where is she?"

"Well..." *How to put this?* "Father, I think there's something very wrong with Mother. It's just, whatever it is, it makes her very interesting to be around. Did you ever notice that?"

He chuckled. "O' course! Why do you think I married 'er?"

304

Becky laughed. "She is wonderful."

"So, she's alright then, wherever she is?" Father asked, eyeing me.

"She's on the moon."

He didn't have a response to that.

"She built a Space Rocket and we flew there together. We just got back."

Still nothing. Father went to speak, then closed his mouth. Then he reconsidered, tried to say something, then shook his head. Finally, he said, "Think you better come in and explain this to me." He turned and walked down the path towards the house mumbling, "I dunno. Kids these days..."

Becky and I exchanged a look, chuckling.

"After you," I gestured her through the gate.

"Thank you."

We strolled down the path towards the little cottage. At the door, I called to Max. "Here, boy! Food!"

He pricked his ears and ran to me. As he bolted through the door, he echoed.

Biscuits!

I closed the door behind me and sat down to lunch.

<u>Epilogue</u>

In the moons that followed, Hale became a lot busier. Word of the dead Wishing Tree spread as far as Joy, and soon people flocked to see the creature for themselves. Hale found itself reconnected to the rest of the southern settlements with a new bridge over the Scar, and a brand new train station at the bottom of the hill.

Suddenly, everyone wanted to visit Hale.

Becky and I caught the maiden train ride out to go on a small adventure. We travelled the length of the train line, hopping off at Fentworth to see George, Millie and the Bighorns. After that, we stopped at Barrow for a few days to offer our hands in the rebuilding process. Maurice's tavern was one of only a few buildings to survive the inferno, but he seldom had any customers these days. Nobody stopped at the husk of a village, and many of the residents had been forced to move to Hooke, or Joy.

"There's not a lot you can do around here," the innkeeper explained, as he showed us around the crumbled ruins of the village. There was an awkward tension between us... He'd tried to kill me after believing us responsible for the blaze, but here we were trying to make amends. "I'd sooner send you to the city to collect supplies. The new Queen has promised to recognise Barrow. Who am I to turn away such an offer?"

We arrived in Joy on the day of the Queen's coronation. Kane's old partner the Black Fedora Man stepped down from his temporary kingship to hand the Joyful Throne over to the leader of the kingsmaids. *Our new queen is a mermaid*, I thought, amused.

"That's the girl I saw in Hooke, the one who talked to me," I told Becky, as we sat on a pew towards the back of the crowded throne room. "She handed me over to Kane!" The memory of the day Kane chopped off Max's tail still made me angry, even after all this time.

The beautiful girl sat in the grand, carved throne dressed in a flowing silken orange and green dress, the colours of the kingsmaids (now renamed the queensmaids), and gave a short speech.

"People of Joy, I thank you for choosing me as your new queen. I vow to serve you well, and put your wishes at the forefront of my priorities. As of today, the destruction of our natural forests is to be toned back, and many of the forges of Anvil Plaza will be closed. The stockpiles of timber that have already been prepared are to be sent to Barrow, where it is sorely needed. Those of you whose forges are to be quenched can have free access to the train to commute back and forth from the village, where you will find plenty of work over the coming moons."

She gazed across the audience, and her eyes caught on me. My heart jumped. She smiled. "That is all for now. If you ever require something of your queen, do not hesitate to bring the matter to my queensmaids. Together, we believe the city can live up to its name once again."

As Becky and I joined the line of people making for the door, a queensmaid stepped in front of us.

"Please, the queen wishes to speak with you both."

I hesitated. *She's probably wondering how I escaped from the Khazi.*

"Okay," I said, hesitantly. She led us to the king's old

bedroom.

The queen waited within, standing at the window overlooking the ocean. The room was much tidier than when I'd last been here. The child king's toys had been removed, and there was a strong smell of seaweed....

"Billy," the queen swept towards us, the orange and green silks flowing in the breeze. "Shouldn't you be dead?"

I reddened as she planted a kiss on both cheeks and embraced me in a hug. Becky's eyes were full of fire, but then the queen smothered her as well. When she stepped back she clasped her hands in front of her in the same way the Train Man used to do, but she made the gesture look a lot more elegant.

"Uh, yeah. I escaped."

The queen's smile was otherworldly in its radiance. "I am glad. The queensmaids owe you a debt, Billy Spudswallop," she declared. "Thanks to you, we were set free."

They want to thank me? Probably for sending all the Fedora Men to Gorlack... "Uh, you're welcome, I guess."

"There is little we can offer you in payment, but know this. Should you ever wish to travel across the seas, we can offer you safe passage through the beasts. Does this offer seem *attractive* to you?"

"Yes it does," I answered, too quickly. Becky shot me a glare. "I mean, yes, thank you. We were thinking of travelling to other regions, the two of us." I put an arm around Becky, and pulled her close.

"Then it is settled. You may take up this offer whenever you like. All you need do is ask."

Becky and I left Joy and rode the train back to Barrow with the supplies. We stayed there for two Blue Moons, aiding Maurice and the other villagers as they rebuilt their homes. When the tavern put on a grand reopening, even the Queen herself showed up, helping to put Barrow back on the map.

With our work done, we made for home, and arrived

back in Hale on a quiet winter's evening.

We lay on the grass atop the old windmill hill, wearing our bobble hats, watching the stars and Terry. Max lay beside us, snoring.

"Hard to believe we were up there not so long ago, isn't it?" I mused.

"Yeah," Becky sighed, stroking Max's head. "Just seeing it makes me want to start another journey..."

"Me too."

Something in the sky glinted, reflecting the moonslight as it fell to earth.

"What's that?" Becky saw it too. She gasped. "Could it be...?"

Max sat up, pricked his ears at the sound.

Ssshhhh-WUMP.

The escape pod's parachute opened and the capsule fell into the trees just ahead of us. Max bounded into the woods after it.

Shortly after, Mother came marching up the hill behind Gorlack. She had a stack of rolled-up papers in one hand and a closed sack in the other.

We both stood at once. "You're back!"

"Of course I'm back! Couldn't stand another minute up there with that pompous, big-headed know-it-all fool!"

"Who, Terry?" I asked.

"Yes, yes, who else could it be?"

Biscuits, biscuits! Max jumped up and down trying to bite the sack in Mother's hand.

"Get down, this isn't for you!"

I smiled at her. "Welcome home, Mother."

"Thank you!"

She embraced us both. "Oh, it's good to see you. Have you got itchy feet yet?"

We laughed. Becky said, "How could you tell?"

"I remember my first adventure! Once I was home, couldn't wait to get on with the next."

"Yeah, we have some ideas," I admitted. "We were

thinking about catching a boat somewhere."

"A boat? Ugh, I'd sooner fly. I've had an idea for the Cloud Cruiser Mark 3." She gestured with the papers.

"Really?" Becky clasped her hands. "When can we build it?"

"Ohh, soon enough, soon enough. I have a list of supplies I'll need you to get first..." Mother glanced around, eyeing the sleeping village. She sighed, smiling. "Anyone else hungry? I brought your father and brothers some *astronaut food*."

We walked down the hill under the moonslight and headed for home.

THE END.

A NOTE FROM THE AUTHOR

Yikes. It's finished. In case it isn't already painfully obvious, that was my first ever novel. Thank you so much for tolerating it, and making it to the end. I'll assume you did, anyway. Otherwise you've just skipped to the thank-you page which is just weird...

Last year, I went through a bit of a rough patch (we all get 'em) and decided to make some rather drastic changes to my life. I ended up quitting my career job and went to live in New Zealand for a year. While I was there, I did all sorts of crazy things like climbing up mountains, bungee jumping, trekking through forests, skydiving, working on a dairy farm... Before this, I was a web-designer, so you can see why I found it such a life-changing and exhilarating experience.

I met all sorts of amazing people as I travelled around, and made some wonderful new friends. I moved from place to place, doing whatever work I could, and stayed in some of the most remote and beautiful places you can imagine.

One day, during a regular shift working on a vineyard, I

had an idea for a prison... "What if there was a big toilet in the sea?" I thought to myself, as I often do. "How would you escape from a place like that?" And so, I had my first 'big idea.' Yes, the story you've just read began out as nothing more than an elaborate toilet gag. I suppose that says a lot about me.

Anyway, that little spark of an idea grew, and as I explored more of New Zealand, my inspiration soared (it's really quite easy to be inspired by that place – you should definitely go there one day) and now, almost exactly one year after I wrote the first sentence, I'm ready to publish this thing. Who'd have thunk it?

As I said, I met many awesome people this past year, and even managed to stay in touch with my old friends back home in England. And many of them deserve some credit for helping me to finish the single biggest creative project of my life.

So, here goes.

Thanks Paul, for being the first person to read any of it and telling me that it didn't suck.

Thanks mum, you were the first person to read it in its entirety and told me that it didn't suck.

Thanks to my regular Scribophiler's, Pauline, Cormac, Leah and Rupali – without your regular, thorough, honest and helpful feedback (not to mention heartwarming encouragement) I would never have maintained the drive to see this through.

Thanks to anyone whose name I stole for the purposes of my characters (you should be able to work out who you are).

A special thanks to Sam for painting me an absolutely awesome front cover.

And last but not least, thank you for reading my ridiculous tale. I can only hope you had a fraction of the fun reading it that I had making it. I hope we meet again sometime, reader.

Farewell, and safe travels out there.

M A Clarke,
June 2014

ABOUT THE AUTHOR

M A Clarke is a 28 year old geek from England who has spent his life playing videogames and watching cartoons. He was also known to make animations of stick men murdering each other back in the day, and has a dangerous addiction to Wispa chocolate bars. He also loves mountains, dogs, dinosaurs and space.
You might like his website: www.mattclarke.co.uk